staying
dead

laura anne gilman

LUNA™
www.LUNA-Books.com

LUNA™

STAYING DEAD

ISBN 0-373-80253-6

Copyright © 2004 by Laura Anne Gilman

First mass market printing: June 2006

First trade printing: August 2004

For Mom and Dad, of course.

And for Mir and ElaineMc,
who have some small blame in all this…

ACKNOWLEDGMENTS

Because no writer works alone,
no matter what it feels like at 3:00 a.m.,
I need to praise and thank the following people:

Jennifer Jackson (agent) and
Mary-Theresa Hussey (editor). Finestkind.

Peter, who understood that there was something I
needed to do, and gave me the space to get it done.

The Cross-Genre Abuse Group, for smacking this
around the room more than a few times.

eluki, who said "yes" to my kids before anyone else,
and Dana and Lynn, all of whom took time out
to pay forward.

The folk in my newsgroup who came up with the info
when I needed it (and the Hounds, who howl on cue).

James, who told me to shut up and get back to work.

Marina Frants, who taught me all sorts of lovely Russian
phrases…some of which even made it into the book.

To you all, if I haven't said it recently,
grazie. Molto grazie.

The Mississippi's mighty, but it starts in Minnesota
At a place where you could walk across
with five steps down...
—Indigo Girls
"Ghost"

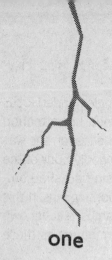

one

"Hey, lady! Move it or lose it!"

The cyclist sped past her, a blur of expensive aluminum, narrow wheels and Lycra-clad body topped by a screaming-orange helmet. He—she? it?—hopped off the curb and dove into the light traffic moving up Madison Avenue, almost slamming into a cab that was cruising around the opposite corner looking for an early-morning fare. The cabbie slammed on the brakes and the horn at the same time, and the bike messenger made a rude gesture as he wove in and out of the middle of the street, heading downtown.

"Oh, for a stick to spoke his wheels," Wren said wistfully, staring after the cyclist with annoyance. The man standing next to her smothered a surprised burst of laughter. Wren blinked. She hadn't been kidding; bicycle messengers were a menace.

Dismissing the incident with the single-minded focus she brought to every job, Wren turned her attention back to the building in front of her; the reason she was standing out on the corner at this ungodly hour of the a.m. on a Monday. What terrible sin had she committed in a past life, to get all the morning gigs in this life? She made a soft, snorting noise, amused at her own indignation. At least it was a pretty morning as those things went.

In fact, Manhattan in the spring was a pretty decent place to be. Winter meant slush and biting winds, while summer had a range of heat-induced smells that ranged from disgusting to putrid. You could live in the city then, but you generally didn't like it. But spring, she thought, spring was the time to be here. The sun was warming up, the breeze was cool, and people were in the mood to smile at each other. Even bad days had an edge of promise to them.

But right now, spring weather aside, Wren couldn't find a damn thing to be happy about. Seven in the morning was way too early, and the job that had sounded like quick and easy money at first was rapidly going deep into the proverbial shitter. She was going to have to do some actual work for her paycheck on this one.

"Maybe that will teach you to answer the phone before six," she said out loud.

"Excuse me?"

Rafe, the guard who had been detailed to "help" her, had a cute little wrinkle between his eyebrows, totally spoiling his until-now perfect Little RentACop look.

"Nothing. Never mind." *Don't talk to yourself in front of civilians, Valere.* It wouldn't have mattered, anyway. Even if she had ignored the phone's ringing two hours ago, before either she or the sun had thought about getting up, the sound of Sergei's voice on the machine would have made her pick the receiver up. She might have the skills that people paid for, but her partner was the one with a nose for jobs that was slowly but surely making them moderately well-off, if not obscenely wealthy. Only a fool would pass up a call from someone like that, no matter what the time.

And while Wren Valere was many things, a fool had never been one of them.

"Rafe? Can you go get me a refill of water?" she asked, handing him the plastic sports bottle she had been holding. He wasn't thrilled at being an errand boy, she could tell, but his orders had been explicit. Give Ms. Valere all the help she needed. Type of help not specified. So he went.

Freed from observation, she sat back on her heels and closed her eyes slowly, holding them shut for a count of ten. She had been doing this long enough that it didn't take her any longer than that to slip into a state of clear-minded awareness. The sounds of early-morning traffic, the smells of exhaust and fresh-budding greenery all faded, leaving her with a clear, concentrated, settled mind. As she opened her eyes slowly, not rushing anything, her gaze went back to the sleek marble foundation in front of her, as though there might have been some change in those ten-plus seconds of blackout.

Nope. Nothing. It still looked as ordinary and commonplace as before, one of any of a hundred-plus buildings throughout the city built in the same time period. No bloody handprint, no chisel marks or dust left on the pale gray surface, no sign of any kind of disturbance at all. Nothing to suggest there was something different about this northeast corner of the building, as opposed to the southeast, the southwest or the northwest sides. The four corners of this building stretched out over a full city block, and she'd just spent the past hour becoming far too familiar with all four.

God, she hated prep work! But you had to check *everything* before you started looking for anything. Even the stuff you knew you wouldn't find. Except, of course, the fact that one corner, or rather one small block inside of this corner, wasn't really there anymore.

A deliberate letting-go of her concentration, and the fugue state slipped away. Wren stood, arching her back to release some of the tension that had gathered there. Magic—current, in the post-eighteenth century terminology—was easy enough to use, if you had the Talent, but that didn't make it *easy*.

Her throat felt like sandpaper. She looked around, but Rafe wasn't back yet with her water. He must have gone all the way up to the executive lunchroom for San Pellegrino.

She clicked on the miniature recorder in her hand, and spoke into it, remembering to speak slowly enough that she would be able to transcribe correctly later on that day. "No indications of newly-made marks or disturbances on the site, not that that means anything—I bet they have a team of sanitation experts who come in every morning and sluice the building down, just in case a pigeon poops on it accidentally."

All right, she thought. *A slight exaggeration. But not by much.* The guy who'd designed this had obviously had some penile issues that needed to be worked out, though.

The building in question was a thirty-eight-floor skyscraper, gleaming steel and glass in the early-morning light. A troop of window washers could spend a full year just wiping and polishing the expanse of windows. An edifice built to proclaim the owner's ego to a city already overwhelmed with capital-P Personalities.

"From the exterior, the building looks intact. This is supported by the engineer's report—" And how the hell had they found someone willing and able to do a full review of the building this morning? Money not only talked, it must have bellowed.

But the report she had found in the folder left at her door by one of Sergei's ever-efficient contacts was clear on that. The missing piece had been removed from within the building, without cracking the concrete and steel surrounds. The building itself had not been harmed in any way by the alleged disruption to its structural integrity. Therefore, it was only her imagination that made the headquarters of Frants Enterprises tilt ever-so-slightly to the left. Cornerstones didn't actually support any weight in modern buildings, or so she had been informed by a quick skim through the multitude of building and construction sites on the Internet while she waited for her coffee to brew. They were there for show, to display the construction date, as tradition. Sometimes, as receptacles of time capsules, or good-luck charms—

Or protection spells.

Wren had been part of the magic-using community since she was fourteen. She'd never once used a protection spell, or known anyone else who did, either. But a lot of people swore by them, apparently. And were willing to pay good money to get them back.

She drummed her fingers on her denim-clad thigh, thinking. Sometimes you needed to know all the facts. Sometimes, knowing anything more than the essentials just clogged the works. The trick was knowing which situation called for what method. She glanced up the length of the building, then blinked and looked away again quickly. The view made her dizzy, not so much from the sunlight reflecting off the glass as the sense of...no, not menace, exactly. But a looming emptiness that was disturbing. As though something more vital than a chunk of rock had been stolen away.

Wren frowned, redirecting her attention to the building's foundation again, squinting as though hoping to suddenly be struck with X-ray vision. Not one of the recorded skill sets of Talent, worse luck. But if a Talent couldn't get the job done, it was time to use your brain, and she had a pretty decent one if she did say so herself. Eliminating the impossible, you're left with the obvious; it would take magic to get the missing slab out without doing major damage to the entire building. And that was exactly the feat someone had apparently mastered on this very building, at approximately 11:32 the night before. So, magic. Which narrowed the playing field not only for culprits, but motives.

She nodded to herself, twirling the recorder absently in one hand. A rather impressive act of vandalism, in more ways than one; it showed off the vandals' abilities without making a fuss the usual authorities could follow, assuming they would even be interested in a case like this; it in no way harmed the integrity of the building and therefore didn't put anyone working there at risk; and it struck deep in the heart of the building's owner and prime resident's deepest, ugliest fear.

It was a hacker's trick, showing how easy it would be

to really harm the target, without doing anything they could easily be prosecuted for. Only in this case, it wasn't all just show. Damage *had* been done, if not anything you could explain on a police report, or an insurance waiver.

Their employer had two very simple questions: who did this, and how soon can you get it back? Right now Wren was more concerned with *how* it had been done. In her experience, once you found the tools, it was generally a simple matter to find the workman. And once they'd found him, the fun part began.

Only problem was, this bastard didn't seem to have left any external traces at all. Wren was—grudgingly—impressed.

Clicking on the 'corder again, she continued making her comments, pacing down the sidewalk.

"The night watchman finished his rounds at 4:45 a.m. At that point, he claims not to have seen anything out of the ordinary—nothing that would have given him even an instant's pause at all." She hesitated, continued. "Which raises the question, I guess, if the theft was done remotely, or if the guard was under the influence of a spell himself."

A jogger went past her at a heavy-breathing clip, and she moved out of the way with the instinctive radar that big-city residents evolve by instinct, but didn't pause in her recitation. Even if the jogger had been inclined to listen in—selective deafness being another big-city survival trait—Wren doubted that he would have recalled it—or her—an instant later. Being invisible was one of the things she did very best. Part of it was by design: her jeans, white button-down shirt and leather jacket were quality enough that she would be categorized as "employed," and the temporary security badge that came with the reports was now hung around her neck, giving her a reason to be in the building. Most people didn't look any further than that. But the real secret to her success was a carefully cultivated result of the genetic lottery. Not a winning ticket; more like a "sorry, try again" one. Her shoulder-length hair was the color that could only be described as "brownish," and her features were unremarkably regular. Average height, average weight, unremarkable measurements—she never warranted more than a swift once-over by anyone, male or female. Her appearance was neither unpleasant nor remarkable. Forgettably average.

Sometimes she wondered if dying her hair bright screaming red, or bleaching it platinum blond would make any difference to the way the world didn't see her. But it never seemed worth the bother to experiment. And why screw with success? Besides, Sergei would kill her.

"The fact that there is no sign from the exterior of the building of digging, or any kind of disturbance at all, confirms the suspicion that it was a purely magical theft."

Well, duh. But you checked everything anyway, just so it didn't come back later and bite you on the ass.

"A remote grab seems more and more probable." And narrowed her eventual list of suspects. Far easier to steal line-of-sight, especially something this size.

Rafe appeared by her shoulder, holding out a water bottle glistening with fresh condensation. Wren shut off the recorder and tucked it into the inside pocket of her bomber jacket, then took the bottle from him and poured a stream of the water down her throat.

"Thanks. Let's go take a look at the inside, shall we?" The *we* was ironic, and they both knew it. Rafe wasn't so cute when he was annoyed. Oh well. She shouldered her way through one of the large revolving glass doors that led to the lobby, and walked inside the building, her eyes scanning the floor and walls with a practiced eye. She was looking for any indication that something might have been chalked or painted on the gleaming marble surfaces. Especially if it was a remote grab, signposts would show up somewhere. Remotes were tough enough, easier to focus if you had something there to guide you in. Leaving something of your own was best, but risky if you couldn't pull it on your way out.

Admittedly, it would have been difficult for anything to adhere to that expensive marble-and-brass slickness, but the lobby would be the logical—easiest—place for the thief to lay a marker. Wren was surprised when her scan didn't turn up anything. Markings were a safer way to do the job than actually being on-site at the time, something you could do well in advance of the job, and assuming that the victim knew enough to call in someone like herself afterward. If *she* had been doing the grab, she would have marked...the ceiling. Wren scanned upward, squinting against the overhead light, and let out a soft triumphant "hah!" There, up on the ceiling behind her, by the door. A faint streak, difficult to find even if you knew where and how to look for it. Wren did a rough calculation and decided that if you followed the end of the streak down and at an angle, it would point directly to where the northeast cornerstone was laid.

"Now, how did you get up there...and is it worth my time to go up and check you out?"

Probably not, she decided. Maybe later, if need be. But for now, the evidence was enough. Nobody was going to go up there and erase it, after all. Not without leaving even more trace for her to follow.

Something beeped. Rafe excused himself, going off into the far corner to talk into his walkie-talkie. He looked upset. Somebody must have seen him snatching the water, she thought with an evil grin.

Nodding to the morning guard at his station, she stopped so that he could compare the code of her temporary security pass against the list in the computer.

"Anyone else come in last night with a visitor's pass?" Overlook nothing; assume the perp was either insanely clever or astonishingly dumb. You never knew when a simple question could get you an important answer.

"Nope. Heard there was a problem last night?" The guard was a short black guy in a standard-issue polyester blue jacket and tie a shade darker than Rafe's. Although the tie might have been silk—he looked like a guy who would upgrade when possible. He sat the long security desk like a command center. Which, based on the number of blinking lights and constantly-changing screens set into the five-foot-wide surface, it was. Like something out of *Star Trek,* only without the nifty beeps and pings and whirring red alerts. This console was sleek and silent, even when a knob flicked red. He glanced at it, flipped a switch, and corrected whatever the problem was, all without taking his attention off her.

"You asking me, or telling me?" Wren asked. She heard the hardness in her voice, and winced inwardly, trying to tone it down a little. *Don't antagonize the witnesses, you idiot!* A slight cock of the head to the right, like the bird she was nicknamed for, and a faint smile that could be mistaken for encouragement softened her words.

It worked enough to take the edge off his initial reaction. "They told me there was going to be a full-scale shakedown later today. That says trouble."

She nodded, shifting her weight slightly to convey interest, and a willingness to hang around and listen to him for as long as he wanted to talk.

"And it had to be last night," the guard—his name tag read Blair—continued. "'Cause when I came in this morning, Joe had already gone off shift, and there were two guys here in way-too-expensive suits, working the desk instead of him. And here you are, full clearance pass, asking to see my log book. So, you with FullTec?"

The name was familiar from her predawn briefing materials. FullTec was the name of the company that had installed the security system for this building back when it was built in 1955, and rewired it every ten years or so thereafter. She'd checked them out online, too. They'd been ahead of their time even then, and were still riding the cutting edge of security technology now. No building wired by them had ever been broken into, held hostage, or otherwise menaced. The upper level executives who gathered for multibillion-dollar conference calls rested easy in a FullTec building. Said so right on their Web site.

But, according to her job notes, they hadn't been the ones to prepare the missing item. Which meant that they—probably—didn't know anything at all about the special protections built into it. That had been Talented work: a mage, probably, or maybe one of the earliest lonejacks. Special protections that kept the owner, the ruler of this little financial empire, safe and secure in his dealings with the outside world.

A protection that had disappeared at 11:32 p.m. last night.

She banished those thoughts for later, returning her full attention to the guard and the here-and-now.

"No, actually, I'm a freelancer. Called in special to double-check some of the systems."

Blair nodded his head, sagely impressed. The tie was definitely silk. "Ah. Watching the watchdogs, huh?"

"Something like that, yeah."

"So, you a tech? Some kind of whiz-kid hacker?"

Wren laughed, thinking of Sergei's caustic comments while he watched her fumbling attempts to upgrade her computer last weekend. Current—the power source of magic—screwed with electronics, so her relationship with her computer was at best user-cautious. "Nope." She paused, a germ of mischief making her tell this poor bastard the truth. "I'm a thief."

Twenty minutes later, she was alone with the main control box for the building's wiring system. The guard had laughed at her words, but the look in his eyes had been cool, and suddenly she'd been given an escort down into the basement. Not Rafe, either. A new guy, still polite but bulkier and much less cute. Not quite a goon, but with definite goonlike tendencies only barely tamed by the neatly pressed blue blazer that didn't quite hide the bulk of a stun gun at his hip. Nor, she suspected, was it supposed to.

"That'll teach me to be honest," she muttered, opening the box and surveying the neatly laid-out and labeled assortment of wires. A stun gun would only take her out for about half the time of a normal human, since her body was used to channeling electrical energy in the search for current, but it would still be unpleasant, if she were taken unprepared. "Sergei's right. Never gets me anywhere except in trouble."

"Did you say something, miss?"

"No, nothing, sorry. I talk to myself when I work. Just ignore me."

And she wasn't really a thief, anyway. She was a retriever, thank you very damn much. A person, as Sergei would say, of specialized skills, who could bring objects back to their rightful—the client was always rightful—owner without the fuss of a police investigation, or the bother of insurance companies getting involved. Sergei had a way of making everything sound so damn high-class.

All right, so sometimes a legality or two got bent out of shape, in the course of a retrieval. But bending wasn't breaking. Not so long as she wasn't caught, anyway. And nobody told her mother.

Reaching out, Wren traced a wire gently, pressing just enough to make it resist her touch. According to the label under it, this section of wires connected to the fire alarm system. Probably not what she was looking for, since those things were notoriously temperamental. Dropping her hand several inches, she came to the security alarm. Again, not likely. That would have been the very first thing they would have checked.

When he'd called with the details, Sergei had made it clear to her that the client wanted this done with an absolute nil of noise. Which meant, ideally, she'd be the only one on the job. But the guard's words indicated, to no real surprise at all, that that was already screwed. If the "mondo suits" at the board this morning hadn't been Mage Council troubleshooters, high-powered magic-users-for-hire, she'd eat her hat, if she owned one. Oh well. Never assume the client's going to tell you the truth. Especially if it involves anything that might actually let you get the job done.

But she had one advantage—high-powered magic-users tended to think in high-powered ways. Which she didn't, as a rule. Start low on the spectrum, work your way up. Nobody uses more power than they have to. Call it Valere's Strop to Occam's Razor.

Closing that control box, she opened the one directly below it and snorted without amusement. The labeling confirmed her initial suspicion: the electrical system for the entire building. Everything that had an On button was initially powered from this one place. She tsked under her breath. Sloppy, sloppy. With the quick close-and-yank of current, she could give every overworked, underpaid secretary a day off.

And then end up explaining to Sergei why the job went south. From a jail cell. Not one of your better impulses, no.

Reaching in, she touched her index finger to one of

the wires, and instantly felt a familiar answering hum in the blood running under the skin. You could describe magic any way that worked, and one mage's science was another wizzart's chaos. It all boiled down to using the existing energy that was generated by almost everything knocking about the universe. Call it electricity, call it life force, or chi: hell, call it Norman if it works. Wren didn't pay much attention to any of the various and contentious schools of magic theory. She wasn't much for schooling, period. You used what you had.

Every human living could use magic—theoretically. In actual practice, only a small portion of the population could conduct the charge, like living lightning rods, and an even fewer percentage of them were what her mentor had called pure conductors. Pures were the elite, the ones who made it to full mage status. They were generally co-opted by the Council, the strongest and most secretive union ever to collect dues. The rest of the magic-using population muddled along at various levels of ability, doing the best they could, finding their strong points and sticking to them.

Technically Wren was a pure, but she didn't see the point in bragging on it. It was like having a high IQ—wasn't much unless you worked it, did something with it. Drawing down the power was easy for her, siphoning off the energy from an external source to flow through her, as though she were running water through her hands. Any source would do, but current that was already tamed and channeled made it so much easier. Like called to like—energy was energy, and where there was one, there was the other. The electronic age was a godsend to magic users, despite what the fairy tales said. If she'd been a little better at channeling out what came in, she'd have been Council material for sure. The thought still made her shudder.

Five fingers now extended, she touched wires at random, discarding anything that sang back to her, looking for a discordant note, something that might indicate a flaw, a clog...or the remnant of supernatural tinkering. In short: look for an elemental.

"Ah-hah!" she said as her thumb grazed a wire that felt different from the others. "Gotcha, you sneaky little..." Pushing with that finger, she listened to the difference.

Elementals were exactly what they sounded like—entities that existed in an elemental state. Very small, and barely sentient, they were nonetheless useful, if you knew how to coax them. Now that she had a handle on one, Wren could sense a flurry of elementals within the wire she had tapped—hardly surprising. Barring a thundercloud, there were few places an elemental flocked to like a live wire; it must be like an amusement park, or an opium den to them, pick your metaphor. Now, to see how long they had been there, and if they'd noticed anything.

"Right. Come to mama..."

Having already gone into the fugue state once that

morning, it was like stepping off a curb to find it again. No thought, no effort, just a sudden snapping into awareness, chasing glittering tendrils up and down her neural paths...

"Excuse me, miss?"

She blinked, shaken out of her intense concentration by the goon placing a paw on her shoulder. He looked nervous.

"Yes?"

"I'm sorry, but, whatever it is you're doing—could you stop? They're reporting power outages on several floors...."

Wren grinned sheepishly. "Right. Sorry." She must have gone too deep, and drained some of the charge down accidentally. She flexed her neck and arched her back as though to straighten out stiff muscles, feeling for the natural current within herself. It hummed and snapped with vigor, confirming her suspicion. She'd gone for an automatic skim, copping a buzz off the charge of magic that could be found even in man-made electricity and storing it in the pool that every current-sensitive person carried, knowingly or not, within them.

Oops. Technically, that would be theft. Never a good idea, to steal from your employers. Probably on the level of office supplies; a pen here, a ream of paper there...Wren shook her head, dismissing that train of thought. It didn't matter. She had gotten what little in-formation was there. The trick now was going to be fig-uring out what it all meant, if anything.

Making nice to the goon-guard so that he would "forget" about what he hadn't really seen anyway took a few minutes. Then she was riding up in the freight elevator, back up to the main lobby. It was crowded with suits now, male and female, armed with briefcases and brown paper bags, some of them already open to let loose the aroma of fresh-brewed Starbucks, or the cheaper stuff from one of the ubiquitous corner bagel carts. The starting bell had rung, and all's well with the corporate world. Wren shook her head, moving against traffic. How the hell did people live like this?

It was with decided relief that Wren left her security badge with the guard at the front desk and went home. Now the real work—the fun stuff—could begin.

two

The message light on her answering machine was blinking, a quick red flash that caught her eye the moment she came in the door. She dropped her keys in the small green ceramic bowl on the counter of her square little kitchenette, her mail next to that, and reached over to press the play button.

Opening the fridge, Wren pulled out the orange juice, pouring a long draught down her throat without bothering to get a glass.

"Wren, it's 9:15." Sergei's perfectly enunciated voice filled the sparse confines of her kitchenette, almost as though he were actually there. "I just accessed your account, and half of your fee has been deposited, as agreed upon."

She raised the O.J. carton in salute to that fact.

"Need I remind you that the client is paying for a timely resolution to this situation?"

Sergei never referred to them as cases, or jobs. No, the "client" had a "situation." Situations paid better.

"Jesus wept, Sergei. Even Christ took three days to rise from the dead! Gimme a break here!"

"And need I remind you that today is the thirteenth? Please mail your rent check today."

"Yeah yeah, I already have a momma nag, I don't need another," she complained to the empty apartment as the tape clicked off. Not that it wasn't sort of nice, having someone to remind her of the stuff that always managed to slip her mind. Like dropping a check in the mail.

That was the way their partnership worked, too. Sergei handled the money side of it, set up the deals, worked the angles. She did the jobs—or, in Sergei's parlance, "rectified the situations." The stuff that took Talent, as opposed to talent. From each according to their abilities, although she had been known to bargain sharply, and Sergei wasn't above getting his hands a little dirty, if needed. She knew for a fact that the man lied with the fluidity and believability of a gypsy prince if it suited him.

A nice skill for your agent to have. It had certainly saved their asses more than once, including one memorable evening where he had played both her father and her husband to two different people in the space of an hour. He hadn't been sure which role was more annoying, especially when she insisted on calling him "daddikins" for the rest of the month.

The memory of that made her smile, the comforting awareness of Sergei as always tucked somewhere along her spine. It wasn't anything particularly magical; just the knowledge born of ten years' partnership that, all joking aside, he was there for her, that all she had to do was yell.

Well, maybe it was a little bit magical. Sergei wasn't a total null, and maybe she'd sampled a little more of his internal energies than she'd ever told him about... but it was only so that she'd be able to pick him out in a dark room, in a crowd, if the need ever arose.

Not that she'd ever admit to needing him, even when she was asking. Bastard would enjoy that far too much. He'd be more than happy to take over handling her personal finances, too, if she let him. It wasn't that he didn't think she was capable. She hoped, because otherwise she'd have to kill him. He just...was overprotective that way. Every way. Sometimes she thought he still saw her as the seventeen-year-old she'd been when they first hooked up, her still foundering in her abilities, and him with a pair of severely pissed-off mages on his tail.

Putting the orange juice back into the fridge, Wren turned out the light in the kitchen with a casual slap of the hand against the switch as she went across the narrow wood-floored hallway and into the main room. She turned on the stereo, letting the soft jazz clear out the silence. The music tugged at the tension between her shoulder blades, pulling it down off her body. A world with saxophones in it wasn't a bad world at all.

Other than the stereo, two huge speakers, and a comfortable brown tweed armchair, the room was empty of furniture. The acoustics of the room were—astoundingly—perfect. It would have been blasphemy to in any way disturb it.

Her fifth-floor walkup had five rooms—downright palatial by Manhattan standards, even if the rooms themselves were tiny. In addition to the music room and kitchenette, there were three shoebox bedrooms against the back wall, each with its own window that overlooked the brick wall of the next building over. A bathroom with facilities that had been upgraded within the last decade sent the rent soaring from barely reasonable to moderately painful.

Okay, so maybe the neighbors weren't all they could be, in terms of minding their own business. The five flights of stairs were murder, especially in the summer. And the sounds of traffic from over on Houston Street could be pretty bad. Wren didn't care. Two years ago she had walked in the door half a step behind the real estate broker, a hyperkinetic woman glued to her cell phone, and had felt a sense of comfort soak into her bones, like walking onto a ley line, those semi-legendary sources of power. This was home. This was her sanctuary. The moment the building went co-op, as every decent apartment building seemed to, sooner or later, she was going to buy her apartment. That's where all of her money went, right into the savings account that was not ever, on pain of pain, touched. No vacations, no expensive toys or impulse splurges.

Well, maybe a few. Mostly, though, she stole what she really wanted. Just to keep her hand in, of course.

Wren was a pragmatist. She was very good at what she did, but no career goes on forever. Especially not one with risks like hers. So she planned. And prepared. And kept praying that human nature would maintain a demand for her particular skills.

So far, no problem on that front. Someone always wants what they're not supposed to have, and someone's always equally willing to pay to get that something back.

Setting the volume level to where she could hear the music throughout the apartment, Wren grabbed the mail off the counter, sorting it as she walked down the hallway into the bedroom that was set up as her office. "Phone bill, credit card, junk junk junk, more junk, political junk." She tossed all but the bills into the recycling bin next to the desk, and thumbed through the flyers that had been stuck in the doorjamb, setting aside one menu and tossing the rest into the bin. That was the third flyer she'd gotten for pest removal. At this point, they were more annoying than her nonexistent cockroaches, current being a great and totally—in her mind—underutilized way to keep a location insect-free.

"If I could only market that little side effect right," she told the photo of her mother tacked to the board on the wall in front of her, "I'd be able to make us both filthy rich overnight. And Sergei, too."

The office was the largest of the three bedrooms, but barely managed to hold the small dark wood desk where her computer and a headset phone reigned, a comfortably upholstered office chair, and a tall potted plant against one wall. The corkboard hung on the wall over the desk was cluttered with papers, takeout menus, and the one posed photo of her mother. Five two-drawer file cabinets marched along the opposite wall, pulling double-duty as a table for an assortment of odd but useful objects she didn't know where else to put. That wall also held a closet. Its door had been removed, and half a dozen shelves installed, to serve as a makeshift bookcase. The window was covered by a rice paper shade, allowing light during the day, but keeping prying eyes out 24/7.

She sat down at the desk and turned on the computer. While it hummed to life, she reached over to the phone, dialing a number from memory while she hooked the wireless headset up, pulling her hair clear where it tangled with the mouthpiece with a mutter of disgust. She hated using the thing, but the phone—like her computer—had been rigged with so many surge protectors to make it safe for her to use on a regular basis that you couldn't move the damn thing without creating disaster.

One ring, and then a crisp, efficient "Yes?"

"It's me."

Sergei's raspy tenor voice changed, so subtly it would have taken someone paying close attention to recognize the new, softer tone for affection.

"You looked at the job site?"

"Yeah, for whatever that was worth." Wren leaned back and swung her feet up on the desk. Her loafers needed polishing. "External was clean, but there was one possible smudge-marker up on the ceiling inside. Although, in retrospect, it could've been there since Adam went figless. Anyway, ruled out anything else. Distance grab, no doubts. A pro."

"But it was definitely a magic-user?"

Sergei was, like so much of the human population, in that nether area between Null and Talent, but after so many years as her partner he was well-versed enough in the uses of it to make certain assumptions. Besides, realistically, what else could it have been?

"Yeah." She refrained from sarcasm. Barely. "Whoever it was used the building's wiring to convey the spell. Probably had every person in the building so hocused, they couldn't have told you what color their socks were."

"And then got the cornerstone out—how?"

Wren's mouth twisted in frustration, making her look

for a moment like a five-year-old given brussels sprouts. "Okay, that part I haven't quite figured out yet. Translocation, probably."

Translocation of an inanimate or inert object wasn't a difficult spell for someone with any kind of mojo and open channels, but the actual performance took a lot out of the caster. Especially if he wasn't present on-site, preferably within eyesight of the object. That was impossible in this case, since the object to be retrieved wasn't accessible without the breaking and entering of a kind that hadn't happened. So. A distance grab of that magnitude would make the hire-price prohibitively expensive, and the cost would increase the further the object was moved. Or it should, anyway. Even the best Talent had to eat and pay the rent, and a Transloc like that would wipe you for anything else for a week. "Might have intended to replace the stone with something else, to maintain volume consistency—" the hobgoblin of all translocations "—but the alarms going off must have wigged him."

"Alarms?" Sergei sounded a little alarmed himself. Wren reached out and sorted the pile of papers on her desk with one finger. Blueprints of the Frants building, cut into twelve-by-twelve squares for easy shuffling, covered with red ink—Sergei's handwriting—and her pencil smudges. "Yeah, alarms. I could feel the echoes when I went into the basement. Nice little mage-triggers. Someone is a smidge nervous down there. I wonder if the perp knew about them before he went down, or if he was expecting a simple grab-and-run, so to speak. And before you panic, no, I didn't set it off again. The parameters were set way too high for little old me."

Actually, that was a lie. She had sensed the threads of magic and slipped under and between them. While she wasn't ever going to be called to serve on the Council—even assuming they lobotomized her long enough for her to agree to sign on—that was more a matter of attitude than Talent. Where she was strong she was very strong, and distracting attention from herself, be it magical or physical, was as natural as breathing to her. Her mentor had called it Disassociation, which was basically a fancy way of saying that she could make people—or things, specifically things like an alarm system—believe that she wasn't there.

The problem, as far as anyone had been able to explain to her, was that for all her undeniable talent she was just a little too dense, magically speaking. The current channeled fine—she had the skill, no doubts there—but it sometimes channeled in weird ways, denying her access to a lot of the major skills like levitation and translocation. Pity, as they would have been damned useful in her career.

"You think maybe the thief meant to use it for blackmail? Or maybe ransom? Hey, got your protection spell here, what do you want to give me for it?"

"Or possibly to open up the door just enough for a direct attack by someone else?" Sergei sounded like he'd given this some serious thought while she was out doing the hard work.

"Maybe. I know, I know, not our problem. I'd prefer blackmail, though. Easier to find someone if they're going to be so obliging as to send back a calling card." If she were a better conductor...ah, well.

On the plus side of that density, the risk of her wizzing out—losing her mind to the magic flow—was probably lower than anyone else at her comparable Talent level. There were always going to be portions of her brain the current couldn't get into.

"They also serve those who hum in choir," she muttered.

"What?"

"Nothing. Look, whoever this was, he's a subtle guy, definitely strong, but not too bright. He squelched the elementals but forgot to sedate them."

"Which, in English, means what?" Sergei did exasperated like a guy with years of practice.

Wren grinned, forgetting he couldn't see her. Tweaking Sergei was always so much fun. He did the staid businessman thing so well, sometimes he forgot to take it off. "It means exactly that, which if you would ever remember anything I've told you about elementals you'd, well, remember." He had the weirdest mental block about certain aspects of current—she'd almost given up trying to figure it out. Then again, non-

Talents *should* be uneasy around current. She shouldn't blame him if even knowing things wigged him out enough to not want to think about it. "I tapped into the wiring, and there was a horde of elementals there. Quiet, but jazzed, like something'd shoved a massive current up their tails, but told them to lay low about it.

"But when I stirred them up, they came shooting out, like they were hoping whatever it was had come back."

And once they had come to her hand, she had been able to stroke them into giving up the residue from that burst of magic. That was another one of her stronger skills—reading magic like some people could read Braille, or maps, or any other code. It made her useless in a really powerful thunderstorm, stoned like kitty on catnip from the overload of power, but the rest of the time it was part of her stock-in-trade. Where one magic-user had gone, she could go, recreating their trail with remarkable accuracy. Well, mostly. Unlike her other skills, which had names and entries in the skillbooks her mentor had shown her, this one seemed to be particular to her and the way her brain worked. Or if other Talents had it, they were keeping just as quiet about it as she was. The end result either way was that she had no real idea how it worked, or why, or how to control it.

Then again, she didn't understand any of that about her computer either, and it still worked fine. Most of the time.

"I skimmed off a decent enough emotional memory

of the thief to recognize him or her again. Pretty sure of it, anyway."

Sergei made an unhappy-sounding noise in the back of his throat. She didn't think he was aware he did it—she couldn't imagine him making it during negotiations with clients, or the highbrow, hoity-toity art collectors who made his gallery so obnoxiously successful, which meant it was a Wren-specific complaint. The thought made her grin again. "Even if you were sure, that doesn't help us unless you actually run into him—"

"Or her."

"Or her, in the near future. Wren…" A sigh, and she knew he was fiddling with one of the slender brown cigarettes he carried with him everywhere and never smoked.

"Yeah, I know. Doesn't help worth diddly, realistically. But what, you expected this guy to leave a calling card? It happens, sure, but not real often. Which is good, otherwise we'd both be out of work."

Sergei made a noncommittal noise that might have been agreement, amusement or a growl.

"Look, all I need is a reasonably-sized list of people with something to gain by the client losing his big block o' protection, and I can backtrack from there. We do a little digging, to see who has the skills, or the money to hire a mage of that power, and then I can retrieve the cornerstone, which you know I can do in my sleep. Easy money. So no worries."

"So, who's worried?" Sergei asked, sounding worried.

Wren hit the disconnect button, not bothering to say goodbye. Swinging her legs back down to the floor, she winced a little at their stiffness. Time to hit the gym—she had gotten a little too out of shape over the winter again. Too many of their recent cases had been deskwork, not action.

She filed the thought under *"when I have a spare hour,"* pulled out the keyboard drawer and went to work composing and sending out e-mails to contacts, some human, and some not quite so, looking for any chatter happening in the *Cosa Nostradamus*.

The one advantage to being part of a community that the majority of the world didn't even know existed was that you didn't have anywhere else to talk about what was going on. So the gossip network was tight, fast, and frighteningly efficient. She'd lay decent odds with her own money that she'd have a lead by lunchtime.

Speaking of which… Wheels set in motion, she sat back and dialed the phone again.

"Hi, yeah, it's Valere in 5J. Medium sausage, and a liter of diet ginger ale. Just slap it on the tab." She listened for a moment, laughed. "Yeah, you too. Thanks." Taking off the headset, she draped it on its stand, running fingers through her hair to fluff it up again.

Her mother's photo managed to emit waves of disapproval despite the smile still fixed to her lips. "Ah, come on, Mom. Breakfast of champions, right? What's the point of having a 24-hour pizza place on the corner if you don't take advantage of it?"

Besides, it was either that or leftover Thai from the back of the fridge, and she'd mentally tagged that for lunch.

She had about half an hour before Unray's buzzed with her pizza. Might as well make it a billable half hour. Pulling the 'corder out of her jacket pocket, she put it on the desk and swung the keyboard into position. With a quick, silent prayer that her moderate use of current while the 'corder was in her pocket hadn't totally futzed the batteries, she hit Play and began to transcribe her notes, wincing a little at the static that had crept into the tape just because it was near her body.

"Come on, brain cells," she muttered as her fingers hit the keys. "Give me something I can use. Momma wants to wrap this up fast and have the weekend free, for once!"

three

The room was remarkable for being completely unremarkable. The walls were painted a soft matte white, the floor made from wide planks of fine-grained wood. The lighting came from discreet spots that directed attention rather than illuminated.

There was one door. No windows. The overall impression was of endless space somehow made cozy. An architect had labored over the lines and arches of this space, a designer had meditated on the perfect shade of white for the walls and ceiling, a feng shui specialist had dictated the ordering of the floor's wooden planks, the exact placement of the three objects which resided therein in relation to the door.

It was for those three objects that the room existed.

In one corner, reaching from floor to ceiling, was a simple green marble pillar, three feet around and seven feet high. Etched onto its surface were crude symbols that hadn't seen the light of day for over three thousand years.

In the opposite corner, an ebony wood pedestal was lit from above, highlighting a chunk of clear, unfaceted crystal that looked as though it had just been pulled from the ground, hosed down, and dropped onto that base.

And in the farthest corner, two men maneuvered a low wooden tray set on wheels into position. It was a mover's trolley, its bed covered with a quilted pad similar to the kind used for fine furniture and grand pianos. Another pad wrapped up over a four-foot by six-foot square, and was sealed with heavy gray tape. The hard rubber wheels moved soundlessly on the floor, despite the weight they bore.

The two men were burly, but not brutish looking. One was perhaps forty, with graying hair cut short. The other was ten years younger, and completely bald. They wore simple white coveralls that had only one pocket in the left sleeve, too small to carry anything larger than a cigarette lighter. There were no names sewn over the chest: no logos, cute or otherwise on their backs.

They finished adjusting the trolley, and the younger man knelt by its side, producing a slender but sharp-looking pocket knife from his sleeve pocket, carefully cutting through the tape, peeling it away from the pad and unfolding the pad from its enclosed prize. About the length of a small bench, the marble's silvery-gray surface was marked and pitted, making the once-glossy surface look dull and battered. A smaller rectangle on the top surface looked as though it had been carved out and then filled in with concrete.

"All this, for that?"

The older man sounded disgusted. No one else was in the room, but his partner cast a worried look over his shoulder, as though expecting someone to appear there and overhear the criticism.

"If the owner says it's art, it's art," he told his older companion firmly. "Let's just get it settled, and get out of here." Personally, the object gave him the creeps. Hell, the entire place gave him the creeps. But he was a professional, damn it. He was going to act like one.

A low matte black platform, installed when the room itself was built and unused until now, waited to receive its burden. The two men took wide canvas slings that had been hung on the trolley's handle, and fitted them around two corners of the marble block. The younger man's hand brushed the surface of the stone where the cement plug was, and he shuddered involuntarily, stopping to look down at his hand as though expecting to see a spider, or something else less pleasant on top of it.

"Will you stop that?" the other man snapped. "Concentrate on the job. I don't need you getting sloppy and dumping it all on me."

Stung, his co-worker glared at him, shook his hand

out unobtrusively, as though to get feeling back into a sleeping limb, and counted to three under his breath, just barely loud enough to hear. On three, they heaved, and with a seemingly effortless movement and a pair of grunts that destroyed that illusion, the stone settled into its new home.

"That's strange. Wonder if it's been hollowed out? I thought marble that size would be heavier."

"Don't complain, man, don't complain! And for God's sake, don't ask," the younger man begged, his eye closed against the sweat that was rolling off his forehead. "We on the mark?"

The stone was square on its base, with a full three feet between it and the walls on two sides; room enough for a person to walk around it, should they so desire.

"Yep," the other workman replied. "Perfect, as always." It was as close to a compliment as they would get from anyone. They were hired via the company's Web site, informed of the details by e-mail, paid by wire transfer, and never knew what any of it was all about. And they liked it that way. Some folk you just didn't want to know any more about than you had to.

Their work completed, the two rolled up the quilted pad and tossed it onto the trolley, pushing it out ahead of them as they left. They didn't look again at the object they had delivered, nor did they pause to consider the other two objects already in place.

No one waited at the door to show them out; they

had been given their instructions before arrival, when they were assigned the job. They would walk down the bland, security-camera-lined hallway they had entered through, down a flight of stairs, and follow a row of lights through a basement maze that would deposit them through a four-inch-thick metal door in a ten-foot-high wall that ran along an unpaved country road. A livery car with darkly-tinted windows waited there to take them back to the city, where they would be dropped off without once having seen another person.

Their employer wanted his privacy. They were paid well enough not to wonder why. And the legalities of what they had done never entered their minds at all.

When the last echoes of the workmen's feet had faded into silence once again, silence reclaimed the building. In another wing, a door opened, and footsteps sounded, walking calmly, with no apparent haste or urgency, the owner of all within those walls. Occasionally the walker would pause to admire a painting, or caress a sculpture, but for the most part the priceless objects were accorded no more attention than the carpet underfoot, or the ceilings above.

Eventually, the door into the white room was pushed open, and the owner of the house entered, walking with those same unhurried strides to the corner holding the newly-installed fixture. He paused in front of it, cataloguing every detail and comparing it to his expectations.

"You're not much to look at, are you?"

The slab of stone didn't respond to the voice.

"But they do say, you can't judge something by its looks. It's not what's on the outside that counts, after all, but the inside. Isn't that right?"

The figure knelt by the cornerstone, trailing one well-manicured finger along its rough surface, shivering pleasurably at the sensation. "But no matter. No matter. I know what you are, what you were. And all that really counts is that you're mine, now."

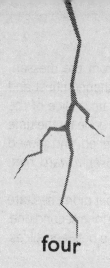

four

"Hey. Babe. Let me in!"

The very first time Wren had met P.B., she had giggled. The second time, she had screamed. By now, when he showed up on her fire escape, she merely flipped the safety latch on the kitchen window, and let the demon come in.

"Thanks. Man, this neighborhood of yours is totally not safe anymore. Some loon started chasing me down the street, yelling something about a cleansing to come. You got much business with Holy Rollers, Valere?"

She shrugged. "You must just bring it out in 'em, pal. You got something for me?"

P.B. shook out his fur, a faint mist coming off him. "Damn, I hate rain. Makes my skin itch." He took a battered-looking manila envelope out from the messenger's bag strapped across his barrel-shaped chest and tossed it on the table, then scooped up a slice of the remaining pizza. The slice was halfway gone by the time Wren had opened the envelope. She sighed, and shoved the rest of the grease-lined box closer toward him. "Here. Eat. You're looking frail."

The decidedly unfrail P.B. snorted, but didn't hesitate in devouring his first slice and reaching for a second one. "I get first prize for speed?" he asked in between slices, referring to the material in her hand.

"As always," she said, licking one finger and using it to sort through the pages, scanning the delicate copperplate that seemed so incongruous coming from P.B.'s clawed hands.

P.B.'s real name was all but unpronounceable. The nickname came from an inauspicious moment back in the early days of their acquaintance, when an innocent bystander had been heard to shriek, "Oh my God, it's a monster!" To which Wren, somewhat short-tempered at the time, had snapped back, "No, it's an effing polar bear!" The description had been apt, and the nickname had stuck.

P.B. wasn't her only source, but he was one of the best. Certainly the most reliable. Demons mostly made their living as information conduits, there not being much of a job market for them outside of bodyguarding and freak-show gigs. There wasn't anything that one of them didn't know, or couldn't find out, and what one of them knew, another would hear, sooner or later.

Sooner, if the money was right. And they didn't play politics: you got what you paid for, no matter who—or what—you were. It was refreshing, in a disgustingly capitalistic pig kind of way. She wished more of the *Cosa* worked that way. But no, the ineptly-named angels had their endless feuds, and the various fatae-clans their more-special-than-thou attitudes, and humans—sometimes she thought humans were the worst of all, with the mages and their rules and regulations and Shalt Nots worse than Sunday School for fear of someone breaking rank and having a little fun. "Someone" in the mages' case mostly being the lonejacks, the Talents who refused affiliation. Unions and scabs, Sergei had described it, but it wasn't that simple, really. Everyone had a different reason for going lonejack.

And, tossed into that mix, always the snarling between the races, like they weren't all in it together, more or less. But some people—humans *and* fatae—just couldn't handle the idea of something shaped or colored a little differently walking, talking and working alongside their precious selves. Wren didn't have much patience with that. You do your job, stay out of her way, she didn't much care if you lived in brimstone or used your hind paws at the dinner table.

Sometimes, she thought it would have been a lot easier being Null. Then she watched the Suits scuttle to work every morning, hustling for a window office, and decided she was happy where and what she was.

P.B. burped, the sound like baritone chimes rising from his rotund stomach. "So what's the job?"

She just looked at him, a wealth of disbelief in her expression. He stared back, his flat, fur-covered face blandly innocent. Anything she shared with him without a for-hire agreement would be sold to his next client before she'd had a chance to act on it herself. Not in this lifetime or the next three, pal.

"Right. Don't tell me anything, just send me out to fetch like a dog...."

She considered responding, then decided that it really wasn't worth the effort. It was enough that she wasn't pitching him out the window already.

Wren had only met three demons in the flesh in her lifetime—that she knew about, anyway. Looks varied wildly, and she was told that some of them could pass for human, if you weren't looking carefully. The three she had encountered weren't those kind. And of those three, P.B. was the only one she could deal with for more than a few minutes at a time. It wasn't that she was prejudiced; she simply couldn't handle the relatively high voltage most of the full-sized demons emitted, like some kind of ungrounded magical wire that set her teeth on edge. Fatae—the elves and piskies and whatnot—were, by contrast, easy on the nerves. And angels never hung around long enough to do more than freak you out.

For a few moments, the only sound in the kitchen was P.B.'s jaws chewing crust, and the scritching-soft noise of paper against paper as she read what he had brought her. Finally she reached the last page, and shook them back into order and replaced them in the envelope, folding the metal closure back down again. Names, jobs, capabilities...P.B. had done his usual bang-up job of getting exactly what she needed. Some of the names on the list were familiar, in the heard-about-them kind of way.

And one was all too familiar, in a gut-clenching way. She forced herself not to focus on it. All the names were equal possibilities right now. Don't jump to conclusions. Conclusions without facts get people killed, possibly even her own very important self. File it, Valere. File it and deal with it later. When you're alone.

"Thirteen names?" She raised an eyebrow at the fur-coated being now lounging in her other kitchen chair.

He belched, then shrugged. "Lotsa folk interested in your boy," he said unapologetically. "He's made himself some enemies. And those're just the ones who have a profile with us." *Us* being the entire magic-using community, the *Cosa Nostradamus*. Human and nonhuman alike. *We might squabble amongst ourselves, often to the point of a passing wave of bloodshed, but in the end it was always us against them—"them"* being what her long-gone mentor used to call Kellers; the Nulls, who were mostly blind and deaf to what was around them.

Not much love lost there. To some of the *Cosa,* her working with Sergei on an equal footing was betrayal. He wasn't too fond of them, either.

P.B. went on. "Probably lots of otherwise upstanding humans who hate his guts too."

"What, he kicks old ladies and molests farmyard animals?" She'd gotten info on the client, but it was all public relations bullshit, not anything actually helpful. Sergei usually did a full write-up highlighting anything she needed to know, but this looked like a time-of-urgency kind of deal. Besides, he was the client, not the mark. They didn't ask too much about the clients.

"Nah." The demon cleared a piece of cheese from between his serrated teeth and flicked it into the garbage can. "Sounds like he gets his jollies the old fashioned way—with money. Preferably other people's money, which he then turns into more money for himself. Real power-hungry, in the nasty-with-it way."

Wren shrugged one shoulder, the tilt of her head conveying supreme indifference. "Most people with power are, that's why they get to stay on the top of the predator heap. Anything I don't already know?"

"Yeah. He's apparently in real bad odor with the local wizzart's gathering."

"Wow." Crossing wizzarts took serious guts. Or a total lack of brains. Possibly both. Unless of course he didn't know what he was doing. If he only knew about the public face the Council sold.... Wizzarts weren't exactly talked about outside the *Cosa*. Not too much inside it, either, truthfully. Mention not, see not, become not.

In fact, "gathering" was an ironic term to refer to wizzarts overall. The only time you got more than two wizzarts gathered anywhere was if they were all using the bathroom. And even then most of them would rather burst a bladder than share space with their own kind. And they weren't much sweeter on other humans. Most wizzarts didn't want to live within a hundred miles of another person. They were all crazy, chaos-ridden by taking too much current into their brain. From what little she'd been able to learn, the entire human race made them feel like she did around P.B., and twice that for another of their kind. It almost gave her some sympathy for them.

Not much, though. Last time she dealt with a wizzart, he'd tried to throw her over a cliff.

"Nice. And the Council?"

Dangerous or not, Wren would take a wizzart over a Council mage any day. Mages—cold, calculating bastards that they were—made her feel like she needed to take a bath after talking to one. And scrub hard.

"Street rumor is he stiffed 'em once, but managed to squirm out of retribution. No word on how, and believe you me there are folks who want to know that little trick, if it's true." The demon extended one three-inch-long claw and dug into the thick white fur on his neck, sighing in satisfaction when he hit the itch.

Wren watched in amusement. P.B. looked like an es-
capee from some demented toy shop, four feet of
thick white fur and button-black nose offset by four
sets of lethal claws and a voice that could scrape tar
off the highway. But if the initial impression was of a
cuddly bear, it was his eyes that were the giveaway to
his true nature: oversized and pale red, with pupils
that were slitted like a cat's. Occasionally, he would don
a hat and trench coat, which made him look like a
diminutive Cold War-era spy, but more often than not
he wore a pair of jeans, and not much else. She didn't
ask how he managed to get around in public like that
without, as far as she could tell, the slightest bit of Talent beyond his own demon nature, and he didn't vol-
unteer the information. Professional courtesy, such as
it was.

"That it?" she asked, indicating the material.

He nodded. "That's it."

"Great." Her tolerance level had reached its breaking
point and she was starting to get a headache. "Sergei
will do the usual deposit. Now get out." She was already
reaching for the kitchen phone, her back turned to him
when she added, "And leave the rest of the pizza."

"Spoilsport," he muttered, but left the box untouched. He also left the window open, in petty retali-
ation, and the sounds of an argument from the
apartment below floated up to her over the pad-clatter
of his clawed feet on the fire escape.

A tenor: voice spoiled and high-pitched by anger. "And another thing, I don't like the tone of your voice!"

Oh wonderful. The couple in 1B were on that rant again. She was convinced the landlord paid them to leave their apartment whenever prospective tenants looked at a place. That had been the last time she hadn't heard them. They were either arguing, or having sex. And one rather memorable morning, they had managed to do both.

Wren held the phone at arm's length, dialing Sergei's number with her thumb as she leaned backward to shut the window. "I have enough drama in my own life, thank you very much. I don't need yours too."

"Yes?"

"Me again," she said into the phone. "Take me out to dinner."

There was a pause. Warily... "And I should do this because...?"

"Because you haven't actually seen me in, what, ten days? Two weeks, maybe, and are worried that I'm not eating properly."

Her partner snorted. She was joking, but there was some truth to it; she had forgotten to eat for two days once when she was on the job, and Sergei had totally freaked when he found out. "And the other, more convincing reason?"

Wren made a snarling noise that completely failed to impress him. She thought maybe once it had. Years ago.

"Look, Genevieve—" She rolled her eyes. He rarely used her hated given name, usually only when he wanted her to think he was pissed off about something. "I have other accounts, responsibilities which require my attention. I can't just walk out when you whistle."

Ooo, someone *was* pissy. Market must be down again. "Yeah, yeah, you're a hotshot high roller. This is work stuff, okay? Do I have to remind you that I make you more on one job than all your other clients, thereby keeping you in your suits and toys, and that—as you're so often telling me—if I don't get the job done—I—and you—don't get paid?"

Sergei made a noise that might have been a protest— or could have been suppressed laughter. You never could tell with Sergei, not even when he was sitting in the room with you. Part of his incredibly annoying charm, and why she was never bored around him.

As amusing as this game was, she didn't want to risk frying the lines by talking too long. "Just get your well-dressed rear up here, okay? Seven-thirty, Marianna's. And bring whatever info you have on the client's business compadres, so I can cross-reference the players before I do something stupid."

"Thought before action. What a refreshing novelty."

"Oh, bite me," she said rudely, and broke the connection before she could hear him laugh. She sat and looked at the phone for a few moments, smiling absently. He was a pain in the posterior, but he was *her* pain in the posterior.

An expensively upholstered chair crashed against an equally expensively-paneled wall, rattling the oversized photograph of the desert at dawn which hung there.

"Idiots! Incompetents!"

The topmost floor but two of the Frants building was split into nine offices around a center lobby. Eight of those offices were large, lush spaces with a commanding view of the city, with a slightly smaller office directly off and to the inside where each inhabitant's administrative assistant sat. The ninth office was twice again as large, and three assistants guarded access like Cerebrus at the gates of the underworld.

At that moment, two of the assistants were cowering in the bathroom, while the third tried to pretend nothing at all unusual was going on in her boss's sanctum.

"Sir, we merely feel that it would be wisest—"

"Don't!" Oliver Frants held one finger up in the younger man's direction, his florid, freshly-shaven face turning an ill-omened shade of pink. "Do. Not. Tell. Me. What. To. Do." Each word was bitten off with precision, as though his perfectly capped teeth were holding back longer, uglier words.

The three executives glanced at each other, uncertain what to say next. They were all in their mid- to late forties; healthy, well-groomed, impeccably dressed. The kind of people you would normally see at the head of a boardroom table, having highly placed people report to them.

But in here, they cowered.

"I will not abandon this building. I will not abandon any of my scheduled meetings. And I will. Not. Hide."

He looked at them each in turn, until they dropped their gaze like chastened children.

"Sir?" The woman, Denise Macauley, had dredged up enough courage to speak. Frants smiled. She had been a particular protégé of his, years ago, and her sharp wits had never failed him.

"Yes, Denise?"

"If I may suggest, sir, that we add to the building's defenses?"

"And just how do you suggest we do that," he asked, "since the mages have made it quite clear that they will not allow their members to work for us any longer? Are you suggesting I hire another freelancer?" When the Council had, after looking things over, refused to help, despite it being their people who had set the spell in the first place, the only alternative had been to look for someone among the so-called lonejack community. The Council's spin would have you believe that they were nowhere near as talented as their own members, but reports had said that one seemed particularly suited for the job, and so Frants had authorized it. But retrieval was one thing. His security—especially his long-term security—was another. "Or do you think that we should perhaps hire a wizzart?"

"No sir," she said, properly dismissing that idea as unthinkable. You couldn't hire a wizzart; they were the flakes of the magic-using world, just as likely to forget what they were doing, and for whom. Or to bring your solution to your enemies, just for kicks. They were too unpredictable for a well-ordered business plan. He could see her mind working at a breakneck speed, choosing and discarding alternatives until she came up with one she thought he could accept. "There has been some talk about a freelance mage down in New Mexico; very powerful, but a little too...creative in his ways for the rest of his kind. Solid reputation—has never once sold out or otherwise failed a client. Council-trained, but no longer under their strictures. He's opened his doors to bidders—I think that we would be able to come to an agreement with him that would be mutually beneficial."

A well-trained, thinking associate was a blessing to their manager. "Excellent. Marco, see that it's done."

One of the men nodded his head, and turned to leave the room. His pace was perhaps a shade too swift for propriety, but Frants didn't call him on it. A little fear, leavened by generous bonuses, made for excellent working conditions.

Denise had stiffened when he gave her idea to someone else, but she didn't allow any resentment or anger to show on her face. Good girl. He would have to reward her when all this was done.

"Randolph?"

The remaining man came to attention, his shoulders going back in an automatic response. You could take the boy out of the Corps, but...

"Could you please speak to Allison in Human Resources, have her write up a press release stating that we had an unfortunate attempt on our security, but that we have every faith in the systems we use, and do not feel that there is any need for alarm, etc. If this bastard *did* take the stone to try and undermine Frants Industries, he will have to work harder than that. Much, much harder."

Randolph nodded and performed a sharp about-face, covering the plush carpeting between him and the door with a steady, measured stride.

"Sir?" Denise said, when he sat down behind his heavy mahogany desk, to all appearances having forgotten she was still there.

"Ah yes, Denise." He looked at her, his pale blue eyes cold, dispassionately calculating. "It may be that this is not the act of a business competitor, but someone perhaps a bit more...directly connected with the particular object which was taken. If that is—an extreme possibility, I agree—but if that is so, then I think that we may need to take further steps than even the ones you had suggested. If you would give me your arm, please?"

Denise had worked for Oliver Frants most of her adult life. She knew what he was asking. And, to her credit, she didn't flinch as he reached into his desk drawer, and pulled out a small, intricately woven straw box with an oddly liquid design, like an hourglass but not, on the lid. He slid the box across the table toward her, and something inside it *shhhhhssssssshhhed* like old grass in the wind.

The assistant still sitting at her desk heard a noise in the main office. A sibilant, sharp noise, like metal on metal. A wet slap, like flesh on flesh, and a muffled moan of agony. And then silence.

She placed her hands palm down on her desk, stared at the well-manicured fingers that cost fifty dollars every single week to keep in ideal condition, and swallowed hard.

Wren spent the rest of the afternoon reading up on the newest generation of motion detectors—not her idea of light reading, but essential to keeping up to date in her particular line of work. Sometimes, for whatever reason, you couldn't use current. Wren refused to be caught with her pants down if and when that happened to her.

Sprawled on the carpet in the third bedroom, which

was otherwise filled with her considerable research library, engrossed despite herself by journals with ten-point type and convoluted electrical diagrams, time got away from her.

"Ah, hell," she muttered when she actually glanced down at her watch. She shuffled the journals into a messy pile and left them there, closing the bedroom door firmly behind her. One finger pressed against the knob and a narrow thread of current flowed from her to wrap around the metal mechanism, locking the tumblers in place. Not that it would keep out anyone determined to get in, but the spell was tied to her just enough to let her know if the attempt was made. She could have coaxed some elementals into baby-sitting for her, to act like a siren if the thread was broken, but the reality was that when *she* saw elementals clustered, that drew her attention to the lock rather than away. And why put up a sign saying "important things behind this door" if you were trying to keep people *out?*

She grabbed her keys from the bowl in the kitchen, shoving her feet into a pair of low-heeled boots as she headed out the door, locking it carefully behind her with the more commonplace and nonmagical dead bolts every New Yorker installed as a matter of course.

Three-quarters of the way down the narrow apartment stairs, she realized that she had left the folder P.B. had given her on the kitchen table.

"Grrrr...urrrrggghh." She reversed herself midstep and

dashed back up, knocking open the four dead bolts and grabbing the bright orange folder. Locking up took more precious time, and she was swearing under her breath in some colorful Russian phrases she had picked up from Sergei by the time she finally hit the street.

With all that, despite the fact that she was only walking a few blocks, it was closer to seven forty-five before she made it to Marianna's. She paused on the street outside the tiny storefront, clutching the folder in her hand as though she might forget it again somewhere, and checked her appearance in the reflective glass door.

She thought about the lipstick she had left untouched on her bathroom counter, and made a face at herself. *You don't need to put on a face for Sergei, for God's sake,* she snarled mentally. He'd seen her at three in the morning, drenched in sweat and splattered with both their blood, and not blinked. So long as she didn't actively embarrass him in a social setting, she could paint herself in blue-and-green stripes and he'd just say something like, "Interesting outfit, Genevieve."

And why did it matter, anyway? If there was one thing she knew, without a doubt, it was that Sergei gave a damn about what was inside, not out. So why did that thought, increasingly, make her feel depressed instead of comforted?

Job, Valere. Job.

Squaring her shoulders, she pushed open the door. Callie looked up from her seat at the bar, saw it was her, and merely nodded toward the table where Sergei was waiting.

Wren shook her head in mock disgust, although she wasn't sure if it was at herself or her partner. Well, of course he was there before she was. Odds were good that he had arrived at exactly seven-twenty-nine, trench coat over one arm, briefcase at his side, taken one look at the restaurant, saw she wasn't there yet, sighed, and requested a table in the back and a glass of sparkling water, no ice.

"Been here long?" she asked, slipping into the seat opposite Sergei. He looked up from his notepad, then looked at his watch. "A little over fifteen minutes," he said, confirming her suspicion.

In a simple but expensive gray suit and burgundy tie, Sergei could have passed unnoticed in the carpeted halls of any brokerage house. Broad-shouldered, with a close-cropped head of dark hair and a nose that was just a shade too sharp for good looks matched to an astonishingly stubborn square chin, he could just as easily have been a former quarterback-turned-minor-league newscaster, or a successful character actor.

What he was, in fact, was the owner and operator of a very discreet, wildly overpriced art gallery. It was through the gallery that he made the contacts who often had need of Wren's services: private citizens, mostly, but also the occasional museum or wholesaler who didn't want to go through the police or—even worse—the insurance companies to reclaim their stolen artwork.

And, on occasion, something a little more...unusual. Like this case. *Sorry,* she amended even though Sergei couldn't hear her thought, *this situation.*

Callie came over, wiping her hands on the front of the white apron tied around her waist, and stood by their table, one bleached-blond eyebrow raised. "Your usual?" she said to Wren.

"Nah, I think I'll live dangerously." She scanned the chalkboard behind the bar with a practiced eye. "Give me the Caesar salad and the filet of sole."

"Which is exactly what you've had the past three times. Experiment a little, willya?" Callie had the flat-toned voice of someone trying to pretend they weren't from around here, but unlike almost every other waiter and waitress in town, she wasn't waiting for the big break to sweep her off to Hollywood.

"And a glass of Chianti."

"Ooo, red instead of white. You are living danger-ously." Not that being a professional waitress made her any more respectful of her clientele. Just the opposite, actually.

"See why I love this place?" Wren asked her com-panion.

"Indeed. A tossed salad and the halibut, please. Nothing else to drink."

"You guys have really got to calm your wild lives

down," the waitress said in disgust, stalking off to the kitchen with a practiced flounce.

"We're such a disappointment to her."

Wren snorted. Callie had been flirting madly with Sergei for two years now, ever since Wren moved into the neighborhood and they started coming here regularly, and he remained serenely unresponsive. Disappointment didn't even begin to cover it. Wren could understand Callie's point of view, though. If she wasn't so sure he'd look at her blankly, or worse yet give her the "we're partners, nothing more" speech, she might have made a play for him, too. Well, maybe not when they first partnered. But lately…it was weird, how someone so familiar could suddenly one day, totally out of the blue and with a random thought, become…interesting. In that way.

Damn it, Valere, focus! "Whatcha got for me?"

Sergei lifted a plain manila envelope out of his briefcase and handed it to her. "The names of all the highly-placed executives, both within the Frants Corporation and at rival organizations, who would have reason to hold a grudge of this magnitude, and the financial wherewithal to hire someone to perform magic of this level. You?"

"Bunch of folk with the mojo to do the job themselves, almost all carrying a mad-on of one kind or another for our client. Strictly low-budget grievances, though." She pulled out a legal-size piece of paper from the file and handed it to him in exchange. It was a copy of the original list P.B. had given her, with her own notes added under each name. "Doubt they'd be in any of your databases."

"Don't ever underestimate my resources," he told her severely. "Many people who think they're invisible often—"

"Leave a fluorescent trail. Yeah, yeah, I know." One of the few "resources" of his that Wren had ever met in person was a former forensic investigator named Edgehill, who was paying off some unnamed but very large favor done in the distant past. He was a slight, frantic-eyed man with wildly-gesturing hands. Listening to him talk was sort of like watching an episode of *CSI* on fast forward while taking speed. But his shit was almost always on the money.

"Would the police have anything on file?"

Wren snorted. "Nobody on this list. Strictly no-see-um talents."

"Noseeyum?"

"Too good to get caught."

"Ah." He grinned at her, the expression softening his face and putting an appealing glint in his dark brown eyes. Behind that hard-assed, hard-pressed agent façade, she thought not for the first time, Mr. Sergei Didier had a real wicked sense of humor that didn't get nearly enough air time. "Kin of yours?"

"Hardly." Without false modesty, Wren knew her

worth, and so did Sergei, to the penny. These guys were good, but she was better. Which was why *she* didn't appear on other people's little lists. Even Sergei, with all his surprisingly good contacts and connections, hadn't known about her way back when until sheer coincidence—and a nasty accident caused by someone trying to kill him—brought them into contact.

Wren's mentor, a man named John Ebenezer, had taught her from the very beginning to keep a low personal profile for a great many reasons, all of them having to do with staying alive and under her own governance. There were three kinds of current-mages in the world: Council-mandated, lonejackers and dead. Just because a Talent had no interest in being under the Council's thumb didn't mean they might not want her there, now or someday later. Better not to take the chance. That was the lonejacker's first law: steer clear of the Mage Council.

Their salads arrived at that moment, and they paused long enough to accept their plates, and wave away Callie's offer of freshly ground pepper.

"I've never understood that."

"What?" He looked at her, his forehead scrunching together in puzzlement.

"The fresh pepper thing. Who puts pepper on their salad?"

Sergei shrugged. "Someone must, otherwise they wouldn't offer it."

"I think they do it just to see who's stupid enough—or sheep enough—to say yes."

"You have a suspicious mind."

Wren grinned at him. "You do say the sweetest things."

"Eat your salad," he told her, lifting his own fork with a decided appetite. Her list lay just to the side of his plate, so he could skim it without distracting himself from his food, or running the risk of getting salad dressing on the paper. Wren watched him eat and read for a moment, then picked up her own fork and dug into the pile of greens. She was going to wait until the dishes were cleared away to go through the neatly-clipped-together, ordered, indexed and color-coded material properly.

"Hey, this name was on my list," he said suddenly.

"What?" That got her attention fast.

"This name." He stabbed one well-manicured finger at the paper as though it were somehow at fault. "It was on my list."

Wren took the paper from him. "Which one?"

"Third from the bottom. George Margolin."

Wren scanned the list, coming to the name he indicated. "Huh. Talent, yeah, but not buckets of it. Not affiliated, not really a lonejack—he's passing." In other words, he wasn't using current in any way, shape, or form that was obvious to the observer, and probably didn't use it at all. At least, not consciously. But you never knew for certain. And some folk were just naturally sneaky about it.

"Great. Move that guy up to the top of the suspects list. Anyone in a suit that P.B. hears about is going to be dirty, one way or another."

"P.B.?" Sergei didn't roll his eyes—that would have been beneath him—but his voice indicated his level of unimpressedness.

"Hey, don't dis *my* sources," she said, pointing her fork at him. "That furry little bastard always comes through, which is more than I can say for some of your people. I seem to recall a little screw-up with IDs that almost got me shot by the cops in Tucson."

"All right, all right. Point taken."

She had to give Sergei that. He was a xenophobic bastard when it came to things like demons and fatae, but he didn't cut humans any slack when they screwed up, either. Especially when it was their own lives on the line.

She flattered herself that he might have been just as annoyed at that snitch if he hadn't ended up in that Tucson jail along with her.

"So how come this guy's on your list?"

"You have the file, you look."

"Why? You've memorized the important stuff already." Wren never understood why people wasted brain-space on anything they didn't need right at hand. That was the magic of writing stuff down, so you didn't have to cram it all in your head. But Sergei was incapable of letting go of anything to do with a job, at least while the file was hot. For all she knew, he did an info dump at the end of every case, mentally shredding all that info in order to make room for the new stuff.

She had a mental image of Sergei running his brain through a shredder, and had to stifle a snort of laughter.

"What's so funny?"

"Nothing." She bit the inside of her lips, made a "go on" gesture. "Tell me about Margolin."

He frowned at her, dark eyes narrowed in suspicion, but complied. "Mid-forties. Computer genius of sorts, chief technical officer for Frants Incorporated. Odd, for a Talent."

"But not unheard of, especially if he's passing. That low-level a Talent, probably enhances the tech stuff rather than shorting it out. Lucky bastard." Wren didn't carry high-tech toys because it was an exercise in frustration, not because she didn't like them.

"According to this, he's smart, savvy, and very very disgruntled. RUMINIT says he felt that he was passed over for promotion because of his religious beliefs."

"What, he's a Scientologist?"

It was Sergei's turn to laugh. "No, agnostic. Rather militantly so. As in 'I don't know, and you don't either.'"

Wren tried to raise only one eyebrow and failed, pretty sure that the resulting expression made her look like an inquisitive owl. "I can see where that could get up someone's nose, yeah. But if he's passing... Yeah."

She checked her notes. "Nope, no real training, far as anyone knows. No mentor ever claimed him." That was how Talents worked, mostly; one-on-one apprenticeships. Went all the way back to when it wasn't safe to work together—or tell anyone what you were, so you tied the knowledge up in secrecy and oaths. "He doesn't have the firepower to do it himself, and I can't see him having enough information without a mentor to track down and hire a mage to do something like this, either." She narrowed her eyes as a sudden thought hit her. "Unless he's from a Talented family that's stayed low-profile, flying under the radar? Neezer said sometimes it ran in the bloodline like that. But not often, not so's you could track it, anyway. So maybe he's not private enemy number one after all." She paused. "I wonder how he got on P.B.'s list."

Sergei squinted at the list, trying to make out the handwriting. "Ursine?"

"Usury. Somebody's got a light wallet, if he's paying out the loan sharks, hey? Odd, you'd think he'd be making plenty of money. Kids' tuition go up? He a gambler? The *Cosa's* not pretty on people who welsh on debts."

"No information on either. And they run some pretty heavy scans on people for exactly that. I'll take it back and see what some determined digging can produce."

Sometimes, Wren wondered about Sergei's snitches. Not their ability—their origins. Mostly they were the usual: artists who heard every bit of gossip that rumbled through the collectibles world, high-rent agents who knew where the money was buried and the bodies bankrolled—that sort of thing. But every now and then she needed information you couldn't get from a cocktail party, or through a discreet inquiry, and then his clear brown eyes would go dark and shadowed, and he'd refuse to say yea or nay…but the information always came through. And unlike his other sources, and her own, the information they gave was always straight-up. Always.

So she wondered, but never pried. For all that they pretty much lived in each other's pockets during cases, weeks could go by otherwise when they only talked briefly on the phone. There was an awful lot about Sergei's life she didn't have clue one about.

Oh, Wren had known back when they first hooked up that her new partner was a man with secrets, not the least of which was how he'd even known about Talents and the *Cosa* in the first place. It wasn't as though they took out ads in the local trades or anything. But he did know, and he never said how, and that had actually made her trust him more, not less. If she was going to let him in on her secrets, after all, she had to respect that he held others as securely, right? But oh, the desire sometimes to crack him open and see what secrets came rolling out…

In a purely mental, informational way. Of course.

She'd seen the women he socialized with, had even met a few of them over the years when their social paths overlapped. Lovely women, Nulls each and every one; elegant and articulate and educated, usually artistic as hell. And visible. Always highly visible. Memorable, even. Unlike her own eminently forgettable self.

And so it goes, Valere. You are what you are. And so is he, and so are the both of you together. Concentrate on the job.

"Anyone on your list you think is likely?" Sergei asked.

Pulled from personal to professional musings without warning, Wren shook her head, replaying his words as she chewed on a particularly leafy green. *Likely as a thunderstorm in summer.* There was someone on her list who had the talent to pull something like this, and the probable grudge and twisted sense of humor to make it seem like a good idea. All she had to do was name him, and Sergei would be able to run a complete dossier. But the words didn't come out of her mouth.

She tried not to lie to Sergei. It was just bad business, and stupid besides. But she wasn't ready to say anything to him just yet. Not before she knew more.

Some things, when you got down to it, were more important than business. Some loyalties you couldn't just walk away from. And anyway, with any luck Sergei wouldn't figure out who she was protecting until she had her answers and it wasn't an issue anymore one way or the other.

Callie came by to take their salad plates away and bring the main course, saving her from having to reply. By unspoken consent they moved away from shop talk while digging into their meals, catching up on the small details that made up each day. Sergei had a new show beginning that week, and he was full of the near-disasters and minor crises that came with every installation.

"So Lowell gestures like he's some off-off-off Broadway magician, only his arm gets tangled in the hangings, which in turn get tangled in the wires. And the wires come down like the wrath of God, sending the piece soaring through the air like it thought it was Peter Pan."

Wren snickered, imagining the scene. "Anyone get hurt?"

"Only the artist, who chose that moment to walk in the door, demanding an update. I thought he was going to have a heart attack."

"You hoped he would have a heart attack," she corrected him. "You could have doubled the prices on everything."

His brief grin made her laugh around a forkful of sole. "Trebled. But there would have been paperwork, and the show would have had to have been delayed, so it's probably best he didn't."

"Spoken like a true patron of the arts. You're a marvel and a wonder, you know that, Didier?"

"I do my humble best, Valere. I truly do. Some day I might even make an honest man out of me."

With perfect timing, they both said "yeah, right" in matching tones of disgust, and his sudden bark of laughter made Wren laugh again as well from the sheer joy of the noise.

He went on to detail the results of the show while Wren finished her meal. Shamelessly scraping the last of the sauce up with her finger and licking it off with relish, she checked to make sure Callie had finally re-seated herself at the bar and was engrossed in a magazine before giving in to temptation and retrieving the file from the floor beside her chair. Sergei continued with his meal, now silently watching her as she skimmed through his data.

"Truthfully, these all look pretty doubtful as our boy," she said finally. "I mean, we need someone who has a pretty major grudge against the client, enough know-how about magic to do the job, and—most importantly—they had to know about the spell in the first place. I'd say that's a triumvirate that lets out all but three or four of these folks. I'd rather concentrate on the ones who would actually have gotten their hands dirty, see if I can't match the readings I took from the site with their signatures."

"Which would mean your list?" Sergei placed his knife and fork down precisely on the table. On cue, Callie swooped down and cleared their table, scraping the crumbs off the tablecloth with a small metal tool and handing them each a dessert menu. She might be an annoying eavesdropper, but she was an excellent wait-ress. "How many of them would fit those criteria?"

"All of them, probably." She pushed aside the menu without even looking at it. Time to tell the truth—if not all of it. "Like I said, they may not be as highly placed, but they all have grudges, and the means to execute them."

"So...?" Oh, she knew that tone of voice. Damn. And twice damn. He knew she was hiding something—he always knew, somehow. Like a vulture knows when din-ner's about to pass over. She looked up into deep brown eyes and wanted to tell him everything. Only a decade's worth of resisting that lure—and seeing it work on too many others—gave her the ability to look away.

Sorry, partner. This one I've got to deal with on my own. You'd only freak, anyway.

"So I'll try to narrow the list down. See if I can't talk to some of them, face-to-face."

Sergei kept his face calm, and only the little tic at the corner of his jaw gave him away. "Any of them wizzarts?" Casual. Too casual. She could hear enamel grind. Their partnership had taught him when to step back and let go, too. He just didn't always—ever!—listen to what he knew.

"A couple. All recent, though, nothing to worry about. I can handle myself, big guy."

She hoped.

five

Although it was nearing noon, activity on Blaine Street, deep in the so-called "artist's maze" favored by trendy galleries, was better suited to early morning, with half the stores just beginning to see an early trickle of customers. The short, narrow street had clearly once been the home to warehouses, metal steps rising up from the curb to oversized metal doors set in otherwise stark brick buildings. But where most of the other converted buildings that now housed trendy stores and galleries had clear glass windows, the better to display their contents in a carefully designed presentation, the narrow glass front on 28 Blaine had been replaced with artisan-made stained glass. The deep blues, reds and greens seemed at first to be randomly placed, but if you stepped back a moment, the wavy striations in the glass and the choice of colors created the appealing effect of an underseascape.

Between the window and metal double doors, a small bronze plaque announced that this was the home of The Didier Gallery.

Inside the gallery, the floor was covered in a muted gray carpet, and walls painted Gallery White were hung with paintings in groupings of three or four, interspersed occasionally with a three-dimensional piece on a pedestal. The works displayed this month were brash, almost exhibitionist in their use of color. A curved counter ran through the middle of the space, and behind it a sturdy wrought-iron staircase rose to the second-floor gallery, where smaller pieces were displayed. A young blond man sat at the desk, flipping through a catalog. He looked as though he belonged in a catalog himself: perfectly coiffed, elegantly dressed and bored out of his overbred skull.

Sergei blew through the door, setting the chime alert jangling. The young man looked up, gauged the expression on his boss's face, and wisely decided not to speak unless spoken to. One look around told Sergei that no one else was in the gallery, and with a grunt that could have been satisfaction or disgust, he nodded to his associate and went to the back wall of the gallery, where touching a discreet wall plate opened the door to his private office.

The door closed behind him, and the young man went back to flipping through the catalog.

"Of all the stupid, harebrained..." Sergei had managed to keep a hold on his temper all the way home from Genevieve's apartment, which meant that by now, although he was just as angry as before, he was unable to let go and have the temper tantrum he so righteously desired.

She hadn't answered the phone when he had called this morning. She hadn't been home when he had arrived on her doorstep an hour later. Not that she didn't have a perfect right to go off on her own. He was her partner, her agent, not her damned keeper. That would have been a full-time job alone. But he had known she was hiding something, damn it. Had known sitting there across from her during dinner, and let it go, and that was his fault.

It hadn't been until this morning, as he was taking his morning walk, that one of the names on the list had jumped out of his brain and thwapped him soundly across the face. He hadn't recognized it at first, because he only thought of the man by the nickname the *Cosa* had given him.

Stuart Maxwell. She was going to confront Stuart Maxwell, otherwise known in Talented circles as The Alchemist. The man so hooked into the current he could turn wishes into water, and water into wine. The man who, the last time Wren encountered him, had tried to kill her. A certified, over the bend, wind whistling through his brains, wizzart.

Wren knew he wouldn't have let her get within a mile of that man ever again, no matter if he had been the first, last, and only name on their suspects list. And so she conveniently forgot to point him out.

He felt his teeth grinding together, and slowly forced his jaw to unclench. His partner only *thought* he was overprotective. And then she went and did something like this that only proved he wasn't damn near vigilant enough!

If she survived—she would survive, she would—Sergei swore to himself, he was going to put her over his knee. And he meant it this time!

Okay, so he wasn't being rational. She had the astonishing ability to do that to him, did his Wren. And it drove him insane.

Exhaling, and muttering a curse under his breath, Sergei finally took off his coat and hung it on the wooden coat rack in the corner, smoothing his hair back and settling himself into his skin. Calm. He needed to be calm. When Wren was in the field, the game was hers. The fact that he could—and had—imagine any of two dozen things that *could* go wrong did not mean anything *would* go wrong. And even if it had—he paused a moment to make a quick gesture with his fingers to avert ill luck—there was nothing he could do about it until she bothered to check in.

He took a deep breath, let it out. This was Wren. She *would* check in. His partner was occasionally reckless, but she wasn't stupid. She knew what she was doing. He had to believe in that. Believe in her. Don't make her asinine fears—that he didn't trust her enough—any worse.

And, in the meantime, he had a gallery to run.

"Lowell," he said into the intercom. "Please bring me the week's invoices, if they're ready? And tomorrow's guest list as well."

The building was more of a shack than anything you could properly call a house. Derelict in the middle of an oversized lot given over to wildflowers and knee-high grasses, the two-story building boasted a wraparound porch and tall windows, but the wood sagged, the white paint was cracked, and the windows were blurred with grime.

"Lovely."

Wren pulled her rental car—an innocuous dark-blue sedan—to the side of the dirt road, and stared at the structure. There was no need to check the address against the information written in her notepad. There wasn't anything else that could be her destination on this isolated road miles from the nearest town. Besides, there wasn't a house number anywhere to be seen.

With a sigh, she tossed the notepad into her bag, slung the strap over her shoulder, and got out of the car. Dust swirled around her heels, the dryness at odds with the riot of greenery on the property. She couldn't feel anything, but that was hardly surprising. You never could—until the trap was sprung, and it was way too damn late.

"You shouldn't have come."

"Max. I want to help you." The Wren-self in the memory was years younger, her hair longer, tied into a braid halfway down her back. Sergei in the distance. Too far away. Far enough away to be safe.

"I'm already damned, girl. Didn't you learn anything?"

His eyes had still been sane, then. Thirty seconds later, he had tried to kill her.

Wren stopped just shy of the border of grass, and sighed again. Then sneezed, her sinuses reacting to the overabundance of green growing things.

"Great. He couldn't have holed up in a concrete warehouse somewhere? Max!"

Approach protocol thus satisfied, she waited, shifting her weight from one sneaker to the other, wiping her palms on denim-clad thighs.

"Max, you shit, I just want to talk to you!"

There was no answer. She hadn't been expecting any, but it would have been nice to get a surprise. Wren was tempted to reach out, to try and feel for the currents she knew were floating around the house, but she didn't. Bad manners, and dumb besides. This was her last stop of the day, and she was tired, short-tempered, and really not looking forward to this at all.

"Max!" A pause. "You mangy bastard, it's Wren!"

A harsh bark of laughter right in her ear startled her, but she schooled her body, refusing to let it jump. Sound waves were easy to manipulate. A cheap trick.

"Come in then, you brat. Before I forget you're out there."

That had been easier than she expected. Suspicious, she stepped onto the grass, watching as the blades bent out of her way, creating a path directly to the porch steps.

Far too easy. She had a bad feeling about this.

The inside of the house was actually quite comfortable, if you liked extreme lo-tech living. The front door opened onto a large room, encompassing the entire front of the house. A fireplace took up all of the far wall, and bookshelves covered much of the other three walls. No television, no computer, no phone in sight. Just books and the occasional piece of what might have been artwork. Not that she had anything against books, but there was only so long you could live in someone else's head. Wren didn't trust anyone who didn't get out and do for themselves.

Not that she trusted The Alchemist worth a damn to begin with. Not anymore. She learned slow, but she did learn. But this wasn't exactly the kind of thing you could do over the phone. Assuming he had access somewhere, somehow, to one. And that it didn't go snap-crackle-pop the moment he touched it. Wizzarts were even more prone to short-circuiting electronics than your average Talent, because they didn't think to be careful.

Some would say that they didn't think at all.

There was no sound at all in the house, not even the hum-and-whir of appliances somewhere, or the clink-clink of water draining through pipes. It made Wren nervous, that absence of sound. So what if she'd grown up in the 'burbs, back when you might still see deer or fox or occasionally a bear in your backyard; she was too much a city girl now to feel comfortable without the end-less background accompaniment of screeching brakes, sirens and horns.

Even the damn crickets outside had been better than this. Silence wasn't a thing; it was the absence of a thing, of noise. And her mind always wanted to know what had swallowed the noise, how, and when was it coming for her.

To distract herself from that thought, she looked around again. Two overstuffed sofas and a leather re-clining chair were matched with sturdy wooden tables, obviously handmade. The plaid upholstery was worn and comfortable-looking, and the floor was wood, scarred with years of use, and covered with colorful cloth rugs scattered with more concern for warmth than style. A large dog of dubious parentage lay on one of the sofas. It lifted its head when she came in, and con-templated her with brown eyes that didn't look as though they had been surprised by anything in the past decade, or excited about anything in twice that time.

"Hi there," she said. The narrow tail thumped once and then lay still, as though that much effort had exhausted it. "Let me guess—Dog, right?"

"Don't see any reason to change a perfectly workable name," the voice said from off to her left. "I'm the man, he's the dog, and we both know our places."

"And his, obviously, is on the sofa."

Max let out a snort as he came completely into her line of sight. He was wearing an old, worn blue cotton sweater and khaki safari-style shorts that showed off knobby knees, red-banded tube socks sagging around his ankles. "That one's his, this one's mine. We stay out of each other's way. Which is more than I can say for you. Didn't my throwing you off a cliff teach you anything? Why you bothering me again?"

Wren hadn't seen Max in almost five years. But for a wizzart, that was crowding.

"Your name came up in very uncasual conversation," she said, sitting down in the chair, but not relaxing into it. Max seemed reasonably rational right now, but that didn't mean a damn thing. She actually had learned a great deal from going off that cliff, most of which involved the fact that she couldn't fly. She wasn't eager to relearn that particular lesson.

"Whoever it was, they deserved killing." He sat down on his sofa and put his feet up on a battered wooden table. His socks were filthy, dirt and grass stains worn into the weave of the fabric, but they somehow managed not to stink.

"No killing," she said. "Not yet, anyway."

"You bring any chewing gum? I could use a spot of chewing gum. So if they're not dead, what's the hassle? And if they are dead, what's the hassle anyway?" He held his hands out in front of him, as though about to clasp them in prayer, and spread his fingers as wide as they could go, staring intently at the space between his palms. The pressure in the room increased, fed by the energies the old man was bouncing throughout his system like some kind of invisible pinball game.

Wren swallowed a third, much heavier sigh. *Wizzarts*.

"Max. Focus."

"I'm listening," he said, cranky as an old bear with arthritis. "Get on with it before I decide you might make good fertilizer for the grass."

He was making an effort for her. That was nice to see. Wren organized her thoughts quickly, compiling and discarding arguments and appeals. Finally, feeling the pressure of his current-games pushing at her eardrums, almost to the point of pain, she went for broke.

"Why did you threaten to kill Oliver Frants?"

The moment the words were out of her mouth, she knew that she had made a mistake. The question was too vague, too loosely-worded. He could answer her without telling a damn thing, whatever obligation or guilt or connection he felt satisfied, and she'd be out on her ear before she got another chance.

"Man's a waste of piss."

And that was it, the sum and total of his elaboration. Typical, she thought in disgust. A wizzart didn't need to have a reason to do something. They thought it, they did it. For that quirk alone Wren could have written Max off the suspect list—this kind of indirect assault on the client required planning, thought—some kind of long-term intent behind it. And nobody in their right mind would have hired a wizzart to do a job like this—there was too much risk that the wizzart would get bored, and deposit the stone in the middle of the local police chief's bedroom, just because.

The problem was, a wizzart simply didn't have anything left over after the magic. Their entire existence was dedicated towards channeling the energies, feeling them as completely as possible, every cell turned towards the goal of becoming the perfect conductor. And that included their brain cells.

Because of that, wizzarts lived in the moment, the instant of action. It made them irascible, ornery, obnoxious—name your adjective and someone would double it without hesitation. "Waste of current" was the popular view. But the Council, in one of its few and far-between acts of mercy, had forbidden anyone to harm wizzarts. There but for the grace of God go you, was their official line. Truth was, Wren knew, the Council used wizzarts. When it came to the major mojos, to understanding the byplay of forces, the correlation of events and probabilities, they were the chaos-theory scientists of the *Cosa Nostradamus*.

Unstable, yeah. But the very fact that they were that unpredictable also meant that Max *could* have done it, either for a client, or a passing whim. The only prediction you could make about the unpredictable is that they're going to do something you didn't even have in the list of possibilities.

"I have a problem," she said quickly, before his attention went into a sideslip. "Someone pulled a nasty job on my client. Someone with a bad sense of the funny. Your name was on the list, and I—" The pressure against her eardrums rose dramatically, and the energies between his hands manifested in zizzing spurts of static electricity. He giggled in pleasure. She had lost him.

A night spent chasing down leads, checking up on suspects' alibis and whereabouts, coupled with a morning of phone calls and in-person follow-ups on local suspects, topped by the two-hour drive to this godforsaken town that wasted even more time she probably didn't have, finally made her temper snap. Ignoring all known procedures and common sense for dealing with wizzarts, she reached forward and slapped her hands over his, forcing the energy into a cage of her own flesh. Energy channeled took on the signature of its user. And right now, trapped between her hands, was a solid buzz of Max-imprinted magic, ready for the scrolling.

hey hey HEY brat. bitch. A flash of herself, much younger, all eyes and ears and good intentions flickering like a beacon from him. She countered with her own self-image, foot tapping in impatience. It was a little like the icons people used in chat rooms, she'd been told. **what what WHAT?**

Irritation came back from him, some resignation—a flash of pride, that she had learned so much since their first meeting. Some disgust, that she sold herself that way, to the highest bidder. And a complete, total lack of information about what she needed to know. He had never even met the client, merely read a newspaper article about the man that annoyed him and spouted off about it in the wrong place.

"Oh, Max."

She released his hands, not apologizing for the hijacking. The formal dance of manners slowed down the mental process, interfered with conductivity.

That was the popular theory, anyway. Sergei had a long-standing, loudly-spoken opinion that Talents were just naturally rude.

Dog yawned, his tongue hanging out of his mouth when he was done. Max stared at her, his blue-green eyes trying to dig under her guard, ferret out whatever he was looking for. Wren ignored him the way Dog was ignoring them, waiting for his reaction. Her body appeared relaxed, but that very casualness was preparedness. Whatever hit, she would be ready to dodge out of the way, roll and slip out of range.

Ignoring the fact that even on an off day Max's range was further than she could run—to the edge of the property, at least, and likely a full line of sight beyond that. If he got pissed, she was screwed. It was that simple. And that was why wizzarts rarely had houseguests.

"You're looking in the wrong place," he said finally, his voice old and scratchy, as though her insight had worn him out in some measure.

"Where should I look then?" If he was going to offer aid, she was going to take it. Her mama might have raised a fool, to be here in the first place, but that didn't mean she had to be stupid about it.

"I don't know." He shrugged, the cotton sweater showing new holes as he moved. "I'll poke through the ether, see what I can find out."

There was a tension about him, in the way the pressure pulled in tight around him, that suggested this little get-together was just about over. Dog whined, and rolled onto his other side, facing away from them. Wren stood, looking across the room at the wizzart. "Why?"

He laughed, a manic sound that made the hair on the back of her arms stand straight up. "'Cause you came to me. 'Cause not killing you's the last thing I managed to do right. Maybe 'cause you're all that's left of John on this green earth."

John Ebenezer. Teacher. Friend. Father figure. Gone, ten years and more. It still hurt, the memory.

"You might want to get out, now."

Wren got. The grass didn't move out of her way this time, instead straining towards the house, as though there was a stiff wind blowing them inward.

There was. Only it was brewing inside: the center of the whirlwind, a black hole of current. Lightning flashed in the clear blue sky, and Wren felt it shiver down her back, like the first stroke of a massage. She got into the car, tossing her bag onto the seat next to her, and almost flooded the engine in her haste to get the hell out of there.

Wizzarts. Jesus wept.

The drive back to the city seemed endless, her brain chasing after one detail or another until she shut it all down with a blast of rock and roll. She might be a jazz kind of girl, but there was nothing like the sound of sledgehammer guitars to get you rolling down the highway. Wren handed in the rental with a kind of regret, patting the hood in farewell as she waited for the attendant to finish checking it out. He was a tiny little guy, bandy-legged, who looked as though he should have been fussing over spindly Thoroughbreds, not standard issue Chevys.

Once he'd given the other attendant the all-clear, she signed off on the X'd line, collected her copies of the paperwork, and caught the subway home, standing-room-only as everyone else headed home from a tough day at the office, too. Normally an irritation, today she welcomed the press of humanity, sweaty and rude though it might be. The fact that she could stand them, could rub skins with the rest of humanity without freaking, reassured her that she still was one of them. Still sane, normal…as normal—

As normal as you could be, with the buzz of magic running through your cells when the rest of the world doesn't feel a thing. When John Ebenezer had first discovered her using Talent to pilfer sodas and candy from the local five-and-dime, he'd dragged her out of the store by one ear. He'd read her the riot act, fed her a lecture on morals, and hadn't let go until she knew what it was she was doing—what she *was*. It hadn't seemed so scary then. He'd been a lot closer to normal then; he'd taught high school, in fact. Biology. Before he too had given himself over to the current, made riding the wave his entire reason for existing. Wizzed out.

By the time she graduated high school, he was long gone; the toll of his own Talent overwhelming what had been his life. But by then, he'd managed to change her life, almost as much as he finally changed his own. *"Maybe 'cause you're all that's left of John on this green earth."*

Sometimes she wished Neezer had just minded his own business that day in the five-and-dime.

Wren wasn't a wizzart. She didn't want to be one, wasn't, for various fate-be-thanked reasons, likely to become one. But how much had Neezer wanted it, back then? Had Max? Had they told themselves, whistling in the dark, that it couldn't happen to them?

"God, woman, stop it!"

An old Chinese man looked at her sideways, his expression clearly showing what he thought of crazy women who talked to themselves.

She got off at her stop, taking the steps up to the street two at a time. The fresh air on her face was like a benediction, and she stopped to draw a lungful in. The sky was just beginning to darken, and the shadows of the buildings shaded into dark blue the way only city shadows could. Yes! Max could keep the countryside— she felt alive in the city, with its constant hum of energy that nonetheless managed to remain completely impartial. Too many people could be better than none, sometimes.

Especially if their presence meant you were sane.

She strode down the street and up to the six-story brick apartment building. It was the tallest building in the neighborhood, standing out against the three-story townhouses and one-story storefronts of Chinese take-out places, psychics, and the ever-present corner delis/flower stores/supermarkets. Depending on what part of town you lived in, they were Korean grocers, or bodegas, or quick-marts.

She thought about swinging by Jackson's to get some fresh milk, maybe play the Lotto, but decided against it. She'd do the shopping this weekend, when she had a little more energy.

But in the instant her feet slowed, contemplating and deciding, her nerves twitched. Back-of-the-neck, millennia of evolution stripped away kind of twitching, what Sergei called the lizard brain. The survival nerve. She sped up again, scanning the sidewalk-side without turning her head too obviously. It could have been one of the kids sitting on the stoop across the street, giving her a too-close once-over. Most people ignored her, even when she wasn't Disassociating—it made her very nervous when someone didn't. Or it might have been something as simple, and ignorable, as a mugger in the shadows, sizing her up as a potential meal ticket. That happened on occasion, but they almost always ended up passing her by for the next person coming down the street.

Nerves, probably. Justifiable, in the aftermath of the day. It couldn't have been anything else. The Wren was invisible, far as most of the world was concerned. She never met with clients, never had any direct contact with them, and she knew damn well there wasn't anything she was working on right now that might have followed her home. And yet...

The question isn't "are you paranoid." It's "are you paranoid enough?"

She spun on one heel, her keys clenched in her left hand in a defensive hold, ready to scrape the face off anything coming up on her.

There was nobody there. Two buildings down, the teenagers made rude catcalls that only increased when she glared at them. A flash of current would teach them a lesson...and be a waste of energy she didn't have right now.

"You're getting as bad as Max," she told herself, turning back and heading up the stairs into her building, praying her words weren't true.

On the street, a figure stopped just shy of Wren's building, watching as she unlocked the door and stepped inside. Wearing a stylish leather coat open over a well-tailored suit, he exuded professional menace that silenced the teenagers even before they noticed the unmistakable leather of a belt holster showing under the coat. Pale eyes looked at them without blinking, and they stared back half in apprehension, half in awe. He smiled at them, not showing any teeth, and they turned tail and fled.

A glance at his wrist to check the time, and he reached into a coat pocket, extracting a small, very expensive cell phone. Staring up at the fifth floor, where a light had just gone on, he touched a button, and waited for someone to answer on the other end.

"Bird's flown home."

He waited while the other person relayed the news, his gaze never leaving the window where Wren's form could be seen, barely, through the rice-paper shade. Then another person took the phone, the deep voice filling the phone's receiver.

"No, she was alone. Should I take care of it?"

The answer was clearly negative. "Right."

He hung up and returned the phone to his pocket. With one last look at the window, he turned and walked down the street, disappearing into the growing shadows as though he had never been there.

Wren tossed her bag on the kitchen counter, and opened the fridge, pulling out a can of Diet Sprite and popping the top. She took a long sip, sighing with pleasure as the ice-cold liquid soothed her throat. Always hydrate, Neezer had told her one summer when she passed out after a particularly exhausting workout. Rehydrate, eat, sleep. You might look like you've just been sitting there half-asleep, but the insides of your body will know they've been abused. If you don't take care of them, they won't take care of you.

Dropping her jacket, she left it in the middle of the floor, walking down the short hallway into her office. No messages on the machine. She'd check in with Sergei later, after the gallery closed. She frowned. No, damn it, today was—Tuesday, the gallery was open late tonight. She'd talk to him later, then. No rush.

She flipped the light switch, then turned on the computer. While it booted up, she flipped through the mail, snorting in disgust at the amount of junk mail and more useless circulars that had been shoved into the front door, making it almost impossible to open. She supposed that hand-delivering them employed someone...she just wished they'd pay attention to the "no menus, no flyers" sign on the apartment building's door! She sorted through them on the off chance something was actually interesting, and spotted yet another pale-blue flyer advertising Village Pest Removal services. "'Let us remove infestations and unwanted visitations.'" Well, poetic, anyway. Then she frowned, looking more closely at the wording on the sheet of paper: *Tired of coming home to unwanted visitations? Concerned about the infestation of your building? Your neighborhood? Call us. We can clean things up for you.*

"Your entire neighborhood?" Hell of a claim, in Manhattan.

A hunch tingled at the back of her head, her brain reaching for two and two in order to stretch it into five. Something about the wording sounded unpleasantly familiar. She put the paper down flat on her desk and reached over to pick up the phone and headset. Dialed the phone number listed on the flyer, pacing as she did so.

"Hello. Yes, I'd like to speak to someone about an... infestation."

The voice on the other end of the line was enthusiastic. Perky. Oh so happy and eager to please.

"Yes, they're huge...winged, too. I just saw them tonight, and then I saw your flyer..." She was a pretty good actress, if she did say so herself. Wren almost believed that her apartment *had* been invaded.

"What? No, I have no idea how they got in, haven't seen them anywhere else. Well, of course, who goes poking about looking for cockroaches—hello?"

The perky, friendly boy on the other line had hung up.

"Expecting something different, were we? Oh yeah. I know who you are now." They weren't here for pests—at least not the way New Yorkers usually used the term. Wren snarled and tossed the crumpled-up flyer across the room, missing the wastebasket by an embarrassing margin.

It was the NYADI—New Yorkers against Demonic Infestation—all over again, she'd eat someone else's hat if it wasn't. They had first appeared about three-four years before, when she was still living uptown, made life hell for everyone, Talent and Null alike, before they finally disappeared as suddenly as they'd arrived.

"Jesus wept, I so don't need this now!" All it took were a couple of newcomers to the city, who didn't know enough not to look directly at the strangers sitting next to you on the subway car, and you got spooked vigilantes trying to save humanity from demonkind. Wren snorted. As though demons were some big threat. She blamed the endless repeats of *Buffy* for that. And *The X-Files.* Some people really just couldn't separate fact from fiction.

But this was way more directed than the ranting street-corner attacks had been. Way more careful, subtle even, which meant someone was thinking. Which was never good when it came to extremist loonies.

"Bastards. If it is them I swear I'll..."

The familiar sound byte of her log-in interrupted her, and she exhaled heavily, forcing herself to relax. Slowly, as though tracking current, she lowered her shoulders, opened her hands, and let the tension slide out through her pores.

Leaving the rest of the mail in a pile on the top of a filing cabinet near the window, she took the headset off and sat down again at the desk. *Work, Valere. Deal with those bastards later. And there* will *be a later....*

Entering in the series of passwords, she logged into her server, downloading the day's e-mail. Most of it was junk and spam, a few were from old high-school friends she managed somehow to keep in touch with, and three were headed "Old Sally." She clicked on those first.

Old Sally was a mare who had been stuffed and stored in a glass cabinet by a grieving owner, way back in the bad old days of battles on horseback. She had gone a-walking one night during a nasty electrical storm about one hundred years ago, caught up in some unknown spell sent out of control.

Since then, she had turned up in a variety of locations across England, most recently in the Dowager Queen's own bedroom. Much like the bansidhe of old, in that she gave warning of terrible times to come. For the Queen Mum, it had heralded the breakup of Charles and Diana's marriage. Not that *that* had required anything supernatural to herald it.

From there, Old Sally had disappeared for several years. Apparently, somehow, she had found her way across the Big Wet to the New World.

As of yet, nobody had been able to figure out what was animating this poor Great Horse so long past her natural life. Nor had they been able to determine her choice of victims, or mode of transport. Mostly, she had been a new tidbit for folklorists and arcanologists to haggle over in irritable and occasionally (but only occasionally) amusing letters to the editor. But now, some crazed collector wanted possession of Old Sally. Enough that they were willing to pay the outrageous sums Wren—via Sergei—could command. Assuming they could locate and get their hands on her, that was. Wren's average job took between three and nine days, from contract to completion. She'd been working this for eighteen months already, on and off, more off than on.

The Wren had a rep for never failing once an assignment was taken. The fact that that rep was as much careful PR as actual fact didn't make it any easier to admit defeat.

"Okay, totally useless, thank you very much." Wren deleted the first e-mail, and went on to the next one. It claimed to be from a psychic channeling the spirit of Old Sally, with a list of demands to be met before she would rest.

"Give me a break," Wren muttered in disgust, using her toe to pull off one sneaker, then returning the favor with the other foot. "She's a horse, and one stuffed with sawdust, making her dumber than the average equine. Which is saying something."

Wren didn't have much use for psychics. There might be real ones out there, just like there might be actual spirits haunting the airwaves, but she wasn't going to hold her breath until someone proved it. Generally speaking, dead was dead, and telepathy only worked in fantasy novels.

The last e-mail had information that might be of more use, involving several potential scandals that might break in the next month or so. Old Sally could be expected to show up at any of them.

Unfortunately, four of them involved people on the West Coast, and another two were up North. She would have to call in too many favors to cover them all.

"Nothing to do about them for the moment," she said in disgust. It wasn't a rush job, thankfully. She could postpone it a few weeks, and worst-case scenario involved somebody getting some bad news a little ahead of the fact. Wren could live with that, so long as the client didn't get too antsy.

God, she hated working two jobs. Surefire way to get something screwed up, make her look like an idiot.

Moving that e-mail into the folder for current cases, she looked at what was left.

One from her mother, without a subject line. Wren hesitated, her finger over the delete button. Then she sighed, and hit the enter button instead.

"Hi, Mom," she said to it. "No Mom, I'm not. Yes Mom, I am. Yes, I will call Aunt Missy. Someday. No, I don't need a loan. Yes, I'm remembering to lock my doors at night...no, I don't want to meet a nice boy. I don't even want to meet a bad boy!"

How could she lose an argument with a woman who wasn't even there? It was a gift, she supposed. A decade past Margot Valere had trusted a well-spoken stranger in a suit and tie to give her daughter a better life than the one she'd had, waiting tables and living in a trailer. For that reason alone—ignoring the first eighteen years of pretty good times despite themselves—Wren knew that she would always owe her mother a debt which made it impossible for her to deny the older woman anything. She couldn't imagine a life in which she wasn't Sergei Didier's partner. Even if he did make her crazy with the overprotectiveness sometimes.

The rest of the e-mail looked innocuous enough: she belonged to several listservs, some professional, some personal, and they all were pretty high-volume during the week. Weekends, they slowed down. The friends, at least, were out having lives.

"I need to get me one of those, some day," she said to herself, pushing the chair back and stretching. Her jaw cracked open in a yawn, and she looked at the clock at the lower right hand of her monitor screen.

Only 8:00 p.m. Then again, it had been a damn long day. And dodging wizzart current took a lot out of you. Getting up, she padded down the T of the hallway to her bedroom, sloughing off her jeans and top and draping them over the end of her bed. The bedroom was the smallest of the three rooms, holding the bed, an old mahogany dresser that belonged in a much nicer home, and a matching table by the head of the bed that held a beat-up lamp, an old-fashioned wind-up alarm clock, a bottle of aspirin, and a slender, worn volume of koans. The walls were painted a dark forest green, and the carpet underfoot was pale green. Her bra and socks made splashes of white lying on top of it. The one window had heavy dark-green velvet drapes that were held off to one side by a gold scarf. She tugged at the scarf, releasing the drapes and plunging the room into complete darkness, cut only by the red glow of the clock.

She turned on the lamp, then sat on the bed and pulled on a pair of cutoff sweatpants and a tank T-shirt. Bed looked damn inviting. But it was too early yet to call it a night. Sleep now would mean she was up at three in the morning, and while this might be the city that never slept, there were limits.

No, a nap was probably a bad idea. Now that she was more comfortable, she'd pour herself some coffee and head back to the computer. Maybe something new would have come in. And if not, maybe exhaustion would make something she had learned today stand out, jump out of her subconscious and tell her where the damn marble block masquerading as a spell was, so she could wrap it up and get some justified sleep.

But by 10:30, Wren had gotten her second wind, courtesy of a natural inclination to evening hours, and a carafe of fresh-brewed Jamaican blend. The office was covered in crumpled-up pieces of paper, and another half-dozen sheets were tacked to the wall, creating an odd mosaic of evidence and theories.

Of the thirteen names on her list, Max had seemed the most probable. He had the grudge and the mojo to pull off a stunt like this, even if his brain stem was a bit too jittery these days to do it clean. He'd only been a full-blown wiz for four, five years now, he might have been able to focus long enough. The energy she had picked up on-site hadn't been all too stable either, a crackpot waiting to happen. Either the thief was borderline wizzing, or…

"Or," she thought out loud, "the snatcher was being influenced by the client who hired the theft in the first place. Stable Talent, crazy client? And it would have to be a long-term-ish relationship, not a once-off deal."

It was a theory, and a pretty wild one, but right now she was flying on theories alone. "I take it back, Lord. I don't want challenges in my life. Nice, boring, easygoing retrievals, that's what I'm after."

She tapped the eraser end of a pencil against her current list, running through the remaining names one more time, beginning with the ones she had checked out today.

"Sandy Hall. Career snitch with the boost—" the ability to use a current of magic to move objects, otherwise known as telekinesis "—but not much in the way of brains." His pattern would fit what she had felt, too. Not a bad fit, except for the fact that according to his wife he was probably dead, anyway. Not that being thrown into a working incinerator was an impossible hurdle to get over, but...

"Emilio Lawson. A better thief than Hall, currently AWOL." Rumor had it an Appalachian cave-dragon had eaten him. If so, strike that name. What the cave-dragons took, they kept. Digested or not.

"Katya Arkady." She had been tossed from the Council's mage roster for conduct unbecoming. Wren snorted. Already she liked the woman. P.B.'s notes suggested she was the one who Frants weaseled out from under. If so, she'd have the grudge motive down cold. Unfortunately, she was currently in the hospital for surgery. While being incinerated might not stop someone really determined, open-heart surgery would probably slow them down considerably. With a sigh, Wren crossed her name off the list, pushing down so hard she broke the point of the pencil.

"Margery and Alexander Freiner. Last seen taking sanctuary from a seriously peeved gnome." They'd be holed up at the Vatican for a while, if she knew anything about gnomes. And no magic was going to get worked under the patrician nose of Rome if they didn't condone it.

She briefly played with the idea of a Papal plot, but gave it up for lack of anything remotely resembling believable logic.

That left seven names she hadn't been able to learn anything significant about, one way or the other, to clear them or move them up on the list. She chewed the eraser tip, then made a face at the taste and started tapping it on the desktop again.

"Seven magic-users with enough mojo and snitch-smarts to pull this off, who were still up and about enough to pull this off without leaving anything more than the reading I was able to scrape up or—more importantly—without blabbing it to anyone else. Damn it, this shouldn't be so tough."

Current made you chatty as well as rude, and people loved to brag. By now, there should be *some* chatter on the street.

"Arrrgh. This is total bullshit," she said in disgust. Dropping the pencil, she stood up and stretched, palms flat and arms reaching for the ceiling. Abandoning the enclosed space and by-now-stale air of her office, she paced down the hallway, her bare feet adding to the furrows worn in the faded brown carpet.

"I'm never going to find out who pulled this off without more evidence. It would take me a year to run through everyone who was in town, much less winnowing out who might have a motive, or who was showing ready green from a job."

Her mother was always after her to get a cat. Somehow, to her mother, talking to a cat was less harmful to one's sanity than talking to oneself. Wren had always thought best out loud, for as long as she could remember, but it had really gotten out of control—in her mother's opinion—when Neezer was training her. Even now sometimes with Sergei, going over a plan, she would pace and walk, while he sat there at his desk and was amused by her. Or, more often than not lately, they would pace back and forth past each other. Wasn't that supposed to be a warning sign of co-dependency, when you start picking up each other's habits like that?

"Screw this. What would Perry Mason say?"

She waited, pausing in her pacing, as though expecting Perry Mason to come to her aid.

"Okay, fine. What would Peter Wimsey say?" Her mother had hooked her on those books, the summer she had mono and had to spend almost three weeks in bed too tired to even think about doing anything more strenuous than turning a page.

She turned left rather than continuing down the hall-way, finding herself filling the tea kettle and putting it on the burner. "Lord Peter would have charmed the guard into telling him the one thing he needed to learn from the scene, and Bunter would have found out the other essential clue, and Harriet would have put it all to-gether in time for a little emotional angst with their tea. Christ, Wren, get a grip." She pulled down a mug from the cabinet, snagging the tea canister as well. "Ignore the evidence, evidence lies. What's the starting point in all this? What's the source? Old man Frants. His build-ing. His protection spell swiped.

"So, logic would say, look to who would stand to ben-efit. One of his competitors? No...one of his underlings. They'd have access to the building, they'd have some-thing to gain from eroding the old man's power base. So...who's hungry? Who's downtrodden?"

The kettle whistled, and she removed it from the heat. She filled a tea ball with pungent leaves from the canis-ter, and dropped it into the mug, then poured the water over it, letting it steep as she stared at it in deep thought.

"You think I'm losing my touch?"

Sergei closed the door behind him, accepting the tea mug from her gratefully. "I most sincerely hope not."

The whole tea-making thing was like a Sergei-alert. He started up the stairs, and she got an urge to make tea. It was deeply weird. But, like so much of the weird-ness in her life, quite useful.

She perched herself comfortably on the counter, watching her partner/business agent sip his tea. He was dressed casually this evening, in dark gray slacks and a white button-down shirt under an expensive leather coat he hadn't bothered to take off. Even though his hair was its usual sleeked-back perfection, with only a hint of the natural curl visible, he looked tired, the skin under his eyes faintly discolored and pouchy. She felt the urge to tuck him into bed, and squelched it. Not only would he not appreciate it, even if he was dog-tired, he also looked pissed. That, plus the fact that he'd obviously come straight from the gallery—she risked a look at the stove clock and amended that; he had cut out before the place closed down, meant he'd finally recognized one of the names on the list. Two guesses which one, and the first doesn't count.

Assuming he'd figured it out by the time he woke up, that gave her a full day's head start on his mad-on. If he only twigged midday, she was in for a meltdown.

"Was your trip today not a success?" he asked.

She did an instant Sergei-translation in her head: Are you okay? He was tired, pissed...but not angry. Not anymore. All to the good. Sergei angry was impressive unless it was you he was angry at.

"Wiped our most promising suspect right off the chart." Wren-translation: I'm fine, the day was a bust.

"Well, that's a success of sorts, I suppose," he said. There was a pause while they both processed the information, then he circled right back to the question at hand. "Why do you believe you might be losing your touch?"

Wren hated having to admit to a screw-up. But better to get it done, and move on. He wouldn't let up until he got it out of her, anyway.

"I let possibilities distract me from the probabilities," she admitted. "I took the most likely suspects instead of the most logical ones."

"Which were...?"

"That you were right. Nearest and dearest having the motive with the mostest."

Sergei shook his head sadly, letting Wren know that her theory was about to get shot down in multicolored flames. He put the mug down on the counter next to her and shrugged out of his coat. Wren caught the collar, holding it for him as he slid his long arms from the sleeves. It was buttery soft, sleek enough to sleep under, which Wren had done on a few notable occasions. Much nicer than her own battered and scarred bomber jacket, but hers could stand up to abuse and shake it off, while his, she suspected, would go into a pout if there was so much as a scratch inflicted on it.

He took the coat back, going back out into the hallway to hang it up in her tiny closet. "At the level of employ where they would presumably know about the protection spell, they're all fiercely loyal to their boss—almost illogically so."

Sound traveled well, and she could hear him clearly as he came back into the kitchen.

"Certainly enough that he hasn't lost anyone to a competitor in fifteen years. Even our Mr. Margolin checks out. He was approached three months ago by InterLox, a rival corporation, offered twice his current salary to come over. He refused. They rise up through the ranks, and they stay within the ranks, disgruntled or no."

He paused, tilting his head in thought. "I wonder..."

Wren sighed, all too aware of the way his brain worked in matters like this. "It's none of our business. Nobody's paying us to snoop interoffice politics."

He grinned. "Yet. Never turn down the chance for some potentially lucrative blackmail material, Zhenechka."

But Wren wasn't appeased by the Russian diminutive of her name. His occasional pirate tendencies made her wonder how horribly overpriced the art he sold actually was. Then a thought occurred to her, and a pained expression settled on her face, creasing the skin between her eyebrows. "So if your boys are above suspicion, and mine aren't panning out...we're out of home-grown information. And you know what that means, don't you?"

Sergei's look was a sympathetic one. "We have to go to the Council."

"Not we." Wren shook her head decidedly. *"You."*

six

It was a spur-of-the-moment thing. That's what Wren told herself, anyway. Normally she tossed the postcards that arrived like clockwork and proved that whatever mailing address one gallery knew about every other one did, too. She was still on the clock, after all. She should stay home, curl up in a blanket and go over...something. There had to be something she could do. Research a little more into methods of translocation, maybe. Or study up on the client's history, to see if she could find a lead on who had a grudge with this kind of expenditure and the know-how to pull it off... Or maybe...

But Sergei had spoken well of the second artist in this exhibit, and while they rarely agreed on matters of art, she trusted his judgment when he said she might like something.

Besides, sitting here alone was making her twitchy, like there were fire ants under her skin. Maybe it was the warm clear evening air, or the noise from the couples and groups walking along the sidewalks and sitting outside sipping coffee. Or maybe it was the fact that she'd spent all day digging through the available information, and had only frustration to show for it.

Whatever the reason, she'd found herself pulling a sleeveless red dress from her closet, piling her hair up in as fashionable a mess as she could manage, shaking the dust bunnies off her high-heeled black sandals, putting on makeup and catching a cab downtown.

The place was, predictably, a madhouse. All the lovely young things, and more than a few who were neither young nor lovely but wafted the scent of money, holding glasses of sparkling wine and grouped around pedestals displaying what looked like large misshapen chunks of Lucite and sailcloth.

"Excuse me." She tried to move around one group, and got no response. "Excuse me!" A little louder, emphasized by a shoulder and elbow applied to the worst offender, a tall, anemic-looking blonde with sharp features. The blonde went on talking as though nobody were there.

Even wearing a screaming red dress I'm invisible, Wren thought in disgust. *Even with cleavage!* She fought down the impulse to give the blonde a spark-charge and instead looked for another way around the chaos.

"Excuse me," a gentle, deep voice said, and the crowd parted as though the speaker were Moses. An equally warm hand touched her shoulder, shepherding Wren away from the Lucite and toward the back of the gallery, where the drink-swilling crowd was thinner. Here, the pedestals were wider, lower, and arranged in threes.

"Oh. Yeah."

Sergei stood back and let Wren join the handful of people who were circling one trio. She restrained herself, with effort, from touching one curving, sinuous stone that begged to be stroked.

"It's alive," she said in awe. "How did he—?"

"He's an artist," Sergei said, accepting a glass of wine from a server and toasting the sculptures with it. "Rare, true, and treasured."

"If one of these were to walk home with me..." she said, only half-teasing.

The man standing next to her coughed on his sparkling wine, and Sergei shook his head in mock dismay. "Don't even think about it, Valere. If you're a good girl, maybe I'll introduce you to the artist and you can haggle out a deal of your own. I won't even take my commission."

"Deal." Not that she could afford it, even without his cut, but it was a pleasant dream.

"Damn." Sergei was looking over her shoulder, his gaze caught on something clearly displeasing. She shifted so that she could follow without being too obvious about it. Nothing seemed out of place...oh. There, by the bar set up in the back to serve preferences stronger than champagne.

"You'll excuse me?"

"I'm not a client, Didier. Go, shoo."

He gave her a distracted smile and moved through the crowd like a Coast Guard cutter. Poor Lowell—*and when was the last time you thought of him that way?*— was clearly overmatched by the statuesque woman in a black silk pantsuit who was insisting to the bartender that she wanted another drink.

"Honey, you've had two too many at least," Wren said to herself as Sergei intercepted the woman with a firm hand under her elbow. They knew each other, from body language. But not a date; he hadn't been serious about anyone since whatshername last summer, and even if Sergei were to bring a casual date to an opening he was hosting—damned unlikely—she would be someone helpful, not a disaster waiting to happen. Not that she was keeping track of his dating habits. Much.

She watched a moment longer as her partner turned the charm on full-assault, then went back to admiring the sculptor's work. Maybe not all abstract work was crap, after all....

* * *

"You told me that it was perfectly safe. You said that the spell-casting done on it was inert, that the magic inside it couldn't escape. Ever."

The woman seated in front of the desk wanted desperately to backhand this sniveling little weasel, but held onto her temper by a bare margin. Slapping clients around was very bad for business, no matter how good it felt personally.

The speaker went on, fleshy pink lips moving in his narrow, sallow face, and that horrible whine coming from his throat, but she tuned it out.

Instead, she looked at her reflection in the glassed-in cabinet behind the client, making sure that no sign of her irritation marred her face. That face could have belonged to a woman anywhere from forty to fifty; brown skin only showing faint lines around lips and eyes, a strong nose and large brown eyes, thick black hair cut short and straight. Never a face to redefine beauty, it nonetheless inspired confidence and a certain sense of security in those she worked with. As it was meant to.

Even the ones who were idiots. Perhaps especially the ones who were idiots.

They were seated in the client's office, a lovely room on the first floor of the mansion they always met in. She assumed it was his home, but had never seen any more of the structure to judge. They always met here: she was willing to negotiate long-distance, but that wasn't satisfactory to this moron. He wanted face-to-face on every damned little detail.

She felt her irritation rising again, and tamped it down, making herself look as though she was paying attention to whatever he was saying. It had been a long day, but that was no excuse. You could also tell a great deal about a client by how they did business. Some insisted on meeting on third-party ground, somewhere impartial. Some never wanted to meet face-to-face, preferring to keep it as distanced as possible. And some— like this fool—kept it close to home, as though that gave them an illusion of control.

It would have been a better illusion if he hadn't called at seven in the morning, bleating like a stuck lamb, demanding that she come out immediately. Whining that the object he had gone to such great lengths—and expense—to acquire gave him, and she quoted, "the creeps." As though the fact that he was her primary client earned him some first claim—more than that, some *sole* claim over her time.

It did, actually. You jumped when the main bill-payer barked. But most had the grace to acknowledge that her skills were worth the courtesy of asking, not demanding, her presence. And "the creeps—" Good Lord, what did the man want? He knew ahead of time the object had magical influences; she had told him herself, once she'd been given the target. He had assured her that he was prepared, had taken the appropriate safeguards.

Arrogant bastard. Even terrified, *especially* terrified, he was still a shit. Still, you had to make exceptions for wealth and eccentricity, especially when they came together in the same package. And so she had rescheduled everything else that day and, despite the eight-hour drive, come out to hold his hand. Metaphorically. He wasn't paying her *that* much.

So now, for the third time in an hour, she tried to inject a note of reassuring confidence into her voice. "We've been over this how many times? That particular spell was woven into the stone at the time of its formation. It is integral to the object, and cannot be removed." It *was* the object, in all the ways that mattered. Without the spell, the item was just a block of stone, mass produced and totally without value. "Unless you intend actual harm to the owner of the building it was taken from, it cannot harm you in turn. We went over this before the initial approach and I warned you of all the possible consequences. I am assuming you still have no plans to harm that person?" Not that she would otherwise care—she knew whose building she had targeted; let the two take each other out and the world would be a cleaner place—but, again, bad business.

"I want you to check it out," the client told her, ignoring her question as though she hadn't even spoken. "Make sure nothing went wrong in the transport."

"That wasn't in our original contract," she told him, leaning backward in preparation for a prolonged bargaining session. But instead, he reached into the desk drawer and pulled out a small brown paper-wrapped packet. He placed it on the desk surface, and pushed it across to her. Her eyes never leaving his, she reached forward and picked it up.

"Half the amount of our original fee, simply for ensuring that the magic within the stone remains inert."

She gauged the weight of the packet, then nodded, tucking it into a pocket of translocation energy she used instead of a pocketbook. It took more maintenance than the convenience was worth, but it impressed the clients when you made things seemingly disappear into thin air. Anything sent there ended up in a safe in her own home, actually. She had been taken advantage of—read that as robbed by her own client—early in her career. Never again.

"All right. Let's get this over with." It was already evening, and there was no way she was going to stay overnight in the place, even assuming he would offer. She stood, waiting for him to lead her to wherever he had stored the object, but he reached into his desk again, and came up with a length of black cloth.

"You can't be serious—" But she could see from his expression that he was. Deadly serious.

More control games. It didn't matter—any half-trained mageling could retrace their own steps, blindfolded, drunk *and* half-asleep. But if it made him happy...

She submitted to the blindfold, but couldn't help a shudder when the client took her arm to lead her out of the office. Now she knew why she had always resisted touching him. Her clients rarely came to her pure of heart *or* deed, but this man exuded some of the slimier emotions—avarice chief among them—so strongly that it was almost a tactile sensation. And underlying it all was a distasteful sense of something dark and ugly, like sludge in a sewer pipe, that made her deeply uncomfortable. Her client, she realized suddenly and for the first time, wasn't what most psychologists would call stable. But freelancers couldn't be choosers. Especially at these pay levels.

He led her down a hallway that echoed their footsteps off the hardwood flooring, then into an elevator that muted their steps with plush carpeting. There was a faint odor in the air which hadn't been there before—orange? No, but definitely citrusy. Something familiar...wood oil. The walls of the elevator were wood, and had been polished recently. God, it was good to have money, wasn't it? She doubted very much he had ever touched a dust rag in his entire life.

They rose one story, then got off and walked down another length of hallway, this time carpeted. The smell of the oil faded under the onslaught of a colder smell—recirculated air. They were in a part of the house that was sealed off from the outdoors. His collection rooms. She had known that he liked to own things—rare things—he shouldn't; had in fact gotten him some of them herself, but not the sheer number he possessed, to require this much space. As they walked, she could feel things tugging at her, faint sparkling touches as appealing as the client was distasteful, and she felt a moment of honest astonishment when she realized their source. Some people collected antique glass, or Impressionist paintings or Pez dispensers. In addition to everything else, the client collected Artifacts.

No wonder he had assured her that he had the proper containment facilities for the cornerstone! But if so, why...and what damage was being done, putting them all in together, where their current might scrape and rub against each other... Was that why the cornerstone was behaving oddly?

Not her business. Not her problem. Do the job and get the hell out, she told herself. And maybe, money or no, you don't take any more magic-related jobs for this particular individual, who was clearly crazier than a wizzart on acid.

Finally he stopped, letting go of her arm long enough to open a door, then he ushered her inside and removed the blindfold. Her attention was snagged immediately by the large crystal to one side of the room that hummed with stored energies. Artifacts. Icons. Almost anything could hold current, but an object made expressly for that purpose, imbued with the creator's own ability...like a Christian cross repelling a vampire, the emotional intent of the object intensified its effect.

Gods above and below, she thought wildly, fighting her body's instinctive urge to flee. *Too much. Too much power. It would consume her, overwhelm her.* She tamped down on the panic as best she could, concentrating on breathing, building up her own defenses until the chaotic current-flows dulled to a distant roar.

A not-so-gentle cough from the client reminded her of why she was there, and the woman forced her gaze away from the seemingly endless planes and angles of the crystal and back to the job at hand.

Mage-sight wasn't one of her strengths, but she had enough to get the job done. Settling herself into a light trance state, careful to work over her defenses rather than through them, she blinked, then looked at the plain gray slab of marble sitting by itself in a corner. Part of her mind found it ludicrous that such an ugly piece of nothing was treated as though it were a piece of artwork, but the majority of her awareness Saw the glitter of magic that permeated the concrete, and knew its value.

It looked exactly the same as it had when she worked the original spell to remove it; red in the middle, where the original activation spell still roiled about, then blue surrounding it, and a paler green on the surface, where the retaining spell was weakest, shining through the concrete plug. Sloppy work there: she would have reinforced it with something a little less porous herself, if she had been the caster. But it was intact.

She was about to break out of trance state and tell the client that he was safe as houses when there was a flicker of light to one side. Frowning, she walked over to get a better line of sight on it. A crooked line of gold ran zigzag through the green, like a Navajo sand painting she'd seen once on display in one of those little art galleries scattered throughout the city.

"Well, well, what do we have here?" she wondered, reaching out with one finger to test it. Even as that one part of her brain told her that was an incredibly stupid thing, she made contact.

A sting of lightning ran through the nerve endings of her arm, straight into her brain. She convulsed once, like a bad sneeze, and a wave of vertigo shivered through her. Then it was gone, and she was standing in front of a perfectly quiescent spellblock, red and blue and green exactly in order.

"What happened? Did it do anything? What's wrong?" The client sounded like a rabbit, and the thought made her smile. The power still whispered through her, attempting seduction. It would be so easy to turn on him, take what was here and disappear... *And then never work again,* the practical portion of her brain reminded her. *The Council already has its eye on you. Not smart.*

Blinking out of trance state, she turned to look at the

client. "There was a slight disturbance," she told him blithely. "But I corrected it. Everything should be fine now."

The client didn't look completely convinced, but whatever she had done had apparently chased away the creeps, because he nodded, and offered her the blindfold again. She took it without hesitation, tying it around her own eyes. The less she saw, the better. She wouldn't give him any reason to turn that craziness on her.

The door closed behind them, and the room settled into silence once again. But deep inside the stone, the red spell energy was suddenly shot through by gold streaks of lightning. The red solidified, pulsing in a fashion unlike its earlier roil, and then stilled completely.

And a mage of moderate ability, listening intently, would have been able to hear a scream of rage and despair rise from the interior of the concrete block.

seven

Sergei looked at his watch, tilting his wrist slightly to catch the light. 10:58 a.m. He was exactly, perfectly on time. He could feel the slight pressure in the soles of his feet that indicated the elevator was moving him upward at a disconcertingly quick speed. It made him, he admitted, nervous. He was all for speed, and power, but he much preferred being the one determining how it was used.

Not that he didn't trust the Mage Council. He did. He trusted them to be cold, calculating, utterly ruthless and completely without a shred of human decency. Perfectly reasonable businessmen. Which was why he was here, in this elevator, instead of his partner. He could hold his own in negotiations, smooth-talk his way through the landmines and hopefully get out with what they needed, not having left too much of himself behind.

Sergei Didier knew from long experience that you didn't need Talent to deal with the mages. Only patience, and a great deal of self-control. His Wren, for all that she was exceedingly good at what she did, lacked a certain level of self-possession when it came to negotiations.

In short, she lost her temper. And everything always, but always, went downhill from there. That was why he was making this call, and not her. Normally, a non-Talent like himself wouldn't be allowed inside the building. The fact that they had allowed him entrance meant that they accepted him as Wren's surrogate. Unusual, but not unheard of.

The Council's old-fashioned, very 1950s patriarchal, except the role of the guy is played by the Talent, and all their dependents, nonmagically, are the wimminfolk and children, used for display to show you're a good provider, if they're allowed in sight at all. Her disgust when she said this had been unmistakable. He hadn't realized, before the two of them started working together, how deep the distaste between lonejack and Council went. Fair enough, since he'd only ever heard rumors of the Council's existence before they hooked up. But they were still all *Cosa* and therefore protected by the rules of the game, such as it was. Because of that, he was perfectly safe here as Wren's surrogate. So long as he didn't do or say or start anything stupid.

He shot the cuffs of his suit, straightening his shoulders so that the suit jacket fell smoothly, the way his tailor had designed it. The finely cut wool slid against the ironed cotton of his shirt, and when he looked down, the cuffs of his pants broke exactly right over his polished dress shoes. Clothes might not make the man, the way his father had always insisted, but they did make the man feel more confident. He was going to ace this. *Keep it cool, keep it easy, and keep it under control. Don't let Wren down.*

The elevator slowed, and then came to a stop. The doors slid open smoothly, without a ding or beep to indicate he had arrived. There were no floor indicators inside the darkly paneled box, no call boxes or emergency phone. You got in because you were here to see the Council, and you got to the floor you needed to reach because they wanted to see you.

A solemn young man, carefully groomed and expensively dressed in a subtle gray suit and cream-and-gray herringbone tie, waited to greet him in the equally dark-paneled, gray-carpeted empty space that would have been the reception area in an ordinary office. They looked like nothing so much as two proper high-risk investment bankers, junior and senior, plotting a merger. Or world domination.

"Mr. Didier. Follow me, if you would."

He was led down a hallway that, like the young man, whispered of power and wealth. The young man could be dismissed. But Sergei believed in those other whispers. The gathered power of seven generations of mages had built the place, and they maintained it to this day. The young man was nothing, merely one cog in the workings of a greater whole. This building embodied the whole.

You're letting your imagination get the better of you, part of his mind tried to tell him. But the rest of him knew the sensation to be true. These were the real halls of power. And Power.

His guide opened a door, standing to one side in order to usher him into a conference room, then shut the door behind him. "Nice to have met you, too," he said to the door, unable to resist. Sarcasm wouldn't be helpful here. But it made him feel better. Had he been like that before Wren? Or did she merely bring it out in him? And why was he chasing that thought now? Impossible questions. Mind on the job, Sergei!

Turning, he took an almost unnoticeable breath, girding himself for battle. The room was not empty. Four people waited for him in the lushly-appointed space; three men, two elderly, one middle-aged, all wearing variations on the young man's grayness. And a woman, white-haired and serene, wearing a deep-blue suit with a large opal pin on the lapel. Sergei recognized the woman at once—KimAnn Howe. She had married a wealthy businessman back in 1968, and therefore been photographed many times in the social papers, keeping her hand in even after the businessman died. She had won herself a seat on the Mage Council fair and square, he recalled, through a combination of ruthless Talent and even more ruthless backstabbing. Petite, but with an air of strength, and graceful, even seated; she was a woman you'd be proud to bring home to Mother, if Mother was a black widow spider.

The others he did not recognize, but it wouldn't have mattered if he did. In this place, at this time, they were not individuals, but the voice of the Council.

KimAnn's presence was unexpected. He was being honored. Or rather, Wren was. He made a note to remember to tell her that. For whatever it was worth. Odds were she'd not take it as a compliment.

"Why have you come before us?" one of the older men asked, after gesturing to one of the four empty leather chairs pulled up to the long polished board table. Sergei waited until they all had taken their own seats before folding himself into his, less a courtesy than an acknowledgement that he sat only by their grace.

A deep breath, as much a centering as he could manage. "I seek awareness."

Not information, for that would give too much weight, too much importance to what he was seeking. Not an action, nothing that would require them to exert themselves on his behalf. Not a favor, for you never, ever requested a favor from a mage, much less the Mage Council itself. Instead, he was asking for awareness: an understanding of an existing situation. And by asking, implying that they had at least a finger in the situation, for why else would he come to them unless they had knowledge, and how would they have knowledge without involvement? And if Sergei—or, more to the point, any Null, came knocking, the situation couldn't be a good one. Flattery and warning, with neither overshadowing the other. He hoped. Byzantine was only one word for Council politics, but it was an accurate one.

A bead of sweat formed at the back of his neck, just under the hairline. *Tiho,* he told himself. Easy, keep it easy...

The four mages sat there, looking at him. He didn't want to put more on the table, not until he had some kind of reaction from them. Some indication which direction the wind was blowing. *Were* they directly involved in the theft?

He had asked the client beforehand, of course, when the initial approach was made. Standard procedure. But the client could have lied. Stupid, but always possible. Not everyone was as careful as they should be all the time, not even him. And he had asked only about the action they were being asked to perform, nothing about the deeper history of the situation. Nothing that wasn't immediately and directly relevant. Had his desire not to know too much in case he needed deniability later put Wren—all unknowing and despite his best intentions—into a direct clash with the Council? It was the one thing she had always feared, always been so careful about avoiding....

Sergei could feel his fingers twitch, and forced them to still. He relaxed a little further into the chair, allowing his exhale to release all tensed muscles, and waited.

"What is it you wish to understand?" the younger man said finally, allowing him this one small victory.

"A casting has been disturbed," he said, not looking at any one of them in particular while speaking to them all at once. Wren had tutored him on this when he first became her partner, drilling him endlessly on the proper procedure. He'd only had to use it once before, when he hadn't fully understood the danger. There were forms to observe, procedure and protocol to follow, and letting himself think of them as four, when they thought as one, would guarantee his failure. "An act of current—" never but never refer to it as magic in front of a Council member; magic was for children and mountebanks "—has been interfered with. Before we take action on behalf of our own client, we seek clarity that this is not as the Council wished."

He was rather proud of that wording, having worked it out on the cab ride uptown. By not giving details, he was implying that of course they knew what had occurred, that he need name no names, make no specific references. Implied as well was the fact that, were it something the Council had decreed, the lonejack involved would of course back off.

And she might. Or she might not.

And if the Council somehow did *not* know what he was referring to, that would tell him much as well.

But he didn't think that was going to be the situation. Wren had once, at three in the morning, exhausted and riding a post-job high, divided the unTalented world into three types: Kellers, those who were blind and deaf to the magic around them; Players, those who were involved in magic, even if they themselves could not manipulate it—himself included—and Jonesers, wannabes and fakes who didn't have a direct connection to the magic but wanted it. Mages, on the other hand, classed everyone as either a Talent or a Null. It was a matter of course that they keep tabs on everyone who counted as a Talent. And yet a wealthy businessman like Frants, who was not only willing to use spells other people could cast but able to afford even the most outrageous fee, would certainly rate a blip on the Council's radar. Even if he was—according to what both he and Wren had discovered—currently on their proscribed list for behavior unacceptable.

And of course they knew who currently employed the lonejack called The Wren—thinking they didn't insulted their entire organization. Especially when the situation apparently involved work performed by a mage, no matter how long ago. Any job a mage undertook was, by default, an act of the Council.

Sergei could feel the weight of the air in the room increase, pressing against his skin as though the humidity level had increased dramatically. That was how the use of active magic felt to him; passive magic, or what Wren called potential, didn't register with him at all, nor did active current outside his immediate, physical reach. Kim-Ann's face remained calm, composed, but the rapid, seemingly undirected eye movements of the others in the room suggested that they were in some kind of communication.

It was, he supposed, too much to hope for that they would discuss anything in a fashion he could eavesdrop. He merely folded his hands in his lap, and allowed his breathing to settle. It wasn't all that different than letting a buyer sell him- or herself on a painting. If you push, they become defensive. Act coy, and they're suspicious. Act as though you know they will come to the proper decision, and eight times out of ten, they will.

"The originator of the first casting held membership within the Council," KimAnn said finally, her fine-skinned brow creased with the hint of a frown. What might be causing that frown, he could only guess. The first middle-aged man looked sulky, the gray-haired older man downright mutinous. Only the white-haired man seemed tranquil, as though what occurred in this room had no bearing on his existence at all. So far, KimAnn was only confirming what he had already said. No help there. Or was it? *Don't think right now,* he cautioned himself. *Listen, and absorb. What they're saying may not be as important as how they're saying it.*

"That mage has since discarded this existence—" died, Sergei translated, as opposed to wizzing or otherwise becoming a disgrace "—and any records of his work have since been purged."

It took Sergei a moment to catch up with what they were saying, matching it with his own understanding of corporate-speak and the endless ways to avoid admitting anything. Purged didn't just mean they had dumped files; they had destroyed the actual *memories* of the mage his- or herself. *Intense punishment, if they're all as much ego-hounds as Wren claims.*

"And the second spell-casting? The removal of the original work?" If they were willing to take responsibility, Wren would insist on dropping the assignment, and he wasn't sure right now he'd blame her. For certain, no one in the *Cosa* would.

"It is not in the interests of the Council to condone discord within." The look in her eyes suggested that Sergei had best figure the rest out on his own. The interview, such as it was, was over. With a careful incline of his head to her, and equal-but-lesser nods to the other men—risky, but he felt that KimAnn would enjoy it, and buttering her up seemed a worthy risk to take, especially if it left them squabbling amongst themselves over perceived slights or favors—he gathered himself up out of the chair and left. The young man met him outside the door and escorted him back to the elevator, which was also waiting. Sergei stood tall as the lift took him down to ground level, eyes straight ahead, hands perfectly still at his sides although he longed for the cigarette case tucked inside his jacket pocket.

It wasn't until he was out of the building entirely that he felt the muscles in his neck and shoulders relax.

"Christ. I need a drink." But first, he had to hand off the bad news.

"That was fast."

"They're not exactly the type to invite you to stay for tea." Sergei draped his coat neatly onto the hanger and hung it in the narrow hall closet. Another month and he'd have to send it into storage for the summer. He made a mental note to remind himself of that in three weeks. He closed the door and turned to see Wren standing in front of him. Hair for once pulled out of her eyes with a barrette, her face was scrunched in the "you've got to be kidding me" look he was far too familiar with. Her arms were crossed, her head tilted back—the better to glare at him—and he was struck with the sudden but not unfamiliar urge to touch the tip of her ever-so-slightly upturned nose with one finger, the way you would an inquisitive house cat. Wanting to keep his hand intact, he again squelched the impulse.

Best to get it over with. "They're clean."

"Clean?" The word, parroted back to him, carried a wealth of disbelief.

"Not responsible for this particular occurrence," he said, amending his earlier words. "In short, and if I'm reading the clues correctly, they don't know who stole it either. And they're not happy about it."

"The theft, or the not knowing?"

"Yes."

"Damn. Some answers would have been convenient." She shrugged, and headed back to her office, presumably where she had been when he arrived. The faint strains of Coltrain rose from the speakers. He frowned, recognizing the CD as one that had gone missing from the gallery last month. A twist of his mouth was the only outward sign he gave of that knowledge. If you were going to work with a thief, you had to accept certain…inconveniences. She couldn't help it. He'd already bought another, anyway.

"Reading between very carefully worded lines, the Council didn't authorize any moves against our client," he told her, aware that she could hear him even over the music. "Apparently, there isn't any profit in undercutting each other's work." He shook his head, his mouth twisting in appreciation. "Nice noncompetition deal they've got there. Wonder if we can get the Justice Department in to investigate?"

A muffled grunt came back down the hallway that might have been agreement, disagreement, or completely unrelated.

"They did, however, perform the original spell. Or at least they're willing to take the credit for it."

"Told you so," she yelled back, and he heard the sound of something heavy and possibly metallic hitting the ground, and her swearing faintly. When a moment passed and there was no further noise, he went into the kitchen and picked up the mug of tea that was steeping, waiting for him and then—having judged enough time had passed for her to recover from whatever minor disaster had occurred, joined his partner in the office. She was sitting on a short stool next to the filing cabinet-table on the other side of the room, fiddling with a large, ungainly lock that looked ancient. He sat down in the only other chair, at her computer desk. A screen saver of parachuting monkeys was activated, indicating that she hadn't used it recently. He turned his back to the monkeys, swiveling around to watch her instead. He should get back to the gallery. Lowell had been borderline snide this morning about his "running off." There was going to have to be a "me boss, you underling" meeting in the near future, he could tell. Christ, he so didn't have time for that.

"That means that nobody under the Council did the grab," she said without pausing in her work. "And no member was approached to do the job, either—since the mark was one of their installations, they would have been bound to report it to the Council." The same as she would, by courtesy, in a similar situation. Probably.

"Would the Council then have told us, now that they officially know you're working the job? And have gone through channels to ask for assistance?" He sipped the tea, chuckling slightly as he saw the logo—it was one of the gallery's mugs, which he bought by the dozen to stock the kitchenette.

"Good question. Probably. They're as susceptible to bad press as anyone. More, actually. So they'd want it back in place too, you'd think, no matter what he and his have done to piss them off since then. It's not like he was the original client, anyway, not unless he's a lot older than his records claim."

"His grandfather, Frants the First. Is that why they're so tight-mouthed on the original job they performed? Or do they just not like to be thought of as bragging?"

She snorted. "Council. They don't like to share the air with us, much less information. It's the principle of the thing as much as the money. My gut, though, says if it's a mage, he or she's a rogue."

Sergei had heard her mention rogues before, but only in passing, and never with a lot of detail attached. "Is that common?"

She gave the lock one last try, then put her tools down on the table next to it. "Common enough—maybe one Council mage every decade or so starts believing their own press, thinking they're better than the others, able to sidestep the Council rulings, that sort of thing. When they catch 'em, which they always do, they kick

'em out—like you said, bad form to have members diss-
ing fellow mages. Especially if they're willing to work
against other Council members."

"Yes. That was the impression I was given." He tapped
his fingers in a tattoo on his leg, less nervous than
thoughtful, trying to sort the pieces in his brain.

"Once they're freelance," she told him, "they usually
fade out of sight. Nobody will hire them, which makes
one unlikely in our case—unless the thief was taking it
for his or her own reasons...." Sergei made a mental
note to follow up on that possibility. "But the Council,
natch, never admits that the mage in question ever
even existed."

"Nobody wants a mage who works on his own?" That
surprised him enough to still the finger-tapping. Lonejacks, Talents who refused to fall in with the Council,
often worked freelance, like Wren. Although from what
she had told him, most didn't work at all, using their
skills solely for themselves, or not using them consciously at all.

Wren made an up-down motion with the flat of her
hand, palm upraised as though she were weighing
something. "Nobody wants a mage who's already
proven himself to be disloyal to the code. When you buy
a mage, they're supposed to stay bought. Would you
want to hire someone your competitor might bribe away
tomorrow?"

"An excellent point." He kept a list, carefully coded,

of all their jobs as well. You wanted to avoid crossing your own path, if you could. "So we're back to—"

An ungodly noise interrupted him. Sounding like a cross between a scalded cat and a howler monkey, the screech came in through the window, rising from the street below. He dropped his mug, catching it again half an inch down, swearing as tea stained his pants. "What the hell—!"

Wren went to the window, throwing the sash up and sticking her head out . "Leave it alone, damn it!" Catcalls responded, male voices, teenagers, probably locals from the accent. She shut the window in disgust. "Mornag."

"Mornwhat?"

"Mornag. I swear to God, Sergei, someday you'll get over that speciesist stick that's stuck up your ass, at least enough to know who's who."

"Or what's what."

"Don't be snide. Mornag're about the size of a mutt, and about as smart as one too. There's a pack that lives in the Park; P.B. uses them as messengers sometimes when he can't get to me. Local kids are a bunch of punks, though. Anything on four legs is fair game. Makes me glad I don't have a pet."

"Or a kid."

"Oh yeah. Although if any kid of mine started running with the sort around here…did I tell you about the newest joy added to my life? Bunch of Neighborhood Watch types, trying to clean up quote—the inhuman trash—

endquote. Started I think with a couple of ranters on a street corner a couple of years back; didn't take them seriously, but they're getting more sophisticated. Masquerading as a pest control outfit now, but they don't want to know about your roach or rat problem. They've been messing with the sub-sentients mainly, mornags, a few piskies. But it sounds like they're escalating."

Sergei didn't seem too impressed by that. If a fatae couldn't outwit a few kids, or well-meaning vigilantes, he should stay in whatever hole he burrowed into.

Wren considered the window, then shrugged. "Well, if he was coming to see me, he'll find a way in later. Business at hand. Your stuff means we wipe the Council itself off the short list."

"And you don't think it's a rogue."

"Nope." She drew the shade again and leaned against the window, arms crossed over her chest. Her hair needed cutting again, he noted. Strands fell into her eyes and she scraped them back impatiently. "Not unless it was a personal thing, taking on a Council client to throw rogue status back in the Council's face. But the setup doesn't feel right. A rogue wouldn't go for such a low-res deal. They like things a little flashier, something to justify their getting tossed. Very 'look at me!'"

"Or, if someone hired them, a juicy enough paycheck to justify the lack of flash. Even mages have to pay the bills."

"I guess. But it would have to be a *major* paycheck.

Ego, Sergei. Mages are all about ego. In fact, the only way I see this as a magus deal is if the mage in question had a percentage in taking our client down, and if he or she or they did, they probably wouldn't be letting us poke our little noses uninterrupted into—"

The lights suddenly dimmed throughout the apartment, and Wren uttered a short, nasty word, diving across the room—almost tackling Sergei in the process—to pull the power cord to her computer. She lay on the floor, panting, the power cord in her hand. The screen saver flickered, then restored as the battery pack setup took over.

Wren sighed in relief, letting her hand drop to the floor as the tension visibly released from her shoulders. Letting go of the cord, she got to her feet, then tensed again as the lights flickered once more. Sergei took his cue from her reactions, his body braced for action, although he wasn't sure if it was to fight or flee. When a Talent was anywhere near any kind of power fluctuation, you assumed the worst.

Thunder rumbled despite a clear sky, and all the lights in the apartment went half-power. "Damn," she said, looking up at the ceiling. "I so didn't need this...."

"Valere. Details?" He hated being half a step behind what was happening.

Wren held up a hand, halting him midinquiry. "Feel that?"

Sergei frowned, shooting his partner an irritated look. "No."

"Oh. Right." She at least had the grace to look some-what embarrassed, he thought, only slightly mollified. She held her hand out to him, and he took it, his much larger fingers engulfing her smaller ones. One thumb smoothed over the back of her wrist without thinking, feeling the goose bumps raised on her skin. The pale hairs along her arm were raised, as though a cold wind had blown in—or as though a surge of electrical energy had run through her.

"Company," she said, too casual to actually be casual about it.

"Dangerous?" Ten years, and he'd never seen her look like this; half-annoyed, half-apprehensive, half-ex-pectant. He kept his hand on hers, not sure if he was giving comfort or taking it.

"Don't know. Probably not." They were whispering, without even realizing it. "Timing sucks for coincidences, though, huh?"

"Not reassuring, Zhenechka."

"Poor baby." She chuckled, despite the strain evi-dent in her body, and he squeezed her fingers gently in support and approval.

The light overhead made an odd fizzing noise, flared brightly, then shorted out. The lamp on Wren's desk made a smaller snapping noise, and the bulb shattered. A handful of sparks shot out from the wall outlets, send-ing a strange blue-white light into the darkened room. Wren backed up, pushing Sergei against the desk, putting herself between him and whatever was forming within her office.

"Great. Now I've got to get those damn protective wards recharged. Not that it matters. This thing's either benign, or powerful enough to short out my protections."

"In which case...?"

"We're screwed."

The sparks had gathered as they spoke, forming a tight ball hovering around shoulder-high to Wren, perhaps three feet away. It shimmered, then coalesced, becoming almost solid, then stretched like Silly Putty down to the floor, and up another foot or so. A twist in the middle, where the stomach might be, and the shadow of features formed over the frame: pale skin, wild, wispy hair, and fierce green-sparked eyes over a high beaked nose.

Sergei took an involuntary step forward, trying to get Wren behind him, but she shoved him back hard.

"Max." There was exasperation and not a little fear in her voice as she spoke his name. "You can't just use the damned phone? Carrier pigeons?"

Sergei reached instinctively for the weapon he wasn't carrying, then checked himself. Old habit. Wren hated guns, so much so that he'd long ago weaned himself out of carrying one rather than make her uncomfortable. And even if he'd had it, damn little good a bullet would do to a current-manifestation. Just put a couple of holes in Wren's walls, which she would not thank him for. And that would be best-case scenario.

The current-manifestation giggled, then coughed, a rasping noise. "Not much time, storm's pulling me out to Canada. Got a line on your boogie. Shimmied down a pipe, caught tail end of the signature you tossed to me. Followed it home and scared the spark out of some halfwit current-hacker. Name of the guy who did the hiring's Matthew Prevost. Good luck, kid. See you in a few decades if you don't get yourself killed."

The sparks compressed, and imploded, sending them both to the floor, hands over their heads in a useless attempt at protection. Sergei rolled so that he was covering Wren's much smaller body, pressing her into the carpet to shield her from the inferno occurring above. *Wizzarts,* he thought in disgust.

Wren was aware of three things. One, that eau d' old carpet was not something you wanted to experience up close and personal on a regular basis. Two, she was being squished flat by something very large, warm and heavy. And three, the smell of burning hanging in the air over them did not bode well for her computer system. *Wizzarts.*

"Showy bastard," she grumbled, the words muffled from the carpet under her face. And four, the rumbling noise over her wasn't a subway, it was Sergei, laughing. Considering his options, she supposed laughing wasn't such a terrible way to let off nervous tension and adrenaline. But he didn't have to sound so damn...amused by it all.

"It's not funny." She used an elbow to make her point, and he obligingly rolled onto his side, letting her lift her face from the floor and breathe again.

"Yes, it is." He looked down at her, his eyes half-shut as he laughed, more quietly now. The smell of his sweat mixed with whatever cologne he used that she'd never quite been able to place; browsing through the men's fragrance counters made her dizzy. "It's really quite funny. One of these days he's going to finally manage to kill you, and he won't even have meant it." His tone was weird: sort of off, like he was strangling on the words.

"Congratulations, you've finally figured wizzarts out. Now get off me, you oversized Russian oaf." She was finding it hard to think, his weight pressed up against her like that. She was tired, that's all. Emotional roller-coaster of a day, of a week. That was why she was having to fight off the urge to topple him all the way to the floor and...

Don't go there. Not with Sergei, who so isn't around for that. It's post-stress somethingorother. That's all. Plus, you need to get laid. Badly. Retrieval played havoc on a social life, especially if you had already run through all the eligible, moderately attractive single Talents in the area. Non-Talents were too risky, mostly, for relationships. She couldn't remember the last time...oh, right, him. Cute but obviously forgettable.

"I grew up in Chicago," he reminded her, getting to his feet and extending a hand to help her up.

"Details, details," she said dismissively. Ignoring the hand—not trusting herself to touch him just yet—she rolled over and sat up by herself, remaining on the floor in order to plug the computer back in. "If he had fried my computer, all of Canada wouldn't have been enough to hide his sorry static butt in."

Her back aching more than it should have, Wren got up and sat in the chair Sergei had discarded when the excitement began, and dialed into her server. She longed for DSL or cable connections, but even if you ignored the cost, she shuddered to imagine what could have happened if she'd been online when Max came to visit. No reason to short out everyone else on the system if you could avoid it. "Prevost, right?"

"That's what the man said."

"Right." She directed the search to include variable spellings, and hit send. In the meantime, Sergei pulled out his cell phone, and dialed a number. "Lowell. Pull up my files and do a search for Prevost—that's P, r, e, v, o, s, t, first name Matthew. Start with the buyers, then go to the miscellaneous file. No, I don't think he's a dealer or seller. Thanks. Right. No, no problems—the name came up in conversation and it pinged my memory. Great. Any messages? Uh-huh." He frowned, a look of anger settling onto his face before it was banished. "No, I can handle it, thanks. Call me back at this number if you find anything."

He closed the cell and replaced it in his pocket. "You want anything to eat?"

"Sure," she said, scanning the list of names her search had returned. "Chinese or Mexican?"

"Forgot to go shopping again?"

"Hello? Who had time? You had me out in Connecticut trying to get a reading on that stuffed horse last week, and then I get home, catch a few zzz's, and good morning, another job."

"You'd rather business was slow?" he asked with a raised eyebrow.

"I'd rather you got back on the horn and called Noodles. Sesame chicken, brown rice, and a Diet Sprite for me."

Noodles was around the corner, a quick walk. Faster to pick it up than wait for a delivery person to get around to them on a weeknight. Sergei didn't bother with his coat, merely taking his wallet out of the inside breast pocket before he left. And if he was a little too eager to get away from the debris of Wren's office, where she was using an ancient Dust Buster to find the last of the light-bulb shards, she was kind enough not to comment on it. Assuming she even noticed—his Wren had the single-minded focus of a mongoose when she was working. Unlike him, whose mind was cursed to go in multiple directions simultaneously.

Idiot. Idiot! Despite what Wren thought, he wasn't totally clueless about his tendency to overprotect. But when Max had crashed in like that, his reaction had been way out of line. What the hell did he think he was going to be able to do? *He* had been the liability in that room, the weak link, not Wren.

Sergei had no trouble letting her protect him, when it came to magical threats, or where current could do more than physical strength. It wasn't an ego thing, as she said about mages. He was pretty sure it wasn't, anyway. But while his brain knew she was perfectly capable in these instances, his body's reactions were slow to catch up.

And his heart, Sergei was slowly coming to realize, staunchly refused to hear. It wasn't a matter of being her protector, her knight in shining armor, or anything as hackneyed as that. But when his heart risked imagining a world where she was gone, it—

Went insane?

That was as good a description as any.

And when the threat came, not from a magical source, but one he was best-suited to deal with, heart, mind and physical instinct were all in accord.

Taking the narrow stairs as swiftly as he could, Sergei left the building and, rather than walking to Noodles, stepped into the shadows where he wasn't immediately visible. With a quick glance upward to make sure that Wren wasn't looking out the window, he took out his cell phone again, entered a local phone number, then a short string of code.

"You left a message?" His voice was calm, with an edge of irritation, like a dog reluctantly yanked to heel.

He kept walking, his eyes scanning the street, as the voice relayed information to him. "You did what?" He stopped short, and his voice sharpened into real anger. "Who decided she was ready for recruitment? My last report..." He listened, then interrupted "—Since when is my word not good enough?"

The person on the other end made placating noises. He scowled, the sharp lines of his face emphasized by the frown. "No. The agreement was that it would be my call. And I still don't think it's a good idea. Leave her alone."

The voice at the other end tried to say something, but Sergei was through listening. He hung up the phone and turned it off, then increased his pace down the street. They wouldn't do anything, not without his signing off on the project. That wasn't the way things worked. But the scowl returned. That was the way things *had* worked. But things could change.

You've already sold your soul, he reminded himself sourly. Why are you surprised that the devil's greedy for more?

eight

"A grazing mace, how sweet the sound, that killed a wrrrrreeetch like youuuuuuu..." Wren could sing when she wanted to, but the horrible faux-Scottish accent she put on made her sound more like a dying cat than a halfway decent alto. The worst of the damage from electrical storm Max cleared up, she was picking up the paperwork scattered all over her office while she waited for Sergei to come back with dinner. She had a faint hope that somehow an orderly room would result in an orderly brain.

At this point, with a name and a focus, it was all about circling in until they had a probable location, and then she could go in and do that voodoo that she do so well.

"I once was lost, but now am found, my amazing mace and meeeeeee."

Besides, filing made Sergei happy, even if it was incredibly low on her priorities. The IRS wasn't likely to come calling when you worked in a cash-and-handshake market. But you never knew when you might need to reference a past job. Like that lock she had been working on earlier. It came from a nasty little retrieval she did four years ago, but she had run into a similar one on the job in Connecticut. Preparedness.

Preparedness was key, and the third completely unofficial, unwritten law of lonejacks. First was: Stay free of Council maneuverings and politics. Second was: Pick your jobs—don't let yourself be put into a no-win situation. And third: be prepared for anything that probably won't happen but maybe might.

There were others, but those three were the really important ones. And at least two were a little bent and battered already by this case. She really, really *really* needed a nonmagical snatch-and-run, something she could do in her sleep, just to up the comfort level a little.

And you're babbling inside your brain. Bad sign, Valere.

She picked up the e-mails she had printed out regarding Old Sally, and slipped them into the neon-green folder she had set up for this job. Green for Sally. Orange for the Frants deal. Mentally she ran through colors. Electric-blue for a file on the anti-fatae movement;

she should have been tracking that stuff already, from the first outbreak, so there weren't any surprises. Or so if she ever felt the urge to yank the entire organization out by the roots...

She put aside that nice thought for later, when her life was a little less hectic.

Hah. And that would be when, exactly?

"Oh, shut up," she told the voice that sounded a little too much like her mother, and forced her attention back to the matter at hand. That left her with the folder options of shocking pink, which gave her a headache, and red. She needed to buy new folders. Maybe ones in a nice soothing pastel shade.

"Who would stuff a horse, anyway?" she asked the worn, ear-battered teddy bear perched casually on one shelf. "Of all the bizarre things to leave to your next of kin!"

Teddy declined to answer, so she straightened the bear until he sat up properly and dropped a pile of old papers into the recycling pile.

Old Sally's original owners apparently took to their legacy, passing her down from one generation to the next just the way their founder's will had specified. And even once they realized that Sal was a harbinger, that her walkabouts always preceded some nasty family disaster, they hung on to her. Wren would have burned the mangy thing herself, but different strokes for different folks. Especially folks with money to pay the bills.

Money. Money was what it all came down to, wasn't

it? Except not always. The Council worked on prestige, the whole concept of face, of respect. You could buy prestige, but prestige couldn't buy money. Could it? She paused. Okay, where was that thought taking her? Why did it feel important?

The sound of the door opening was followed by the unmistakable smells of Chinese food wafting down the hallway, blowing away whatever chain of thought she was constructing.

"Plates are on the counter," she yelled.

"They threw in an order of sesame noodles," he told her, juggling a large brown paper bag in one hand, plates and chopsticks in another. "I think Jimmy's got a letch for one of us."

"Works for me," Wren said cheerfully, indicating the cleared-off section of her desk as a staging area. "I have no objection to selling your virtue for a mess of Jimmy's noodles."

Sergei set the bag down where she suggested, and handed her the plates. He seemed calmer now, although she sensed a tightly focused simmer happening underneath. She thought about pushing a little, to see if he'd open up, but decided not to. If it was work, he'd tell her. If it was something else...anyway, she needed him focused, not exploding.

"Anything turn up?" he asked.

Wren took a quick look at the screen, where the most recent search results she had run on the name had come up while she was cleaning. "There are a couple of M. Prevosts on the East Coast, three in the Midwest and seven in the Pacific Northwest." She extracted her food from the bag and settled cross-legged on the floor to eat. "You?"

Sergei shook his head to indicate that he hadn't heard anything, then a faint red stain touched his cheekbones as he pulled his cell phone out of his pants pocket and turned it on again. The tension in the air eased slightly.

"That's an ooops," she said in mock-sad agreement, just as it rang. "You firing on all cylinders tonight, Didier?" It was so rare to catch Sergei doing something blatantly stupid like turning off his phone when he was expecting a call, she actually couldn't enjoy it. Well, not as much as she'd like to, anyway. Not while they were working. Time to tweak him on it later, when he was a little more mellow.

"Didier," he had answered in the meanwhile. "Right, thanks. Uh-huh." He made a scribbling motion at Wren, who got him a pencil and the back of a used envelope. "Right. Okay, thanks. No, that was what I was looking for, thanks. Right. No. Everything's fine here. No, we don't need your help. Uh-huh."

Wren made a circling motion with her hand, and rolled her eyes. Lowell. It had to be Lowell. The dweeb. There was no love lost between her and Sergei's gallery assistant. She thought he was a suck-up with a fetish for electronic toys, and he considered her a parasite without any redeeming social graces. Sergei did his best to keep them at opposite ends of the city. *Dweeb,* she thought again. *If he only knew what his oh-so-artsy boss did in his spare time!*

Sergei hung up the phone, and looked at her, a faraway look in his eyes, what Wren called his thousand-yard stare. When his gaze was cold, it made people tremble in their shoes and back away with minimal breathing so as not to catch his attention. It had taken her several years to get over the urge to run, when he got like that. And another year or so to realize it would never be turned on her. When it went hazy like it was now, though, it meant he was running through a hundred different possibilities, calculating the odds. The latter look was only marginally safer to be around than the former, and it *did* get used on her every now and again.

"What? Tell me it's not the government again," she pleaded. The first and only and hopefully last time they had trod on the toes of the FBI, even Sergei's best contacts had been forced to do some very fast talking to smooth things over. The government's top-secret official position was that there was no such thing as magic, no such thing as Talent, and absolutely no such thing as the *Cosa Nostradamus.* But they came down pretty hard on anyone using that nonexistent Talent anywhere near them.

"No, not this time. Our motive is greed, pure, and not-so-simple. Not financial—aesthetic. I was right, Prevost is a collector."

"How do you know that? And how do you know it's the right guy? We got a couple of Prevosts on this coast—he's been to your gallery? We have an address? Wait a minute, collector of what? Fine art and chunks of concrete don't exactly match, hanging on the wall. Even the weird-ass shi—stuff you sell."

"A collector of things other people don't have," he clarified, ignoring her usual slur on his artists. "He came off the broom—" Sergei's less-than-fond way of describing the Players, or magic wannabes, who came into the gallery "—a few years ago, trolling for items that might be one of a kind. Items of a magical provenance. Which means that he was plugged in enough to know I might be a source, which means he'd also know enough to keep asking in the right places. And he would keep at it—he had those vibes, which was why I remembered him. He'd keep digging until someone actually was stupid or hungry enough to give him what he wanted—or tell him where and how to get it. It seems a damned likely match, yes?"

Wren stared at him. "Yes. Damn, yes. Which means you were right, if this guy's not a Talent himself—"

Sergei shook his head. "I'd lay money he's not."

"—then our thief was probably on retainer, maybe had been from when you first encountered this collector-guy, or soon after. A steady job, no need to advertise his or her abilities, which would explain the lack of flash." She shook her head, considering all the ramifications. "A collector. Great. I hate this job. Have I told you how much I hate this job?"

"Not yet," he sighed, sitting back down in the chair. "But I suspect I'll be hearing it a great deal."

A good retriever could get into any building ever built. And Wren was the best retriever working in the United States, maybe in all of North America today. Some locations might take less time, some might take more, but they were all accessible if you had the Talent. But collectors were an entirely different animal. As Sergei once pointed out, the true collector has read the evil overlord's rules, the most important one being "don't gloat about your plan in the face of your enemy, captive or not." And the second most important being "pay your hired help well, so they can't be bought out by rivals."

Plus, a real mental-case collector—the obsessive, aggressive, doesn't mind breaking the law to own something type—kept his spoils well-guarded. In fact, he didn't care if anyone else knew he owned something or not. What's important was that *he* knew that he owned something that no one else could have, either because it was one-of-a-kind, or impossible to obtain, or some variation on that theme. He wouldn't need to advertise, to show off, or to gloat. So there would be fewer weak chinks in his armor for Wren to wiggle through.

But there was money at stake here. A lovely lot of money, even if Sergei had, in retrospect, underbid the deal. And if there was one thing that could motivate both of them, it was the thought of that money sliding its way into their own pockets. Well, that and the challenge of it all.

Sergei and Wren grinned at each other, a little anticipation mixing in to go with the aggravation. One of the things that had bound them from the very beginning was an awareness that it wasn't enough to be the best. You had to prove it. Not just to others, but to yourself as well. Council, Wren admitted ruefully, weren't the only ones with ego.

Money. Prestige. Face. Ego. A little hamster, racing in her brain. *What's the connection, what's the thread that binds it all?* Let it rest, Wren, she warned herself. Let it unravel in its own time, its own pace.

"Noodles?" he asked, offering her a plate. She took it, and a pair of chopsticks, and started shoveling food into her mouth. It was going to be a *very* long night.

For the next few hours the only sound to come from the office was the sound of chewing, paper turning, and the tapping of Wren's fingers on the keyboard. She couldn't remember how many late-night sessions they'd had like this, hunting down some detail that would make a puzzle piece fall together. Sometimes a case—*situation*—was a question of trolling, like she had been doing with Old Sally, sending out lures and waiting for the answer to fall into your lap and close the case. But more often a job prep session involved chasing down dead end after dead end, until Sergei started to mutter the most interesting curses in Russian, which was how she discovered that a particularly pungent and heartfelt curse *could* and *did* sear the air with an interesting shade of blue electricity. Prep wasn't fun, even if this was more enjoyable than the earlier know-nothing, assume-nothing stages. But prepping every step of the way was how you got the job done. Going in half-assed, as Sergei was forever saying, was the mark of an amateur or a glory hound.

The fact that he usually said this right after she had gone in half-assed was beside the point.

Tonight they had split the workload: he was sorting through gallery records his assistant had—under protest and with a few comments about overtime not quite under his breath—brought over, while she searched the Internet for any mention of one Matthew Prevost, art collector and obscenely wealthy person. Occasionally one of them would find something of interest, and put it in the "follow-up-on" pile. That pile was depressingly small, but around 10:00 p.m. Wren thought that she might have gotten a pipeline into his main home on this coast.

"Real estate records have an M. Prevost signing off on the loan. It was buried…looks like he did it through a second party or something." The house was in upstate

New York, north and west of Albany. Far enough away from the original site that his pet mage probably couldn't translocate the stone directly—unfortunately reducing the chance that someone like Wren could sniff it back to him—but close enough that they could transport it by normal, and less traceable means, rather than use the effort of translocating it again. And that meant there should be some record of it. Or not, she thought, if they hauled it themselves. Better to burn that bridge when and if they came to it.

She squinted at the screen and frowned. They needed a Realtor on-call, to help them figure this mess out. "Okay, does that make any sense to you?"

Sergei leaned over her to look at the display, one hand resting lightly on her shoulder. "No…maybe." Out came the ubiquitous cell, and he punched in a preset phone number.

"Good morning. It's Sergei."

"Good morning?" Wren mouthed at him, one eyebrow raised. She did the math quickly in her head. Too early for London, unless this person was a *real* early riser: Asia? Her suspicion was confirmed when Sergei switched into what sounded like Chinese. She hadn't even known he knew any Asian languages, although once she thought about it, it didn't seem too strange at all.

Makes me feel about as smart as a rusty nail, though. That's four languages he knows, English, Russian, French and Chinese. That I know about. Wren could barely manage a smattering of French, and knew a handful of words in Spanish, most of them rude.

To make herself feel better, she drew down on the current humming in the walls and made a fortune cookie rise from the debris of dinner, stripped the cellophane from it, and sailed it through the air into her hand.

Sergei shot her a glare. "Sorry," she mouthed. Active current—even controlled doses—did terrible things to cell phone reception, which was why she never bothered to carry one.

She unrolled the slip of paper in her hand, and read her fortune. *It is not the dying which is so bad, but the staying dead.* Confucius say "huh?"

Jimmy had a seer writing his fortunes. Made for occasionally unnerving experiences. She considered the slip of paper and then tossed it into the garbage. Sometimes you had to let the really obscure ones go. It would make sense when it made sense, and probably not an instant before, if she knew anything at all about seers. She had enough trouble dealing with today, much less what might happen tomorrow.

"Okay, thanks." He replaced the phone in his pocket and leaned forward, as serious as a man six foot three inches tall could look, sitting on the floor.

"So?" She prepared herself for the worst, not knowing what she thought that might be. The room smelled stale, her mediocre ventilation not handling the layers of Chinese food spices and sweat.

Unexpectedly, he laughed, his smooth chuckle washing out over the room and easing muscles she didn't know had tensed. "You look like I'm about to bring an ax down on your neck, Genevieve."

"Bastard. Who was that? What do you have?" Something clicked in her memory then. "That was Stephen?"

"It was indeed." Stephen Langwon was a former Treasury agent—and occasional art collector, preference for watercolors and a damn good eye, according to Sergei—who had retired and gone into, of all things, real estate. They did have a Realtor on-call after all. "He's in Seoul for a family reunion."

"Bastard," she said again, with more heat, realizing that he'd spoken whatever that language was just to piss her off. "You messed with me on purpose!" Wren kicked out at him, surprised when her bare foot actually managed to connect with his thigh. He grabbed her heel and held on to it with one hand as he continued.

"Stephen thinks that our target probably bought this house through a corporate blind, something to keep taxes off his back. And maybe deflect attention from any suspicion he might be under."

"Right." She tried to pull her foot away but he held on to it. "So who does own it?"

"Nobody?" He shrugged. "Maybe a holding company, I'm not sure how it works, and I didn't want to keep him on the line that long to explain it to me. Besides, static was terrible."

She ignored the slam. She had already apologized, what more did he want?

"So if it's owned by some corporation, can he weasel out if, say, stolen goods are found there?" Wren whistled. "Sweeeeet. But where does that leave us?"

"With a place to look for answers." He yanked on her foot, and she slid out of the chair with a startled yelp, landing on her ass on the floor. Before she could recover, he had unfolded himself and stolen the chair.

"Where're we going?" she asked, recovering enough to stand and lean over his shoulder. Sergei accessed a Web site with a .gov suffix and then dove deeper, past a flurry of password demands and allegedly invader-proof protections. He wasn't a hacker any more than she was, so Wren assumed that meant Stephen had given him the details. Tsk. Bad Stephen. Then she blinked as names, addresses and taxpayer ID numbers scrolled by. "Whoa. Is that…gimme that." He fended her hands away with ease. "Hey, it's my computer, I'm the one going to jail they trace you back. At least let me have the fun of it."

He found the information he was looking for, and clicked on the link to access the file. Wren practically danced behind him, aware that he found her impatience amusing but unable to stop herself. When he printed out the information and then closed the window, she whined in disappointment.

"Serrrrrggggggg…"

"God. Never do that again." She just grinned, pleased to discover another thing that could put his teeth on edge, and filed it mentally under "just in case," sub file "extreme measures." In some ways it might be easier to work with someone who didn't know you so well—fewer buttons for the pushing—but what was the challenge in that? He stood up and gestured her back to her seat. "Stephen took a risk, and gave me that information for a specific use. I'm not going to abuse his trust. Not without damn good reason, anyway. You have your road map. Follow it."

Wren lifted the printout off the printer feed and scanned it as she sat down. "Okay, yeah." Now they were in her territory, more interesting than having government reports. She clicked the mouse, bringing up the browser and scrolling down to a bookmarked page. The header read Anything for a Price. In smaller letters the webmaster advertised "Information for the Discerning Seeker."

Typing one-handed, Wren entered her access code, then the information off the printout. Hitting enter, she turned to hand the paper back to her partner. "See what you can dig up on that company, the ones who set up the alarms. Start with their bonding licenses, work from there. I want to know who they work with, if there are any contacts at all to anyone in the *Cosa*."

Sergei nodded. Dealing with the *Cosa Nostradamus*—especially but not limited to the Council—

was very much like dealing with the mob in the non-magical world, in several ways. The first and foremost was that you gave them respect. For retrievers, that meant asking permission before hitting something that belonged to them. They had done the equivalent of due diligence earlier, clearing the background with the Council. But now that they had a target, every p and q had to be lined up before Wren went in.

The computer screen had changed to an expectant cursor blinking in the middle of a plain dark-red screen. It hurt the eyes to look at it directly for more than a moment at a time. Cracking her fingers like a concert pianist with pretensions, Wren held her hands over the keyboard, focused her inner current, and began to type. The red screen flickered, and an odd, four-dimensional effect seemed to stir within the monitor. Sergei, taught by experience, looked away until it had flattened into something a little more bearably two-dimensional. Wren held the tip of her tongue between her teeth and coaxed the swirling display to form and hold the proper connection.

Using current on electronics was, putting it mildly, stupid, and possibly dangerous. Certainly to the electronics in question, probably to the person using it. But the system didn't seem to have suffered any aftereffects from Max's visit, and she'd protected it as best she could figure how, and it was just so damned *useful*. And the unknown person who had set up this Web site didn't accept any other key. Tricky bastard.

Taking a deep breath, she rested a hand palm down over her chest, feeling her heart beating a little too fast under her T-shirt. *Mellow, mellow...* Gathering a coil of current from the inner pool up her spine, down her left arm and into her pinky, she gently touched the center of the display.

Electricity crackled around her, and her awareness *fell* into the database.

Behind her, Sergei shook his head, sitting down on the floor so that he could work while still keeping an eye on her motionless body.

Sometime around one in the morning, Sergei, finished with the papers he had been searching through, reluctant to make any more phone calls at that hour and bored with looking over her shoulder, started to get restless.

"Go home," Wren said, her fingers flying over the keyboard. The remains of dinner had been stacked in a pile on one corner of her desk, and she occasionally took a pull off the liter of soda at her elbow, barely aware that it had gone flat and gotten warm more than an hour before. She had come out of the database around midnight, and had begun typing what she had learned, working faster than she had thought she could type. You basically got an infodump, and then it was up to you to sort through it. Problem was, if you didn't get it down one way or another real fast, it went zip out of your brain and all the money you'd put into the meter was for nothing.

Not to mention the fact that data-dipping made her cranky, sore, and hungry as a bear after hibernation.

"I'm fine." Sergei shifted his legs under him again, and swore as several papers fell off the lap desk he was using and onto the floor.

Wren shot him a Look that had no effect except to make him go pace the hallway instead. Ten minutes later her fingers finally started to slow down, and then stopped. She shook them out to see if there was any nerve damage, pushed back from the desk, and stretched hard enough to hear things creak.

"Didier!"

He leaned into the room. "Done?"

"Mmm, I think so. Need to let it sit and then come back to see if it's in English. Come on. I feel the need for dietary disaster. It's ice cream time." She took him by the hand and dragged him out of the apartment and down the stairs.

"I don't want ice cream," he said, trying to dig his heels in. "It gives me gas."

"*You're* giving me gas. So if you won't go home or at least take a nap, then shut up and walk with me. Ice cream helps me think. You can just keep me company, okay?"

They left the building, Sergei taking her hand off his forearm and enfolding it with his own much larger hand, an apology for his behavior. His fingers were warm, their palms sliding against each other with the smoothness of flesh-to-flesh, and Wren leaned her head against his shoulder briefly. "See? You feel better already."

"I was fine," he said, shoving her away with a nudge of his arm, as though embarrassed to have her leaning on him. His fingers remained laced with hers.

"You were fine. Now you're better." The night air felt wonderful on her face, and in the distance she could hear late night traffic, and the occasional chop-chop-chop of a helicopter flying overhead. Maybe a news crew heading out to New Jersey, or a Coast Guard crew on patrol. A few other couples were strolling along the street, coming off the bar scene in Greenwich Village a few blocks away.

"Besides, you've never had Marco's gelato. It's awesome, in all the best ways. He makes it with—" She stiffened, her hand convulsing around his before her fingers fell slack and dropped from his grasp.

"Wren?" He stopped, startled. "Wren? WREN!" His yell attracted the attention of a couple walking towards them. The man slowed down, as though to swerve and avoid them. His companion glanced over worriedly as though afraid to see violence break out, then let her date drag her to the other side of the street. Sergei noted them, but paid no attention whatsoever. Everything that mattered was staring at the lamppost with blank eyes and a worse expression. His worst nightmare, piled on top of the events of that evening, was too much for him to deal with. He shook her, hard, his fingers probably leaving bruises on her arms. Panic sucked the air out of his lungs, and he thought he was going to throw up.

"Wren! Come on, what's wrong? Wren? Genevieve! Come back to me, Genevieve. Come on, look at me. Wren, look at me!"

His heart contracted, then she blinked, and animation slowly returned to her expression. "Whoa. Shit."

"What the hell just happened?" His question was shy of a roar, but only just.

"Someone tried to tag me."

He blinked, stared at her. "You brushed it off?"

"Not sure 'brushed' is the right term, but yeah. Told whoever it was in no uncertain terms to go bother some-one else, I didn't have time for head games. Sheesh. Whoever it was, had serious mojo."

Tagging was the act of challenging a current-user, one lonejack to another. Typically it occurred during a turf battle, when lonejacks quarreled over a patron, or to scope out the local competition. Or, more often according to Wren, as the start of a practical joke among friends.

Wren didn't have any friends who could and would do that. Not anymore. And she didn't have a patron to fight over, the way Council mages did.

"You want to go back?" he asked, already swinging her around to face the way they came, but she swatted him on the arm.

"Screw that. He or she or it wants a rematch, I want my ice cream first." She shrugged, walking forward again. "Besides, it was probably just someone testing the waters. I shook 'em off. That's probably all they wanted to know."

Sergei sighed, rubbing the bridge of his nose as though he were the one with a killer headache forming. "There are days I really wish there was a rulebook for all this."

"Council frowns on that. Heavy. But what the hell, write it." She took his hand again, the casual appearance betrayed by the sweat on her skin. "We could make a fortune selling it out of the trunk of your car before they took us down."

He smiled at her flippant tone, but his eyes were shadowed. "Seriously. I don't like this. Not when we're on assignment."

"You think this is connected to the case?" She let out a short sharp laugh. "No offense, Sergei, but that seems damned unlikely. Who would care?"

"The person who took the stone," was his answer, as reasonable as he could make it, considering the way his instincts were still screaming to get her off the street, as though her apartment was proven to be any safer. He also noted, almost as though watching someone else, that he had gone into what Wren called watchful predator mode, like the hawk alert for someone who might try and take his kill. From the expression on her face, she had noticed it too, and wasn't sure if she should feel protected or insulted.

"It's unnerving me, Wren. This whole situation is starting to unnerve me, and I don't know why, which unnerves me even more."

"Yeah." She paused, her hand holding his a little more tightly. "It's probably just coincidence. Some newbie wanting to see what's in the neighborhood."

"I don't buy into coincidences. You know that."

"And you know damn well that current plays merry hob with the usual laws of probability. So lighten up. Come on, I want a double scoop of mint-chocolate-chip-cookie-dough ice cream, and I want it now."

The brittle tone in her voice, more than her words, convinced Sergei to lay off the topic. For the moment.

Marco's was still open, as Wren had predicted. It was a narrow storefront, barely wide enough for the glassed-in display. Farther in the back the store widened enough for two small tables and eight chrome-back chairs, like something stolen from a cheap diner. A teenager with long shiny black hair down her back was behind the counter sullenly serving out cones to a group of kids even younger than she was. When she looked up and saw Wren, though, her expression brightened. "Jenny, hi!"

"Heya Sandy. Didn't know you were still on night shift." She didn't bother, as usual, to correct the nickname. It stopped bothering her around seventh grade.

"Yeah, got my classes switched to the afternoon. Sleep in the morning. Sucks to be me."

Wren laughed. "Give me a—"

"Double mint-chocolate-chip-cookie-dough. And

you?" She turned her gaze onto Sergei like he was a cone of something she'd like to eat, and Wren instinctively stepped closer to her partner's side. She realized what she was doing, and felt herself flush, but couldn't help herself. It was one thing what he did on his own time, on his own turf. But he wasn't to hunt on her home ground. Ignoring the little voice in her head that pointed out a) it wasn't Sergei giving the come-hither looks and b) what say did she have in who he hithered to?

"Vanilla, please."

Sandy's gaze flicked from Sergei's face to Wren's, and something in there made her step back. "Right. Two cones. With tax, that's six twenty-five."

"That's side street robbery," Sergei muttered, reaching for his wallet.

"Isn't it though? But worth it." Wren accepted both cones, turning to hand the vanilla one to him, when a terrible shriek filled the air.

"What the hell was that?" one of the kids seated at the back tables demanded. Sandy had paled, and Wren's eyes went wide. Sergei had enough presence of mind to grab her cone before she was heading out the door. "Stay there!" she shouted back. Sergei assumed she was talking to him, since Sandy had jumped the counter and was following already. In passing, he noted that although shapely, her legs ended in hooves. *Cosa,* although no fatae he was familiar with. Not that that meant much. Wren had forced him to confront his own xenophobic tendencies—and that had been an ugly scene—but there it was and he had to deal with it. Mainly by letting his partner deal with the fatae as much as possible. Although occasionally, as now, he found himself wondering how many times he had encountered fatae without knowing it. Not a comfortable fact, which led him back to another uncomfortable fact, which was that his partner had just gone out into possible if not probable danger...

Stay put. She said to stay put. His resolution to heed her order lasted all of three minutes. It might just be a random mugging. Or it might be whoever had taken the magical potshot at her earlier. In which case he'd be of no possible godly use to her, but... "Stay where you are. Don't move, if anyone except us comes in the door, get down." The seven kids nodded, clearly unnerved but confident in their ability as New Yorkers—and teenagers—to handle whatever happened. Sergei looked for a place to put the cones down. Seeing none, he pushed open the door with one shoulder and went outside anyway.

He found them in the alleyway halfway down the block. Wren was crouched next to something large and faintly... Sergei looked more closely. No, the figure was definitely glowing, in a sort of hazy, pulsing light. Closer, and he saw that Sandy was sitting cross-legged on the pavement, the glowing thing cradled in her lap. As he watched, the glow pulsed one last time, then went out.

"Damn. Damn and...damn."

She's furious, part of his mind noted with detached curiosity. *When she's just angry, she gets creative.* He couldn't recall ever, in ten years, seeing his partner so upset she couldn't curse, mostly with words he had inadvertently taught her.

Sandy bowed her head over the figure, her long dark hair falling to cover both of them. Wren reached out her hand as though to stroke her hair, then rose to her feet and stumbled away, bumping into Sergei almost blindly.

"An angel?" It was the only thing it could be, with that glow.

"Yeah. Someone...bastards must have jumped him. Threw something in his face, it was all...all melted." She swallowed hard, then set her own face into determined stoicism. "Lye maybe. Cleaning fluid. That would...it would fit. Then, when he couldn't see to protect himself, they stabbed him. Bunch of times. Even an angel can't survive that much cold steel."

Sergei whispered a brief prayer for whatever soul angels contained. They might not be the godly messengers he had been taught in catechism, but nothing deserved to die like that. Not even a fatae.

"Okay, this has got to stop. It was one thing when they were just preaching, or making life awkward, but how am I supposed to get any info if half the *Cosa's* afraid to stop by? I picked this neighborhood because it was weird-friendly, damn it!"

Sergei, not knowing what else to do, handed her the now-dripping cone. She took one look, and started to hiccup, the laughter fighting it out with the tears. Her hand shook, but she took the cone.

"They? The...pest-control group you mentioned?" He didn't know what to do, to make it better, so he fell back on the old standby—work. Keep her thinking, keep her moving.

"Yeah. Have to be. Who else—" Her voice caught. It wasn't death, he realized suddenly—she had seen dead bodies before, had seen people die in front of her. But this... *Never a fatae.* She had never seen one of the fatae die before. Knowing they were mortal was different from having it proven to you. And there was just enough day-dreaming little girl left in Wren that the proving was painful.

Behind them, Sandy stood, leaving the rapidly-cooling body of the angel in the trash.

"His brothers will come and find him soon enough," she said. Her eyes were red, but her voice was steady. "I'd rather we not be here when they do."

"Right." Angels weren't all that fond of humans. Or...whatever Sandy was.

"You going to be okay?" Wren asked, obviously thankful to have someone else to focus on, rather than her own—perceived—weakness. They were both on emotional bungee cords, it seemed, being pulled way too tight and dropped from way too high.

"Yeah. Or, no, but whatchagonna do?" And with that, the sullen teenager mask fell down again, and she shrugged. "I got to shut down the store. Marco will be by at closing. I'll have him walk me home. You, go."

They went.

nine

There were thirty-eight floors in the Frants Building. It was by no means the tallest building in the city, even post-9/11. Nor was it the most attractive, or the most striking, or the best situated in terms of prestige or ease of commute. But for many years, it had the reputation for being the best maintained, the safest. No false alarms dragged the local fire engine company out to investigate, no cops had to come and investigate any robberies, any B&E. It was, all told, considered an excellent place to work, in any of the thirty-six floors that held the offices of nine different companies and two multipartner law firms.

Oliver Frants would be quite proud of it. If he ever gave the matter any thought.

"Why are you wasting my time with this?" He strode into the private elevator, dressed in a gray sweatshirt and jogging shorts, both damp with sweat, speaking into the cell phone microphone clipped to his collar. His bodyguards moved with him; one before, one after. They weren't necessary within his own building. Rather, they *shouldn't* have been necessary. But recent events had changed all that.

The elevator doors closed, the cage sliding smoothly up. Frants continued to talk; the elevator shaft had been wired to ensure there was no interruption of service. "Do I not pay you good money? No, better than good money! All I expect is that you do what needs to be done. Is that such an impossible burden?"

The person on the other end of the line mumbled a response that did not mollify his boss.

The top two floors of the building were used for a distinctly different purpose than the levels below. Completely renovated a decade before, soundproofed and insulated from the office space, on a separate electrical system, they were both apartment suites, but there the similarity ended. The uppermost floor was filled with clutter, almost homey in the scattering of glossy porn magazines and dog-eared paperback books, the battered black leather sofas placed around a widescreen television, the occasional slightly wilted plant near the windows, and the debris of food and dishes in the large, open-plan kitchen. Seven rooms led off the main space, each one with a closed door. In the floor of the main room, at each corner, there was a trap door. Opening one would reveal a curving chute or a sturdy ladder, both made of thick plastic. No metal, no electronics, nothing that could possibly be magicked by current, or jammed by high tech.

Those trap doors gave instant access to the living area directly below, a mansion reconfigured onto one floor filled with the very best, most luxurious mahogany and leather furniture, glass-fronted cabinets, Persian carpets and high-end electronics.

Seven bodyguards above, on rotation to protect one man below.

"Call me when you actually know something, then!" Frants terminated the call and exited the elevator. One bodyguard moved ahead, opening the door to his boss's living quarters. He stepped inside, did a quick visual scan while his partner ran a check with a handheld scanner.

"All clear," the second one announced, his readout returning nothing that shouldn't have been there. The first guard nodded, his physical check confirming the electronics.

"Fine. Go."

The two guards looked at each other, then Number 1 shrugged and stepped back. If the boss wanted to be alone, he'd be alone. One of them would stay outside, in case he changed his mind. The other would go upstairs, and the third of their team had remained below, in the basement gym area. Nothing could get into the private portions of this building without them knowing it.

"Honey, I'm home." Frants laughed, kicking off his trainers and leaving them by the entrance. His valet would come by in the morning to have them sanitized. The cell phone was unclipped, juggled in one hand. A tug on his sweatshirt with his free hand, and it was tossed into the hamper, followed by his socks. His valet would attend to them, as well.

He walked on the silky-soft rug, barely feeling the texture from familiarity but aware of it nonetheless—the awareness of ownership. Naked but for his shorts, he went into the kitchen and poured himself a glass of the high-protein drink that was waiting in the blender, freshly-made for him. It tasted disgusting, but it did the job.

Oliver Frants took pride in the fact that he rarely slept. A combination of drugs, herbal extracts, and iron self-control kept him going, his mind sharp. Time, he believed, was too precious to waste: there were only so many hours allotted to a man, and he had things to do in every one of them.

His father had owned a home in the suburbs, beyond the noise and congestion of the city. His grandfather lived in a townhouse off Astor Place, and used to walk to and from the office every evening. *I lair where I hunt,* their son and grandson was often quoted as saying. *You*

*can't be out of touch when there's business to be done.
And there's always business to be done.*

"Peter?" His drink in one hand, the cell phone in the other, he wandered over to the widescreen video display and watched the overseas markets scroll past. "Where do we stand on the McConnell deal?"

He could practically sense the bodyguard outside, the rage of having to depend on someone else for protection a smoldering ember in his awareness. His insurers insisted on their presence, but it annoyed him. It was like an itch that you can't quite reach, knowing that ignoring it won't make it any more bearable. Even worse, since that damn spell had been breached, they'd upped the guards to two at all times rather than simply when he left the building.

Oliver Frants had not left this building, save for closely-guarded public appearances and PR tours, in almost a decade. Less agoraphobia and more obsession: this building was all he needed, the control panel from which he manipulated the world to his liking.

But that self-determined universe had been shaken, badly, by the bastard who dared put sticky fingers on his belongings. His security. No matter what his people said about the likelihood that it was probably only a joyrider, a thrill-thief taking something that was supposedly impossible to take, Frants knew it for what it was—a slap at him. At everything he was, everything he had built.

The fact that the lonejack he had hired to retrieve it had yet to succeed left him with even less desire for sleep now. Things to do. Thieves to crush. Universes to be put back to rights.

"Now you tell me this?" he said to the man on the other end of the line, his tone exasperated, irritated. "Now, a week after the drop-deadline?"

He wasn't risk-adverse. Far from it: he'd built the company his grandfather had started into a multinational empire. All by taking risks. Calculated, considered risks. Having a madman running about with his protections—bought and paid for, thrice over! It was not acceptable. He would not rest until it was returned.

Because now, when he closed his eyes, nightmares crept in. *No,* he thought, banishing the idea of exhaustion. *Better to stay awake. Stay on top. Stay in control.*

"Stop making excuses. There's no way they can make any profit with a bid that low. What are they really getting out of this? Well, find out! What the hell do I pay you for, if you don't know shit?"

He flipped the cell shut, then reconsidered, opening it again and jabbing a button. "Wilkinson. Keep an eye on him. If he screws up, by so much as an inch, remove him. Rawkey. Yeah, Rawkey's due a promotion. See to it."

Satisfied, he placed the phone down on a hand-inlaid mosaic table, and strode over to the glassed-in walls. The city was spread out below him, like candies on a plate. If he wanted it, it was his. But he didn't want it. Let lesser men claim land, buildings, *things*. He wanted...more.

Behind him there was a noise, a faint, almost kittenlike sound. Frants turned to consider the body sprawled in the off-white sheets. An observer might think she slept peacefully, but Frants noted the sweat on her skin, the faint twitch of her limbs, and smiled in satisfaction.

He wasn't a cruel man. He didn't mistreat his toys. He simply preferred them...compliant.

And he had plans for Denise, as soon as the time was right. When he had everything in place. Plans far beyond the minor amusement she gave him in bed. A good corporate soldier, Denise would fulfill the vow she took when she accepted the terms of employment, and truly give her all for the company. For him.

Smiling at the thought, he turned back to watch the city slowly come back to life.

It was a dream, only a dream. More, a memory she was dreaming. Old, dead, harmless. Knowing that didn't make it any easier....

The lab room was empty, the only light the afternoon sun slanting in through the second-floor windows. Behind her, down the hallway, Wren could hear the sound of the girls' soccer team running wind sprints in the nearest stairwell, the heavy fire door propped open. The noise of their sneakers, the heavy breathing and oc-

casional yell or catcall or burst of laughter could have come from another planet.

She took another step forward, could feel the change in air pressure, still standing in the hallway. Like walking into a sauna, the heaviness of it repelled her, made her want to back away and never come back. Like a horror movie, only it was all around her, not flat, on a screen. Nervously she chewed on the nail of her middle finger, tugging at the cuticle. Danger, it whispered. Every prickle on her skin urged her to back away. Leave the building; hide, stay low, stay unseen. She had survived for so long, being unseen. Fading into the woodwork. Letting predators—of which there were too many, in high school—look for more obvious prey.

"Mr. Ebenezer?" The voice that came out of her throat was faint, hesitant, squeaky.

She knew he was there. She could feel him, even through that heavy air, the gentle hum in the currents that identified John Ebenezer to her as vividly as sight or sound. Magic, like everything else, left its mark in the environment.

Sometimes, she thought, the mark went too deep. It caught you unawares, tugged you from the shadows, made you think there was something better...and then slapped you for assuming too much.

Closing her eyes, Wren braced herself, counting backward from ten to settle her emotions. Never go into anything half-cocked, she could hear her mentor say. Think before you charge.

When her pulse beat with the same tempo as the currents in the air around her, she opened her eyes. Her slender, pale face was set in determined lines new to her, a decade too early.

Resolved, she walked steadily into the heaviness, into the classroom and straight on into the back of the room; raised her hand and pushed open the lab office door.

That room was in darkness, too, save one small desk lamp. It illuminated the intent, dreamy-eyed face of a man in his early forties. Black hair, hazel eyes, pale skin. On a good day, those features snapped with intelligence and vigor, a lively sense of humor that swept his students along with his enthusiasms. His hands were held over the lamp, palms facing each other, straining as though forcing something obdurate between them. His fingers shook from the effort, and his body language—hunched shoulders, bent legs—screamed tension of another sort. The pressure in the air came from him, shoved against him; a storm front waiting to happen.

"Oh, Neezer…"

Her mentor, still dressed from class in his khakis and lab coat, stared into the space between his palms, not acknowledging her entrance or her words. Not aware of either, she knew.

"There's a line we dance on. On one side, control. On the other, chaos. Both are terribly, terribly appealing. But neither is safe, and neither's very smart, either. Either one of them will suck you in, and never let you go."

Neezer's voice, three years past. She was fourteen again, sitting in the diner, drinking a bottomless glass of diet Pepsi, listening, but not really hearing. When you're fourteen, the idea of losing yourself like that seems impossible. Unthinkable. It hadn't seemed much more real at seventeen, either. Not until it happened to Neezer.

"There's a price to be paid for magic. That much of every story is true." Too much control and the joy dies. You can't create, can't improvise. Current becomes a tool, not a gift. That was the road the Council walked. Wren knew Neezer would have slit his own throat rather than go that road. But chaos...

Chaos meant wizzing, turning yourself over to the currents of magic. Letting it overwhelm you until there was no "you" left, not really. Until you were a current junkie, unable to separate from the magic at all. Not wanting to, at all. Endlessly creating, dissolving, creating...

Her breathing was harsh, strained. Pale brown eyes filled with tears, itching as if she had a sudden attack of allergies, hay fever in the middle of winter. She blinked the tears away, reaching for that balanced edge of control.

Ground. Focus, find the center within her, where her own current lay coiled, waiting. Know it, manipulate it. Reach out to the currents humming within the building, laced into the walls, twined into the electrical wiring of the high school. Power to power. She touched it, felt it

*gentle under her touch, calming her own nerves in re-
turn. Wren wiped one sweaty palm against her jeans,
then covered his fingers with her own. They were cold,
tingling.*

"Neezer?"

*He didn't respond. Panic wound in her stomach, spit-
ting acid.*

"Neezer, wake up!"

In the real history, he had woken, at least for a little
while. But in her dream he stayed silent, still staring...

No! I will stop this now. I will wake up NOW.

Her eyes shot open and she stared up at the ceiling.
It was dark, the still-quiet that comes before false dawn,
the only time a city can ever be said to be quiet. Sweat
dampened her skin, clumping her hair and making it
stick to the back of her neck. Tears pooled in the corner of her eyes, and her throat felt tight not with fear,
but sorrow. Sorrow, and loss. A dull aching pain that
never, ever went away, not any moment she was awake
or asleep. *Don't leave me alone....*

It was the angel. That's all. That's enough.

Rolling onto her side, Wren kicked the sheets away,
letting the night air cool her skin slightly. The sense of
emptiness lingered. Her left hand reached out, almost
without conscious thought, and lifted the phone off her
nightstand. Speed dial number one, and the sound of
ringing filled her ear.

"Didier." A sleep-drenched sound, groggy. He had

only left her apartment three hours ago. Even with his usual difficulty catching a cab, at that hour of the morning there shouldn't have been any traffic. More than enough time to make it up and across town to his apartment, peel off his clothing and fall into bed. He wasn't much on bedtime rituals when he was that wiped out.

Suddenly guilt washed over her, making her voice almost too soft to be heard. "Bad time?"

"Never." She could hear him moving about, the sound of pillows being fluffed and the creak of the bed as he shifted his weight. "I was only sleeping. Who needs too many hours of that?"

In the darkness, his voice in her ear, she could almost pretend he was there with her. Imagined his weight sinking the mattress, his too-long legs taking up half the bed. She knew he liked to sleep sprawled on his back, while she curled on her side. More than once they had both managed to fit onto an undersized motel mattress, or—once—a tarp spread under the leaking roof of a falling-down woodshed. It hadn't always been contracts and bank accounts and reputations doing half the work.

"Bad dream, Zhenechka?" His tenor was like caramel, the normally clipped syllables softening. His nighttime voice, she thought of it. The voice he used only for her, and the cat he didn't want anyone to know he fed, in the alley behind the gallery.

"Yeah. No. It...." She hesitated, her free hand playing with the edge of the sheet. *Silly, this hesitation. Stu-*

pid, to call him and then not talk. But she couldn't find the words right away.

"I dreamed about Neezer," she said finally. "That... that day." The Day, she thought of it. The day her mentor had finally admitted out loud what they both knew, that he was on the edge of wizzing—of becoming a danger to himself, and to her. The day when being a Talent had stopped being a game, and gotten deadly, dangerously serious.

She listened to the long, warm sounds of Sergei's breathing, and felt oddly comforted, as though he had put his arms around her and cradled her to him.

"I'm scared," she said finally. And she wasn't referring to just the aftermath of the dream. Something was happening. Things were changing. She could feel it, like thunder in the air, even if she didn't know the cause.

"I know. So am I." He wasn't talking about the dream either.

And that was what she loved the most about her partner. That in the dark, separated by half a city, connected only by the faintest wisps of technology, he could make her feel better by giving validation to her fears. The thought struck her as horribly funny, and she started to giggle for the second time in five hours.

"Wren?" But there was no real worry in his voice now, only understanding. "It's okay, little wren. Let it out. It's been an impossible day, even for a tough little bird like you."

Something grabbed her inside the ribs at his words, grabbed and clenched and caught her short of breath, aching and expanding in the hollowness. "Don't ever leave me," she asked, not even aware of what she was saying.

There was a long silence.

"I won't. Not ever. Now go back to sleep, Zhenechka. I'm here. I'll stay right here."

With that promise, she curled herself around the receiver, and slowly slid back into a dreamless sleep.

"Don't leave me..." A whisper, a child's terrified command. Or a woman's heartfelt request.

He could stay with her...or he could protect her. He might not be able to do both, not anymore.

Give the devil his due, he protected what was his. And right now, some insurance didn't sound like such a bad idea.

On the other side of the island, Sergei Didier lay in his bed, staring out his window at the pale pink light creeping into the sky, and knew what he had to do.

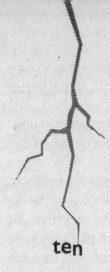

ten

In a building without any identifying signs or the usual indicators of occupancy, on a street that nobody in the city thought to walk down without a good reason for it, the Fatal Friday cocktail party was in full swing in a room off the second-floor lobby.

The room itself was warm and inviting, paneled in cherry-stained wood and filled with glossy-polished furniture. Thick cream carpeting muffled the sound of heels and conversation alike. Easily two dozen men and women moved about the glassed-in room, drinks in hand and gossip on their lips. It could have been any group of lawyers or accountants unwinding after a tough week in the system. Could have been, but wasn't.

They were the Silence. What one well-placed insider

had once called the real world's answer to MacGyver: two-hundred-plus operatives armed with nothing more than their wits and a pocket knife.

And the resources of a multimillion-dollar endowment, renewed annually by donors who remained distant and unnamed.

But for the operatives for whom Fatal was a tradition, albeit an ironic one, the who and the why of the Silence's benefactors wasn't something they thought about every day, if at all. It was enough that they were there, doing what they did. And part of what they did involved appearing in front of the Action Board on the third Friday of every month.

The Silence took no fees, accepted no credit, courted no publicity. A truly secret society in a world with a long history of pretenders to the name. But there were always holes, always flaws. No organization had perfect security, perfect information. And so the Silence regularly drained their direct operatives of whatever info they held, no matter if it seemed useful or not at the time.

And to that end, every Handler on the continent, and a few who had to fly in from overseas, stopped by to unload their month's worth of reports in person, and get a grilling on every detail in return. Praise was allocated, and occasionally blame or reprimands.

The cocktail party afterward was a civilized veneer on the heavy drinking which invariably followed those reports.

It used to be a looser affair, but after the one "safe" bar in the neighborhood burned down during a labor disagreement, the Silence brass established this in-house gathering. Free booze was better than stuff you had to pay for, and the Silence had a way of keeping tabs on who was saying what in their drunken stupor.

Sergei hadn't been to one of these gatherings in almost seven years. Purposefully absent, as though least in sight would mean least in mind, the minor flow of information he used to maintain his and Wren's freedom fed to them over the phone, from a distance. Obviously, that distance hadn't been enough. A phrase from *The Godfather* sprang inevitably, ironically, to mind. "Just when I thought I was out, they pull me back in."

But there was never loss without gain. He hoped, anyway.

The press of a body nearer to his than was comfortable was his only warning. "What is your deal, anyway?"

"Excuse me?" Turning, Sergei raised one eyebrow, and looked down his admittedly patrician nose at the much shorter speaker, to no effect. He prided himself on the ability to freeze out unwanted conversational interlopers, but Dancy had never been able to take a hint. Sledgehammer or otherwise.

"Take the promotion, man." Dancy leaned forward, the alcohol plain on his breath. Five foot nothing, squarely muscled like a bulldog, he had been around forever, gone up the ranks from messenger to Handler, and the scars of it were in his eyes. "You know they get what they want anyway, and they want your girl, bad. So why not take the bennies too?"

The Silence's interest in Wren was open gossip. Bad sign. But it was their obvious need that gave him the leverage he was here trying to use. That didn't make Dancy's comments any easier to take. "Get. Away. From. Me." His teeth didn't quite grit together, but it was a near thing. He did *not* like being talked about. He never had, even in his glory days as an Active. He liked it even less when Wren was involved.

Dancy blinked, taken aback by the other man's re-action to what he had intended as friendly advice.

"Right. Still the same old team player, huh?" That stung, more than it should have. More than he should have let it. "See you around, Softwing."

Softwing. His nickname in the Silence. He'd always found that...amusing. Ironic. The owl and the wren. Birds almost of a feather.

Sergei took a cigarette out of the silver case he al-ways carried and rolled it between his fingers. Fifteen years since he'd inhaled nicotine, and the urge was still there, a smoky siren's song. He tested himself, every day, some days every hour. Masochism? Martyrdom? Was there really much difference between the two?

He shouldn't have been so hard on Dancy. You couldn't be in the game and not get talked about, and that's what this all was, a very deadly serious game. And the moment he walked into the building, people knew. He might call it gossip...active Handlers would call it intel. Their lives sometimes depended on it.

"Didier?"

He turned, bracing himself until he saw who the speaker was.

"Adam."

"I never thought I'd see you at one of these again." There was an unspoken question on Adam's lean face, a concern that dated back twenty years, when they were both raw recruits in the Silence's ongoing battle. Adam never seemed to age, damn him. A little more silver in the reddish hair, a few more lines around the eyes and mouth, but still the same. His companion, a younger woman with dark brown ringlets and an open, curious face, watched the two of them as though she had her eye to a microscope.

"I had need of the Library. Sheer bad luck to pick today, but figured as long as they were pouring..."

Adam pursed his mouth. You didn't go to the Library unless and until you had exhausted all your usual resources. But Sergei had just enough of a reputation as a renegade that he might do anything at all.

"Did she let you in?"

A twist of the mouth that might have been a smile. "Sent me to Douglas."

"Ouch." The Library was harsh on people who wasted her—its—time. But Douglas was almost worse. "Was it worth it?"

Sergei shrugged. "Won't know until I know."

The Silence was small by most corporate standards, but it still had an organizational chart with three branches: Action, Information and Operations. Douglas *was* Operations. He pulled strings, and Action—the branch that oversaw Handlers and their agents in the field—danced.

Douglas knew where the bodies were buried, how deep, and what it might take to dig them up again. You went to him only when you had something of value to trade.

Adam looked at Sergei with renewed interest, but his companion finally had enough, and elbowed Adam in the ribs just hard enough to make her point.

"Ooof. Right. Sorry. Clara, Sergei Didier. Sergei, Clara Maroony."

"You were a Handler," she said, sizing him up with a cool eye he might have found appealing at another time, on another day.

"Not anymore."

"Not right now," Adam said, and returned Sergei's glare with a cool eye of his own. "He's freelancing at the moment. I'm thinking of taking him as my mentor."

Clara snorted, and turned on her heel, leaving them in search of more interesting conversation.

"Heard of me, has she?"

Adam made a "what can you do?" move with his hands. "There are those who still like to talk about the lad who told the Silence to take a long walk off the short pier. If it helps, most of the young'uns haven't a clue who you were. Still are." He held up a hand to stop anything Sergei might say in response. "Spare me, okay? We've been friends for too long to fight over this. Even if you are stingy with the Christmas cards. Just remember that you do still have friends here." His expression grew intent. "And that you can do more with friends than enemies."

"Thank you." There really wasn't anything else he could say. And friends were always good to have. He might have need of them. Soon.

Adam clapped him on the shoulder, and turned to follow Clara. Sergei stood in the middle of the growing crowd, feeling it swirl around him in an intricate two-step of office politics. Sharks and lampreys, circling, looking for something struggling in the water.

An ugly image, and probably not fair. The Silence operatives were the good guys. He had to remember that.

If Sergei was going to be honest with himself, there was a lot of truth in what the two men had said. If he were to return to the Silence, bringing Wren with him, he would be their golden boy again, a position he'd held for most of his adult life.

Look at it logically, old man. On the one hand, if he agreed to be Wren's Handler, he would be in a position to help her adjust to the...particulars of the organization. If he balked, and they coerced her anyway, he would be locked out. The Silence would make sure of that.

The thought of her turning to someone else, taking guidance from someone else, made his stomach twist. Ten years they'd been partners. Three times longer than anyone else he had ever worked with. A truer partnership than anything he'd known before.

Those thoughts brought up memories he had been repressing since he walked into the building, the memories that had driven him out in the first place. Poor Jordan. Young, Talented, eager. So eager to please, he claimed he could do more than he could. And current wasn't kind to those who overreached themselves.

Wren thought that there wasn't anything worse than wizzing. He had seen that there was. The Silence had asked that of Jordan. Had demanded it. Taken it.

Destroyed all that talent, that eagerness. And he, as Jordan's Handler, had been complicit. Guilty.

Wren wasn't that compliant, that obliging. The very thought made him grin in relief and memory as he raised his glass to his mouth.

But if everything he'd planted today grew as it should, he would have to return here. That was the offer he had made to Douglas: he would return to the fold, and they would leave Wren alone. Return to the thing that had almost destroyed him, to protect the thing that had saved him.

Douglas had promised to consider it, to take the partial victory rather than lose entirely. Sergei would still be free to continue his association with Wren, after his responsibilities to the Silence. And that association would earn her the Silence's protection as well. But active status would put a strain on their relationship, their *partnership:* one he wasn't sure it could survive.

And how long would the trade hold for? The Silence wanted Wren—how much time could he buy her, realistically? Was it a trade worth making, or would he be selling himself for no real gain?

He would do it, in a heartbeat, if he felt that it was the right move. If it were a winning move. But he didn't trust the Silence anymore. And, in this matter, he no longer trusted his own instincts.

Sergei kicked back what was left of his drink and left the glass on the table. Suddenly the amber liquid didn't taste as appealing as it had before. The cocktail party was building in energy. There were people arriving whom he hadn't seen in years, people he had once considered allies, but he didn't want to mingle, didn't want to talk to anyone else, and have to decipher what games they were playing, what agendas they were pursuing or alliances they were building. He pushed through the crowd, nodded to the few people there he respected, and went out the door and down the escalator—the Silence didn't like elevators, too easy to tamper with—and out to the street.

The question lingered, like the aftertaste of the Scotch. Why was he trying so hard to avoid the inevitable? Adam thought the Silence could be useful to him, Sergei. And Douglas believed that Wren could be useful to the Silence. That message came through loud and clear. She could probably write a half-decent ticket for herself, maybe stay out of the worst of the assignments.

But there was always a price to pay for power. In this case, Wren's freedom. The chance for her to remain a lonejack, answerable to no one save herself. The option to do or not, as she felt best.

In short, what was at stake was her soul. It was clichéd, old-fashioned, but he didn't know any other way to express it.

He glanced back up at the building, its façade innocuous, unthreatening, almost not there to the casual passersby. There was a price to pay for everything. Wren might, given the choice, think losing him, at least for a little while, a fair price to pay. And yet he had promised never to leave her. Did this qualify or not? And if it came to that, would he be able to honor that promise?

Too scared to risk everything on the roll of the dice, when you know someone else had the loading of it. He was *too old for this. Too unwilling to rock the small, patched boat he had fashioned for himself.*

Walking down the street, he forced the tension out of his shoulders, breathing in the soft spring air and letting it settle in his lungs, carrying away the smoke and cologne-scented air from inside. What-ifs and maybes were theory. He wouldn't borrow any more trouble than he already had to hand. And right now, with Douglas appeased for the moment, that trouble was the current situation.

Wren had taken off earlier that afternoon, saying she had a few things to deal with before doing the job. Magic things, he knew. It was frustrating, being left out of that part of her life. Oh, he'd gone along on a job a time or three, but almost always as an adjunct, or a distraction. He didn't delude himself into thinking that what he did wasn't important—they were a functional team, neither side as effective alone. But the fact of the matter was that she was the Talent, the retriever. He was just...the money man. The dealmaker. The borderline Null.

He knew the bitterness in his thoughts was silly, and he also knew its source. There was a canker of worry eating away deep in the pit of his stomach, and not all the confidence in the world in their abilities could soothe it. Not about this case, or at least not only, but about what the Silence planned to do. Wren sensed changes in the air, things that frightened her. He hadn't told her that fear came from him, that she was picking up on his own emotions. He had been a successful agent because he could sense threads being spun around him before they were visible, could take action against them before they became a problem. But he couldn't get a grip on anything right now.

He had made promises: to his partner, to her mother, hell, even to Neezer, although he'd never met the man. And tied into all that, the growing fear that he wasn't thinking clearly when it came to Wren Valere. Was he honestly trying to keep her safe? Or just keep her dependent on him?

"You don't want to be controlling her?" Douglas had said. "Then stop controlling her."

A five-year-old memory surfaced, brought up by the events of the previous night and the sudden reemergence of The Alchemist in their lives. *Wren, bruised, battered, grinning from ear to ear. "You were fabulous!" Her voice was shaky, her eyes bright with the adrenaline rush of having been thrown over a cliff and dragged back by the sheer power of his one hand on her ankle, almost too late. He wanted to bury himself in her static-wild hair, and never come out. Never face a world again where he could see her falling, falling down to the cliffs and the water below…*

"Gahhh…" Shaking his head violently to rid himself of the image, he shoved his hands into his jacket pockets and strode off with renewed energy down the street. Too many years ago, too many scrapes and close calls, and that was still the nightmare that made him break out in a cold sweat. *Overprotective? Me?*

He would talk to her. Tell her what was going on. Somehow. And then it would be up to her to decide. To judge his choices. And he would put his own fate into her hands as well.

"Only you would find walking down 8th Avenue at one in the morning to be relaxing."

Sergei chuckled, a low, contented sound. "Look around you, Wren. Hookers and johns, drug dealers and buyers...and cops. Everyone's out on the street watching everyone else. This is the safest, most interesting place to be in the entire city at night."

"You're insane," she said, just to hear him laugh again. He'd shown up at her apartment around midnight, pacing and fidgety like a cat overdosed on catnip. When she tried to get him to tell her what was wrong, he'd grabbed coats in one hand, her arm with the other and said: "Let's take a walk."

"And you're with me," he said now. "What does that make you?"

"Your bodyguard." She nodded at a cop who was talking to two hookers, an Asian transvestite and a skinny little redheaded girl who looked all of fourteen and was probably twelve. The cop stopped in midlecture and gave them both a professional once-over, then nodded, the action a little more than casual.

"One of yours?" Sergei asked in a low voice.

"Uh-huh."

There were Talents everywhere, some of them barely functional, others rivaling Merlin at his prime. Of the ones who were aware, active and trained, about one third were lonejacks, the freelancing scum of the universe. According to the Council, anyway.

The cop went back to his unwilling audience, and Wren and Sergei walked on without any further interaction. You noted, but you didn't out a fellow Talent. It was rude. And possibly dangerous.

"Hey hey hey. In for a night on the town?"

Sergei froze the huckster with one chill glance, and he faded back into the garishly lit doorway.

"I thought the mayor had gotten rid of that."

"You can't get rid of sin, Wren. Not while there's blood and breath."

"Not the theaters, the talkers. Aren't they supposed to stay off the sidewalks?"

"More laws are observed in the breaking than the following. But I don't need to tell you that, do I?" A stranger's voice. The cop had followed them after all.

"Just walking, Officer...Doblosky," she read off the badge that was clipped to his NYPD windbreaker.

"Just talking," the cop replied. He was a big guy, built like a linebacker, with close-cropped blond hair and faded blue eyes that squinted naturally. "You sassed the cleaners come to town?"

A frown, then comprehension. Did she know about the vigilantes. "Yeah. You know 'em?"

"They're sloppy. They can tag their grime okay, but the mop slaps everyone, you know? And sometimes I'm not too sure they know grime from honest dirt." He nodded once, his eyes still squinted into some nonexistent light. "Walk careful-like."

"Plan to. Thanks."

The cop faded back into the night-flow of pedestrians, and Wren shivered even with her jacket over jeans and T-shirt. Sergei moved closer to her, as though contact would ward off the nonexistent chill. She leaned against his arm, resting her head against his shoulder briefly. "I didn't know they were in more than my neighborhood."

"Makes sense. Lot of the fatae hang around Central Park, right? Probably along Riverside, too. Go where the hunting's good is probably their motto. Sorry, where the cleaning's good."

"You're such a bigot." She shook her head; it was an old argument, and one they weren't going to get anywhere with tonight. "Not all the fatae are like the polevik your grandmother told you nightmare stories about. You'd actually like P.B. if you ever tried to talk to him."

"I'll pass, thanks. Look, I don't wish them ill. You know that. I just..."

"Don't like them."

"Yeah."

"Okay. So, you said you wanted to walk and talk. We're walking..."

"We're talking." He shoved his hands into his pockets, and stared straight ahead, the comfortable closeness of a moment ago chilled slightly.

"Uh-oh. Sergei's going all Mister Didier on me." She slapped his arm, not gently. "I thought I'd broken you of that habit years ago. You only do it when you've got something to say you don't want to say and once you do that I know you've got something ugly to say so you might as well say it."

"It frightens me that I didn't need a translator to follow that." He was delaying, and they both knew it.

"Know me, love me. Talk to me."

He didn't want to, she could see that. Had probably, honestly, known it the moment he suggested taking a walk. *Men,* she thought in disgust. "All right, we're going to be that way." She tucked her arm into his and intentionally matched her pace to his longer stride, so they were walking in unison. "So we can talk about... hrm. The stock market? Nah, too scary. The government? Scarier. Job's just about set, so there's nothing more to gnaw over there. Oh, I know! We can talk about the fact that my fricking rent is going up. Again. Is it always wrong to kill people? I mean, landlord-like people?"

"Yes." This too was an argument they'd had before.

"Darn. Okay, then let's talk about the case anyway. I'm set for tomorrow, only need to—" A homeless person weaved too close to them, and Sergei swerved, pulling Wren with him. They'd had a bad experience with a homeless person, a year or so before, and he was still a little wiggy about it.

The swerve had brought them into an open doorway, and Sergei turned his head, frowning at a faint noise.

"What?"

"Probably nothing." He looked over his shoulder for

the cop, but he was gone. There was another probable cop, in a similar windbreaker, down the street, but too far away to call without attracting too much attention.

"Stay here," he said, his right arm pushing Wren against the wall as his left bent, his hand reaching to the small of his back.

Gun? All that talk about how safe it was and he brought that damn gun?

But his hand came away empty, so either he hadn't brought the pistol, a nasty-looking thing she hated with a passion, or he had second thoughts about pulling it there and then. "Stay," he said again, like he was talking to a mostly trained dog, and slid noiselessly into the open doorway.

Wren waited all of three seconds before she followed. *Stay my Aunt Petunia.* She actually *did* have a Great-Aunt 'Tunia. *Oh yeah, partner, we're so going to have to talk someday real soon about this overprotective thing you have going... Between this and the whole not telling me things, we are so going to have a talk.*

But conversation was going to have to wait, Wren realized when she caught up with her partner. He was struggling with a guy—a kid—dressed in jeans and a hooded sweatshirt. Another teenager was on his knees, bent over. Wren could sympathize—Sergei had taught her the move that left you like that, and it wasn't fun for a woman, either.

As her eyes adjusted a little more, she realized that

the shape she had taken for a pile of rags or something was moving. A pale, narrow-fingered hand reached up to grasp the wall, pulling itself up bit by bit. First a shoulder, curled in, then a straightening spine, and then a head, square-shaped, with a fine Roman nose and an impressive rack of antlers, six pointers, with shards of velvet still hanging from them.

Fatae. One of the rarer types, too. Not one you'd ever expect to see in the concrete jungle. The fatae shook its head, as though its slender, slightly pointed ears were ringing, then curled its shoulder again and head-butted—antler-butted?—a third assailant who had been drawing his leg back to kick the fatae while it was down.

Wren winced as the human hit the wall and bounced off. He didn't look quite stunned enough, so she wrapped a ball of current around her fist and threw it as hard as she could, recalling every softball game she'd ever pitched. She'd been a lousy pitcher, but current was forgiving, and it caught the guy directly in the breastbone, barely an inch above where he'd been gored by antlers.

This time, he went down and stayed down.

The fatae turned to look at her, and she saw its brown-lined eyes widen in alarm just as she felt her arms being grabbed and held from behind.

"Interfering witch." The voice was accompanied by incongruously sweet-smelling breath, as though he had brushed and flossed before heading out for a night of fatae-bashing.

"Wren!" She heard Sergei call, and then the grip in her arms was loosed and she whirled, another ball of current forming in her fist. But the attacker was down, and she was confronted by a man, coffee-skinned and on the older side, dressed too well to be either a cop or a street person, and with too direct a gaze to be either john or druggie.

"Thanks," she said, gesturing to the junior-sized base-ball bat he held in his hands.

"No prob," he said, his eyes wary. She realized suddenly her palm was still sparking and fizzing, and damped the current immediately, reabsorbing it as quickly as she could. "That, um, I..."

The stranger shrugged it off. "After a while, you see stuff, you can't blame the drugs for it, man. Just didn't want to see you or the deer-boy get bashed by some fucking out-of-towners."

Sergei limped to her side, watching as the dealer hooked the bat into his belt and went back out to the street to finish his business. "I love New York. Such an insane town. And what's most insane of all is that it's perfectly sane."

The fatae got to its feet. It was taller than both humans, but not as much as Wren had expected. Of course, just about anyone or thing past puberty was taller than her, so that scale was skewed a bit.

"My thanks," it said. "I was…uncertain if I would be able to take all three."

"You probably could have," Sergei said. He was favoring his right hip a little, and Wren tried to move his jacket aside to take a look at it. He slapped her hand away, gently. "I just hate seeing those odds in a fight."

"You're all right," she asked it. "Can we…well, can we help you get to where you are going?"

"I live here," it told her, then grimaced as though aware that the empty hallway, its wallpaper faded and peeling, didn't quite suit it. "I needed to be in the city for a few days. Business to conduct. This is…known as a safehouse."

"Not anymore," Sergei said grimly.

"No. Not anymore." It made a futile attempt to knock some dust out of its pelt. "I will inform the owners of this in the morning. For now, again, thank you, and good night."

"What, no granting of wishes? No handing out of gratitude?" Sergei had meant for his comment to be for Wren's ears only, but the fatae lifted its head and stared at him with outraged dignity.

"I am a Leshiy, not some Disneyfied djinni. I do not spend my life adhering to human-dreamed rules of how magic works."

"Actually, they're more suggestions than rules," Wren said, stepping forward to help the fatae dust itself off. "And we prefer that you call it 'Talent,' not magic."

The fatae turned its heavy, antlered head toward her. "That is bullshit. *You* have Talent. The thing you have a talent for is magic."

"Oh, great, magical semantics in the middle of a crime scene. If you're going to split word-hairs with me—" and she poked it in the middle of its pelt-covered chest "—I have a skill for Retrieval which is part of how my Talent manifests."

Sergei snorted. "Magic. And they're all faeries."

"Thank you," the fatae started to say. And then "Hey!"

Wren rolled her eyes. Men. Antlered or otherwise.

Back out on the street, Wren turned to say something pointed to her partner about dragging a poor defenseless lonejack out into the middle of chaos and then never actually talking about what he wanted to say, but the moment she opened her mouth her body betrayed her with a huge, jaw-cracking yawn. Great. Of all the times for her rush rush panic crash lifestyle to catch up with her.

"Go to bed, Wren." Sergei didn't look much better than she felt. His face was always lean, but now it looked drawn, and his skin tone had an ashy tint to it, even discounting the street-lamp lighting.

"You okay?"

"I'll be fine. I just need a full night's sleep and a few sales to keep the artists from whining at me."

She laughed, as she was supposed to. "There's still this conversation we were supposed to have—"

"Later." He was too determined not to talk about it, after dragging her out to talk about it in the first place. The fight had put walls up between them, somehow, and she didn't know how to pull them down, or even if she should, right now.

"Sergei..." Something told her that this was important, maybe even more important than the job, but he moved his hand so that his thumb covered her mouth, gently silencing her.

"You need sleep. Focus on the job." He hesitated, then reached out and tucked a strand of hair behind her ear, his hand resting on the side of her face. "Everything can wait until that's done."

He refused to talk about it any further, seeing her onto the subway heading downtown, standing on the platform watching as the train pulled away.

She trusted him. What other choice did she have?

eleven

Wren could feel the tingle run along her arms and down her spine. Nothing physical—this was a pure mental kick. Anticipation jiving with readiness. Matthew Prevost wouldn't know what had hit him.

It had been late afternoon when she finally drove up to the site, and dusk had moved in while she got into position. She was dressed for work in a clouded gray bodysuit; camouflage for the shadows. When she worked in urban areas, she wore a more conservative gray or black fleece jogging suit, to better blend in, but there was no reason she could invent that would cover being caught out here in the boonies, in a building that was never open to the public. Sergei kept promising one of those chemically-triggered chameleon suits, but so far it hadn't turned up under the Christmas tree. Just as well, probably. Whatever favors he'd have to call in or promise to get his hands on it wouldn't be worth it. Nothing ever was.

She sat in the vee of a decent-sized tree, hidden behind a fall of small, spear-shaped leaves that shifted and turned in the occasional breeze. The target's home looked quaint from the exterior; a pretty little white two-story building in the middle of seven acres of rolling lawn. There was the main farmhouse-style building, circa 1950, plus two wings added on by the current owner in a similar enough style to look natural. The entire property was framed on three sides by a man-height stone wall with sharp-cut metal shards set into the top, and backed on the other by a wooded patch that led into another private enclave that was patrolled on a regular basis by armed guards. Nasty neighbors, Sergei had reported: not the kind to invite over for a picnic. But the target wasn't much for socializing. Parties were occasionally held, written invite only, black tie not optional. Money, money, and more money. It was enough to make a girl salivate.

There were two ways in and out; through the huge iron gates at the end of the long, winding driveway, or through the equally impressive iron door that was the only break in the wall. The door was locked by remote control, with a mechanism that looked very pretty, and very unfamiliar, and nobody went through the gates without a digital pass that was scanned five feet in front of the gate, under the watchful eye of screened-in surveillance cameras.

So Wren wasn't going in through either entrance.

The mark was smart enough to keep his landscaping trimmed—no convenient tree limb close enough to the wall to swing over on. "Why is nothing ever easy?" Dropping gently out of the tree, she landed on her heels and palms. Keeping to the low brush that did grow there, she edged closer and stopped about ten feet from the wall.

What the hell...?

She had already noted the stirrings underground, where the electric cables were run into the house. He probably got premium cable, too. But the ground muffled the current, making it a background sensation, like the crickets and the peeper frogs. She could probably pull power from it, if pushed, but it would be more effort than it was worth, even in an emergency.

No, this was different. This current was live, and practically twitching with energy. It was like waving a candy bar under a chocoholic's nose. But where was it coming from? Could a mage have left a storage cell somewhere on the grounds? But why here, with a mark that hired out all his work? It didn't make sense. No, this had to be a natural source, somehow. Maybe a lodestone, or—

Or the goddamn stone wall was hiding a nasty electrical alarm system. And she bet those metal shards carried a charge, too. Tricky, tricky. Very nice. Bastard.

"Thank you sir, may I have another?"

She had two choices. She could try to use magic to untangle all the strands, figure out how the alarm worked, and try to shut it down. Thereby likely alerting whoever was manning the system that there was a problem, and taking up lots of valuable time off her schedule, even assuming she could figure it out. Or, she could stick to her original plan, to vault the fence, and pray that she didn't set off any charge that floated above the wall as well. He had hired a mage to steal the client's possession, why not use one to protect his home as well? It was unlikely—people who know that mages can be hired tend to shy away from magical defenses; what can be bought can be sold—but still a concern. Or—

"Monty, I'll take what's behind Door Number Three."

Moving backward on her hands and knees, Wren retreated almost to the road she had come in on. A pastoral country road, with large trees lining its winding length, it looked like something out of a Jane Austen novel. At any minute now, a horse and buggy could come clomping around the corner.

"Or a cop car, making his patrols. Get a move on, idiot!"

Her own car, boosted from a used car lot that night, was down the road several miles, tucked into the scrub on the shoulder. She had lugged her equipment from there, hiding it until now. A web-and-cloth utility belt, strapped down like a gunslinger's holster, carried her tools. A slimline headset fit over her left ear, the antenna almost hidden in her hair. It was set to open receive, with a very limited field, meaning that she should be able to pick up anything transmitted within the house—like an alarm, or a phone call.

A quick check on the ties of her shoes, the Velcro closures of her suit hood fastened, and she was ready to go.

Hiking down the road, she had seen several deer flitting through the trees, foraging in the dusk light. And the memory of that sight had given her an idea for assault option number 3.

The push was the first skill she had manifested, back as a preteen. It had grown so gradually, so naturally, that she had been a full year into her training before she realized it was magic at all. Neezer had called it empathic coercion. Once she knew what she was doing, it felt uncomfortably like rape.

But with animals, she justified to herself, it was no worse than any other means of control.

Power was easy enough to draw down, once you knew what you were looking for. After that, it was all a question of focus. Wren sat cross-legged on the ground, her palms flat in the dirt, and concentrated.

"Ground, child. If you're not grounded, it will snap you into cinders like some dumb bug."

John Ebenezer's voice in her head. The first lesson. The most important lesson. You couldn't rush it. A deep breath in, then an exhalation, then in again, and she could reach inside and touch the core of energy stored within her, feeling the pulse of magic respond to her call. Visualizing it as a cleanly-rolled ball of glowing cord, she pulled gently at one strand, unrolling just enough to suit her need. The tip split off into a baker's dozen individual threads, each one reaching out into the forest in front of her, searching for something of the right mass.

Like a fishing pole, one thread jerked, then began reeling itself in, enticing the creature at the other end to follow it.

Grass. Fresh grass. Sweet grass.

It came in closer, passing within a handbreadth of Wren as though it could neither see nor smell the human. A deer, full in the chest and shoulder, looking like a bow hunter's wet dream. Okay, maybe a little more mass than she needed. She turned to watch it, keeping her hands firmly in touch with the grainy, reassuring solidity of the earth. Wait...wait...

When the deer had almost reached the stone wall, Wren closed her eyes, and flicked the end of the strand on the deer's hindquarters.

Flee!

The deer, panicked, shied and ran away from the feel of the lash, side-slamming the wall with one powerful shoulder and falling away slightly stunned. It reeled for a moment, then bounded away, taking clear, powerful jumps that—at any other time—Wren would have been tempted to admire. But she was already moving, taking advantage of the momentary distraction to scramble up the wall, find tiny finger holds in the mortared niches, and vault herself over the dangerous top to land with a sold thud in the grass on the other side, falling flat on her face and praying that her suit would protect her from any visual scan of the area.

Any security system in this kind of setting, she reasoned, had to make allowances for wildlife. She hoped.

A moment passed, then five, each counted off in her head like a metronome counting out piano practices. Then another five. Almost off-schedule...time to risk it.

She raised her head, scanning the area. Nothing moved. Nothing sparked, or otherwise indicated watchers.

"Oh, screw this," she said in disgust, hauling herself up and sitting back on her haunches. Either she'd get shot, or she wouldn't.

She didn't.

The first barrier passed without confrontation, Wren settled comfortably on the grass. Her weight was balanced evenly, her spine relaxed and flexible, like a gymnast ready for the next set of tumbles. You can't rush things, not if you want it to work. Don't force the moment, let it flow...

Without warning, she felt a presence behind her, then another in front of her. Low to the ground, not towering man-height. Two more came in from the sides, with a fifth waiting just off to the right and forward, almost out of range. By the prickling of her thumbs—not to mention the distinct aroma of wet fur—she knew what they were. No real surprise on that. She just hadn't expected so many.

Five hellhounds, she thought in disgust. *This guy just has way too damn much money.*

Quarter-breed hellhounds, actually, about half their grandsire's estimated size. Nobody she knew of had ever seen a purebred hellhound. Or if they had, they hadn't been in any condition to talk about it afterward. But their offspring showed up often enough to prove that they existed. Those pups usually came to a quick, bad end. If their own dams didn't smother them, disgusted owners or annoyed ASPCA workers did it.

Hellhound crosses were *mean.*

But enough breeders had seen the potential, crossing those pups with a calmer breed—Saint Bernards were popular—and selling them to very selective owners as the ultimate in guard dog. Quarter-hounds were smart, aggressive, and trainable. Barely. They were also strong enough to take down a person, one-on-one. And she had to deal with *five.*

And they were starting to get restless.

"Sergei, I'm blaming this on you," she said in a calm, even voice. "And if I get torn to bits, I swear every single bit is going to come back and haunt you."

One hound snarled at the sound of her voice, and the others shifted, but they didn't attack. Yet.

The thread of energy she had used to call the deer

to her was still loose. She picked it up, mentally, and extended it toward the closest-in hound, on the odds that this was the alpha. Canids were pack animals. One brain, many bodies. Please God let that hold true.

Nothreat. Noalarm. Nodanger. Noprey. It was more wordlike than what she had used with the deer, playing on the animal's reasoning and training to direct it where she wanted its brain to go. All concern, all wise-ass comments faded into the back of her brain. Dropping focus meant losing control of the current, and losing control meant ending up like Neezer. Or, in this case, torn to shreds physically before her mind shattered. **I'm no threat to you, no danger...no reason to be here, no reason to stay...**

There was a heavy wuffling sound way too damn close by, the wet smack of jaws snapped together, but she didn't let it distract her. **Nothreat. Noalarm. Nodanger. Noprey.**

A whine, then the furthest-away hounds backed off a step, then another. And the alpha let them do it. Another step back, out of immediate lunging range, and all five were gone into the shadows, dismissing her as insignificant.

Okay, thank you, God. I do truly appreciate it, and know that you're telling me to get my ass in gear, which I will do just as soon as my heart gets itself down out of my throat, and my stomach picks itself up from my knees.

According to the information she had been able to

sneak out of the local police department mainframe, the digital gate and dogs were the only protections the mark had outside the house. But the legal stuff was usually only the surface. He was a collector. Think like he thinks. How would he safeguard his pretties, so that no one could take them away from him? Think like the nice crazy person, Wren. Get into his head and make yourself at home.

Wren got to her feet and started moving toward the house, keeping alert for any noise or sound out of the ordinary. Security lights every twenty yards, easy enough to skirt around. Low to the ground, look like one of the dogs. Any camera will only pick up a shadow, any heat sensors could mistake her outline for one of the equally-sized dogs. If he had anything that picked up pulse rates, she was cooked. Don't think about it.

The information Sergei had pulled together said that the mark had some kind of alarm system set up in the house proper, but no human guards. Made sense—if you have something to hide, why invite strangers in? Likewise, the mark wasn't hooked up to the local police department's monitoring system. If you don't want strangers, you doubly don't want strangers with badges, and FBI-supplied downloads of stolen art.

She was close enough now to see that the white clapboard had been painted recently, likewise the deep blue shutters. A low hedge of holly bush ran along the foundation, preventing any would-be burglar from getting too close. She removed a slender plastic tube from her belt and extended it to its full twelve-inch length. The lens at the end adjusted for the darkness, and she was able to focus in on the nearest window. There were plain white curtains hanging from either side, and the suggestion of white furniture. Recalling the blueprints spread out on the kitchen counter, Wren decided that this must be the sitting room off the kitchen. Which meant that she was on the wrong side of the house.

"Damn."

Changing the magnification on the spyglass, she inspected the window itself. Faint lines ran through the glass in a meshlike pattern. That ruled out a first-floor entry, but she hadn't been planning on one, anyway. "Not a duckling, but a swan," she said, raising the spyglass up further, passing the second floor and continuing on up to the roof. And what she saw there made her smile.

The sleeves of her bodysuit were flexible, like the rest of the material, until it came to her wrists. The cuffs around each hand hid several layers which extended to cover her palm and hooked into the microfiber of her gloves. The palm of each hand was now covered with five powerful-looking claws—sharp enough to find purchase in anything short of concrete. Also sharp enough to tear her suit, which is why she hated using them. But so equipped, the wood shingles of this house would be easier to access than climbing the tree, earlier. In fact, it took her five minutes, only because she was muffling

her motions, keeping her weight spread like a spider's—
not the ideal conditions for a human to climb under. But
five minutes later, she was at the nearest second-floor
window.

The mesh was absent from this pane. The lock was
electromagnetic, probably wired throughout the house
and tied into the master control box. The only way to
unlock the window would be to enter the key code into
that box, and Wren would be willing to bet her paycheck
that the mark was the only one who had the key.

Whoever had sold him the system had given him a
pretty good household system, especially when tied
into the first-floor precautions, and the external defenses. But they hadn't accounted for someone like
Wren. She moved further on up, onto the roof, and lay
down to regain her breath, and still the shaking in her
arms. Once her body was sufficiently under control
again, she swung herself over the roof, head first, until
she had eye contact with the locking device. Once the
image of it was secure in her mind, she closed her eyes
and reached for the tiny twelve-volt hum that was coming from it. It was like some kind of surreal virtual reality race, chasing one spark of power through the
thousands of relays that made up the house. She ignored
the feel of blood rushing to her brain from her physical
position, and the distractions of a more powerful hum
of electricity from the generator hidden somewhere
under the first floor, falling into a warm campfire glow of

the dedicated security system. She could feel a backup generator there as well, but no other power source. Just as well—this way she didn't have to be delicate, for fear of triggering a blackout throughout the neighborhood. Those tended to be messy and attention-catching.

With the portion of her self still inside the system, she gathered up as much energy as she could take. But instead of storing it within, the way she had at the Frants building, she punched it up into a ball, and released it back into the system like a fastball pitch.

Seven seconds later, the entire lock system had shorted out, and Wren was in through the now-unlocked window. *Fail safe* had another meaning entirely for those on the breaking and entering side.

Wren took a few seconds to let her body recover, and to orient herself. The mark might be some kind of hot-shit collector, but he wasn't much in the way of interior decorating. The room she had entered through was almost astonishingly bland. A business traveler could be down here, and expect to get a newspaper under his door in the morning. Moving through the room, she kept off the area rug, staying to bare floor as much as possible. The door to the hallway was ajar, and a light shove with her shoulder pushed it open.

She spotted the cameras almost immediately. They weren't hidden—it was almost as though the mark was making a point, putting them where anyone could see them. And the light was on, indicating they

weren't in the same power loop as the locks. "Great,"
Wren muttered. "He likes to watch." She reached into
her belt pouch and pulled out a small bone charm.
Yellow with age, and lined with a thousand hairline
cracks, it had a strange warmth to it, almost as though
it were alive. It was a one-shot, but a very efficient
one. Clenching it in her fist, she felt the cracks give
way, the charm crumbling into dust. She opened her
hand and flung the dust at the camera lens. A spoken command—"puzzle"—activated the charm as the
dust clung to the lens. Somewhere in the house, the
bank of monitors would only be showing a fragmented
picture, as though static had gotten into the wires
somehow.

But it wouldn't last forever. Time to get a move on.
She recalled the floor plans again. "I'm...here...and you
are...there. Right." Satisfied, she set off down the white-
painted, white-lit hall without hesitation.

Even without the floor plan, Wren wouldn't have had
any trouble discovering which wing held her quarry.
The trouble was getting to it without making any un-
scheduled detours. While the guest wing she had entered in was well-appointed, the private wing was a
thief's buffet. Delicate silver sculptures made her fingers
itch to caress them, and paintings which triggered her
hodgepodge memory of Sergei's lectures on the Mas-
ters practically sang for a cutting blade to liberate them.
And the tall, blue-white marble figure set in the corner

of one room made her swear under her breath. Did the Museum even know they were missing a piece?

But all those were mere distractions compared to the pull she could feel, in the part of her that recognized the presence of magic. Faint, but undeniable, she was drawn down hallways of polished wood floors and priceless artworks to a closed door at the end of the camera-lined corridor. The door looked like all the others; no handle, indicating a magnetic lock. A nice piece of machinery, to ensure that the house could be locked down from a central control. Assuming, of course, someone hadn't already shot down the control getting in. Ooops.

This was it. She was somewhat surprised that the stone was giving off that much power, but she wasn't here to make judgments, just to get it back to its rightful owner. Let Mages squabble over the technical details.

She paused for a moment, kneeling at the door. A faint buzz of electricity, remnant from the alarm she had already disabled. Nothing else. The back of her hand pushed at the door, and it swung open without a sound.

"Hello, baby," she whispered as the magic stored in the room hit her. As though in response, the currents running through the room thickened, raising the hair on her arms. The space was practically overpowered by the Artifacts stored there, and Wren had her answer about the mark's abilities—only someone completely Null would have arranged them like this, fully charged. Null, or remarkably arrogant.

"Easy there, fellows," she said, the way one would to a growling dog you were pretty sure wasn't going to attack. She was anthropomorphizing horribly, of course—Artifacts weren't alive, not even in the most basic way. They absorbed the energy they stored, that was true, but the way Tupperware might absorb the smell of the food stored within. Nothing more.

She kept telling herself that as she edged carefully past the green marble pillar that, to her eyes, almost pulsated with energy. It was old. Very old. And very much not for the likes of her.

Not for the likes of him, either, she thought, resentful on behalf of the pillar, then circular-filed the thought. She wasn't here to rescue anyone else's talismans. Not if they weren't paying her.

The clear crystal, on the other hand, actively repelled her. Contrary, she stopped in front of it, trying to see into the depths. Taking precious seconds she didn't have, Wren let her eyes unfocus, then clicked into a working trance. Not as effective as a fugue, it should nonetheless allow her to gather more information about the stone. Reaching out with the ability that made her a Talent, Wren touched something slick, sweet and disgusting. Her eyes widened and she snapped back the probe in that instant of contact.

Blood.

Wren grimaced, trying to get the taste/smell/feel out of her brain. Current was flavored by the user, the more so the longer it was held, and so were the spells they made with it. This was nasty, particularly nasty. And...what was the word? Malevolent. All she wanted to do was find a nice nasty thunderstorm somewhere and let a few lightning bolts slam through her, to wash the taint away.

Backing away from the crystal, she turned to face the concrete slab she had been hired to retrieve. A pocket flap on the arm of her bodysuit gave way with the *snick* of Velcro and she pulled out a slender ivory wand the length of her finger. It might, in fact, once have been someone's finger. You didn't ask too many details when you were buying someone else's work.

Wren was lousy at making talismans. Unfortunately, she was even worse at translocation. So she'd had to rely on someone else's skill. Pointing the wand at the cornerstone, she rubbed the ivory between her fingers until it began to warm up, then said the incantation under her breath. Haste made disaster, but the awareness of that crystal at her back created an intense desire to be gone from that place. Subconsciously she moved closer to her target, and the wand dipped dramatically, like a dowsing stick hitting pay dirt, tapping the cement once, sharply.

Wren barely had time to moan in dismay before a thick black smog came out of unseen vents, turning the air into an impenetrable barrier. A basic security system—confuse a thief, make it impossible for him to see his goal and nine times out of ten he'll flee empty-handed.

No time to flagellate yourself now, she thought. *Finish it.* Holding the wand more firmly in fingers suddenly slick with sweat, Wren completed the incantation. But even as she felt the current wave itself into the proper patterns, something felt off. There was too much magic in the room, and her concentration had been fouled. Something was wrong....

"When I bid you—go!" she cried, trying to gather her own magics as a protection against whatever might be happening. There was a terrible noise, like the scream of a dying man, and a flash of electric light shot upward from where the cornerstone lay, up toward the ceiling.

In that instant, she felt the spell snap into place, and the cornerstone vanished, leaving behind the usual rush of incoming air that indicated a successful translocation.

And in its place, rising tall and solid in the space where the stone had been, a figure formed, shaking crumbs of concrete off its incorporeal shoulders.

Aaahhhhhhh

It was less a sound than an exhalation of pure energy. If Wren thought she had been spooked by the crystal, she hadn't known the meaning of the word until then. This was old, and dead, and not quite human any longer—

And it was very, very angry.

Wren came back to awareness as her feet carried her down the hallway, the talisman room already a distant memory. Her lizard brain had taken over, reading the blueprints in her memory and directing the body through her escape route. An alarm was bleating throughout the house, and she had a vague memory of it going off when she first touched the cornerstone, but nobody came out of the walls to apprehend her, and she wasn't about to question things that went right. Not now. To the other side of the house, out the window, sliding down the wall like a squirrel in free-fall, up and down the trunk of a tree, landing with a bone-jarring thump on the ground and jinking and dodging toward the trees without hesitation. The gate would definitely be juiced now—trying to get over it would be suicide, even if she had the time to prep. And who knew what the hell was happening back at the house? No, safer to risk the madmen with guns next door. All they could do was kill her.

Ghosts! Nobody said a damn thing about ghosts, she thought with justifiable irritation. Not that it would have mattered worth a damn if they had. She didn't know a thing about ghosts, or poltergeists, or anything of the undead variety. Nobody really did, or if they did they weren't talking. Common theory was that the soul was dispersed after death, not inducted into any kind of afterlife. Holding someone after that had to be some seriously wicked mojo.

"Great. Next thing, I'm going to run into vampires. Okay, ixnay on the jinxing of self!"

The car was a darker shadow in the night. She opened

the door and slid inside, fumbling for the keys, since she'd disabled the overhead light before leaving it earlier that night. Her arm trembled as she turned the ignition, and she was suddenly aware that her entire body was shaking.

Get home, she told herself. *Get home, and then you can collapse.*

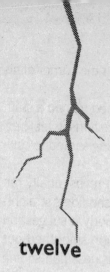

twelve

For once, Matthew Prevost's office was not immaculate. An entire folder of papers were splayed across the expensively-carpeted floor, their arc indicating that they had been swept off the desk with a significant amount of force. A pile of small beige and brown colored chips were all that remained of an ancient Navajo pot. And half a dozen books, their leather bindings cracked and pages scattered, were mute testimony to a temper tantrum of extreme proportions. Prevost himself wasn't in much better shape, standing in the middle of the office and raving like a madman. Although he stood in one spot as if locked into place, his arms flailed wildly, his face twisted like a Halloween mask while he roared his anger, paused to grab a deep breath, and then started again. All that was missing was froth at the corner of his mouth to finish the picture.

For once, for the first time, he wished he had a staff, so he could kick a few of them to make himself feel better. His foot jerked, as though imagining someone cowering in front of him.

After another half an hour of this, Prevost finally ran down. His fingers unclenched, and his shoulders straightened, giving his slight, desk-jockey body a suggestion of authority once again. His expression smoothed out as well, the face of a prosperous businessman sliding down over the rage that had been there a moment before. The sudden calm would have been more frightening to an observer than the madness earlier.

He exhaled, then went to sit behind his desk, ignoring the mess underfoot. Picking up the phone, he dialed a number from memory. Why the hell did he have a magician on call if she couldn't get the job done?

"Your precautions failed," he said without preamble. "Someone got in tonight and took it. I don't know how. I don't care how." His voice started to rise, and he paused long enough to get it back under control. "They took the cornerstone."

The voice on the other end of the line asked a question.

"Of course I want it back!"

His well-manicured fingers began to drum on the desk as the other voice spoke again. His eyes narrowed as she finished speaking, but his voice remained even.

"I'm perfectly aware of this. The amount I paid for the original acquisition is a more than reasonable fee for the same job, despite the higher profile. You agree?" It wasn't a question. "Good. Contact me when it is done."

Hanging up the phone, Prevost leaned back and surveyed the room, but his mind was clearly elsewhere. His little mage was starting to show too many signs of independence, questioning his requests, dragging her heels when he summoned her. He was going to have to do something about that, and soon. But not tonight. Not while he still needed her. And right now he had more important matters to deal with. Whoever had broken into his home tonight had defeated not one but two security systems. And his highly-trained, extremely expensive dogs had run off, howling at the moon and not responding to their collar-summons. The loss of one of his possessions was enough to drive him into a rage, but this breach of security left him with a deeper, colder anger. This was unacceptable.

Picking up the phone once again, he dialed a different number. "Your system was compromised. Fix it."

Beth Sanatini had been freelance for almost twenty years. Halfway through her apprenticeship she had realized that the Council and she were going to butt heads on a regular basis, so why even bother trying to toe the line? But before she left—went rogue, in their eyes—she had studied the layers of power, judged who was an up-

and-comer, who was there for the long haul, and what they might do in order to keep their power. And once you knew that, there was no need to cut all ties completely, no matter how rogue you were. Just good business, after all.

But in the end, it had been the Council itself that came calling. Or, rather, one member in particular. They had offered a deal Beth couldn't refuse, and it would be funny if it weren't so damn annoying. It was that member Beth contacted now.

Three rings, as always. Someone was tapping into the line to see who it was. Caller ID was a piker compared to a magical tap. Beth crunched on the carrot stick, and waited until someone cleared her ID code, then picked up on the other end.

"Apparently, someone took Mr. Prevost to the cleaners tonight."

"Really?" The voice on the other end of the line didn't seem at all surprised. Just once, Beth wanted to be able to give them something they didn't already expect. If you were going to be a stoolie, however reluctant, you should at least be a useful one. "And I assume that he has asked you to retrieve said object once again?"

"You would be correct," she admitted. Suddenly the carrot didn't look anywhere near as appetizing as the chocolate chips stashed in her freezer. It was horribly unfair that you couldn't magic off excess weight.

"You will not accept this commission."

Beth watched as her fingers clenched so hard on the carrot that it broke in two. Not a surprise, really. If they could have stopped her from taking the original job, they would have. The Council didn't like to be embarrassed, especially by escapees like her own little self. "Will I be compensated for the loss of that commission?" she asked, already knowing the answer.

"We allow you to operate without interference," her contact told her. "Do not presume upon that goodwill."

Goodwill. Beth would have smiled, if she weren't so damn tired. That translated to "we're not going to yank the leash we keep you on—yet." If they'd had anything to do with the retrieval—and she suspected they did, from sheer pride if nothing else, they would be determined to have it end here, now. You didn't trespass on Council deals. Except she had, and lived to tell the tale.

Maybe it was time to twist that smug bastard once, just because she could. "Were you also aware of the fact that the item Mr. Prevost recently acquired through my services was showing signs of breakage?"

There was the sound of someone sitting upright in a chair. "Details," the voice ordered crisply.

"He brought me in to judge what he perceived to be leakage of the spell. He was correct—apparently our Mr. Prevost has a touch more Talent than anyone suspected. Barely enough to notice, but it did alert him to the problem. It also, I suppose, explains why so many of his pretties have a magical element to them."

"Did you correct the damage?"

"I patched it. But that's not going to last. And if someone else has it now, odds are their workings—"

"It is no longer your concern."

The line cut off, replaced by a dial tone.

"Well, damn." She hung up the phone, and leaned back in her own chair, twirling one of the carrot halves between her fingers. Someone was playing games. Big, ugly, complicated games that were going to get people killed.

She smiled now, and bit into the carrot with a satisfying crunch. Just so long as it wasn't her.

The security camera showed a van pulling into the driveway. Dark blue, with a discreet white logo on the doors. A transmitter placed inside the car signaled to the security box at the front gate, and they passed through the checkpoint without a hitch, the doors opening smoothly for them. As they moved down the graveled driveway, the headlights caught flashes of large bodies loping on all fours alongside the truck before deciding it wasn't a threat and falling away.

The van pulled up in front of the house, and two men dressed in dark blue coveralls got out, one of them going around back to open the sliding door and retrieve a small toolbox. The other man waited for his companion to rejoin him, then pulled a cap out of his pocket, fitted it to his head, and together they went up the stairs.

They rang the doorbell, then waited patiently until the door opened.

"I thought I told you people to use the side door," Prevost groused as he opened the door. "Well, come in, come in. I wasn't expecting you for another hour or two."

"We were already on the road when the call came in," one of the men said, exchanging a glance with his companion that clearly indicated his opinion of the man in front of them.

Prevost, already leading the way through the house to the command center, didn't notice. "Well, as you can see, on the surface everything is working, but someone managed to break through nonetheless. And I refuse to sleep here until it's all been checked out, and fixed!"

"I don't think that will be a problem, sir," one of the nameless men said, as he took a soft cotton scarf from his pocket, and looped it around Prevost's neck, yanking the unsuspecting man backward with one jerk of his arms.

The other man took a large curved knife from his toolbox, and stepped in front of the struggling Prevost, calmly slicing open his throat, a wide gash from one corner of his jawline to the other, with one slash of the blade. Prevost's body arched forward, so the blood spurted on the ceiling in an artistic spray, only a few drops landing on his assailant's face and coverall. Then Prevost slumped forward, collapsing to his knees as his assailant let go of the scarf. "You've become the problem. Sir."

The knife-wielder wrapped the blade in a cloth also taken from the toolbox, and replaced them both carefully, locking the lid. Only then did he pause to wipe the blood from his face with his sleeve, the crimson fading into the deeper blue of the fabric.

"Get started down here," the first man said, rolling up his cloth and replacing it in his pocket. "I'll go check out what's upstairs, see if there's anything they want back, now that we've found him."

"Right. Give a yell if you find anything—I'll only be a few minutes down here." He picked up the box and went back out to the truck, leaving Prevost behind on the parquet floor, gaping like a fish as he died.

Ten minutes later the house was in flames, and an unmarked blue van was making its way through the streets of the nearest town.

thirteen

Sergei was waiting for her at her apartment when she finally got home, two hours after dawn the next morning. The stolen car was abandoned in the driveway of an unsuspecting suburban household an hour's drive west of the estate. She had walked through the predawn gloom several miles to the local Greyhound station, catching the next bus south to D.C., where she had paid cash for a seat on the first Amtrak express train back into Manhattan. By the time she arrived, the sweats she had put on in the car looked far worse for wear, and she could have easily passed for one of the discharged mental patients who wandered the streets waiting for a medication time that never arrived. She came in the door like a load of walking lead, hands outstretched for the mug of coffee he had ready for her. It wasn't well-made, but it was hot, and it had caffeine in it, and it was manna from the gods.

What day was it? Saturday? No, Sunday, that was why the trains had been few and far between. God, she needed to *sleep*. "I'm not getting paid enough for this."

He pushed her down the hallway toward the bathroom, turning the shower on and shoving the knob all the way to hot. She took another gulp of coffee, and felt some of her synapses start to fire up again. "I'm *really* not getting paid enough for this. How much am I getting paid again?"

"You want to check your balance again?"

"Couldn't hurt. Might help."

He took the mug from her, and when she might have made a whimper of protest, placed it on the counter and tugged at her sweatshirt. Her arms went up, and he pulled it over her head, dropping it on the floor. She took the hint, shucking out of shoes, socks, and sweats in short order. Bra and underwear followed, any sense of modesty in front of him long gone in her exhaustion. She managed another gulp of coffee before he was moving her into the shower. The hot water and steam hit her at the same time, and all she could do was moan in gratification. Her hair plastered to her head, she leaned into the jets, feeling the grime and dust and dirt washing away. It was almost always the same way after a Retrieval, this bone-deep, beyond-exhaustion weariness.

Hot water helped. She wasn't recovered, not by a long shot, but now she finally felt like she might be able to sleep, at least.

The shower curtain pushed aside, and Sergei handed her the coffee mug, freshly topped off.

Or not.

When she got out of the shower, a towel was waiting for her. Sergei wasn't. She wrapped herself in the terry-cloth, squeezed the excess water out of her hair and finger-combed it, then went in search of her partner. He was sitting in the main room, occupying the one chair. The stereo was on, playing music she didn't recognize. Low bluesy sound, and a woman singing like a prayer, in French.

Always a bad sign, when Sergei went to Paris.

She left him there, and went into her bedroom. A quick rummage through her dresser turned up underwear and a pair of jeans. A sweatshirt left at the foot of the bed smelled clean enough, and she slipped it on, pulling her wet hair out from under the collar. Fortified, she went back to the main room, and sat down cross-legged on the carpet across from him. He tapped the remote, and the music shut off.

"Okay. What?" Yeah, his jaw was way too squared for it to be anything other than ugly news.

"The spell returned the cornerstone to its proper location, as per our agreement. However, the client claims that we did not finish the job."

Wren blinked. Thought. Looked up at her partner. "This wouldn't have anything to do with a ghost, would it?"

Sergei's face went through a sea change of expressions, from perturbed to disconcerted to resigned. "Start from the beginning. All the gory details."

It took almost as long to tell as it had to perform, with Sergei constantly interrupting and asking for more, more specific details. But finally Wren got to the point where the wand struck the cornerstone.

"What happened to the stone then?"

Wren shook her head, tracing her fingers along the design of the rug. "Damned if I know. The smoke was everywhere, I could barely see an inch in front of me. But I know where you're going with this—I thought about it a lot on the way home. Yes, I think the ghost came from the stone. No, I have no idea how it got there."

"It was part of the spell."

Sergei's voice was dry. She looked up at him in disbelief, half expecting a joke. But while his finely-drawn lips were curved in a smile, there was no real humor behind it.

"What?"

"The ghost was part of—"

"I heard you, I heard you. They tied a person into a spell? I mean, a real live person?"

"A dead person, actually, otherwise it wouldn't be a ghost."

"No, Sergei, you don't get it. If there was a ghost trapped in there, I think they—the person who cast the spell—had to have used the person. I mean, the living person. Who then became a dead person."

"Murder." He didn't say it like a question. "They couldn't have, I don't know, called up a ghost from someone already dead?" Sergei offered the possibility without any real sense of optimism.

"Maybe. Hell, I don't know a damn thing about raising the dead, or using spirits in magic at all. Not exactly in the playbook, if you know what I mean." Not in the playbook at all. Not any one Neezer had ever told her about, anyway. Then again, Neezer had been a pretty straight arrow. That didn't sound like anything he'd want to talk about—or want her to know about. Admirable, but a real pain now when the info would be useful.

Wren got up, pacing the length of the room and then back again, gesturing with her hands while she thought her way through the problem, like a professor lecturing before a class. "Okay. Work it through. According to most magus theories, spirits are pure energy tied to flesh for the duration of a life. Where that energy comes from, you're moving more into religion than magic, and a whole different headache. Now, I was taught that at the moment of death, the energy, or spirit, dissipates, goes back to the elemental flow."

"In which case, no ghost." Sergei leaned back into the

chair, managing to look totally relaxed even though she could feel the alert tension in his half-lidded gaze.

"Normally, yeah. But that's why I think this person had to be alive. When the spell was cast, anyway. I'm not sure exactly when they'd have to kill him. If they could catch the spirit as the flesh died, and trap it then—" Wren shuddered. "That's nasty. That's really, really nasty. Killing's one thing. Trapping something like that—what if it was claustrophobic? Ick."

"It gets worse," Sergei told her. "According to our client, we were hired to retrieve the entire cornerstone—the spell contained within the stone, as well as the stone itself. We failed. He is therefore refusing to pay the final installment of the fee." That fact clearly angered him more than the fact of a generations-dead murder victim, however tragic.

Wren stared at him, thinking it through as quickly as she could. "And if they used the energy of the death to create the spell, somehow, or activate it, or whatever...which means it's probably tied to the ghost..."

"Then if the ghost isn't recaptured, our contract is technically void, and they have every right not to pay us."

Wren threw up her hands in disgust. "Christ on a Popsicle. You couldn't have told me that little detail before?"

Sergei met her eyes squarely, not a little irritated. "I didn't know that little detail before. And even if I had, what could I have said? I'm not the one who's the expert on magic here, am I?"

Wren ran her hands through her hair, pulling at the ends in her frustration. He was right. Damn him. That was one real and dangerous flaw in their system. Sergei didn't know enough, couldn't, for all his reading and questioning, know enough about magic, or current, to know when he was being yanked around in negotiations. "Okay, new rule number one. We know all the facts *before* we take a job. No reconnoitering after the fact. Even if that means you have to put them on hold and call me if something—anything—seems hinky. Okay?" He hesitated. *"Okay?"*

They stared at each other for a long, drawn-out moment. Then Sergei exhaled, nodded. Wren snorted. Great going forward. But for now...

"I suppose bowing out of the contract is a no-go?" His glare was answer enough. Screw up one job, and your reputation was shot. Especially when the screw-up was through your own stupid fault.

"Right. All we have to do is figure out how to track down a ghost and shove it back into the marble, and we can collect our paycheck. Piece of freaking cake."

As though to mirror the mood inside, the day turned overcast early on, and before midday, the faint patter of rain began hitting the roof and windows. It was a mild front, nothing brewing in the clouds, but it brought a pleasantly fresh smell to the air, of ozone and clean dampness that Wren appreciated.

Wren turned on every light in the third bedroom, which she used as the library/storeroom. Every wall was covered with bookcases that went to the ceiling, and the floor had boxes filled with things magical and inert from past jobs and research that she didn't know what else to do with. Half, maybe more of the books, she'd never read past the cover flap, just shelved for a possible need later on. Well, later was now. She rummaged through the bookcases for any title which might possibly touch on the subject of ghosts, while Sergei sat in her office and ran through search engine after search engine, bookmarking any site that looked as though it had potential.

"At this point," Wren directed him, "we don't pass anything up, no matter how crazy it looks." Much to her surprise, death current was a well-researched, if frowned-on topic. Weird that she'd never heard about it before. Or then again, maybe not so weird. You sort of had to have a specific question to go looking for these answers.

The real problem, they quickly discovered, was that even within reputable magical sources ghosts were mostly a theoretical debate. There was no way to prove that an alleged encounter was a spirit, or merely the effect of a subconscious magic-user, or even a deliberate hoax by a trained mage.

"Or," Wren said glumly, "a wizzart just losing his mind." She looked at the piles of books and printouts surrounding her, spread out all over the music room's floor. Sergei had kicked her out of her own office when her running commentary on the idiocy of several writers had become too much for him to concentrate.

The truth was, most written texts on the supernatural were completely useless. Ninety percent of anything people believed grew out of their own fears and superstitions, not reality. Historical figures like John Dee and Agrippa Von Nettesheim, alchemists and scientists and self-proclaimed "magicians" rarely if ever touched on the truth. And those who did know rarely—call it damn near never—felt the urge to share that knowledge with outsiders.

Oh, there was some truth to the "other magics," as the texts called them. Herbal craft. Faith-based "miracles." It was as real as current, but with far less reliability. Sometimes they worked. Sometimes they didn't. Less to do with ability than sheer luck, really. There were speculations, ranging from alternate world power bleeds to Divine intervention, but for the most part it was left to folklore and Nulls trying blindly to create what was beyond them.

But the one thing Wren had gotten from her rather reluctant attendance in college—two years, associate degree, and gone, and only because her mother insisted as part of her going to work with Sergei right out of high school—was the fact that you could sometimes find useful information in unexpected places. Placing aside an old text on necromancy, she instead picked up a modern paperback on spectral visitations, a pop science book written by a popular "ghost hunter," who claimed to have the reports of over five thousand sightings in his files. Bypassing the section on haunted houses, she went straight to the back of the book, to the chapter on the ghosts of murder victims. Unquiet haunts, they were called.

Most of the chapter seemed to focus on ghosts that were merely reliving—so to speak—their deaths, or haunting the specific area of their demise.

"Not the case here, more's the pity." The apparition she had encountered was clearly aware of itself, and just as clearly no longer bound to the stone. Might it return to the actual site of the murder? But they had no idea where that might have been: a drawback, not knowing the spell used to create the protection. And somehow Wren didn't think that the Council would give that detail up, even if Sergei hadn't specifically said they'd purged that file. Would the ghost think to return to the building? And even if it did, what would it do there, haunt the lobby? Wren smirked at the thought of Rafe and his buddies trying to escort an unruly ghost out of the building.

A pain started, just behind her left eye, and Wren winced. Closing her eyes to rest them for a moment, she did a few deep-breathing exercises, trying to chase down the pain and squash it. Although she had met a few people who could use current to heal serious wounds, she had never been able to pick up more than the basics of burn-ease and pain-reduction—nothing a few aspirin, a cool compress or a good massage couldn't do just as well.

And asking Sergei for a quick massage was out of the question, too. Normally he'd oblige, but recent events had made her shy away from asking for physical contact. She shoved her hair out of her eyes, impatient both with it and herself. Although even without that she might not have bothered him. Her partner was tense about something, too. Wren didn't want to ask; if it was job-related they'd just start feeding into each other worse, and if not...if not, then it fell outside the established partnership rules, and that led back to her own reasons for not wanting him to touch her and...God, what a freaking *mess*.

A twitch of the energies flowing through the apartment, and the stereo came on, thankfully set low from Sergei's use. Another twitch, and the dial moved until it hit the local soft jazz station. She caught the tail end of a commercial, then the music came back, a horn instrumental with a light, catchy repeat to it. Nothing that demanded her brain pay any attention to it. Wren let herself float along with the sound for a few moments, then pried her eyes back open and refocused on the page.

* * *

Sergei heard the music come on, and paused a moment to listen, then put it into the background, barely audible to his working brain, and went back to his Web-surfing. He had three windows open at once, running down links as swiftly as he could. Wren's refusal to spring for a DSL line was a sore point, although he couldn't fault her desire to save money.

Links that led to Web sites that looked reasonable on the crank scale he bookmarked, the others he shined on. This sort of skimming was a strange type of research, and one he had come relatively late to, but it suited the way his mind worked on several different tracks at once.

And while one track was dedicated to the job at hand, another segment of his mind was replaying the conversation he'd had, unwillingly, the night before. He had been working late in his office—dithering, he admitted to himself—while waiting for Wren to contact him, and let him know everything had gone off as planned, or not. But shuffling invoices and re-plotting gallery displays would have been preferable to having his cell phone ring and picking up to hear, not his partner's voice, but a masculine tone from years in the past. Matthias. North American branch coordinator for the Silence. The man who used to hand down Sergei's orders. Emphasis on the used to.

"We're taking the matter out of your hands." A

protest, barely formed, was overrun. "You're not im-partial in this anymore."

Douglas had promised to consider his offer, himself, his abilities, in exchange for Wren. Was the old man not as powerful as he'd once been? Or were things that urgent, that promises made to their own people now meant nothing?

But then, he wasn't one of theirs, was he? Not now. Not until he folded himself back into the mix officially. If he ever did—if his half-spoken promise to the old man wasn't just a bluff to gain more time, the way they both half suspected it might be. And until then...until then he was just a chess piece like everyone else.

Sergei took a moment to gather himself, to lock his emotions into the box built for them. The box men like the one on the other end of the line had shown him how to build. Steadied, his response was cool, in control of himself and the moment: "It was never about impar-tiality. It was about judgment. And my call is still that her skills, while impressive, are too limited, not worth the risk. Nor is she well suited to the...discipline of what would be required.

"You've not questioned me before. Has there been a reason to suddenly, now, doubt my evaluation?"

A final, formal vote of no-confidence from the voice on the other end of the phone line meant more than a sudden career-change for both of them. He had wanted to hold his breath, hang on the next words. But instead he breathed normally, back relaxed against the support of his ergonomically correct leather chair, arms resting by his side, the very picture of open body language, as though that would somehow transmit over the phone. *I have nothing to hide, I have nothing to fear.*

"Sergei. Please don't insult my intelligence. We've humored you for several years because we could afford to. But it's time to come home now."

"Go to hell, Matthias," Sergei said softly.

But as he ended the call, staring blankly at the painting on the far wall of his office that normally brought him intense emotional satisfaction, he felt tendrils of fear stir, wrapping themselves around him until he could barely move. His thoughts were like pigeons, scattering as soon as they landed, over and over again, until he wasn't sure what he was thinking at all.

The computer pinged to indicate an incoming e-mail, and Sergei broke himself out of the memory, wrenching his brain back to the chore at hand.

Action was the only cure for fear. Action was the only way out of the threads he could feel closing more and more tightly around them both. If only he knew what the right move was.

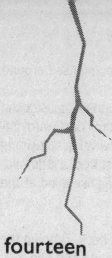

fourteen

He was sitting in a tropical bar, breathing the smell of night-blooming flowers and salt spray. A soft breeze kept the humidity at bay. His drink smelled of gin, and the ice cubes clinked pleasantly as he took a sip.

A hand touched his shoulder, running light fingers across the back of his neck. He shivered in pleasure and reached back to capture the hand, intent on pulling her forward, and onto his lap.

There was a faint noise in the background of his dream. It was familiar, category nonthreatening, sub-category comforting. So he ignored it, concentrating on the elusive woman behind him....

"Oh no you don't," he heard the nonthreatening voice murmur, and a sudden mental alarm went off—too late to keep the icy-cold hand from wrapping itself around his neck.

Sergei let out a shriek and bolted upright, causing the office chair he had fallen asleep on to roll backward, hitting the wall and rebounding, the swivel seat twirling slowly until it finally came to rest. He stared, a little wild-eyed, at his partner, who was grinning like a kid at the circus.

"You're so cute when you freak."

His hand went to the back of his neck, rubbing the skin as though to try and bring some warmth and feeling back into it. "Bitch."

"Hey, you're the one drooling all over my keyboard."

"What time is it?" He had fallen asleep some time around three in the morning, based on his last recollection. Sergei vaguely remembered being able to handle the odd hours of a case better than he was feeling this morning.

"Almost seven. Had a passing recollection of you saying you had to be at the gallery this morning. New installation, right?"

"Yeah. Thanks." He stifled a moan as his joints woke up fully and started sending urgent messages to his brain. "I'm getting old, Wrenlet. Old and achy."

She flicked him a glance, clearly assessing how much of that grousing was for show.

"Poor baby." She shifted the baggie of ice from hand to hand as though to keep her hands cold in case he balked. "I do have extra pillows, you know. Next time, use 'em. That chair is not comfortable to sleep in, even for me. Much less your ancient bones."

"Hah. So funny."

"Any luck with whatever you were doing?"

Sergei shrugged, then winced when that movement set off more internal complaints. "By the time I fell asleep, I couldn't have told you what I was looking at, much less looking for," he admitted, unbuttoning his sweat-sticky shirt and taking it off. "I'm way out of my league when it comes to the supernatural stuff, you know that."

"You're learning, grasshopper. You're learning. It's just—"

"Tough if you're not born to it," he finished for her. "Yeah, I know." Sergei rolled his shoulders, then clasped his hands and stretched his arms straight over his head until he heard something crack and felt his spine move back into alignment. "Ah, God, that's better." He turned to see Wren staring at him. "What?"

She started a little, a flush coloring her cheekbones. "Your hair is standing on end," she told him, then giggled. "Looks cute."

He grumbled at her, then headed off to find the spare toothbrush and a comb.

Wren watched him walk down the hallway, enjoying the visual as one of those unspoken perks of her job.

Sergei in dress slacks and nothing else was a sight no red-blooded, breathing, hetero female should miss. It wasn't so much that her partner was built—he wasn't, really. Big guy, yeah, very nice shoulders and his fore-arms made long-sleeved shirts a crime, but he wasn't ex-actly underwear model material. But the muscles he did have were clean and smooth, and he walked like a tiger.

Nice to look at. And so warm... She giggled, remem-bering his reaction to her iced-up hand. The skin on his neck was so sensitive, he told her once, that he had to use a special shaving cream to keep the razor from irri-tating it.

That ice cube was cruel, but effective, she thought. There really wasn't any other way to wake a man who slept that deeply. Not when he knew he was here, safe: not without letting a stranger off the street come in and stand behind him. And then pity the poor stranger.

Drawing in a deep breath, she exhaled, feeling her own tension start to creep back into her shoulders. De-spite a full night of sleep, in a comfortable bed, there was still a gut-deep unease riding her. They needed more information. Fast.

Tossing the ice bag into the kitchen sink, she went into her bedroom and got a shirt from out of the lowest drawer of the dresser, added a pair of dress socks and boxers to that. Stacking it into a pile, she stuck her head into the bathroom to make sure he was safely in the shower.

"I'm leaving fresh clothing on the toilet," she told him, raising her voice to be heard over the water. She assumed the muffled groan she heard was acknowledgement. "I'm gonna run down to Unray's for a calzone. You want anything?"

The groan this time had a distinct negative to it.

"Okay. Back in ten."

By the time she got back, he had boiled water for tea, and was ensconced at her breakfast table, reading the newspaper. Reading glasses he denied needing were perched low down on his nose, and his eyes darted back and forth, scanning the articles, mining them for anything of interest. When his eyes slowed down, she made a mental note to read the article he was studying.

She sat down on the only other chair and unwrapped her breakfast. The smell of warm cheese, dough and tomato sauce filled the air, and her stomach rumbled. By now, Sergei was used to her odd eating habits, if not reconciled to them, and he ignored both her and the smell.

Finally he folded the paper, put it down on the table, and folded the glasses and put them away. "What's the game plan for today?"

She shrugged, mopping up the last of the sauce with a scrap of dough. "Poke around. See what pokes back."

"Be careful," he said. "I don't think the client is very happy with us right now, and I trust him about as far as I can throw that damn building of his."

"Gut feeling?" Nice to have confirmation, even if it was of bad news rising.

An exhalation through the nose that might have been a laugh. "A little. Maybe. If you think maybe you're getting onto shaky gossip-ground, back off."

"I'll be delicate as a butterfly."

"And the beating of your wings therefore causing a typhoon in China. Not reassured, Wren."

"Go do your sober business guy thing," she said, flapping a hand at him. "And leave the real work to the Talent."

After Sergei left, Wren took a quick shower, then put together a plan of attack. She needed fresh veggies anyway, so that was a place to start. Grabbing her oversized shoulder bag, a lime-green monstrosity she hadn't been able to lose for almost five years now, she shoved her sunglasses, the mini-recorder, a protein bar and her wallet into it, got her keys out of the bowl, and hit the stairs. It was gorgeous out; blue sky and warm air, and the scent of new leaves and early flowers drifted over from the park. The tension didn't leave her shoulders, but it did shift a little to let a moment of pure enjoyment in, and she swung around the corner and down the street with more energy than she'd thought she had in her half an hour ago.

"Charlie! Morning!"

The young man putting cans away in the back of Jackson's E-Z Shopper looked as though he'd had a worse night than Sergei. Or maybe a better one, the way he winced at her greeting.

"Whoops, sorry," she stage whispered. "Why don't you do something for that hangover?"

"Can't," he said. "No focus."

She looked around, saw that the only other customer was at the front of the store paying for her purchases. "C'mere." He leaned forward, and she rubbed her hands together briskly, feeling heat build in her palms, then placed the palms on either side of Charlie's skull. She might not be great at it, but even a mediocre healer was better than none at all. After a moment or so, he sighed in relief, and she let her hands fall away.

"Thanks." His eyes were already brighter, his skin a healthier tone. "What can I do ya for?"

"A bunch of almost-ripe bananas, the best tomatoes you're hiding from the rest of the customers, a pound of coffee and some information."

Charlie's skin lost some of its color again, and his eyes shifted to the left and up, the giveaway of a liar, or someone about to lie.

What now? Wren thought in irritation.

Four hours later, Wren was in what could be best described as a flaming snit. Charlie had actually been the most welcoming of all her contacts. Not that anyone had shied away from greeting her, but the moment she tried to dig even the faintest butterfly touch, they got skittish and silent.

And that is just so not Cosa *style.* She paid for her coffee and looked around the tiny, crowded Starbucks for a place to sit down. A couple got up to leave, and she snared their table quickly, ignoring the irate looks from another couple who had also started for it. *No, not the usual at all. More often you can't get them to shut up! Especially if you're admitting you don't know something they might. I should have just gone to the damn simurgh up on 80th and bartered something for the answer. More expensive, but a hell of a lot faster.*

Wren frowned, that thought tapping into something else in her brain. She had been sticking to the human contacts at this point, simply because they were easier to meet in public, but now that she thought about it, stirring a packet of sugar into her coffee and stirring absently, she hadn't *seen* any of the fatae recently. Not even P.B.

"Mind if I join you?"

She looked up into wide-set black eyes, and grinned. "Think of the devil—sure, please, save me from the coffee-swilling masses."

"We *are* the coffee-swilling masses," Lee said, folding himself into the molded plastic chair. At 6'5", Lee Mahoney was almost Wren's polar opposite. With his shock of white hair contrasting with golden skin and ebony black eyes, there wasn't any way you could *not* see him in a room.

It served him in good stead at gallery openings where

the press honed in on him like bees to pollen—she had in fact met him through Sergei's studio, where he had been part of a group show. His sculptures, for the most part, made the critics happy. His appearance made the reporters happy. And both made Sergei happy, for the money he could command for a Mahoney original.

Wren was happy because Mahoney was the first lonejack she'd met on moving into the city. Which meant that they had been friends now for almost five years, and a happy successful friend was a useful friend.

"How goes married life, Tree-Taller?"

"It goes," he said, taking the lid off his coffee and sipping carefully. "Although she told me she'd divorce me if I ever came to her studio again."

Wren snickered.

"Not funny. All I meant to do was help them move some furniture, so I gave a little *push*, and—"

"Let me guess, shorted out their entire signal?" His wife was a morning DJ for a local alternative station. They operated on a shoestring, probably including skimping on anything but the minimum practical protections. Not that anything Wren had encountered did a hell of a lot of good against major current-usage—she had once burned out an entire shopping mall—but it would have deflected a minor push like that.

"Not quite that bad. But close. Radio stations are way sensitive, Wren. Way sensitive."

"I'll keep that in mind." Five or six years ago she'd had

to retrieve something from a building next to a power station. When it went bad and she had to pull down current hard and fast…well, that power grid had needed overhauling anyway.

"So, what've you been up to?"

And that was another reason Lee was so refreshing. Unlike most of the *Cosa*, when he said he wasn't interested in gossip, he meant it. And when he *was* interested in you, it meant, well, that he was interested in *you*.

"Job turned scurvy," she said glumly. "So, you know anything about a guy named Frants, or maybe a Talent who had a mad-on for him?" So much for butterfly wings, she heard Sergei sigh in the back of her head.

Lee stirred his coffee with maybe a little too much deliberation.

"Ah Lee, not you, too? What? Did I step on someone's toes? I checked with all the usual suspects beforehand, I swear I did."

"No, nothing like that. At least, I don't think so. You know me, Wren, I'm not exactly in the loop."

"Then what is it? Lee, I swear, I'm getting the cold shoulder from everyone. Even you. What did I do?"

Lee looked at her, unhappiness plain in his expression. "It's not you, Wren. It's just…Council's been squirrelier than usual, last month or so. They've come down hard on their own people—they shut whats his name, Blackie, over in Staten Island down entirely—mage-locked him in his house for an entire week!—and I think everyone just expects them to come down hard on us, too." Us being lonejacks. "And, well...odds are you're going to be the first they come down hard on. As an example."

Wren sighed. "Great. Round up the usual suspects. Why me?"

Lee took the question seriously. "Because you're good. The best, not to feed that ego of yours too much. And because you hang with everyone. Lonejack, fatae, wizzarts...you've even got friends who are mages."

"One," Wren corrected. "And I'm never really sure if we're on speaking terms from day to day."

"She spoke for you back during the Fleet Week debacle."

"I seem to remember a few other people at this table being involved with that." Not their finest hour. A prank gone out of hand, and people got hurt. They'd both sworn off pranking after that, otherwise Lee would have been the first suspect in that tag attempt earlier in the week.

"Point is, they remember you. And now you go and get involved in something the Council's watching—yeah, I've heard about Frants. He hired a lonejack 'cause he's already too far in debt to the Council, rumor says."

Wren nodded. She'd heard the same thing, doing her prelim research. She had run across a lot of rumors. Half of them contradicting the other half and the half that remained usually weren't true anyway.

"So suddenly nobody wants to talk to me, 'cause

they're scared the Council's going to think they're linked to me and treat 'em to the same heavy fist?" Could that have been what the tag was about, someone looking to take out a potential problem? But why? And who?

Lee shrugged. "Lonejacks," he said. "We're a selfish, self-centered bunch." He patted her hand. "If it makes any difference, everyone, well, mostly everyone respects you. We just don't want to be thought of as...in the same league of trouble as you."

"So everyone will send flowers, but nobody will come to my funeral, huh? And you're not afraid of being over-heard telling me all this?" Her stomach did a slow roil, the acid from the coffee churning into full-blown indigestion.

He shrugged, taking his hand back. "I'm an artist. All my current goes into my work." His sculptures had been described as "electrifying" by one critic. Since he actually molded the steel with current, that review had given them all the giggles for an hour. "And my connection to the fatae is limited, since I don't use them in my work." Null-tempered steel responded better to current than one that had already been molded or shaped by a Tal-ented worker. "Short version, the Council doesn't care about me or mine. Suddenly crossing the street when you show up would raise suspicions, not stopping to have a coffee and a chat.

"Hey, if it's any consolation, this too shall pass. Like you said, the Council's always getting squirrely somehow or an-other. Just hang tight, stay low, and we'll all be right as rain."

"Yeah. I'd love to do that. I really would." *But there's still a job to be finished. One that's already got Council fingerprints all over it, even if they do claim to be quits with it. Maybe after that I can talk Sergei into a vacation somewhere that's not here.*

"Thanks, Lee." She stood, picking up her bag from the floor at her feet. "Really. For everything."

He nodded. "Stay low," he repeated. "And I'll see you around."

Wren forced a smile, and walked out the door. "Idiot! Idiot, idiot masquerading as a target!" But by the time she'd walked the three blocks back to her apartment, she was almost resigned to the entire situation.

Maybe the Council does have their fingers in the Frants job, despite what Sergei said. It's also entirely possible that this Council brew-up has nothing whatsoever to do with the case. The Eastern branch has been on our backs for decades; hell, long before I was born.

By the time she had climbed the five flights, the endless loops her thoughts were taking her in had turned her resignation into amusement. "Wren Valere, scourge of New York City," she said out loud. "The woman strong Talents fear to gossip with."

Talk to Sergei, she decided. He probably wouldn't have a clue what to do about it, either, but then again, maybe he would. He'd gone nose to nose with the Council, after all, twice now. Maybe he had some insight a lonejack would be too close to see.

And maybe he'll know a nice city somewhere we can relocate to, when—if—the storm actually breaks. She left her bag on the kitchen counter, checked to see if there were any messages—there weren't—and went into the music room to put on some careful thinking music.

"Hey. Hey!"

Wren had just been starting to bliss out to the sounds of Rick Braun's "Night Walk" when she heard the banging on the window. One eye had opened, then closed again, but the noise didn't stop. Heaving a sigh, she picked herself up off the floor and went into the kitchen.

"I'm going to get you your own key," she grumbled, letting P.B. in through the window. The pleasure she felt in his casual manner—so different from the humans of the *Cosa* today—made her tone less irritable than usual.

"Really?"

"Not a chance in hell."

P.B. sniffed the air. "Oh yum. Any leftovers?"

She gestured to the fridge. "*Mi casa es su casa,* apparently. Claws off the orange beef, that's breakfast tomorrow."

"That's disgusting."

"Excuse me? You eat carrion by nature, P.B. Or have you forgotten that little detail?"

"Hey, nobody asked me when they designed my ancestors."

Literally. Demons were the only members of the *Cosa* to have documented origins. Sometime back in the eleventh century, according to the journals of one H. Buchanon, sick but Talented bastard. Wren had wondered once what sort of creatures he had used as the base stock for his creations. The probable answers so disturbed her she swore never to think in that direction ever again.

"Did you have a reason for showing up, or were you just looking for someone's day to ruin?"

He stopped with his paw inside the carton of pork fried rice. "Whoa, someone got up on the wrong side of the smiley face this morning."

Wren sighed. "Right, sorry. It's been a long week, a long damned day, and I had a headache to begin with."

"Oh, sorry." He shuffled back a step or two, and she smiled at him. That small a distance didn't really make much of a difference to the vibes his kind put out, but it was sweet of him to try.

"And yeah, had a reason. Was at the Firehouse last night, got some good gossip. If you're not too cranky to indulge…"

After the brush-offs she had been getting from her human counterparts, Wren almost pounced on this indication of normalcy. "Sit. Spill."

He chuffed laughter, and Wren had a vaguely unsettling view of his teeth before the black-lined lips closed again. "You may not be so happy to hear what I've got to say when it's said."

"That would sort of fit with the rest of the day, that I

finally get gossip and it comes with a warning label. Never mind, go on, tell me anyway."

"There's talk about maybe this vigilante group is being funded by the Council."

Wren boosted herself up onto the kitchen counter and stared at the demon. "Use a fork," she suggested absently. "Otherwise you'll get spices under your claws and that's going to burn. Why would they do that? Okay, so the Council isn't exactly fatae-friendly, but they've always been *Cosa. Always.*"

"Except when they're trying to shut us down, put their rules on us. Hell, you're a lonejack, you know what it's like."

Wren snorted at the timeliness of that comment. Everyone had a mad-on for the Council this week. Not that this was anything new. The Mage Council had been founded to keep a check on human magic-users. The first lonejacks had told them where they could stuff those checks. It had been pretty much subdued one-upmanship ever since then, seven generations of sibling rivalry, with the Council always but always having the upper hand.

"They've always claimed dominance over us, yeah." None of P.B.'s business what was going on within the lonejack community, if he hadn't sniffed it out already. "But I don't get the logic of this. Even if they wanted to—okay, assume they want to, even if they thought they *could* somehow control all of the fatae, why would they fund a bunch of bigoted head-knockers as part of their plan?" She shook her head. "I don't buy it. Maybe a mage or two—hell, maybe even a lonejack or two, we're not all comfortable with the more, hrmm, outré of the fatae, but not as a Council-condoned movement, no."

"They're human. We're not. You really think that doesn't matter to the Council?"

She rolled her eyes at him, as theatrically as she could manage. "Sheesh, and people say we're a bunch of bigots!"

"What, you thought that was only *human* nature?" He shook his head, sharp-pointed ears twitching, something she didn't remember ever seeing before. *He must really be nervous.* "Face it, Valere, there's going to come the day when the Council goes too far. When they show their colors, put off the mask, whatever cliché you want to use. Where are the lonejacks going to stand then, huh?"

Oh God, I'm being felt out for a rebellion! The thought came and went in an instant, as did the quick *Do they know the lonejack gossip, that I'm going to be the Council's whipping boy? Girl? Whatever?*

"You're assuming a group consensus. Unlikely, with us. Even if you're talking about just the East Coasters." She was *not* going to get caught up in this. Not with her own problems already breathing fire.

"I'm serious." Beady black eyes stared into her own and she was reminded in their red-flecked depths that P.B.—cute fur and button nose aside—was called a demon for a reason. "What's it going to be? Human to human? Or the side you know is right?"

Time to shut this discussion down. Hard. "When the time comes, I'll choose. Why are you in such a rush to have that moment arrive? Do you *want* to see the *Cosa* broken?"

"I'm not rushing anything. Just telling you what I see."

"I got eyes, too, P.B."

"Right." He looked down, seemingly astonished to see that he had eaten his way to the bottom of the container. "You got eyes, but they're human ones. Guess it makes a difference." He put the container in the trash, gently, and turned to look at her. "See ya around, Wren."

"Damn it, P.B...."

"No, I mean it. I'll see you around. You're okay. For a human." He shrugged. "Everything else...we'll see, right?"

"Yeah," she said, watching him climb out onto the fire escape and slip down the ladder. "Yeah, we will." *Those whom the gods wish to destroy, they first set among factions.* "I need more aspirin."

The sky was splashed with pinpoints of stars, untouched by moonlight. The softness of warm air, and the sigh of leaves bent by the night breeze. A house behind him, lit from inside by bright white lights. Nothing felt real, or right. This wasn't where he had been. This wasn't right. He was...who was he? What was he doing here?

A tremor of panic wrapped around his brain, and he forced it away, forced himself to think clearly. He stood in the middle of the wide, sloping lawn, his back to the house, and stared into the night, oblivious to the pack of hellhounds circling him several feet away, uncertain whether to strike or not.

Where was he? What had happened? He looked at his hands, fingers open, palms facing upward, then brought his left hand slowly up to touch his mouth, his jaw. They made contact, then flinched away in discovery.

He had been a handsome man, before. It was a justifiable vanity which had made him take such care when getting dressed in the morning. Now, his cheekbone felt soft, giving way under his touch, and his pale blond hair was matted and caked with gore on one side, and dusted with cement dust all over. His worsted wool trousers were badly rumpled, and a rip in the knee distracted him for a moment, for he certainly would have recalled tearing his clothes! His hat was gone, his favorite hat, which he knew he'd had with him when he left…this morning? was gone, and he felt a moment's worry about that—his head uncovered, like some young boy at play! His waistcoat was covered with that same gray dust as his hair, and there was another tear in the left sleeve of his shirt. That arm was clearly broken, hanging at a horribly awkward angle. But he felt no pain, wasn't even aware there was anything wrong until touch and sight informed him of it.

He blinked, tried to organize his thoughts, tried to recall his last memory before waking here.

Nothing. Only the cold waiting space of eternity, a hollow pain that ate everything else. Think, damn it! Dust. Cement. You were on a site, looking over a project. Karl had been behind you, holding your briefcase while you checked on the marble slabs to be set into the foundation. Something had been wrong with them, one had been damaged.... And then the memory rose as though out from deep lake water, to reclaim the air—save no air filled his lungs or formed his exhale. No breath...

And it came back to him, a sudden screaming howling rush that overran his brain, knocked down walls and took up residence like a flight of harpies. Logic fled. Dark blue eyes unfocused, then sharpened again in madness. Where he was no longer mattered. What he had been no longer mattered. Memories consumed him, and pain, and the only thing which concerned him was getting back to where he had been. And killing the man who had killed him.

His battered, staved-in face was further torn by a feral snarl that had the hounds stepping back carefully, so as not to catch his attention. He strode forward, his feet planted firmly on the earth in the ground-covering stride of a man with a destination. But the well-manicured blades of grass poked through the dusty brown leather of his shoes, through the pale skin and bone. Not like physical objects might pass through a hologram, but as though two solid objects somehow shared space with each other, two universes meshing imperfectly.

Left behind, one of the hounds whined, a low, worried, confused sound. Then, as one, the pack turned and fled in the opposite direction.

The ghost walked faster, ignoring the trees around him, the wildlife that fled from him, his death-crazed brain throwing image on top of image, memories colliding with nightmares. The feel of paper beneath his fingers, of fine wood and cool glass, rough-hewed stone and polished marble. The sharpness of a knife at his throat, the putridity of smoke and burning flesh. The touch of skin to skin, the sound of laughter low in the throat and whispers and shouts of joy. The sensation of falling, of landing. The satisfaction of completion interrupted by pain. Laughter, low-voiced laughter as he lay in his own blood, as they poured darkness on top of him, heavy darkness, and left him screaming until he smothered beneath his own voice...

Not heaven, not hell, not even the endless turning of some judgmental wheel—forever held suspended within his tomb, the energy of his death sustaining the spell until the structure it was tied to—His structure! His creation!—crumbled and fell.

But he was out, now. Free of that damned crypt, if not of this world. But that was all right. That was better than all right.

He stopped, something inside him orienting itself, and then he nodded sharply, and changed direction, this time heading south. He knew what had happened. He knew where to go.

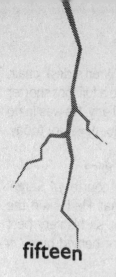

fifteen

They were waiting in his apartment when he came home from the gallery that night. Two of them, high-rent suits and subdued silk ties, shoes polished and haircuts perfect. A chorus of Warren Zevon's "Werewolves of London" went through Sergei's brain before he ruthlessly clamped down on it. Now was no time for whimsy.

Their timing was, to put it bluntly, horrible. And it didn't help to acknowledge that he had brought it down on himself; going to Douglas had started a chain of inevitability, this visitation the logical progression from the phone call the night before. Client, Council, Vigilantes, Silence. Disparate threads; somehow becoming a web. A large, nasty, sticky, mostly still unseen web.

The problem was, it had been a long day on top of

damn little sleep, and waking up in Wren's desk chair, which had been adjusted for someone a full foot shorter than he was, hadn't helped his mood any. He was in no shape to deal with a confrontation. Not now. Not today. Not yet.

But they weren't giving him any choice.

"So much for locks. Or common courtesy." Sergei kept his voice dry, ironic. Professional. He locked the rage, the fear deep down inside, put on his very best mask and closed the apartment door behind him. *I'm going to get an ulcer.*

"We waited outside for an hour. I think your doorman was about to call the police. So we decided discretion was the better part of not being arrested." The older of the two, the familiar face, had made himself at home on the long brown leather sofa. The other, standing behind him like a soldier at parade rest, was an unknown. Insurance, Sergei decided. Not muscle—the Silence wasn't that foolhardy, to force the matter like that. But a guarantee that whatever happened it would be two to one. A compliment, if you took stock in things like that. He was disgusted to discover that he still did.

"And leaving a note to say you'd stopped by never crossed your mind," he murmured, shrugging out of his coat and hanging it in the closet. Dusk had already settled, and he touched the control pad that turned on a scattering of lamps throughout the space. His apartment was an open space; no alcoves or half walls a shadow might hide against. What had started out early in his career as paranoia had evolved, over the years, to a personal preference. One wide archway led to the kitchen, while a metal spiral staircase led to the sleeping alcove. The fourth and seventh steps creaked.

Sergei tugged off his tie and looped it over the staircase's railing, slipping off his oxblood loafers and leaving them on the floor beside the lowest step, dress socks following, tucked inside the shoes for easier carrying. He kept his back to the two men all the while, a dual insult; "I'm not afraid of you" coupled with "you're not important enough to deal with first." But his pulse was too fast, and he was wishing he had gone to the cocktail party he'd been invited to that night instead of coming directly home. Standing around dealing with enforced laughter and unwanted innuendoes would have been preferable to this.

"A note might be lost, or disregarded. Face-to-face, it was felt, was...wiser."

Sergei straightened, spent a moment staring up the staircase, contemplating. Counting heartbeats until he felt reasonably balanced, and couldn't risk any more delay. Only then did he turn to face his unwelcome visitors. Andre Felhim. Tall, lean, black, with a sprinkling of gray in his close-cut hair. He was probably in his late sixties by now, but his face was that of a man a decade younger. Andre had helped to recruit Sergei, in the way back when. They'd never gotten along, but there was respect there. A good choice to send, Sergei acknowledged. Well, nobody had ever said the Silence was stupid. Far from it.

"What, so I can tell you to get lost face-to-face? Fine. Get lost. Better yet, get stuffed."

"Now, Sergei Kassianovich…"

"Leave my father out of this." Scraping old wounds, using his patronymic. No, the Silence wasn't stupid. But they did take risks. "When you wait for an invitation before appearing in my home, then I will be polite. When you come here to threaten—"

"There have been no threats made!" Andre shot off the sofa like an uncoiled spring, sounded truly outraged. His companion, a short but strongly-built redhead, looked as though he regretted not being the one to have made the threat. Sergei didn't ask Andre the other man's name. Didn't care to know.

"You're shadowing my partner. Making not-too-veiled comments about my failure to, what was it they said—ah, 'my failure to bring her to heel.' Like she was a dog I was supposed to train." He glared at the older man, his shoulders squared and his mouth set in stubborn lines. "Pushing me to make deals. No. And again, no."

"Will you hear me out, at least, before you throw us out of your home?"

Sergei locked glares with him for a long moment, then relented. "All right." He made a seemingly careless gesture with one hand. "Make your pitch."

"I'm not here to harass you, my boy. Nor to discuss your...ongoing negotiations with Operations."

Right. And pigs fly.

"I merely wish to discuss a possible intersection of interests."

"And for that you had to bring a companion?"

Andre smoothed past that comment as though it hadn't been said. "It has come to our attention that you have taken on an assignment that runs parallel with a situation we ourselves have an interest in." He reached into his suit jacket and removed a handful of photographs, which he then handed to Sergei.

Sergei looked, then dropped them onto the coffee table between them. They fell face up, fanned out as though for display. Two of Wren in the early morning light as she was working outside the Frants building, another one of her standing next to a car he didn't recognize, and two more of the house their target lived in, taken from a slight distance but showing astonishing detail.

They had been tailing her. Suspecting it was different from having proof, and he had to force back the beast that now rose, snarling, in his throat. *Hold, hold. Don't lose it. You can't afford to lose it.*

Unaware of the danger he had been in, Andre fell into lecturer's pose, knees relaxed, arms behind his back, as though he were addressing a class of eager freshmen hanging on his every word. "Before you get indignant,

I assure you we haven't made a habit of being voyeuris-
tic. We merely—"

"Yeah, I know," Sergei interrupted, still seething. "I assume that you have a file on Frants?" And then *oh, good
going* he snarled inwardly, turning the beast on himself.
A tyro's mistake, to allow anger—any emotion—to push
him into such a stupid error. You never, ever gave away
information—in this case, their client's name—without
an equal exchange. Never assume they know anything.
Their poker face might just be better, that's all.

"We do, yes," the older man said in a tone that re-
buked him for asking such a foolish question, "but our
interest is rather more with the man who...acquired
your client's item."

And Wren thinks I dance around the topic, Sergei
thought without showing any of his momentary amusement. But the break allowed him to regain his calm, to
step back a half step and get some perspective. *So they
followed her. Think of it as unexpected backup. They
weren't going to harm Wren. Not intentionally. Not while
they still think I can be used to manipulate her into
working for them. And not after, not unless they take us
both out. And there's no reason to do that. We're potential benefits, not liabilities.* "Why?"

Irritation broke through Andre's calm exterior. "Oh,
come now, Sergei. We taught you better than that."
Sergei gave himself a point for the lapse. Maybe a point
and a half, the way the vein in Andre's neck pulsed.

"You knew about this 'collector' and didn't think to tell us." The redhead spoke for the first time. His voice was Eastern Seaboard boarding-school perfect, his accent just as clearly disgusted. With Sergei, with the situation, with having to waste his time in this apartment on a matter that should never have become a matter at all, if people had just hewed to orders and regulations and Told All the moment they learned it. A True Believer. Sergei wondered if he'd ever been that bad. Probably.

Time I took back control of this situation. Taking off his suit jacket, he draped it over the back of the leather recliner. His favorite reading chair, with a gooseneck lamp perfectly positioned to shine the best illumination on a book. He resisted the lure of its cushions, wanting to remain on his feet and alert. "What was there to tell? A lot of people think they want to rub up against the magical. Most of them wouldn't know it if they got slapped in the face with a true Artifact. I had no reason to believe that he was any different."

"It's not your place to make judgment calls like that. You should have reported him—and any other individual who came looking for items they should not have."

The hell I should have. "Andre, get your dog off my ankle." Sergei knew he was screwing this up; they had gotten him on the defensive, second-guessing his own actions, but there was a spark of righteous indignation fueling him now, in addition to the anger and fear. Where the hell did they get off, harassing him like this? *They're desperate. There's blood in the water, somewhere.* And he cursed himself again for dropping so completely out of sight that he didn't know the gossip that was going around the Silence. Didn't know what had driven them to push so hard for the thing he'd told them they could never have—Wren. He should have read the tone of Fatal Friday better. Dancy, Adam; they had both tried to warn him. So had Douglas, in his own rat-bastard way....

"I'm just one man. You telling me no one has been assigned to tracking things like this, that you have to rely on one burned-out Handler and a twenty-something lonejack to solve your problems?"

"You're hardly burned out," Felhim said, trying to soothe the roiled waters like the diplomat he had once been.

"I am," Sergei said without rancor, the calm coming at the cost of sudden, total exhaustion. "And you know it. That's the only reason they let me walk away ten years ago. First, you wanted me to report in—then, to report on what I'm doing, report on what I'm seeing and hearing. And now, suddenly, you need more. You start to order me around, like I was one of you again. Are things really that bad...." He paused, purely for effect, then decided the hell with it and went for the kill. "Or is it that you know Genevieve won't go anywhere without me?"

"You so sure about that?" the redhead asked, a challenge.

"Jorgunmunder," Andre said, warning him off that

avenue of attack. But Sergei didn't even have to process the question.

"Yeah. I am."

Yeah, he was. It was astonishing, really, how obvious it should have been to him, this sureness. Like a chair when you desperately needed to sit appearing directly behind you, as though by…and now he did chuckle. *As though by magic.*

"It's a simple enough proposition, Didier." Having failed to intimidate, Jorgunmunder was trying for reasonable like a shirt he knew wasn't going to fit. "Find out who was giving this Prevost fellow the direction of so many Artifacts. That's all. We'll do the rest, if you're too mercenary to deal with it."

By "mercenary" he meant working for a living, not lapping at the Silence's teat. And by "deal with it," he meant exactly what it sounded like. The Silence was named that for a reason. Nobody talked.

Sergei refused to rise to the bait. He leaned against the wall, arms crossed comfortably across his chest, watching the two of them with a carefully upturned quirk to his lips. Just because he hadn't played the game in years didn't mean he had forgotten how. And with Wren to practice on for all that time, he knew for a fact that the expression on his face was guaranteed to frustrate anyone it was turned on.

"Christ," Jorgunmunder went on, reacting to Sergei's body language as though he'd read the script beforehand, "it's in everyone's best interest that the information be shut down, before someone who isn't content to just look at his pretties gets hold of too many!"

And that, Sergei thought ruefully, *was always the problem. Everything the Silence did was reasonable. Was for the better good of humanity—as the Silence saw it.* And for the most part he agreed with their goals, their reasons.

It was just the way they used up their people. People who saw too much, did too much. Cared too damn much. *And all the doing and seeing and caring doesn't do more than stem the tide.*

He would have done anything—had done everything—to keep that weary, bitter awareness out of his Wren's eyes.

And yet...they had a point. He'd worried about Wren's description of what she'd seen at the mark's house, too. "Look. I'll get what information for you I can. I always have." Without him, they'd still have nothing more than rumors about the Council's existence. "But back off. No more shadowing, no more harassing. No more manipulating. If you've talked to Douglas then you know the most you're going to get is me, not her. Leave Wren alone. She's not to be any part of your plans."

"Don't you think maybe that's for me to decide?"

All three men jerked to attention. Sergei cursed both his inattention and the standing order that, no matter what time of night or day it was, a woman matching Wren's description would always be allowed into his flat, no questions asked. He had meant it to be for her safety. *Another good plan gone to hell. Seems to be a theme for the day.*

She stood in the doorway, arms firmly planted on her hips, and stared at them. No way to tell how much she'd heard. No matter, it was all damning.

"All right. Since I've crashed the party, do I get an invitation after the fact?"

Andre turned so that he was facing her completely. "This is Genevieve?"

Sergei gave him an "are you kidding?" look. "Would you believe me if I said no?"

Andre didn't bother replying to that. "Ms. Valere. My name is Andre Felhim, and this is my associate, Poul Jorgunmunder."

"Generally speaking, people who have associates who look like that tend to say things like 'I'm gonna make you an offer you can't refuse.' That your deal?" She ran her hand against the wall, as though testing the texture of the paint. Sergei recognized the move for what it was, a gathering of current from the wiring that ran behind the plaster.

"Wren…" he warned, even as Felhim rushed to reassure her.

"I assure you, there will be no need for…violence. On either side."

She flicked a glance at Sergei, asking for feedback, which reassured him somewhat. She might be angry, but it wasn't out of control. Yet.

"It's okay, Wren."

Her hand dropped from the wall. Sergei hoped that the Silence agents didn't make the mistake of thinking that meant that she was unarmed. No Talent ever was, a lonejack even less so. Paranoia was how they stayed clear of the Council. He should have been paying more attention to that lesson. He sighed inwardly. Douglas had been right. He *was* better suited to working within the system, not without.

"Right. Felhim and Jorgunmunder. Harassing my partner—" A subtle emphasis on the words, a touch heavier on *my*. "Talking about something my partner—" Again the emphasis, this time on *partner.* Sergei hid a wince. She was definitely angry. "—doesn't want me to know about." She moved farther into the room, her boots making solid noises on the hardwood floor. Of the four in the room, Wren should have been the one overwhelmed. She was barely five-four—five-six in those boots—and hid her gymnast's strength under a deceptive softness. The unthreatening, unmemorable look she cultivated was so effective that you hardly ever saw her standing right next to you, and could rarely describe her five minutes after she left the room.

Sergei could, though. He knew where she was every minute they were in the same room, the same apartment. He knew the color of her eyes, and the shape of her chin, and the way that she stood, the way she slept. And he knew that underestimating her was the worst mistake anyone in this room—himself included—could make. He held still, as though a cobra had him in her gaze, and prayed he would survive uneaten.

"Secrets. Whispered conversations. Threats. I find things like that...very interesting. So talk to me. Who are you, Felhim and Jorgunmunder?"

The muscle shifted uncomfortably, but nobody bothered to look at him. "It's very simple, really," Andre said. "I am an old...friend of your partner here, come by to see if he—and by extension you—would be interested in a business proposition."

Sergei growled at the inclusion of Wren in his comments.

Wren raised an eyebrow at that, but said nothing more. Encouraged, Andre went on.

"We work for an organization that has a vested interest in...ah, call it neutral good, if you have any familiarity with Dungeons and Dragons."

"None whatsoever." Wren rolled her eyes as she answered. *Why did everyone always assume that Talents were all geeks and role-players?* Why would you need pretend when you had the real thing?

"Ah." He was a little nonplussed, but recovered fast, she'd give him that. "Then say that we are more interested in the long-term balance of the world, rather than righting specific wrongs, although we do take action on cases as needed."

"And we are...?" She prompted him. Felhim looked at the redhead—Jorgunmunder, his name was—who made a "get on with it" gesture.

"The Silence."

Like that was supposed to mean something.

"And...?"

"He never told you about the Silence." Jorgunmunder laughed, a short, harsh bark. "Figures."

He, meaning—"Sergei?"

Her partner, leaning against the wall, shirtsleeves rolled up to his elbows, his hair finger-combed until it was standing on end, refused to meet her eyes. Suddenly his unhappiness at the two men showing up made a lot more sense than just him declining a business deal. That was, technically, his job: to deal with offers. Except what was this group offering? Who were these guys, and what else had her *partner* been hiding from her?

"Mr. Didier has been an associate of ours for quite some time. It was he who first brought you to our attention, in fact."

Wren didn't trust this guy—he was too smooth, too sincere—but she wanted to hear him out. Mainly—she admitted to herself—because Sergei obviously didn't want her anywhere near the others. And right now she was pissed at her partner. Royally, majorly pissed, so much so that she could feel the current stir within her involuntarily.

It wasn't just that Sergei had kept secrets. She'd known there were depths in him, secrets, past stuff. Whatever. It wasn't the fact that there were secrets that made her so angry. It was that someone *else* should be telling her about them. A betrayal of some vows she didn't even know they'd taken. Her gut seized up, her eyes burned, and she wanted equally to hurt everything in her path, and hurt herself as well. Physical pain had to feel better than the glass shards tearing their way inside her, right?

The last time she had given in to that urge was when she was fourteen and Paul whatshisname had stolen her bike and then dared her to do something about it.

Then, she had caused the tires of the bike to blow out while he was riding away on her bicycle, sending him careening into traffic where a car hit him, leaving him with a concussion and a broken leg.

Sparks danced around her hands, which were clenched so tightly her close-trimmed nails were about to draw blood from her palms.

And somehow her partner knew she was close to breaking point, because there he was, moving like the Wrath of God toward the older guy.

"Get out." Calm but cold. And maybe not so calm underneath.

Jorgunmunder made a dismissive gesture. "Didier, I know you're upset but—"

"Get out!"

It was a roar this time, and the redhead took an involuntary step backward. "We'll call you...."

Felhim edged Jorgunmunder toward the door, one hand on his companion's elbow. "You'll call us," he said calmly. "When you've made your decision. Ms. Valere. Sergei." And the door closed softly behind them.

There was silence in the apartment. Sergei stared at the seascape watercolor on the wall over the sofa. He had bought the painting with his first paycheck, too many years ago to think about. The artist had gone on to command seven times the sum for one of her pieces. He had the eye for talent. And Talent. It had always been a double-edged sword.

"Wren..."

"No. Just...no. Don't...don't talk to me right now." She glared at him. "Arrggghhh." It was a long, strangled noise, then she stormed out of the room. He could hear her in the kitchen, opening cabinets and slamming then again while she looked for things. The sound of glassware, the refrigerator opening and closing.

She was angry; well duh, to use a phrase Wren had thankfully grown out of. He'd if not lied to her, then certainly omitted information. And possibly endangered her as well, although she couldn't know that. Or maybe she was angry because he was withholding a job possibility from her? But that was his job, to winnow through the offers and only bring her the ones he thought were worthwhile. So she couldn't be angry about that, could she?

Maybe he could have done things differently. But it had made sense at the time, keeping the parts of his life separate. He hadn't wanted to be Softwing anymore, hadn't wanted that life anymore. *There's always a price to pay.* His own words, twisted but still true. He only hoped the cost of this revelation wasn't more than he could afford.

He just had to trust her. And wait.

It didn't take more than ten minutes.

"How long?" She stormed back into the main room and stood there, one hand on her hip, the other holding a Diet Sprite, glaring at him. "How long have you been tied up in this, whatever this is, and not told me?"

Oh. Sergei rubbed his palms against the fabric of his slacks. Whatever he said, she was going to be unhappy.

"Sergei? Come on."

"You never wondered why a mage wanted me dead?" Their very first meeting, when Wren had used her Talent to save him from a car accident caused by a mage seeking to hide some nasty doings.

"Yeah, yeah. You were poking around in his business. Mages get peevy about that, especially when they're not being good citizens." She paused. "Since then? Since before then. You bastard!" Sergei had been prepared, but the soda can still nicked his ear as he ducked, and the stream of Diet Sprite splattered across his shirt. He controlled his instinctive reaction, keeping his hands loose and still by his side. Any movement right now would be risky. He said a quick prayer of thanks that Margot, Wren's mother, had instilled in her daughter a firm grip on her temper, and risked a glance at his partner.

She was seething. Literally. The nearest lamp flickered and then the bulb popped, the glass breaking with a faint crack. Sweat tracked under his collar, and he suspected that if he could see current, he would be close to wetting himself. *Stay calm, Zhenechka. Stay calm and we'll both make it through this intact.* Normally he could talk her down. But he'd never been the target before. Not like this. He could feel his little boat not only rocking but capsizing under his feet.

"Ten years. Ten years you've been working with these people…"

"No." He risked interrupting her, to head off that misunderstanding before it got worse. "Not *with* them. I've been inactive—I haven't worked any jobs for them in almost eight years. Not since we went full-time." He willed her to hear him, hear what he was saying.

She did, he could see it in her expression, but she wasn't cutting him any slack. And her fists were still clenched.

"Why? Why couldn't you tell me? I'm your damned partner, right? Why did this have to be some deep unspoken secret?"

A memory, the two of them sitting in a diner in New Jersey, the rain coming down heavy outside. She was so young, but her eyes were already shadowed with loss. "Partners?" *she had asked.* "Partners," *he had agreed.* "Although I'll be handling the money....."

Senior partner. Why hadn't he—hadn't either of them—realized that the balance had shifted?

Because you were afraid to look, his conscience told him. *Because once you looked, you might see other things.*

"You don't know them, Genevieve. I wanted to keep it that way. They're not..." He hesitated, thinking of the best way to phrase it. "They're like the Council, only more so. You don't want to get tangled in them. Not ever."

"You saying they're the bad guys? You working for the Dark Side now, Didier?" He'd taught her how to use sarcasm, but she'd taken to it like a pro.

"No. No, they're not...bad. They're good—but they're not neutral, no matter what Andre was trying to claim. They have an agenda, and they'll do whatever it takes, use whoever it takes, to create the result they think is best."

Wrong answer. He could see the current rise in her, creating a flush under her skin as she finally turned on him, not with magic but with her fists, hammering against his chest with enough force to leave immediate bruises. He let her.

"Damn it, Sergei, I'm not eighteen anymore! Stop treating me like I'm still a little kid who needs to be protected!" Her voice cracked on "little," losing the anger and was instead filled with the tears her eyes wouldn't release. The spate of violence ran its course: he rested his hands gently on her shoulders, wanting to comfort, but she turned away.

And that was the crux of it, wasn't it? He had made so many promises to keep her safe…. Douglas's words came back to him. *Stop controlling her.* "You were the oldest eighteen-year-old I ever met."

Again, the memory of that afternoon in the diner. Her hands folded in front of her, brown eyes steady on his face as he laid out the proposal that led to the formation of their partnership. She had never been a kid. Not with everything she knew, everything she had been through even before they hooked up.

She knew what he was thinking, exactly what he was remembering. "I knew what I was getting into then. I *chose* it." She wheeled on her heel and stared at him. "Can't you trust me now the way you trusted me then?"

Time for truth now. Look into it, and admit it. "It was easier then."

"To trust me?"

Sergei suddenly felt older, so much more tired. "To risk you."

Wren hadn't ever known how quickly anger could turn into fear, and fear into pain. And she'd never known that affection could feel like heartburn, heavy and sour in the gut, like an elevator going down without warning. "Ah, hell, Sergei…"

She reached out, touched the side of his face with two fingers. The touch she'd been needing, not allowing herself. His skin always felt scratchy, no matter how closely he shaved, and the familiar warmth made her want, stupidly, to cry all over again.

This is Sergei, you idiot. Sergei. How could you ever think, for even a moment... And she hadn't, really. It was all screwed up, everything; her, them... She had always trusted him, even when she was so angry she could have shorted out every electrical appliance for a city block. When she didn't trust herself, for whatever reason, she still trusted Sergei. It was humbling, in a way, to realize just how much.

How much she loved him.

Valere, you have the world's worst timing for being honest with yourself, you know that?

Love, love. Not just hots-for-his-bod love. Or even hots-for-his-mind love, which—honestly—had always been there, from the very first. Had been the thing that made her listen when he talked about a world she'd never imagined...

He might have leaned into her touch, or not. The next moment the contact was broken, and they were watching each other, surrounded by the question.

"Tell me about the Silence, Sergei."

He sighed, collapsing into his chair like someone had pulled the bones out of his body. "Short version?"

"If you'd be so kind." Her words fell into the air between them. She had meant it to be sarcastic, but they just sounded...tired. God but she was tired.

"The Silence was founded in the 1900s by a bunch of white men with guilty consciences." His voice was the same casual, slightly singsong voice he used to brief her on jobs. "The name's pretentious but obvious—they are silent workers, responding to those who cannot otherwise call for help. Quote endquote. The agency—society, call it whatever you want—has expanded over the years—I'm not sure how large it is now but there are offices in at least seven countries that I know of. Probably more. Primary mission—to right wrongs. Secondary mission—to keep wrongs from being committed."

She snorted. "And who defined what was wrong and how it should be righted?"

He shook his head. "You're going to lecture someone else on comparative morality? Genevieve—"

"Right. Nose duly slapped. Go on."

"None of the founding members had any Talent at all, but they like to recruit those who do. Only they don't call it that—they say 'magic,' and don't sneer at the term. A number of the wrongs they right have to do with misused powers, to the point where it's become a bit of a specialized sideline."

"Ah. And you...?" She sat down on the sofa opposite him, leaning forward to rest her chin in the cup of her hands, elbows resting on her knees.

"Me." He sighed. "There are layers to the Silence. You

don't get to see the inner workings, ever. I was being groomed as a Handler, the liaison between home office and an agent in the field." He paused, then let the other shoe drop. "Specializing in Talented agents. Minor ones, all they could get, although at the time they didn't know why, didn't know about the Council."

"At the time." She absorbed the dual blows, bit back the obvious comeback. "And then...?"

He sighed, met her gaze squarely. "And then I woke up one morning and didn't give a damn anymore. I wanted out. And then I got into a car crash, met an astonishingly Talented young thief in the making who helped me complete that one last mission, and I walked. No regrets."

His eyes were clear, his gaze steady. Wren knew there was more to it...but then, she'd always known there was more to Sergei than what he showed. *Not many gallery owners carry a handgun, or know how to drop a tail in city traffic.* Her own fault if she'd never wanted to probe too deeply, right?

He reached across the coffee table, took her hands in his own. She hadn't realized how cold her fingers were until his much warmer ones enfolded them. "You don't have to make any decisions this instant, Zhenechka. Think about it. Sleep on it. They've been waiting for years. No matter how urgent they claim this particular case is, they'll wait a little while longer."

"And you?"

Their gazes met, and the tears she'd been resisting were echoed by the ones glittering unshed in his eyes. "I'll be here," he said. "Whatever you decide."

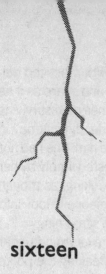

sixteen

The woman holding court had been beautiful in the fresh-faced, athletic way when she was younger. Now her face held a kind of regal authority that was more rare and more impressive than beauty. She disdained a desk, making herself comfortable in a brocade armchair. On one side a laptop rested on a mahogany tray-arm that swung away and back at her slightest touch.

The rest of the room was likewise decorated, a rich mahogany server taking up most of one wall, heavy bookcases the second, and a sofa and love seat placed under the large glass windows that showed the skyline of Chicago.

Oliver Frants sat on the cream-on-cream brocade sofa across the room from her, equally at ease. His well-manicured hands held a coffee cup with practiced delicacy, and his suit looked as pressed and sharp as if he had just shrugged himself into it, rather than surviving a ninety-minute plane ride after a long, difficult day in the office. Denise Macauley sat beside him. She had not been offered coffee, and her hands rested limply by her side. Her face was placid, pleasant-looking, as though listening to gentle music. But were someone to look into her eyes, their dark depths would be screaming.

"I thought that you said you had everything under control?" their hostess said finally, breaking the polite silence that had fallen after casual chitchat. As frustrating as Frants found it, he could not rush the issue. Not here, where he was very much not in control. He had scorned the Council years ago, using a go-between to get around their prohibition on doing business with Frants Industries, and paid the price for that deception. Was, in fact, still paying that price. The fact that Madame Howe was willing to meet with him at all now was due only to his rather blatant bribe.

Galling though it was, in this situation he needed her aid. Rather desperately.

"We did," he replied. "But the stone was returned to us in damaged condition. The spell has been…dislodged."

She snorted, a surprisingly ladylike sound. "Dislodged? Say what you mean, Ollie. It's been broken. That will teach you to try to work with amateurs. Hiring a lonejack, what were you thinking?"

They both knew what he had been thinking. A Council mage had installed the spell, and been dispatched by Council order immediately after they discovered the nature of the spell. No mage had worked for Frants Industries since, until his ill-fated attempt twelve years ago to use current to take his father out of his way. It had been stupid, to use magic to do something more ordinary means could have accomplished. But he had wanted to make a point, that no man—or woman—could say no to him.

And the mage hadn't. More fool her.

He had thought he would never have to worry about the Council's anger so long as he stayed within the building. The ban held: no Council mage would touch that building, for good or ill. They could no sooner go against their order than they could take back the original spell which had caused it. But they could, he hoped, give him help in other ways. It was, after all, their work. They should have some pride in it.

"The spell no longer works, even with the cornerstone returned. It needs to be repaired."

"I'm not sure you can blame the lonejack for that," Kim-Ann said, placing her coffee down with a gentle clink of china against wood. "But either way, the fact is that you're screwed." Even the obscenity sounded polite in her mouth. "Really, the theft and resultant breakage is hardly surprising. What did you expect? You left anger, pain in your wake with that spell. Only the weight of the building kept it in check for this long."

"Not me, my grandfather," Frants objected. "He was the one who commissioned it."

"You believe that that makes any difference to magic?" She was elegantly scornful. "You reap the benefits, directly, so too do you reap the costs."

"That spell bought protection against ill will." Ill will, in that particular case, to cover everything from envious competitors to disgruntled union organizers, and any other conflict his grandfather, no innocent when it came to the underbelly of big business, could name.

"You cannot use the spell against the spell itself," she said in return. "And money, even a great deal of money, cannot outrun death's hatred. Your grandfather knew the risks when he purchased our work." "Our," although the Council still denied any involvements. Which was why she alone met with him here in Chicago, rather than a full quintet on their own turf, as was usual. This meeting was not happening on any level. "You should have paid more attention to the details when you set all this in motion."

Frants wasn't sure if she was referring to himself or his grandfather. The old woman was old enough to have known the bastard personally, but her mind seemed clear enough to tell the difference. He repressed a shiver. Mages. They were all damned spooky, and only a fool trusted one.

"And, to make matters more complicated, there has already been some inquiry from outsiders as to our part in this matter." She made a moue of disgust. "I'm not very happy about that, Ollie," she continued. "Part of our agreement at the time—the reason we allowed the spell to remain intact—was that we be kept out of this entire sordid mess."

The reason they had left the spell was because they had kept the money the mage had been paid for it. "And you have been. For over fifty years—"

"It's not enough," she told him. "There is a risk now, and that is unacceptable. Clean it up, Oliver. Or we will be forced to clean up all of it." The emphasis in her words left little question but that she included him in that mess.

He narrowed his eyes, as though gauging her strength, one jungle predator to another, then relaxed. The illusion was that he had made the decision not to challenge her, but it was only an illusion.

"It's being handled," he assured her.

"Good. Then we have nothing more to say to one another. Once you have the materials back in place, someone will be assigned to correct the breach and reapply the protection spell. We—however reluctantly in this instance—will honor our warranties."

Frants stood to leave, holding one hand out to Denise. A heartbeat, and she took it, sluggishly, as though uncertain how to make her body move any longer.

"And Ollie," the older woman added. "Don't bring

your toys here again. I don't want that kind of filth in my presence."

Frants merely smiled, and inclined his head to her as they left.

Seven candles lit the edges of the room, their flames oddly still, giving off narrow shafts of pale yellow light. Five of the wax pillars were white, two dark red. On the black marble slab in the center of the room, seven more candles, these black, with a harsher white light, illuminated a female: naked, painted with sigils and signs on every part of her body. A rope was loosely bound around her ankles, and a long, sharp blade was pointed edge-first into the valley between her breasts.

"Hear me,
With blood the line is drawn.
With blood the barrier is drawn.
Barrier of strength, which none may break.
Barrier of power, which none may annul.
A trap without escape, for malign intent."

The blade cut into the woman's skin, but she did not react. A harder push, and blood began to flow from the cut.

"Hear me,
With blood the line is drawn.

With blood the barrier is drawn.
Barrier of strength, which none may break.
Barrier of power, which none may annul
My will commands. My will commands."

A pause. Another, longer pause. The candle flames didn't so much as flicker, much less change color as they were supposed to do once the wards were in place.

"Damn it."

The black-robed figure dropped his arms and strode to the wall, slapping angrily at the light switch with the hand that did not hold the athane. His bare feet peeked out from under the hem of the robe, and the neatly-trimmed, buffed toenails only added to the surrealism of the scene.

Frants put the knife down on the slab and shed his robe, tossing it aside without a thought to the cost of the material. Beneath, he was naked, his body graying and worn but still in reasonably good shape.

Despite the overhead light now flooding the room, the body on the slab of black marble still did not move. Only a shallow movement of her rune-dabbed chest, and the warm blood trickling over her rib cage, indicated that she was still alive. Her eyes were open, staring without focus up at the black-painted ceiling, and every great once in a while the lids would blink.

"Another worthless spell. Another *damned* worthless spell!"

He'd paid good money for this one, this and all the others he'd tried. Traditional magic, the way most people thought of it, the Voodoo and witchcraft and magics dark and light. Their methods might be sneered at by the mages and their oh-so-scientific "current," but it *worked*. Magic was magic, it didn't care what your philosophy was. And, more to the point, those traditional methods could be worked by someone other than a Talent. All you needed was to *believe*.

"I believe," he said to whatever might be listening, watching. "I believe!"

He had to. It wasn't as though anyone else was going to protect him, not with his so-highly-recommended lonejack hire screwing up the retrieval, and this evening the Council giving him ultimatums. Him! And already, the scavenger fish were nibbling at his heels. Small deals only, for now. But he could sense the tide turning. Soon everyone would know. And then they'd turn on him.

He left Denise where she lay, opening the camouflaged door in his interior room and closing it carefully behind him. The air in the rest of his living area was much cooler, and he shivered a little in the sudden temperature drop, but didn't go into the closet to put something on. Instead, his attention caught by the view outside his windows, he moved to take a closer look.

Dark clouds swirled in the sky to the west, contrasting starkly with the morning sunlight glinting off buildings on the other side of the city. A front was coming in.

A spring storm, moving fast. Probably filled with thunder, lightning...electricity. *Current.*

"Whore mages and their bastard current." He spat the words, raising a fist to slam against the shatterproof glass. "Damned elitist mages...but I'll best them. I'll show them they don't treat me that way."

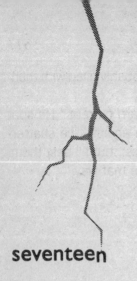

seventeen

"You know, I can't believe I've never been to your apartment before."

Sergei shrugged, breaking four eggs into a bowl in quick succession and tossing the shells into the garbage. "I don't throw many parties."

"Yeah right. You don't throw *any*. At least not that I've ever been invited to." She paused, but he didn't take up the conversational bait. "So how come I never just stopped by? Watered plants while you were away? Fed your cat? More pepper."

"I don't have a cat. And the plants are on an auto-mated watering system." He had kept her away, he sup-posed. Part of that distancing thing, one last refuge where she wasn't. Fallen now, the way so much had, to her presence in his life. Why had he fought it for so long? To what purpose?

Sergei ground more pepper into the egg batter, then tossed in an extra pinch of paprika before pouring it into the oversized skillet. His kitchen was small, but the breakfast counter let visitors sit and talk while he cooked, which was what Wren was doing. They had been talking all night, actually. Or rather, he had been talking, telling her everything about the Silence he could remember, while she paced around the apartment, running her hands across his belongings like she was blind and learning them by Braille.

This *had* been a refuge. Now everything had her touch on it.

Now his past had her touch on it as well.

Both things were going to take some getting used to, he suspected.

"More to the point," he continued, "is why did you happen to stop by on this particular night?"

Wren fidgeted in her seat, clearly wanting to deflect that particular question. "Um…would you believe a premonition?"

"No." Her foresight skills were, to put it bluntly, non-existent. Purely in the here and now, was his Wren.

She shrugged as if to say it was worth a try. Pouring a glass of orange juice into the tumbler, she contemplated its sparkling clear sides. "Why can't I ever get my glasses that clean? Mine are always cloudy."

"Wren..." He shook his head, smiling a little. She was like a five-year-old sometimes, trying to avoid topics.

At the exasperated tone in his voice, Wren felt like giggling. Some things might change, but some things didn't. Wouldn't. It was still fun to tweak Sergei's chain.

"P.B. stopped by yesterday... Christ, yesterday afternoon. Only then? Anyway. Long talk. *Cosa* stuff." She wondered briefly if she should tell him, then decided against it. Yeah, okay, she was invoking a double standard, since she'd spent the last six hours digging his past out of him, but...*Cosa* stuff. He wasn't involved in that, even by virtue of being her partner. Not really. She ignored the little voice that reminded her that Sergei—her partner—had been her surrogate to the Council, and she'd been more than happy to let him do that. It always made him uneasy, anyway.

And the other stuff, the lonejack stuff...it could wait. God, bad enough when she had two reasonably simple jobs, not—she tried to gather all the strands around her now—job, Council, fatae, and now this with the Silence, and felt her brain whimper in protest.

No, put that aside for now. She was distracted enough; they both had way too much on their plate right now. No need to add something more in when it might not even be anything at all.

Wren had a sneaking suspicion she wasn't making the brightest of decisions, but...it wouldn't be the first or last time she'd done that. And...there was just the tiniest, sneakingest uncertainty in her brain. How much of what he had learned *had* he told this Silence? How much of what *she* had told him had he passed along? There were loyalties here, and they were all tangled up, and she needed time to sort them out.

"Anyway." What had they been talking about? Oh, right, P.B. "Made me need to take a long walk afterward."

"Across town? Must have been quite some talk." But he didn't push the question further, as she'd known he wouldn't. Especially not tonight. This morning. Whatever.

"Yeah. But I got tired and realized I'd gone out without my wallet, and…"

"And then you realized that you could just drop in and borrow subway fare?"

"Well…I was sort of hoping for cab fare, actually…" She tried for kittenish; yawned instead and felt the exhaustion drag at her. Internal and external. She checked, an automatic reflex, and the pool of current barely stirred inside. Bad. Very bad. She could call on external sources if she needed to do anything flashy, of course, but it was like…it was like trying to go on no sleep for a week, was the closest she could have described it. Being able to do something didn't mean it was a good idea. She was going to need to recharge, and soon. Being caught in an emergency and draining someone's building was really bad manners.

He slid the omelette out of the pan and onto a plate, then sliced it neatly in half and transferred one section to another plate. On cue, the toaster popped, and the scent of warm bread almost overwhelmed the eggs. Her stomach rumbled, and he laughed at her.

"Eat first. Cab later."

He sat down next to her, their legs bumping under the counter, and picked up his own fork. Wren followed suit. Neither of them were anything more than okay cooks, but she was *starving*.

By the time they had cleared the dishes and put everything away, it was almost eight. Sergei went to take a shower, muttering something about an appointment later that afternoon.

Wren could have used one herself, but she had no spare clothes stashed here and the thought of getting clean and then climbing back into her dirty clothing was, well, disgusting. She could live in the same pair of jeans for a week, if need be, but once she was clean she wanted to be clean *all over*.

She was, however, willing to steal a fresh pair of socks. And it had nothing...well, maybe a little to do with checking out Sergei's bedroom.

After putting on another pot of coffee, she climbed the wooden steps up to the loft, and looked around. It was interesting, in a sparse, sort of Japanese way. A low bed covered by a dark red comforter and two feather pillows. The bed was weirdly squared off; full, not king-sized like she'd expected. Then again, it wasn't like there was a huge amount of room in the loft to fit a larger bed in. An armoire and a low dresser, both of the same honey-blond finish as the bed frame, were up against the wall, and a laptop desk on rollers stood by the bed, lacking a laptop but piled with papers and a blue and white cup and saucer that looked too expensive to be left there. And that was it.

Wren would have investigated—all right, she admitted, call it was it was, snooping—further, but just then she heard the water from the shower shut off. She took a guess at which drawer her partner kept his socks in, grabbed the first black pair that came to hand, and skedaddled down the steps. She grabbed her boots from where she'd left them by the sofa, and grabbed her jacket off the banister she'd used as a coat rack, and then went back into the kitchen. Sergei was already there, pouring himself a mug of the freshly-brewed coffee. He was wearing dress slacks and a crisp white button-down shirt, his hair still wet and slicked back, and she suddenly felt grungy and disgusting in a way that had everything to do with needing a toothbrush and about ten hours of sleep. She took a quick look out the one narrow kitchen window and saw that the predawn clouds had thickened. Wren's eyes widened, and she could practically feel her nerve endings coming to attention. "Damn. How did I miss this one coming in?"

"You were a little preoccupied last night?" her partner suggested mildly, getting up to rinse his mug and put it in the dishwasher. She accepted the truth of that.

His building was modern and heavy and really well insulated; add in her own emotional distress, and it wasn't all that surprising she hadn't picked up on the storm tendrils reaching into the city. "A front moved by just to the south of us last night, according to the news, but it probably wasn't close enough to get you hungry."

Which she was, now. Starving, in fact, for something no amount of food could ever satisfy. Sergei took one look at her face and hustled her downstairs. The doorman whistled them up a cab and packed them into it, Sergei coming along with her. She didn't even bother to argue. There had been an incident almost five years ago, involving a storm and a narrow balcony, that she was never, but ever going to live down.

By the time they got downtown to her building it was midmorning, and the air was heavy, thick, as though trying to recalculate itself into a solid. Wren dropped her bag off in the apartment and then climbed the fire escape up to the roof. She stood a safe distance away from the railing, surrounded by other brownstones and storefronts, the landscape of her neighborhood. She was hyper-aware of the rising noises of traffic from the streets below. The smell of the city in springtime, the sharp tang of ozone coming down from the sky competing with the harsher exhaust rising from the street. But in her mind she was standing on a hill, with grass underfoot, and the fresh, clean breeze of an oncoming storm tickling her skin, watching a front move closer to where she waited.

It was more difficult in the city. But difficult wasn't always a bad thing. Having to work for something meant you were more willing to follow protocols. Protocols—the structure for drawing down power—eased the difficulty. They also meant that you were less likely to get caught up in the current surrounding you.

Less likely to wizz.

A low rumble of thunder sounded again, the growing darkness overhead promising a spring thunderstorm. The wind had picked up in the past few moments, and Wren's T-shirt billowed where the wind caught at it, making her thankful for her leather jacket. But even without the signs, the accumulation of cumulonimbus clouds earlier during the day, or the thunder just now, or the warnings on the news, Wren would have known a storm was coming. Known it in the way the hairs on her arms and neck tingled. Known it in the edginess which invaded her system, and the way her breathing kept wanting to speed up without having exerted herself.

Like calls to like. An electrical storm carried with it power in a multitude of forms. Benjamin Franklin hadn't been looking for a new way to light up houses when he went out with his kite and his metal key. For most Talents, man-made electricity was the only way to go. Pick your source according to your ability, your need, and siphon off what you want. It was already tamed, controlled. There was no risk it would sweep you over, snap the bindings that kept you inside your own head and send you flailing into an uncontrollable wild current.

Less risk. Less satisfaction. Less chance of addiction. Wren could tell herself that she was merely on the roof in order to get some fresh air. That she only wanted to feel the pressures shifting as the storm front rolled in. But if she didn't lie to Sergei often, she almost never lied to herself. Her eyes closed, face lifted to the east where she could feel the front coming in from New Jersey.

Long ago, they used to blame changes of weather for people's moods, a pseudoscientific theory popular enough to affect the outcome of criminal trials. With any luck, a nice small thunderstorm would be enough to recharge her both magically—depleted after the house job—and emotionally. Then she could go back downstairs and deal with the ongoing assorted disasters without snapping at Sergei again.

What remained of the morning light faded into gloom as the clouds arrived overhead. Lights snapped on down below on the streets, and windows began to glow with lamps and overhead lights. A slow roll of thunder, much closer, and a light rain began to fall in the city. She took off her boots and socks, and tossed them back to the small shed that housed the emergency stairs, trusting that they would fall under the overhang and not be ruined by dampness. She thought about putting the jacket there too, but kept it on despite the sweat prickling under her arms and down the line of her spine. It was comfortable. Comfort was important, too.

Now. Center yourself. Feel the ground under your feet. She could hear her mentor's voice in her ear, although the memory was over a decade old. And although there was tar and concrete underfoot, and more concrete beneath that, she could feel her connection to the earth intact, taking her down past the bedrock which made up the island of Manhattan, spreading runners and setting roots in the solid strength of the living dirt, anchoring herself in the memory of atom to atom, mud to mud. Center. Ground. Anchor. All words meaning the same thing: remember yourself.

When the first flash of lightning cut through the sky, Wren was ready for it. Deep in a receptive state, she reached up to touch it. But it was too faint, too quickly faded for anything other than a pleasurable sizzle. The rain increased, quickly soaking Wren through to the bone. Her jeans and jacket were a sodden weight, but she didn't feel it. Her toes curled, as though digging themselves into rich, muddy loam. Her head tilted back, her hair slicked to her skull, rain washing her face as she laughed up into the storm. Another roll of thunder, then a crack of lightning. The storm was closer, sailing into Manhattan like a queen ascending her throne. Elementals buzzed in the wires, singing their happiness as static. Wren could feel it building inside her, a tension from stretching too far, anticipating too much. Back off a little. Wait.

Center. Pause. Check grounding. Wait for the thunder. Focus. Reach.

It was like sticking your tongue into an electrical socket, the adrenaline of a roller coaster's free fall, the instant of solitary orgasm. The reason wizzarts chased the essential moment, the philosopher's stone of transmutation, crude flesh into something transcendendant. Raw power filled her, surged through her body. The temptation was there to ride it, just let it take her where it would.

No. Control. Focus. Bring it in. And slowly, slowly, painfully-pleasant, Wren forced the current to go where she directed it. They quarreled, and she held firm. It resisted, a tangible, almost-alive force, then submitted to the power of her will, and the protocol-raised walls.

The rain slowed to a faint pattering. The clouds still hung directly overhead, but the sun was beginning to glint again across the Hudson River, and the darkness was cut through by slightly less threatening-looking clouds moving in. Wren drew in a deep breath, feeling the answering surge of magic settling into her body and pooling into the reservoir she had made for it. Satisfied and satiated, she raised her arms high overhead in a full body stretch. And, as though in sympathy, a narrow rainbow appeared, arching from dark cloud to lighter one, almost directly overhead.

"How do you do that?" Sergei asked, part in awe, part in irritation.

Wren shrugged, not surprised, having sensed him somewhere in the back of her brain, when he came out to join her. "Magic."

She wasn't kidding. Mostly.

He made a sound that might have been a snort, and she felt him coax the wet jacket off her shoulders, tossing it aside with a sodden *thunk*. Then his arms wrapped around her, fitting his dry suit jacket over her wet skin. For a moment, she let herself relax into it, the warmth and the security it promised. His jacket was cat-soft, the way expensive wool could be, and smelled like Sergei, a mix of salt and mint-spiced cologne that she could pick out in a crowd, if need be.

It didn't matter what he didn't tell her, she realized almost lazily. They'd hurt each other before. They were going to do it again in the future, no matter how much they didn't want to. You couldn't get that much under someone's skin, that much in their blood, and not know exactly how to hurt them, even without trying. But the bliss...the bliss that you could create, in that closeness... She giggled with the thought of it. Maybe not now. Maybe not even soon. But it was there. Waiting. Like current, coiled inside them.

"Feel better?" he asked.

"Oh, yeah. Come on, let's get back to work."

The second front arrived about an hour later. All around the city people cursed, struggled with umbrellas, dashed into the nearest overhangs or ran, newspapers over their heads, for subway stops and building lobbies. Sergei, at Wren's request, opened all the windows in the apartment to let in the cool, wet air. She was still riding a high from the power feed, pacing the apartment like a caged tiger, occasionally stopping by a window to sniff the rain-laden air.

"Something's going on," she said suddenly, stopping by the kitchen doorway.

Sergei, printouts and notes spread out over the kitchen table, looked up at her over the rims of his reading glasses. "How so?"

"I don't know." She continued pacing down the hall. "But I know."

"Well, let me know when you know what you don't know how you know," he said, not expecting an answer. She had sucked in so much power, her blood was probably vibrating. He wouldn't get anything useful out of her until it had all settled in and been absorbed. And the storm being overhead would make it worse, not better. Anything could be going on in the city right now. And, knowing the city, and the players in it, anything probably was.

But none of it was likely to concern them.

The Frants lobby was still as pristine in its marble and chrome as it had been almost a week before, when Wren had been brought in to investigate. The storm—

now directly overhead—muted the light coming in through the high windows, casting a subdued hush that seemed to mute the security guards sitting behind the desk, talking over the previous day's baseball scores.

"Please. A lucky play. If he'd fooled the runner into thinking he'd caught it—"

"In your dreams. Face it, there ain't gonna be a post season for those jokers this year."

"Least we're still in the running. The Mets couldn't get a wild-card slot if you gave 'em Willie Mays in his prime back."

They continued wrangling quietly, eyes trained on the monitors with the casual ease of professionals. One even still sat like a cop, left hand dropping to easy reach of a nonexistent gun in a nonexistent holster. The only other motion was the occasional employee coming back very late from lunch, or leaving early, heels clicking on the marble, or thudding soundlessly on the all-weather runners put down to protect people from slipping on wet marble. A siren wailed, a few streets over, and the voice of the ambulance driver hailed cars in front of him. "It would be nice if you got out of the way." New York courtesy—the "asshole" unspoken but heard anyway. The quality of light shifted, as though a cloud had passed, allowing a flash of sunlight to escape, then the foyer was shadowed again. The former cop stopped, rubbing his right hand across the back of his neck, as though something had prickled the hairs there.

"Did you..." he started.

"What?" His partner looked at him curiously.

"Never mind. Must have been a draft or something."

The ghost moved past the humans, dismissing them from its narrow focus of concentration. They were workmen, hirelings. Not the one he was looking for. The surroundings were wrong, different, but he knew the lines of the building, the feel of its structure, the soul within its walls—literally. This was his building. It had called him from where he had been, drawn him to the place where it began.

The place where it would end.

He simply had to find the one who had caused all this. Find him. Punish him.

Destroy him.

eighteen

The message was waiting for her when she got back from the gym the next morning. Wren's natural inclination was to sleep, not exercise, but recent events had reminded her that when you never know when you're going to have to outclimb, outrun, or outdodge in the course of a job, it pays to have given some attention to your body. And it gave her something to do that didn't involve worrying at the various nets that seemed to be closing around her. Council. Silence. And this damn job, still unfinished and hanging over her head like a nasty, sharp blade.

Yeah, a couple hours of heavy sweating, just her and the weights and the treadmill, were exactly the thing for her situation. Although living in a walkup was its own sort of mindless exercise. She reached her floor and sagged against the apartment door in exhaustion. The city was warm today, unseasonably so, and the fact that the gym had blasted the air-conditioning made it worse, not better.

Unlocking the door, she started peeling off clothing the moment she made it inside, dropping things in a trail behind her as she went into the bathroom and turned the shower on full blast.

Heaven is good water pressure. Thank you, God, for the blessings of good water pressure. Her building would never be featured in *Architect's Weekly,* but it had excellent plumbing.

Something pinged at her memory and she frowned, trying to remember what it was she needed to deal with.

"Oh. Right."

Grabbing a towel off the rack she wrapped it around herself and walked back to the kitchen where she had seen the message light on her answering machine blinking.

"Miss Valere. This is Andre Felhim. I was calling to see if you would do me the honor of having dinner with me tonight." There was a pause. "I have not cleared this with Sergei, as I suppose I should have—"

"He's my agent, not my keeper," Wren told the answering machine in irritation.

"—but I was not sure if he would be pleased at our having direct contact. I do, however, feel that it is needful, as you, I am sure, have questions that Sergei may not be able to answer."

The old curiosity lure. God, like that's not so transparent.

And so effective, a voice that sounded a lot like Sergei's replied.

And so effective, she agreed without hesitation. *Hey, they become clichés for a reason…*

She picked up the phone, and, ignoring the shower waiting for her a few minutes more, dialed the number he had left.

Wrapped in a thick plush towel grabbed off the top of a pile of mostly-folded laundry, Wren sat down on the side of her bed and started to comb her hair out, careful of ever-present snarls. She really needed to remember to braid it, not put it into a ponytail.

Sergei liked it braided.

Right. So much for putting all thoughts like that on the shelf until you're a little less busy. As though she'd be able to. He was in her thoughts on a daily basis before; how did she think she was going to banish him now, when there were more things to think about? Like the thought that maybe the affection she'd always felt under his heavy dose of senior partneritis might be more than just, well, affection?

Or it might not be. She had to deal with that thought, too, before things got way too weird.

"But later. Later." Jumping off the bed, she tossed the comb onto the dresser and pulled on her underwear, then a pair of jeans and a tank top. Seeing the laundry still sitting there from weeks ago reminded her that there were other things she had to deal with today, and top of the list was the one she dreaded doing the most.

Cleaning.

For a small apartment, she thought twenty minutes later, the place could get *bad*. It wasn't that she was a slob, exactly. *I can just think of half a dozen things I'd rather be doing. A full dozen, even*.

On the worst-last theory, she attacked the kitchenette first. Once the counters were cleared away and she had washed everything in the sink, she was about to head into the bathroom, armed with a scrub brush and Lysol, when a pile of drab green tossed into a corner caught her eye.

Her rucksack.

"Damn." In the exhaustion after the job, she must have put it there, or maybe Sergei had. She retraced the steps in her memory, and determined that Sergei had been the one to take the rucksack from her. Frowning, she put the bathroom supplies down and sat down next to the bag to sort through what was in there.

"Bodysuit, filthy. Into the wash. Underwear and socks, likewise. Whew." She sweated a *lot* on that job, apparently. Something felt hard under her fingers as she sorted through the cloth, and she frowned, patting through the fabric to find out what it was. From the arm pocket, she withdrew the ivory talisman, now broken in two unequal pieces.

I don't remember that. Or saving it. But then, there was a lot after the ghost appeared that she didn't remember. Just the wand tapping the stone, and then...

The wand had touched the cornerstone. A glimmer of an idea came to life in her mind, and Wren closed her hand around the talisman. "Bingo!"

Scrambling to her feet, she left the other contents of the rucksack scattered in the hallway, going into her office, then looking around, shaking her head, and heading back up to the roof.

She thought maybe this needed fresh air and open space if it was going to work.

The sky was pale blue, with just a few storm clouds scudding along over the river to her west. But Wren wasn't looking for a storm—she still had enough in her to work this particular spell.

She didn't have any words ready, and nothing was coming to mind. Neezer had frowned on improvisation, but sometimes you just had to make do.

Holding her palm open and facing the sky, the smaller of the wand pieces—the tip that had touched the cornerstone—resting on her fingertips, Wren reached inside and pulled out just the thinnest strand of current. It wrapped around the ivory almost without command or direction, wrapping it in a faint pulse of blue-green power.

All current took a user's signature; the longer it was held, the deeper the impression went. The wand had touched the cornerstone, which was deeply imprinted not only with the original mage's power, but the current she had sensed in the ghost itself. So, with any luck, the wand would have retained a hint of that signature. Maybe enough to "tag" the ghost.

Cosa forensics. She wished now she had been nicer to that cop, Doblosky? Maybe she'd stop by and do some shop talk, some night.

With her frustration distracted by that thought, the words came to her.

"Bone within casing
Bone long removed from its skin
In sympathy, connect!"

The glow zizzed at her, then sank into the ivory piece, disappearing...but not dissolving. She could feel it humming if she concentrated, working its way through the atoms that made up the bone, searching for that signature, that connection. When it found it, with luck...well, she didn't know what would happen, actually. That was the problem with making spells up as you went along. But once the connection was made, she should be able to use the ivory to track the ghost.

"*Should* being the operative word."

She pocketed the ivory, and forced her shoulders to

relax. Their client didn't want to pay them, the Council was maybe—probably—out for her hide, her partner had been hiding deep dark secrets, she was about to have a late lunch with a guy who was doubtless very very bad for her, and she was pretty sure the reason she'd never dated anyone seriously since she moved into Manhattan was because she was in love with afore-mentioned secret-keeping partner, who might or might not feel the same way about her.

"I really do love my life," she told the pigeon sunning itself on the ledge without the slightest trace of irony. "I really do."

Wren had chosen to meet at Marianna's, thinking that it would be her home territory. But the moment he walked in, it felt more like some weird kind of betrayal. Nobody should be sitting at this table with her except her partner.

From the way Callie handed them the menus, she wasn't the only one to think that.

"Nice place." He shook out his napkin, placed it on his lap. Horn-rimmed glasses made him look like a college professor, or a politician playing the academic side.

"It is. Don't think about coming here on your own."

"No, I think not," he agreed easily. "Our waitress might poison me."

"Probably," Wren agreed, not even bothering to look at the menu. This guy was hard to dislike. Anyone that smooth, that easy to talk to, Wren didn't trust on principle. And when you added in what Sergei had said...

Suddenly, she wanted very much not to be here. Not even for a free meal.

"My partner doesn't like you." *Might as well cut to the chase.*

"Is that you meaning me, or you meaning the entire organization?"

"Yes."

Felhim closed his eyes, visibly gathering himself. "I did walk directly into that one," he admitted. "Are you going to take his dislike for your own, or make up your own mind?"

Wren snorted. "You really don't know me well at all, do you? For all your snooping and your spying—oh yeah, I know you've been following me, harassing my partner—you don't have a clue about me, Wren, the person, as opposed to The Wren, lonejack." She bit at her thumbnail, thinking, then looked directly into his eyes. "Learn this right now, and everything will go a lot smoother. You tried manipulating me via Sergei. It didn't work. You won't be able to manipulate him through me, either. We're partners. So if he doesn't like you, or your organization, I'm going to assume that there is a good and logical reason to not like you as well." She saw a faintly surprised look in his eyes. "Neither of us is exactly even-tempered, not when it comes to people trying to headcase us."

"We're all a team now, Genevieve."

"Ms. Valere. You don't get to call me by my birth name until I say otherwise." Casual acquaintances could call her Jenny. And only family and total strangers got to call her Wren. She waited to make sure he'd gotten it. "As for teamwork...don't assume. Ever. I haven't signed on any dotted line yet, and I may not ever. I'm a lonejack, remember? I don't play well with others."

"Your partner excepted."

"My partner excepted," she agreed.

Seeing he had closed his menu, she gestured Callie over. Andre ordered a salad and the fish. Contrary, Wren decided on the spur of the moment to have the hanger steak. Callie almost dropped her pencil in shock.

"Never think you know someone," was all she said as she walked away. Wren was pretty sure Andre had gotten the point.

"So tell me about the Silence," she said after Callie had delivered their salads. "Your take on it, not the official PR brochure."

"We don't have any PR," he said. "We take our name rather seriously."

Okay, no real sense of humor about the organization. Noted.

"Not the official line. You want me to make my own opinion about the Silence? Accept the fact that I'm not impressed by Ideals and tell me what really goes on."

He put his fork down and considered her across the

table. His skin was slightly mottled over one cheek, she noted; the light played on the faint tracings of lighter skin, as though there had once been markings there.

"I always feel as though I'm channeling *Men in Black* when I say this, but...we are the court of last resort. Not only because we're the only ones who can deal with certain cases...but because oftentimes we're the only ones who know about it."

Pretty much what Sergei had said. And she got the feeling they were both leaving things out, each for their own reasons.

"Sort of like a multinational Star Chamber, huh?" She sniffed at his surprised look. "Again with the assumptions. Okay, only an Associate degree. But I do read, you know."

"I apologize. My surprise was unwarranted."

"Damn straight."

No need to tell him that Sergei had typed the phrase into a search engine and let her read up on it that night in his apartment. Another difference to keep in mind when she was looking for someone to get mad at. Felhim wanted to woo her over by sheer force of whatever. Sergei wanted her to make up her own mind. Well, mostly.

"And in response to your question, only in the widest sense."

"Yeah. You guys authorize killing. The original Star Chamber didn't."

Not that Sergei had said so much, in so many words. But it made sense.

And Felhim didn't deny it.

Wren supposed that if she had any real delicate sensibility, she would refuse the meal, refuse the deal, and walk out. Do the whole "I may be a thief but I have some standards" routine. She did a systems check, just to make sure there wasn't anything she was missing. *Nope. All quiet on the outrage front.* Not that she didn't disapprove of killing. She did. But she was also very much against getting killed. And if it came down to it, she thought she might have less trouble with being a killer than being dead.

Besides, she was a thief. Her specialization was in getting in and out without conflict. And it wasn't as though she'd have a lot of contact with the Silence, beyond getting assignments, right? Sergei dealt with their clients, not her. It was a good business model.

You're rationalizing, Sergei's voice said to her. She could hear the resigned amusement in the tone, see the raised eyebrows, one higher than the other, softening the otherwise severe lines of his face.

Bite me, she told her hallucinatory partner, and cut into her steak.

It was, after all, very good food.

The teakettle was whistling when she opened the door. She'd known, anyway—the moment she started working the locks on the apartment door she'd felt the urge to boil water herself.

That was probably why she resisted picking up the tea habit herself. Better to know it was him causing it, and not some weird craving of her own.

But the time delay of opening three different dead bolts gave her a chance to come up with a cover story. Where had she been? What had she been doing? Telling him would only upset him, for no reason. Even if it was a perfectly innocent meal.

"Have a good meeting?"

She blinked at him, mouth open.

"Jorgunmunder told me. He took great pleasure in it, actually." Sergei pulled at the string of the teabag, watching the water darken as though that was the most important thing on his mind. "He's so blatantly obvious it almost takes all the fun out of it."

Wren remembered to breathe again. She closed the door behind her, reactivating the locks out of habit.

"Why?"

"Why is he so obvious? Because he lacks imagination, I think. Or maybe it was beaten out of him as a child."

"No. Why...play the games? Lunch, head games... why do they bother? Why isn't 'no, go away' enough for them?"

"Partially, I think, because that's the way they oper- ate. Nothing is as on-the-surface as it seems, nothing is as easy as it should be. They operate in the shadows, so they think everyone else does, too. Metaphorically as well as actually, Wren," he said when she opened her mouth to point out that she did, yeah, work in shadows. "Also...they think I'm going to fight them for you. Make their...acquisition of you difficult."

Her temper, kept in check all lunch, flared. "I'm no-body to be acquired!"

Sergei smiled, sipped his tea. "Just so. And yet, you did go to lunch with Andre."

Wren narrowed her eyes at him. "All right, mister. Into the kitchen." She didn't wait for his response but brushed by him, going through her arrival ritual—keys in the bowl, bag on the counter, start the coffee ma-chine—only to discover that Sergei had anticipated her.

"Bless you. I so wanted to get lunch over with I didn't bother having coffee afterward."

"Andre was less than charming?"

She snorted rudely through her nose. "Andre couldn't be less than charming if he was nailed in a pine box with a ghoul on his chest." She dumped sugar into the cof-fee and took a long drink, swallowing with relish. She could swear she felt the caffeine hit her brain like a sy-ringe. Then the weight of recent events dropped back down on her shoulders, and she put the mug down and turned to look at her partner.

"I don't want to get mixed up in their games. Not when there's so much else going on—and stuff I haven't told you about, either." He gave her a Look, a cross be-tween curious and disappointed. "I know, and I will. It's nothing urgent, though. I don't think. Just...making it difficult to focus. Damn it, we need to get this job dealt with and done before anything else." She ran one hand through her hair, tugging at a snarl she found near the end, then muttered a curse as she felt the hairs break and give way. She really should have braided it. "They're not going to go away, are they? The Silence, I mean. They're just going to stand there and push and push and push...."

Sergei must have heard the despairing tone in her voice, because he put his own mug down on the counter and reached for both of her hands, holding them between his and looking her intently in the eyes.

"They will give up. Eventually. We just have to...hold firm against them. I've told them no for so many years now—the two of us should be able to shut them down once and for all."

He sounded less than convinced, or convincing, but Wren couldn't work up the energy to challenge him on it. Easier to pretend. "Damn straight. And you should have thought of that before you kept secrets. Damn it, Sergei..." She pulled her hands free, paced around the confines of the kitchen, which took her all of five steps. She ended up facing her partner again, who stood so still she could tell that he was keeping himself on tight rein, not wanting to say or do the wrong thing.

"God, we so don't have time for this right now." Too much else going on, things maybe she really did need to tell Sergei about. She slid her hand back into his, this time lacing their fingers together and pulling him in close. When he was within satisfactory range, she reached up to touch the end of his aquiline nose with the tip of the index finger of her other hand. "I know what you're scared of, partner. And so do they. So listen up, and listen good. You're *mine,* stupid actions and overprotectiveness and the entire deal. What you said the other night...it goes for this end too, okay? You're stuck with me, got it? So they can go as big bad wolf as they want and it won't do them any good. Right?"

He swallowed hard, his gaze meeting hers like a physical impact. "Right."

"Right," she echoed softly. *Okay, breathe, Valere. Breathe! And then let go of fingers, let go of partner, step away...and breathe!*

But she couldn't seem to let go of his hand. It was too warm, too firm, too...right. And the look in his eyes was making promises she hadn't heard...or given...yet.

"So," he said finally, an ironic, self-aware, self-mocking smile turning his lips at the corners. "Did you make any headway on figuring out how to force the ghost back into the stone?"

"Yeah." Speaking seemed to release her muscles; she slid her fingers out from his and took a step back, turning to reclaim her now-cooled coffee. "Lemme show you."

She led the way back to the office. It was the same as it ever had been. The same as it was just a day before, a week before.

And it wasn't. At all.

Wren wasn't sure she liked this new awareness; the feel of him a step behind her, the same emotional sense of him, but now coupled with a physical *location*. She'd always thought of him as a man, as an attractive man, as, hell yes as a sexy man.

But now he was...

Hers.

She thought about that for a while, as she sat down in front of the computer, and smiled, an expression disturbingly similar to the one on Sergei's face earlier.

Yeah. She could live with that.

"Okay, here's the deal. It all depends on how they actually got him into the cornerstone in the first place. If he was willing or not, I mean. Also how they actually did it, but intent is really key."

Sergei leaned over her to look at the screen, his hand on the back of her chair. A part of her brain noticed, but the rest was focused on what she was explaining to him.

Partners, she thought. First and foremost. Anything else—if there really was anything else—is gonna have to wait.

nineteen

The last of the rain had moved out into the ocean overnight. Wren woke to discover that Sergei had, at some point, carried her to bed. She had a vague memory of his hands pulling off her jeans, tucking her into bed. "Sleep, my wren," he had said before turning out the light and closing the door behind him. She thought. That part might have been a dream, right?

She also discovered that he had left all of her windows wide open in order to catch the breeze. Normally she'd like that. But the air was surprisingly cool, as she discovered to her shock when she pushed the covers away.

"Great. Thanks heaps, partner," she grumbled as she moved through the apartment, shutting and locking the windows. Clad only in a pair of cutoff gray sweatpants and a boxy pink T-shirt, she used the back of her hand to cover a yawn, then continued grousing. "What, you think some kind of honor code's gonna keep me from getting ripped off? Not a chance of tha—aiie!" She jumped back when a large, furry white arm reached in to prevent her from closing the kitchen window. "Jesus, P.B., you scared the hell out of me. What the hell are you— Oh, God. Get in here!"

She helped the demon crawl through the window with none of his usual energy. The fur on his left side was filthy and matted with blood, and he stood as though something in his gut hurt.

"I was waiting for tall dark and prissy to leave, and I guess I kinda passed out," he said, sitting gingerly in the nearest chair. "Didn't want to deal with the disapproving stare thing. Not today."

Wren was already busy, wetting a dish towel with warm water and wringing it out. Sitting on the table in front of P.B., she wiped carefully at the worst of the muck around his eyes. She ignored his usual slam at her partner, having heard Sergei call P.B. much worse over the years. Some males just couldn't get along. "What trouble did you get yourself into this time?"

"Crazy vigilantes," he muttered, not moving under her ministrations, even when she hit a particularly sore spot. "I think you're right, Wren. Council's not involved in this. Or if they are, it's way deep, so these guys don't know they're being played." He shivered. "Too nasty, they'd think the Council all sons of the devil, too. And not the way we usually mean it, either. They were screaming all sorts of weird shit, slogans, like they were having a rally. Mostly folk were ignoring 'em.... Then one of them spotted me over by Eighth Avenue, minding my own damn business. Decided I'd make good doggie treats."

"You hadn't heard Eighth Avenue wasn't safe anymore?" Wren said in disgust, using her fingers to comb through the fur and make sure the cut underneath was clean as well.

"I heard, yeah. But this is my city too, isn't it? Aren't I as much a New Yorker as they are?"

"They're crazy, P.B. I don't think they get the whole demons-have-rights-too gig." They'd taken out an angel, tried to seriously damage an adult leshiy. And now they had attacked P.B., who looked pretty damn fearsome when he wanted to. They were escalating. And based on the comments the member had made during their fight, she wasn't confident that they were going to stop with the fatae members of the *Cosa*.

"Hey!"

"Sorry." She took the towel away and inspected his face again. "Okay, turn."

P.B. obligingly turned in his seat, allowing her access to his side.

"Looks like you took a slide in a gravel patch," she said. "I'm assuming the dog looks worse?" She shook her head violently when he grinned evilly, showing all his teeth. "No, never mind, don't want to know. It wasn't the dog's fault, you know."

"You'd feel better if I ate the human?"

"I said I didn't want to know!" she yelled. "And yes."

"I'll remember that next time. Speaking of which, do you know you've got a shadow on the house?"

"What?" She handed him the towel, now almost saturated, and stalked to the window to lean out.

"You can't see him from here."

Wren pulled back into the window, her momentary ire fading into a calmer consideration. A shadow was a stalker, a watcher, not someone who made direct overtures. But he would be reporting back to someone.... Before recent events, Wren would have just shrugged and ignored it. Before, it had been her and Sergei against whatever situation they were working on, and they could handle whatever came up between the two of them. Now...they could still handle anything that came up, but it was way more complicated, and that was making her a little jumpier than usual. "Pro?"

Might be Silence, still. They'd been the ones giving her the creeps, according to Sergei. Might even have been behind the tag attempt, if they had Talent on the payroll, although she still liked the Council for that. Besides, Sergei had said most of the Talent they recruited was low-level. And anyway, if it was them, why would they be lurking so obviously now, when they were all out in the open and reasonably aboveboard?

"Yeah, he's too good to be an amateur—but not *Cosa*, not the way he's fidgeting. Flatfoot, would be my guess."

"A cop? Oh hell." Wren threw her hands up in the air in a perfect mimicry of Sergei at his most indignant. "What have I done to piss off the cops lately?" That would be all she needed, for the city's Finest to finally start putting two and two together and coming up with 3.5. Unless it was whatsisname, Doblosky...no, he'd let her know if he had some reason to be lurking. Right? I mean, after giving her the warning and all.

"Not asking, don't tell," P.B. said, getting up stiffly to run the towel under more water to rinse it out. "You got any aspirin?"

"Yeah. I'll go get it." She left him dabbing at his side and muttering about stringy terriers, and went into the bathroom. Opening the old-fashioned medicine cabinet, she shook out two aspirin into her palm, then reconsidered and took the whole bottle with her. "Here," she said, going back into the kitchen and tossing him the bottle. He caught it in one clawed hand and flicked open the childproof container without effort, shaking half a dozen tablets into his palm and dry swallowing them.

"So tell me about this shadow," she said, reseating herself on the table and letting her legs dangle, feet several inches off the floor.

"Nothing to tell. Saw him while I was trying to get up the fire escape—and did it never occur to you to live somewhere with an elevator? Anyway, he ignored me when we passed on the street, even though I know for a fact he saw me, then did a start when I got to your window, so it's definitely you he's looking for. Unless you-know-who's got someone's panties in a twist."

Wren considered it for about half a second. Sergei had said that the Silence was pissed at him, too—the thought that he might be in danger made her stomach seize up for an instant, then she started thinking again. The Silence knew where to find Sergei if they wanted to. And, despite her partner's words last night about their motives, she didn't think they would hurt him to get her cooperation. They didn't seem that dumb, not even Jorgunmunder. And certainly not after her little conversation with Andre over lunch. "Possible, but unlikely."

"Job-related?"

She had already considered that. "Also unlikely. Client's probably not happy with us right now, but he knows we're still on the case, so I doubt he'd go to the expense of shadowing me personally. Besides, if he did, he'd never be able to get another Talent to work for him ever again, and he strikes me as somebody who is right now way dependent on what we can give him."

"Which leaves us with the cops," P.B. said. "Fine. That's your problem, not mine."

"A cop who saw you and didn't react?" Talents on the force were notoriously even more bigoted than Sergei when it came to the fatae, and especially demons.

P.B. looked like he would have shrugged, if he didn't

think it would hurt so much. His black eyes twinkled, and Wren was reminded suddenly of the abominable snow monster from those old *Rudolph the Red-Nosed Reindeer* cartoons. She shuddered to get rid of the image. "Cops are the least of my problems."

He dropped the now-filthy towel into the sink, and went to her fridge, clawed paw sorting through the contents with a depressing familiarity. "Do you ever go food shopping?"

"Don't you start," she told him. Going back to the window, she rested her palms on the sill and felt the morning air against her skin. Despite her words to the demon, she wasn't so sure her client hadn't set the shadow after all. He had a very good reason, one she had been too crazed and emotionally off-kilter to think of before. The ghost had been inside the cornerstone. And, more importantly, the client had known that. Which meant that the client was—in all likelihood—an accessory way after the fact to murder.

Okay, so that wasn't anything you could prove in court, not after this long. And she wasn't about to go to the legal system anyway. But it was enough to make any cautious man nervous. And from what Sergei had said, their client was nothing if not cautious.

And if a mage had *done the original spell under specific Council orders*... Thinking hard, she was reaching up to shut the window when something burned the side of her neck. She flashed back to the summer she had disturbed a hornet's nest under the eaves of her grandmother's house. It had been one of the few visits they had made, her grandmother a stern old woman who disapproved of her daughter's lifestyle choices, not the least of which were centered on the little girl whose father she refused to name. Wren had been sent outdoors to play while the two women argued. She had climbed up the drainpipe—even then, she had been agile and stupid—and discovered the hard way that stings can hurt.

This didn't hurt anywhere near as bad. But the second sting, sharp to her upper arm, did.

Then P.B. was on top of her, the damp, bloody smell of his fur gagging her.

"Shut up!" he snarled in the vicinity of her ear when she protested. He was shaking, she realized. And that fact was enough to quiet her down immediately. Unable to move, her brain clicked into fast-forward. *Someone shot at me,* she realized. *Damn it, someone* shot *me!*

Out of habit, Sergei checked the street outside Wren's apartment building, scanning the sidewalks and stoops casually. Nothing triggered his warning system; the usual number of kids were hanging around, the same shopkeepers leaning in doorways watching foot traffic going by, the usual sounds of traffic and slams of doors. But something was off. A sound, or a lack of sound, a smell, or a feel...whatever it was, it made him want to break into a run. Instead, he forced himself to walk at his usual stride, neither slowing nor hurrying. His left hand slipped into his coat pocket, touching the reassuring weight hooked to his belt through a carefully-sewn slit in the fabric. Damn Wren's phobias. The Sig-Sauer looked like a toy, and practically disappeared in his palm—but when a situation got ugly, you generally didn't need a howitzer to do the cleanup. Small and deadly was the trick.

He forced his shoulders to relax. It might be nothing. It could be anything. Wren wasn't the only person to live on this block, by a long shot. He could name half a dozen residents of that building who could be in trouble at any given time, either with the police, or a less uniformed organization. Taking the three steps of the stoop one at a time, he unlocked the exterior door and headed for the staircase. Even without his daily regimen at the gym, the walk up to his partner's apartment would keep him in shape, he thought. They were narrow, but surprisingly well-lit, so he didn't complain. Good footing on the treads, combined with visibility, made for a staircase he could live with.

Two feet from the door to her apartment, he could hear the muffled swearing. His hackles rose, even as the tension reduced further. Whatever was wrong had already happened, the threat either gone or neutralized. The pistol was in his hand when he opened the door anyway.

Blood was splashed all over the kitchen floor, although someone had made a halfhearted attempt to mop it up. A scuffle of footprints, then a disgusting-looking towel and Wren's sneakers in a pile by the kitchen doorway. He followed the noises to the bathroom. From the sounds, he could pretty well guess what he was going to find inside.

The sight that greeted him confirmed his pessimistic guess: Wren was sitting on the toilet, shirt off, wrapping a gauze bandage around her arm. His entire body tensed again, the anxiety level skyrocketing until he saw that she was clearly more annoyed than injured.

"Do I want to know?" he asked as gently as he could. "Or is this one of those things where I'd be happier not asking?"

She snarled at him, not looking up from the mess she was making of the gauze and tape. Blood loss apparently made her testy. He took both materials from her, unwinding what she had already done in order to get a good look at the damage. Expecting a slice, or at worst a burn, his expression hardened at the sight of the ragged flesh torn away from her triceps. Someone had treated the wound with less than surgical precision, tearing her arm up further in the process. There'd be no way to avoid scarring. But a hospital was out of the question—they'd recognize a gunshot wound as easily as he had, and then there would be questions Wren wouldn't be able to answer.

He touched one long red scrape on the side of her arm, leading to the wound, and she hissed in pain. He'd seen marks like that once before. A sniper's weapon. Neat, precise: not deadly unless used by a marksman. So was this meant to be deadly...or a warning?

"P.B.?" His voice was flat, cold. Being fair, the demon had done as good a job as possible, considering—the site looked clean, and any germs he might have been carrying on his claws wouldn't take in a human; that much even he knew. But that didn't mean Sergei had to like the thought of the ugly little fur-face using those claws on Wren, even in a good cause. She nodded, and he moved on to the next logical question. "Shooter?"

"Gone. P.B. spotted a shadow, I made like a moron and went to look. Less shadow, more assassin. Who'd want to kill me?" She was pissed, you could hear it in her voice. Pissed, but curious. And more than a little angry. "If it was our so-called client, I swear, I'm going to find that ghost and ram it down his murdering little throat, and client privilege be damned."

Despite the cold anger that was growing in his own gut, Sergei chuckled. That was his Wren; business was business, but make it personal and she wouldn't ever let it go. Unfortunately, he was going to have to put the kibosh on that. Unfortunately, because the more he learned about the entire situation, and their client specifically, the more he was inclined to agree with her intention. Even if it was shockingly bad business.

"I don't think it was the client," he told her, cutting fresh gauze from the roll and expertly winding it over the injury site, putting just the right amount of pressure to keep it from bleeding again, while still allowing it access to fresh air. "Not if it had anything to do with the stone or the ghost. Our client wants the ghost returned to the stone, right? Can't do that if you're—" He hesitated, unable to say the word.

"Dead?"

He swallowed hard. "Right. Anyway, no point offing his best hope of that." His voice was shaking, and he could feel her eyes on his face as he focused on making sure the bandage fit perfectly.

"Yeah, my thought, too. Frants may be many things but I'm thinking he's not dumb. Or at least his people aren't. They might hire someone to off me, if they really were pissed at my screwing up the retrieval, but they couldn't risk alienating every other lonejack around. And word *would* get out; it always does." Wren took pity on her partner, looking away while she tested the bandage by moving her arm carefully. She was the one who got shot, and he was the one who was freaking out. Love was strange. "And the Silence wants me alive, if leashed. No, it feels right, this being related to the job. What if there's someone else—a competitor, maybe, like we thought originally might have done the grab—who doesn't want that restoration to take place?"

"That was my next thought too, yeah. Someone who has an ax to grind against Frants, who might have pointed our original thief to the cornerstone in the first place?" He cut a piece of tape off, and secured the bandage. "Do you still have that sling around here?"

"I hate wearing that," she complained. "I feel like a cripple."

"You're not going to be doing any work until that heals," he told her. "So deal with it."

She grumbled, but indicated the storage area under the sink. He opened the door and rummaged past boxes of tampons and unopened bottles of mouthwash and shampoo until he found the triangle of mesh and cloth, and had her arm adjusted to his satisfaction within it. Then he escorted her to the kitchen, and set about boiling water for tea.

"I don't want any," she told him petulantly.

"Tough. You're not Bogey, you're not going to drown the pain with booze."

"Spoilsport," she said in accusation.

"Guilty as charged. There's more, which is why I think something hinky is going on with the situation. Prevost's dead."

That stopped her mid-complaint. "How?"

"A rather pretty slash across the throat, followed by arson to take care of the house itself. Since several items were noted to be missing from displays in the rubble, based on the display stands still intact, the local police are assuming that the thief killed him, then set the fire to cover his tracks."

Wren muttered something unpleasant under her breath that he pretended not to hear. "Theft and arson...you think the client—I'm being set up for murder?" Fire would destroy magical traces better than anything except being dropped to the bottom of an ocean for a hundred years or so. Current came from nature, and so nature took it back into herself.

Sergei shook his head. "If so, he still wouldn't have a reason to kill you—he'd want you alive to take the fall."

"Yeah, unless it's still two different players? Damn! No, then they'd kill me, so I *couldn't* go to trial. The ghost remains at large, Frants is left to swing in the breeze, unprotected, and nobody ever gets called to account for anything. Y'know, between this, your Silence...teaching school's starting to sound like a better career choice all the time."

He started to pace, two steps into the kitchen, turn, another three to take him into the hallway, then back again. She watched him move, fascinated enough that the pain in her arm began to recede. They really *had* taken on each other's habits. That was scary. "It's too messy," he said as he paused in front of her. "Too many strings and unknown players. Murder's usually much simpler than all this. Passion, greed..."

"I had been thinking...could it be that Frants has just decided that the sooner everyone who knows about the murder which caused the ghost is silenced, the safer he will be?"

"The client wasn't even born when the ghost died," he reminded her. "He can't be held responsible, can he?"

Wren tried to shrug, then winced as the pain came back with a sharp blast to her shoulder. "Legally? None of this holds up legally. But I don't think the ghost, for one, much cares," she said, jumping a little when the kettle began to whistle. Another wince.

Sergei got two oversized mugs down out of the cabinet, two herbal teabags from the jar on the counter, and poured the water with the concentration of a sommelier at a four-star restaurant. He'd rather have had caffeine, but that was the last thing either of them needed right now. His brain already felt as if it was vibrating at too high a speed.

"And you know damn well the cops won't care," she continued. "But there was murder committed, in his grandfather's name, if not his. It's not exactly habeas corpus, but the rumors are more dangerous to a businessman than an NYPD investigation. Especially a businessman who has traffic with the *Cosa*."

Since he was the one who had taught her that, back in the early days of their working arrangement, he couldn't argue the point. Handing her one mug, he got the sugar out and carefully measured three teaspoons into his cup, stirring until it was mixed to his satisfaction.

Her mug was white, with small red paw prints along

the side. A Cheshire grin stared back at you when the cup was empty. His mug was blue, with the Chinese symbols for warmth and comfort stamped in white on the surface. An entire cupboard filled with mugs, and not one of them matched. And, he suspected, not one of them actually legally purchased. He wondered what she had thought of the black jasper Wedgwood china in his kitchen. *Probably thought you were gay,* he thought glumly.

"Wait a minute."

Sergei looked up, and could almost hear the pieces falling together in her brain, like locks clicking. "Yeah?"

"You said only some pieces were taken?"

Sergei nodded.

Wren blinked. Then blinked again, her normally pink-flushed skin taking on a ruddier tint with anger. "Figures. Betcha I know which ones, too. *Bastards!*"

Wren slammed her mug down on the table, causing the tea to slosh over the sides unheeded. She stood, pushing the chair back with too much force, her entire body an expressive declaration of disgust. "We've been played."

"What?" Sergei was pretty sure he had heard her correctly, but he wanted to be sure.

"It wasn't the client," she repeated, enunciating clearly. "All of this—the theft, my being hired—it was the *Council.* They want me to think it was Frants, setting him up to take the fall for everything. Bastards are cleaning up their own mess—and I'm the damned mop."

She went on to tell him the gossip, everything from the rumors on the street, the Council's increasing paranoia, to P.B.'s comments about the fatae maybe finally having had enough.

"Even their meeting with you—they were setting the stage. Giving us enough rope to hang us *and* Frants.

"They did the original spell—or one of their own did, which makes it Council business even if they didn't authorize it beforehand. They might have balked at ritual murder, at least officially. But what's done was done, until Prevost started sniffing around. I'll lay good money they pushed him toward the cornerstone. Maybe they just meant to leave Frants vulnerable; sort of a payback for putting them in that position in the first place. Council's big on eye for an eye. Everything else—him hiring us, the ghost actually escaping—could have been taking advantage of the situation. But if the retrieval failed, Frants was left open to attack, my reputation is damaged so I'm less of a perceived threat to them, and hey, maybe the ghost and I will take each other out in the meanwhile. And the Council sits there and washes their hands clean."

Sergei considered that as he took a sip of his own tea, almost but not quite too hot to drink still. She had a good theory. A damned disturbing good theory. "So what do you want to do about it?" he asked her, taking a seat on one of the chairs and looking up at her, one brow raised in the manner he knew drove her crazy, because she couldn't do it. At this point, you took whatever release valve you could.

"What do I want to do? I want to find that damn ghost, and squeeze it back into its box so we can get paid." He could almost hear the "duh" in her voice, though she refrained from actually saying it. "And I want the Council to know it's been done and that I know what they were trying to do, even if I have to take out a damn ad in the trades to do it. Let them chew on that, for a little bit. Make 'em wonder if maybe lonejacks aren't the second-class Talents they've always claimed. And then let them stew about maybe I'm going to go after them next. Money is money, but when you shoot at me, it gets personal."

"Nice plan. How realistic is it?"

"Not very," she admitted, deflating a little. "But it's good to have goals."

She took a sip of her own tea, then put it down and reached for the sugar canister, dumping in a heaping teaspoonful of the sweetener. He was pleased to see that she managed the maneuver without the slightest hint of awkwardness. She had been training herself to be ambidextrous ever since she fractured her right thumb during a Frisbee game in the park last summer, but he'd had his doubts as to its effectiveness. She still wouldn't be up to picking locks any time soon, though. Or climbing over walls.

"But we do have to take care of that damned ghost,

one way or another," she said, breaking in to his thoughts. "So where the hell is it? I put a catch-spell on it, but I have no idea if it will work. And I think it would require the ghost to manifest, the way it did when I first saw it, to trigger the spell. Which, who knows if it will do?" She put the mug down, adjusting the sling to rest a little more comfortably. "Any luck turning up potential spook gathering places?"

"Actually, yes. Considering the fact that ghosts seem to be the second most widely ignored topic next to the whereabouts of Jim Morrison among the so-called magical intelligentsia—"

Wren snorted. "I keep telling you, he got himself sucked into a tornado being too wizzed to come out of the wind."

"—regardless," he went on, "a contact of mine came through with some interesting information. Ghosts are tied to this plane by one of three things. Unfinished business, ties of strong personal emotion—a loved one or thing—and a nasty little curse that doesn't seem to be the case here, as it was able to actually leave the stone once it was cracked open."

"Great. A lot of help if we knew who it was when it was at home. Failing that, let's go with unfinished business." Putting the mug down, she chewed on the thumbnail of her left hand. "Almost everything we've learned about ghosts is alleged and hypothetical. Fine. Allegedly, a hypothetical ghost would appear at the place where he was killed, not where he was buried. But our ghost was tied to the cornerstone by his death, yes?"

Sergei nodded slowly, thinking along with her.

"I'd been assuming they did a ritual interment, maybe some bones, some blood. But what are the odds that our boy was killed on-site, as it were, rather than being brought there for disposal?"

"Before the foundation was laid, allowing his killer easy access to a place to dump the body? You'd know more about the specifics of spell-casting than I would, but I'd say it was probably pretty likely."

Wren spat out a bit of fingernail, looked at her thumb, then went back to chewing on it. "Or it all might just have been a crime of passion. Y'know, see person you hate, bonk 'em over the head, toss the body into a specially prepared block—the world's most grotesque time capsule, never meant to be opened. If—"

"If it weren't for the spell," Sergei finished for her.

"Right. That's one thing that's not hypothetical. Again constructing out of maybes and what-ifs, but from what we've found out it sounds like blood magic is nasty and unpredictable, but if it works it's a surefire way of making something last. Hollow out a receptacle, cold-cock the victim, create the spell, seal it to freshly-spilled blood and use the power released in the instant of actual death... Quik-Crete for a spell of intent. And if the person killed had some kind of connection..." She raised her face to look at him, at the same moment he stopped, mug halfway to his mouth, to look down at her. Sergei didn't have a shred of magic to him, but he could have read her mind at that moment. Without another word, he got up and headed to the office, Wren half a step behind him.

"1953, 4...when the hell was—"

"1955," she supplied, pulling the number from the file he had sent her a little over a week ago. "Damn. You think there'll be anything archived from there?"

"Not obits, no. But we're not going to look for the obits." He sat down at the computer and logged on to the Internet, long, capable fingers moving over the keyboard like Mozart on speed.

"Please tell me you're not hacking into the NYPD records again?"

"All right," he said agreeably.

"All right, you won't, or all right, you won't tell me?"

"Yes."

Wren grinned. Their definition of "law-abiding" was remarkably flexible, she thought, not for the first time. If you looked at it too closely, it would probably make you froth at the mouth. Her mother would be horrified.

"Oh, hell."

"What?"

"I forgot to call my mom. You keep doing whatever it is you're not doing. I'll be back in a bit."

Wren went into the bedroom, where the other phone line ran, sat down on the bed, and prepared herself mentally for talking to her mother. Deep breaths. In...out. Don't mention the gunshot. Don't mention the storm. Don't mention...

The list was too long. She loved her mother dearly, but it seemed as though they were always walking across a minefield with each other. A minefield someone else planted, at that.

Letting out a last breath, she picked up the phone, held it awkwardly with her left shoulder and dialed. "Mom? Hi! Yeah, I know, I'm sorry—Sergei had me working on a project for him, and you know how he gets. I know, he's a horrible slave driver, and in no way deserves me." Wren leaned against the headboard, adjusting her arm in the sling more comfortably against her body. "No, same kind of thing. Someone wanted to authenticate a piece of sculpture."

Well...it wasn't exactly *untrue*.... Margot Valere knew what her daughter was—tough not to, considering the way her talent manifested when she was a kid, in the middle of a screaming mother-daughter fight. And Neezer had insisted on honesty; the teacher-student relationship raised enough eyebrows, when the student was a teenaged female. But her mother pointedly chose not to know what Wren did with that talent. As far as her mom was concerned, Wren was a researcher and general dogsbody for Sergei, who was merely an eccentric but well-off gallery owner.

Everyone was happier that way.

* * *

When she came out of the bedroom ten minutes later, the only thing on her mind was hitting the kitchen for something sweet. P.B. had made her drink half a gallon of orange juice before he left, but the post-stress munchies were hitting hard, and she was craving Oreos. Preferably dunked in chocolate milk.

Sergei was on his cell phone, speaking urgently in a language once again Wren didn't recognize. It wasn't Russian—she'd heard enough over the years to recognize that, nor was it Spanish, German or French. She thought. More guttural, for one thing—a little like German, if it were spoken by trolls. Another damned language in his damned repertoire. If she didn't love him so much she'd—*and backtrack that thought. Hold it for later.* Way later.

He saw her, and made an urgent gesture that translated into "stay where you are, don't move." She obediently stood still, leaning against the wall and watching him pace in the limited space. Even on her grumpiest days she had to admit he was nice to look at. And today, his jacket off, shirt rumpled and a little bloodstained, hair sticking up in the front where he'd obviously been running his fingers through it—okay, was it weird that she thought that was sexy?

Yeah, probably, she decided. *Blood loss, Valere. Blood loss and stress.*

And also nice the fact that he liked her mom. Not that

it mattered or anything, but it was nice. As long as she was going to indulge in a little blood-loss thinking. Odd, though. In the decade they'd been working together, she'd never heard him mention a significant other, or any family other than the mother who had died when he was in college, and a father who stayed behind in Russia to make sure they got out.

Okay, fair enough, she didn't as a rule share with him much of what went on in her life outside the job, either, but...suddenly, she wanted to know. Wanted to share. She had almost died today, might have if P.B. hadn't been there, and then all the stuff that had been kicking around between them would have been...

Nothing.

It was all the ghost's fault, she decided, a little freaked by the direction her thoughts were going in. She was thinking about dying, and hereafters, and things she had no business contemplating. Here and now, that was always their motto. Focus on the moment. In fact—

Something stung against her leg and she yelped. Slapping at her pocket with her bad arm, and then yelping again as she remembered why it was in a sling.

"Bloody be-damned stupid..." She managed to dig into her pocket and pulled out the ivory talisman, which was glowing a deep ugly red, and stinging her skin like a handful of nettles. She held on to it through sheer willpower, trying to focus on anything it might be able to tell her.

"Where are you?" she asked it.

"There's a disturbance in the Frants building."

Distracted, Wren looked up, almost dropping the talisman. "What?"

"That call was one of the cleaning staff. I left a sizable request for information, if anything happened. Cleaning staff's usually the best source for information, and they work cheap."

"And?" The talisman was pulsing now, and she could feel it doing...something. Could the two be related? How could they not?

"Loud thuds, screams and a broken window, but nobody can get onto the executive floor to check it out. According to the log-in sheet, the only ones there are Frants and three of his bodyguards, a security guard who was doing rounds, and one of his top-level executives."

Wren swore. "There's no way in hell I can get there in time, if it is the ghost—damn, damn damn!" She kicked the talisman in frustration. "Right. Stand back."

"What are you going to do?" She ignored him, getting a piece of chalk from the office and drawing a small square on the floor in the middle of the hallway. "Genevieve?"

"I'm going to transloc, okay? I don't have any choice." She put the chalk aside, wiped her hands, then went around the apartment turning on all of the lamps and overhead lights. Sergei had never really noted before how many light sources she had.

"I'm glad I had a chance to recharge," she said, almost

to herself. "This sucks major stores enough on its own, I don't want to have to do it running on empty."

Sergei wanted to argue, but couldn't come up with anything that didn't sound both stupid and overprotective. Translocation was not a talent Wren could manage well; transporting oneself was the simplest use of it, and about all she could do, and that only with risks, so there was no point in demanding to go with her—he'd have to take normal routes, and arrive long after he could have been any help.

She came out of the kitchen, having turned on all of the appliances. "Okay. Now or never." She took the sling off and handed it to him. "Don't bitch. It was only a scratch, really, and I may need to use both arms for...something."

He looked at her, then nodded, taking the fabric from her. "Be careful, Zhenechka. This isn't worth dying over."

"Not a hell of a lot is," she said in easy agreement. "Hold the fort."

He touched the side of her face with two fingers, looking down into her eyes as though searching for some sign, some indication of uncertainty. A brush of his lips—dry, soft—on her forehead, and she almost cried at the promise implicit in that touch. "Mind the arrows," he replied in turn, and stepped back.

Drawing a deep breath, Wren closed her eyes, found her center, and visualized the Frants building, tying that picture to a sense of *where* she wanted to go, so she didn't end up in the elevator shaft, or something equally unpleasant. Then she reached out in a way she had never been able to explain to Sergei's satisfaction, and *yanked* all the threads of electricity being funneled into her apartment.

To Sergei's eyes, Wren appeared to glow for an instant, an electric blue streak sizzling around her like a silhouette, then there was a painful "zzzsssst" sound, and everything in the apartment shorted out at once.

By the time he had found the flashlight she kept by the door and turned it on, Wren was gone.

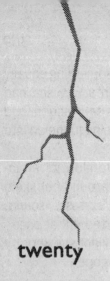

twenty

She landed in darkness, the static charge still zipping along her skin. For a moment she was disoriented, fighting down the urge to puke that came with translocation, then the crash of something obviously breakable nearby reminded her where she was—and why. The darkness wasn't just because she had her eyes closed—none of the lights were on. She reached out, crawling forward until she found the wall, then searched until she found a switch and flipped it. Nothing happened.

"Damn," she whispered to herself. The power must have shorted out here as well. Not surprising, if the ghost was—likely, if not certain—tapping into the current to give itself more form, more power. Not surprising, but inconvenient as hell. For a moment, Wren wondered if they were going to have yet another city-wide blackout as fallout from this. If so, she was never going to hear the end of it.

Pulling whatever current was left in the quiescent wiring into her against the probably inevitable need to come, she moved forward, keeping her injured arm to the wall, just in case. There were no windows; faintly glowing emergency lights picked out darker shadows, indicating where furniture was placed. She was in a reception area, just behind the heavy desk that greeted visitors as they came out of the elevator.

"Pick a direction, any direction," she told herself, trying to remember where the sound of breaking glass had come from. A man's guttural bellow echoed from down the hallway. "Okay, pick that direction." Staying against the rough-papered wall, she moved down the hallway, flinching when her shoulder came into contact with the corners of framed pictures. Bruises were going to be the least of her concerns when this was all over, but it bothered her no end that she couldn't add a medical rider to her contracts to cover hospital bills. Or at least a nice long visit to Jay, the masseur who worked down the block but was too expensive to indulge in.

Focus, you idiot.

There was light coming out from under the double doors at the end of the hallway. Not steady, clean light from overhead fixtures, or even the flickering glow of sunlight through office windows. This light was colored, like an aurora borealis, shifting blue to red to green to yellow without any particular pattern. And every now and then, an angry spark of metallic silver sizzled through, burning a jagged line in the carpet and leaving the smell of burned fibers and ozone hanging in the air.

Guess I've found my ghost. Or one really, really pissed, heavily charged mage. She pondered a moment about which would be worse, forcing herself to move closer to the door against every instinct which told her to turn tail and run.

The door handle was cool, causing her to jump a little. She didn't know why she had been braced for it to be hot, but apparently she had. Closing her hand around it more firmly, she turned, and pushed the door open.

To her surprise, it swung freely, causing her to stumble a little over the threshold. And there she stopped, caught in the scene that met her eyes.

This had once been a beautiful office, filled with heavy wood desks and upholstered chairs, and decorated with high-ticket artwork. All the furniture was crashed against the far wall now, the frames and canvasses of the artwork shattered against it like so much storm wrack. The plush carpeting was zigzagged with burn marks, and the air was filled with acrid smoke and the smell of charred wires. A step farther into the room, and all that was wiped out under the load of another unmistakable odor—burnt flesh. A figure lay sprawled facedown on the carpeting, the blue blazer jacket identifying him as building security. *God,* she thought. *Not Rafe. Please...* One arm was outstretched, as though trying to grab at whatever had fried him. The skin was bubbled and crisped until you couldn't tell if the person had been white or black or Asian. Another leg lay half under a chair...unattached to a body. Three legs, total. And another arm, heavily muscled, flung over a desk, blood pooling where it lay. Body part...the bodyguards Sergei had mentioned? Wren felt something gag at the back of her throat, and fought to keep it down. Throwing up wouldn't help anyone, and now was not the time to have screaming hysterics. Later. Assuming she was still around to enjoy them.

The swirl of building energy brought her attention up, off the body, to the others remaining in the room.

"Oh, shit." She thought she whispered it. It might have been a whimper, though.

An older man she assumed was Frants was backed up against the wall, his nose bleeding and probably broken. His white dress shirt was shredded, as though something with claws had raked across the front, and there was blood dripping down one arm as well. A woman huddled at his feet as though she had been tossed there and then forgotten. Her hair was wildly disheveled, covering her face, but her body was perfectly still, like a mouse hiding from a hawk. Neither had so much as glanced at her when she came in, and Wren couldn't blame them.

The apparition she had encountered at the mark's house had been mostly ephemeral, more energy than substance, and it had scared the piss out of her. The figure in front of her was very much solid, with color and texture, from the mud caking its—his—pants leg, to the faint shadow of stubble on his chin and cheek. Disturbing enough, that it had somehow managed to anchor itself that well in the living world, but what was even more frightening to Wren was the low-level aura which flickered and snapped around him. That was the source of the strange light—and the probable cause of the dead man's imitation of a bucket of KFC.

The dead guy might not have been a mage, but he'd obviously been floating in the current long enough to pick up a few tricks. Interesting. If she lived long enough to follow up on it. Right now, it was just another thing on a very long list of things that were pissing her off about this case.

The ghost looked directly at her, and she sucked in a breath of shock and fear. Nothing sane lived in those eyes, if anything lived at all. His pupils were wide and fixed, and within them flickered the agony of a human system overwhelmed by magic.

Wizzed. He's wizzed. I never knew a Null could wiz… never knew anything dead could wiz…I'm dead. So very, very dead. Almost without her willing it, she grounded herself deep into the steel and concrete of the building, reaching for the bedrock deep beneath, praying that her ability would go that far. Praying desperately that her training would be enough to hold against whatever undead skills this thing had brought back with it. *And why the hell didn't anyone ever write down anything about ghosts interacting with current,* she railed to Sergei in her mind. *I may not go by the book but damn it, there's supposed to be a book!*

To her astonishment, however, the ghost turned away from her, rubbing one hand against his muddy pants leg as though trying to brush it off. He had dismissed her, somehow, and even though it was what she had wanted, the thought of it made her illogically angry.

Don't let him finish whatever he's started.

"Hey!"

The ghost turned again, and his face moved, almost as though he were trying to say something. It might've been a good-looking face, once, before the death blow turned half of it into tapioca. The jaw didn't seem to be working, and the ghost-thing gave up finally, returning its attention to the other humans in the room.

No, Wren realized. Not both. Just one.

"That's it. That's why you're here. Duh!" God, her brain must have gone on vacation the minute she took this job. It wasn't about haunting, not the way they'd been thinking, anyway.

Fuck. Like lightning into her system it all made sense. Revenge. Damn it, they should have figured on the whole revenge angle...or they had, but they were thinking about the human, living side of it. Not the one who was most wronged. *Legally? None of this holds up legally. But I don't think the ghost, for one, much cares.* Her own words, just that day.

The ghost wanted revenge on those who stuck him there—and failing the mage who was long dead and gone, where else but on the man who bore the name of the building he was trapped in? Okay, so it wasn't the guy who had built it in the first place, but that's why they did that whole thing about the sins of the father, yadda yadda yadda. Revenge...

Yeah, she had been right, she'd swear to it—the Council had set it all up from the very beginning. Frants challenged them, dissed them, and so they decided to take him down. They'd tipped Prevost—probably others, but Prevost took the bait—about there being an Artifact practically unguarded and for the taking. Then, when Frants yelled, they refused to get involved, probably told him he was on his own, so he'd hire an expendable lonejack to get it back.... Expecting—hell, *knowing* that the stress of translocation would be enough to crack the seal of the spell. And then when she not only survived but stayed on the job, they had tried to take her out so the ghost would remain free. Free to take his revenge on his killer—or close as made no difference—and get rid of a troublesome former client at the same time. And a troublesome lonejack, too, once their sniper missed. The proverbial two birds, and someone else's stone, so their hands, to all the *Cosa,* remained clean.

Only who was to say what the ghost would do once they—she and Frants—were gone? Had the Council thought that far ahead? About what it might do if it figured out that a Council mage had been the one to cast the spell in the first place? The Council might have purged that mage's name from their ranks, but the knowledge of it happening survived; that was the thing about memory dumps, someone had to remember it had been done, and why. So there was still a trail to the Council.

But while she was congratulating herself on being so clever, if a little late, the ghost had gathered power in again. To Wren, safely grounded, it felt as though a stiff breeze had started from within the office. The dark-haired woman, however, was thrown against the wall behind them, slamming hard and crumpling without ever moving to defend herself. Frants, on the other hand, grabbed on to what was left of a desk and refused to budge.

The ghost raised one arm, fist clenched, and gestured at Frants, who snarled back at him in defiance. Another window shattered, clearing a man-sized hole, and Wren reacted before she could think about it.

"No!" she screamed, pushing her unwilling body directly at the ghost. She half-expected to impact something, but instead went into a forward roll right through him. It was like flying through severe turbulence, jolting her physically and sending her adrenaline levels skyrocketing even faster. She landed and turned almost in one motion, only then discovering that her action had put her directly between the ghost and his intended prey.

"Oh *shit*," she said again.

"Hold it still!" Frants ordered, his bravado quickly dissolving back into the arrogance of a man who was raised to give orders. Client or no, this guy was really begging to get hurt. Unfortunately, dead client meant no payments at all. Sergei would be pissed.

Trying to remember anything she had ever learned about deflecting hostile current, or anything else that might save her ass, Wren had the sudden visual of Sergei trying to explain some weird-shit sculpture thing. What was he saying?

The artist meant it to show how we all take from those around us, every moment of the day. All human-ity is one life form, broken up into smaller mobile parts.

All one form. All one energy. All current comes from the same source....

And the ghost hadn't been substantial long, his cur-rent might still react to the spell she had cast to track it.

"Bone within casing
Bone long removed from its skin
In sympathy, connect!"

Even without the talisman in her possession, the spell worked well enough that she could slowly siphon off some of the ghost's stolen energy, using the connection between her current and the spell, and the spell and his current. It was hard, damned hard, but she could feel it working. More current flowed, and her gut felt warm and tight, as though she'd just consumed a particularly rich meal. She was going to pay for this overload tomorrow, assuming she didn't get killed first. There was only so much a human body could contain before it burst, and she was dangerously close to that now. But it was the only safe place to put the energy: shielded, he wouldn't be able to get to her to retrieve it.

At least, that was the theory.

The ghost faltered then, eyes narrowing, tried to pull back the current. It was the weirdest tug-of-war she'd ever been involved in, nothing like the lessons Neezer had put her through—

"Energy without will is just energy. Power you can't use isn't power at all. Now, can you feel the current when I do this?"

She had yelped as the static charge passed from his fingers to hers, a thousand times worse than anything she had felt before. "That hurt!" she had cried out, indignant.

John had shaken his head. "Of course it did, Jenny-wren. It doesn't like being mastered. It will fight you every chance it gets. But you can't use it until it bows to your will. You must control it, channel it. Otherwise it's useless, and you're powerless. Now do it again. And concentrate this time!"

Concentrate. Control. She exhaled, inhaled, letting the energy she had taken in sink lower, until her legs felt like lead weights, like part of the steel of the building. A mantra, taking her back to those early days of basic channeling... "As I will it, so let it be. As I see it, so let it be. As I channel it, so let it be."

The chant soothed her, twined the power with her own signature until her body hairs stood on end, and her spine tensed and arched from the pressure building within.

"Now, let's discuss this properly—" she started to say to the ghost when a sharp suction of energy from behind her pulled Wren off balance. She whirled to face Frants, completely forgetting the ghost for a dangerous instant. "What the hell are you doing?" she demanded, feeling her grounding shudder under the two-pronged assault. He ignored her, forcing his lips to form words that didn't want to come through his throat. Wren grabbed at him, latching on to his shoulders and shaking him until he lost his last threads of concentration and fell silent.

"What the hell are you doing?" she yelled at him again.

"Damned spell won't work without the sacrifice. That's what I've been doing wrong; they don't want blood, they want *everything*." He shook free of her grip and reached down behind him to haul the woman to her feet, obviously intending to pick the spell up from where he had left off. The woman's eyes were aware and terrified, but she seemed unable to help herself.

"Blood to blood, bone to bone!
Soul to soul, spell contain!
Take this gifting, double hold—"

Bastard, Wren thought, realization dawning as she tried to make sense out of what he was saying. He was trying to force the ghost's energy into the woman's body. But how? A spell was only a recipe—the magic had to be done by someone with Talent. He would have to be letting someone else channel Talent through him while he said the words. Stolen Talent. *Some of the bodies…they must not have been complete Nulls. It wasn't the ghost—the bastard killed them and stole what little current they maintained!*

Wren howled in conjunction with the ghost's scream. It was an abomination, a travesty of everything she had been taught, to rip current that way from unwilling innocents. And in order to actually recreate the spell that way, he'd have to—

"Bastard!" She screamed at him, the ghost completely forgotten at this point. In order to recreate the spell, he would have to use the same elements. Suddenly the woman's presence made sense: he would kill the woman as well, releasing not one but two souls into the magic. Repeating the sins of the father—grandfather—and adding a half-dozen more to the mix.

Screw you, Frants. And screw the paycheck you rode in on. All her concentration narrowed to the man in front of her. The woman sagged in his arms, nobody at all home in her eyes. And it wasn't likely she was a willing participant, not the way she was hanging there like a broken Barbie Executive Dress-Up doll. Wren dropped the threads of current binding the ghost, and cast them toward Frants. If the ghost wanted to take revenge, goody for him. She was getting Barbie Doll the hell out of there. She balled that thought up into a tight little wad, and shoved it with all her slight empathic talent into the ghost's aura. Either he'd get it, or he wouldn't. She couldn't worry about it anymore.

He had woken up that morning, the world in his hands. Stopping by the pier mirror in the entranceway, he'd tipped his hat at a rakish level and grinned at his reflection, then adjusted it to a more sedate, respectable position. His coat just so, his hat just so, his world just so, he'd stepped out the door of his home...

A voice, from out of nowhere. A woman's voice. *Kill him if you want. I will not let you have the girl. No more innocents.*

In the depth of his madness, the man who had once been heard the words as though the speaker were inside with him, safe in the eye of the electrical storm that surrounded him.

"I don't want to kill anyone," he told the voice. "I just want to go home!" Home, with its polished wood furniture, and the white gauze his Sarah insisted on coating every window with. The heavy rugs, and the soft bed he so hated to get out of every morning...

Sarah was gone. The house itself was gone. Everything was gone, save the building he had given his last days to. The building which had taken everything from him. And the man in front of him, his features, his name a direct inheritance from the man who had ordered this building created. Had ordered one life taken to protect his own miserable, worthless one.

The tiny portion of what was left of Jamie Koogler went up the stairs of a long-gone townhouse, drew the curtains, and took his beautiful wife by the hand.

And the ghost bared suddenly-sharp teeth at his victim. "See what granddaddy left you?" he asked, his voice horrible and stained with madness.

Wren managed to grab Barbie Doll by the arm and drag her away from Frants. The ghost ignored them both, the current breaking around them harmlessly as they moved toward the door. The woman's flesh was cold, almost as though she were dead, but the farther they got from Frants, the more vitality Wren could feel inside her.

In the hallway, Wren propped her against the wall and knelt down so she could look into the woman's eyes. Sure enough, there was still a bare spark of awareness there.

"Stay here," she told Barbie Doll. "You got that? Stay here, stay low, don't move or blink or whimper or anything, no matter what, and you may just live through this. Okay?"

A faint, jerking nod was all the answer she was going to get. Wren patted the woman's head once, then got to her feet and stared at the door. A man's scream, and the soft thump of flesh hitting something hard came through the open doorway.

Oh damn it, damn it, damn it...

She couldn't do this.

Charging back through the door, she pulled deep within, to the places Neezer had shown her back in the first days of their training. The cells that made up her body, the current which animated those cells. She reached deep and down and *into* herself, dragging everything out and shaping it into a ball, stretching it out until it was man-sized, and throwing even as she yelled *"Stop!"*

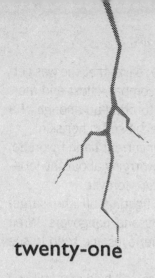

twenty-one

Agony! All there was in the universe was agony. Absolute, endless head-spinning pain that had no beginning, no end. All that existed, all that was, was agony.

Empathy was another so-called magical ability that was more common in fantasy novels than among Talents, but the moment she passed through the doorway, Wren was on her knees with the overload of emotions. A second longer, and it sorted out into distinct threads: a wave of pain: sharp talons, digging into the flesh of his throat. Hot bile, burning his gut. Crashing tides of aching loneliness, a bowel-tightening yearning that could never, ever be soothed....

Fight it, Valere! A stern voice commanded in her head. Sergei's voice, his inflection, but her own brain. It took Wren precious seconds to realize that she was getting it from both sides of the combat, ghost and mortal. And a few more seconds to bring up enough of a barrier that she could only feel herself in her skin.

Seconds that, if her blast of current hadn't worked, could have stopped her from worrying about the job—or anything else, for that matter—forever.

Raising her head slowly, fighting off the surge-headache that felt like a thousand hangovers, Wren blinked the tears away from her eyes and tried to see why she was still alive.

The two figures hung in place, still held immobile by her blast of current. The ghost hovered over its victim, a recognizable human form zizzing and shorting with current, a hazy yellow-green tinting its unreal flesh. Frants had fallen in front of it, one arm up to shield his face, the other reaching behind him as though searching for a weapon. She saw the glint of dark metal against the carpet, and recognized the shape of a handgun, its steel more blue than shiny.

Wren hated guns with a passion. You couldn't outtalk them, you rarely could outrun them, and, as she now knew from experience, bullets hurt like a sonofabitch. A push of current, and the insides melted just enough to make it unusable.

It was stupid waste of current, but she felt better immediately.

Frants stirred slightly, as though he'd felt what she

did, and she tightened the freeze-spell. It wouldn't hold, was barely holding now, but for the moment she'd kept them from doing whatever it was they were going to do to each other.

At least until she could figure out what the hell she was going to do next.

The ghost turned to look at her, and she shuddered. **You said I could have him.**

A hiss, even without sibilants. A low wind moaning through the trees. Everything of loss and pain and emotions, knotted so tight it could never be undone.

I did. I was wrong. A private correspondence, instinctively. The ghost was as much current as anything else, held together by magic and sheer still-human stubbornness. Talking to it along the current was as easy as talking to herself.

The ghost didn't like her response, turning its red glare back to Frants. The mortal was on his knees, sweat pouring down his pasty-white skin. The ghost's normal-looking human hands had grown talons, somehow, somewhen; sharp, black-tipped claws that rested one at Frants's throat, the other on his face. Like the caress of a rabid tiger.

I'll have him anyway.

And with a slashing movement too fast to follow, the ghost tore five terrible scores down half of Frants' face. Shreds of skin clung to the claws, and Wren stared, fascinated, as the ghost raised one hand for another blow. **Let him suffer as I have suffered....**

Don't...

She said it out loud as well, she thought. She might even have screamed it. "You'll regret it," she said rapidly, getting up off her knees and moving forward as carefully, as non-threateningly as she could. Out loud, to appeal to whatever might be left of his humanity. "You're not like him. You never were. Not if you were a builder. You were a builder, weren't you? You created this building. Imagined it. Dreamed it. Drew it."

She was playing a hunch, the one she and Sergei had shared that moment before all hell broke loose here. For the magic that tied him into the protection spell to work, disgraced, out-of-favor magic that depended not on the caster herself but on taking and making deals with greater forces, there had to be a connection on both sides.

Frants's grandfather, on one end, desiring protection at any cost. And the victim, with an equal desire to see the building defended, successful.

A builder, maybe. A dreamer, certainly. The architect, most likely. Sergei had almost had it; if he'd only been given a moment longer to get into those files....

At the thought of her partner, she felt the warmth tingle low at the back of her spine. He was on his way, she could feel him racing there on foot, a madman on the street.

Not enough time, and he couldn't do anything except be in danger too, but he was coming. She could count on him. He wouldn't leave her alone. That knowledge made it a little easier to coax the current-charged monster in front of her. Affection. Appreciation. Love. The things that bound humans—living things—together.

"You made this building be what it is."

I did...I did...for this one! The ghost started to turn its attention back from her to the sobbing, bleeding Frants. **He did not deserve it.**

Wren didn't have time or energy to explain to a mad ghost that he was two generations too late. "No. Not for him. For them." She risked a glance over her shoulder. At the poor guard, the dismembered bodies. And then further out, to where Barbie Doll stupidly huddled in the hallway, unable to move any farther away. "For everyone who uses this building. Do you know how many people work here every day? It's a good building. A safe building, because of you."

All the things she had learned about the building from her basic research, came tumbling to her lips. The security systems. The wide, carefully lit stairs. The failsafe air ventilation system. The care and upkeep that went into it, every single day, so many years after it was first sketched out on paper.

I want...

"I know," she told him, real regret in her voice. She'd want the same thing, too. "I know." She flicked a glance at Frants, cowering in an almost fetal ball on the carpet, and inspiration struck. "But there's—maybe—another way to do it."

The ghost was listening to her now. So was Frants, uncurling enough to look at her, his eyes pleading underneath the streams of blood. Human eyes. *But who was the victim? Who had the right to ask for justice?*

Tell me. Quickly.

"Go back into the stone—"

The ghost turned on her, sharp needle teeth gleaming as he raised a hand toward her. **Never!**

She was dancing on cracking ice, her mind working faster than she thought possible, her skin tingling with the effort it took to keep them both still. "Go back for now. For a short time, a time you'll barely notice." She assumed. She hoped. "The length of a mortal lifetime."

And then? He thought he knew where she was going with this, she could tell by the way his ruined lips were beginning to smile. It was terrible, and she repressed a shudder.

"And then he'll take your place."

Frants yelped a protest, and they both turned to stare at him.

"He'll take your place—" an unspoken threat to Frants, to shut up and let this play out "—and you'll be free."

You can do this?

"When the time comes, it will be done." If she had to get every damn lonejack to hold the bastard down while she brought the knife down on him herself, it would be done. And the Council could just sit and spin. They had set her up to hide the fact that a member of their damned coterie used blood-magics in place of current, committed murder to enforce a spell. And Frants knew all about it, had to, and had used her to strike back at the Council's refusal to help him now. Why the hell should she care about any of them?

"Hell no I won't," Frants said. Or tried to say…his face wasn't in much better shape than the ghost's right now, and it came out soft, as though he'd lost a bunch of teeth at some point, too.

You would rather die now, and find hell that much faster? The ghost sounded honestly curious, and Frants's eyes widened. He shook his head once, blood spraying across the room. Wren noted almost in passing that while the ghost was solid enough to do damage, the blood drops went right through him.

Swear to it. Swear, when the years pass, you will submit. You will replace me, and complete the spell.

Frants looked at Wren, who looked back at him as emotionlessly as she could. He could die now, or die later. It was up to him now.

"Yeth. I thwear it," he said.

Wren felt her shoulders sag a little in relief. She didn't think she could have stopped the ghost again, wasn't sure she would have even if she could. It was a dilemma she was glad not to have to face. *Frants will spend the rest of his life trying to find a way to wrangle out of the promise, by logic or magic or any other means he can find. His using Barbie proved that. But that's a worry for later. For someone else.*

"*Satisfied?*" she asked the ghost privately. It considered for an endless moment, then dropped Frants, its claws retracting into normal-looking fingers.

It's cold in there, it told her. **And lonely.**

"It's not forever." And it was the best she could do.

The ghost nodded.

"What was your name?" she asked him suddenly.

Jamie. And there, overlaying the ravaged face, the maddened red eyes and needle teeth, she saw him. Young, vibrant. A serious expression, almost studious, but with the enthusiasm of a man in love with his work and his life. The ripped fabric swathing his body reformed into a handsome fifties-styled suit, the shirt underneath gleaming white.

Brown eyes under heavy brows sparkled at her, and he raised one calloused hand as though to tip a hat perched on his short-cut hair. He seemed surprised that there was no hat to touch, and looked around for it with an air of distraction, then shrugged in apology.

He looked once more at Frants, pointing one slender, groomed finger as though to say *remember,* and then he faded into the current and was gone.

Gone from the room. But not entirely. Wren was still grounded in the building. Now that she knew what to look for, what to feel for, there were threads of Jamie throughout, like a parent watchful over a child on the playground.

It made her feel safe, protected. And as she slowly disengaged from the building, she could swear that she felt him acknowledge her in return. Then even that faint awareness faded, and she was totally herself again.

A clunk and a whine deep inside the building, and the overhead lights came up again. The sharp click of computers rebooting came from somewhere down the hallway—the one in this office would never work again, not fried as it was—and somewhere deep in the steel she could hear the whine and wail of an alarm.

The elevators were running again. They didn't have much time left.

"Come on," she said to her client. "Get up."

He cringed away from her, scrambling backward like an animal.

"Get *up,*" she said, infusing as much command into her voice as she could manage. He didn't stand, but did stop cowering. "People will be here soon. Do you really want them to see you on the floor?"

She personally didn't give a damn. But better they rush to him for answers than look to her as the only person still standing.

The appeal to his pride seemed to work, as she thought it probably would. Grabbing the edge of a still-intact table, Frants hoisted himself to his feet, using the back of his arm to wipe away the blood that still flowed from his face. He stared at the blood left on his sleeve as though he had no idea where it came from.

That's going to hurt once he comes out of shock, she thought, not without some sympathy. "Come here," she said, rubbing her hands together and trying to find some remnant of current left in her system. It stirred, sluggishly. The building was too weak, still, to pull from, and there were no other sources available, so it would have to do.

When he—understandably—refused to come any closer, she sighed and stepped forward over the wreckage of what had once been an antique chair and reached out to touch the side of his face. "Hold still, I just want to make sure you're not going to bleed to death standing there, okay?" She'd read somewhere that scalp wounds bleed worse than they actually were, damage-wise, but she didn't know if that held for facial wounds, too.

"Slow, breathing steady
The body repairs itself.
Cells reknit, blood clots."

A standby she had been using since high school, something even her limited Talent could make work reliably on surface cuts and abrasions like this. If he was bleeding internally, they were both just shit out of luck.

She winced as her arm reminded her that Frants wasn't the only one injured. It would have been damned useful if the healing cantrip worked on her, but self-healing with current was a major no-no. You were too close, things could get overwhelmed and go wrong way too easily. Neezer had told her horror stories of organs fused together by a Talent who got carried away feeling the inside of his or her body. It still gave her major jeebies, just thinking about it. No thanks.

Taking her hands away, she frowned. The blood had slowed, anyway. *But that's going to scar pretty badly. Good.* She wasn't feeling too charitable toward the bastard right now, for all that she wouldn't let him get killed.

A familiar-sounding chime pinged out in the hallway, and the rumble of voices indicated that the cavalry had finally arrived. She picked out Sergei's lighter bass out of the worried-sounding cacophony with relief.

"In here," she called, and two very serious-faced cub scouts rushed in, followed by their father. She blinked, and the boys refocused into still-young paramedics, who zeroed in on Frants. They knelt in front of him, pulling out instruments and bandages, and doing other paramedic-like things. Their "father," she assumed, was building security, since he immediately started talking into his walkie-talkie, giving updates to someone somewhere else.

She ignored him, turning to the nearest, far too baby-faced paramedic. "There's a woman out there—"

"Someone's with her," the older-by-hours paramedic assured her, then did a double-take. "Ma'am? Are you okay?"

She looked down at herself. The sling was long gone,

and the bullet hole had begun to bleed again under the bandages. She hadn't felt anything until he mentioned it.

"I'm okay," she said, willing it to be true. "He's the one who got hurt."

"Holy shit," Security Guy said in tones of awe. She looked up. He'd discovered the body parts.

Think it's time to get the hell out of here. There was barely enough current left inside her to hotwire a car, but she managed to wrap herself in distraction long enough to slip out the door.

Sergei caught her by the elbow of her uninjured arm as she entered the hallway, and she noted absently that her distraction spell didn't work on him very well anymore. Curious. Something to follow up on. Some other time. Whole lot of things for some other time.

"What happened?"

A reasonable question, she thought. What the hell *had* happened? Another paramedic was kneeling on the floor by Barbie, taking her pulse and checking her eyes. She looked reasonably alive, if not quite alert.

"Lessee. Saved her, saved the client, at least for a couple more years, laid an unquiet spirit to rest for a while longer, anyway. Oh, and earned us the last of that damned fee 'cause Jamie's back in the cornerstone. Don't forget that. No way Frants is gonna weasel out of paying us now, no matter what deals were made."

She had no idea, now, how she was going to realistically enforce that, but she would do her best. Jamie deserved that much from her, at least. Nobody else alive knew him. Nobody else, really, would care.

"A gentleman to the last," she said, and Sergei stared at her, the look on his face almost amusing in its concern. She must sound as though she were babbling, probably incoherent, hallucinating. Maybe she was.

I promise, Jamie. I promise. Nobody's going to screw you over again.

Another security-type was standing by the elevator bank, talking into *his* walkie-talkie, and a woman in a severely tailored suit was stalking down the hallway toward them, taking notes.

Of course, she had also in effect sentenced a man to death (however deserved), and probably set herself up for the Council's extreme wrath (even more than rumor claimed). Those facts didn't bother her too much, even though she knew they should be giving her the screaming meemies. She wasn't feeling much of anything, actually. Brain, like body, was numb. Very odd.

You're drained. Stupid, stupid girl. Neezer's voice? No, Max. *You can't afford to get that drained, girly. Not anymore. Not with the enemies you've been making.*

Sergei must have seen something in her expression, because he drew her in close, his arms heavy around her shoulders.

"It's all right, Genevieve," he murmured. "It's all right." Wren turned her face into his chest, and closed her eyes with a sigh. It wasn't all right. Not by a long shot. But for a moment, just a moment, she could pretend it was. That the case was wrapped up with neat little ribbons, and nothing waited for her outside this embrace but the usual sleep-for-two-days aftermath.

The warmth of his embrace made her begin to feel human again, his natural energy leaching into hers. Just a little. Just enough.

Just enough for all the hurt to come flooding back into her system.

"Take me home," she said.

They took a cab back to her apartment, Wren tucked into the crook of his arm the entire time. He could feel her shivering slightly, despite the day's warmth, and he pulled her closer, trying to share as much of his own warmth as he could. Her skin was too pale, and there was a faint sheen of sweat on her face, as though she was running a fever, but her skin felt cool to the touch. In all the years he'd known her, she'd never even had a cold.

"It's depletion," she said, so soft he could barely hear her. "I'll be okay once I've rested." He ended up having to carry her up the stairs, almost dropping her when a shadow rose to meet them at the fifth landing.

"She's okay?"

"Yeah. Just worn out." For the first time he looked P.B. in the eyes and saw only concern there. "Get the door for me, okay? Keys are in my pocket." The clawed hand felt odd, brushing against his jacket, but the demon had the keys out quickly, racing up the last flight of stairs to turn the locks and open the door so he could carry Wren in without stopping, going directly into Wren's bedroom. P.B. turned the covers down, and Sergei laid her onto the sheets.

"Bunch of worrywarts," she said sleepily, her eyes barely open.

"That's us, yeah." P.B. sat on the edge of the bed while Sergei stripped off her shoes and socks. "Word's out on the street, Wren. Everyone's talking. Rumor says Council's shitting bricks. Nice going."

Sergei frowned at that news, but Wren waved a lazy hand in the air as though to say it was nothing. "Gotta sleep now," she told them. "Sleeeeeeeep and I'll be fine. Promise. Go'way."

Her partner nodded, pulling the cover up to her chin. She grabbed his hand, tugging him down closer, then slid her hand up to the back of his neck, managing even in her exhaustion to find his lips with her own.

It wasn't a graceful poetic first kiss, but there were sparks. Literally. Wren's eyes opened wide again, and she smiled sleepily up at her astonished partner. "Gonna haff ta talk about tha, too."

"Later," he promised, echoing her own words. "Sleep, Wrenlet."

Sergei—gently—kicked P.B. out of the apartment, and went about brewing a mug of tea. He picked the largest mug in the cabinet, rinsed it with warm water, and then pulled the tea ball out of the sink and filled it with the loose tea she kept in a tin on the counter. While the water boiled, he sat at the kitchen table and fiddled with the spoon, dipping it into the sugar bowl and stirring the white granules around. He pulled his cigarette case out of his inside jacket pocket, looked at it, then put it away.

The case was over, for the most part. But all that meant to him was that there was time to worry about everything else. The things they had put off. The things he couldn't avoid thinking about any longer.

His Wren had made powerful enemies with this case. Too many people knew that the Council had a hand in what went down, with the death of the architect and recent events alike, even if they didn't know the why or how. Reputations were at stake, and he didn't think they would be willing to let bygones be bygones. Especially not if what she said about the split in the *Cosa* between Talents and fatae were true.

And, he admitted it, the attack on her life was still making him see red. Which was another problem. Things had changed. Not for the worse…he didn't think. But definitely changed. And they were going to have to deal with that, too.

He picked up the cream-colored business card on the table in front of him, turning it between his fingers for a long moment, then tucked it back into his pocket.

Deals. Deals were what he knew how to do.

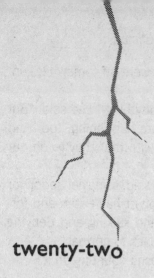

twenty-two

Two days later, Wren had finally regained enough strength to demand to be let out of her apartment.

"No."

When raising enough current to throw a steady stream of paperback books at Sergei's head left her limp and exhausted, they compromised. She could get out of bed and sit in the music room, and maybe, if she was able to handle that, they'd go for ice cream.

"Tyrant," she complained. But since she said it while he was making her breakfast, he just smiled and told her to drink her orange juice.

Three days later, Lee and his wife Miriam had stopped by to see her, filling the two of them in on the latest gossip. The Council had apparently agreed to

talk to fatae leaders, and they were off somewhere unknown, holding conversations.

"It's not going to come to anything," Lee said. "But
it's keeping anything else from happening, too. And
while the Council's occupied with that they're off our
backs as well."

"I give them a month," Wren said, using her spoon for
emphasis, the container of yogurt half-eaten and forgotten. "A month of yelling and sulking and denying
everything, and everything's back to normal."

Sergei hoped so. But he wasn't counting on it.

She still had nightmares. Of Jamie, his face staved in,
falling forward into the wet cement prison. Of Frants,
groveling for his life as she held him at the chopping
block. Or Barbie Doll, eyes vacant and mouth screaming as the spell sucked the life out of her marrow. She
woke from every one coated in sweat, Sergei holding her
in the darkness. He sat beside her every night as she
fell asleep, and was there when she woke. And they
never talked about...anything.

We're so screwed up, she thought ruefully on the
fourth day afterward. Before, they'd at least had denial
on their side. Well, denial on her side and obliviousness
on his. Or was that the other way around? But now...

But did it really matter? She combed out her hair,
consciously plaiting it the way she knew Sergei liked. Did
it matter if she said anything, or if he did?

Yes, damn it.

She laughed at herself, relieved that it was morning, the sun was shining, and he had finally agreed that she could go for a walk. "A short walk," he had added. "Around the block, no more." You couldn't push Sergei. Well, you could, but you wouldn't get far. Enough that he knew that she knew and she knew that he knew. They'd work all the details out later. When she had the strength for it.

Her mood sobered suddenly. When other things were dealt with once and for all.

"So?" she said as they walked down to the corner the next afternoon. Strolling, really; all she could manage, although she refused to admit to it. Sergei had matched his pace to hers automatically, wordlessly, so there was no need to pretend.

He had been gone the night before and this morning as well, talking to people, and she had missed him when she woke up. Wren pushed her sunglasses farther up on her nose. The sun was warm, and brighter than she remembered after so many days inside. "We should talk, I guess." She glanced sideways at him as she spoke, and he nodded.

There was a little coffee shop down the next street that always had the same three old men sitting at the counter, and a young woman reading the newspaper at one corner table. Wren had never been in there before—it was a little out of her usual route—but the windows and table were clean, and the regulars looked well-nourished, so it seemed as good a place as any.

"Coffee," she said to the waitress, a middle-aged woman who looked as though she had been born in her uniform. "Black, no sugar. Tea for him." It would be disgusting, the way restaurant tea always was, but he'd drink it anyway.

He had pulled out the cigarette case, and was extracting one of those damned cigarettes from it, rolling the brown paper between his fingers.

"So?"

"I made them your counteroffer," he said, staring intently at the cigarette.

"And?" She frowned. "Don't make me pull it out of you, Didier. And I mean that literally."

He almost smiled at that. The counteroffer was one they had worked out, in the long early-morning hours of her recovery, waiting for the nightmares to recede. She—they—would work for the Silence. But on her own terms. If Wren was on a job already they couldn't yank her off it, if their job conflicted with her lonejack ethics ("don't you dare laugh," she had warned Sergei, her head resting on his shoulder and feeling the laughter shaking his body although he didn't make a sound) she could refuse it.

"And…they accept. With a few conditions of their own."

"Of course. Nothing's ever that easy." Making this

counteroffer hadn't been easy at all. She was giving up so much. "So? What are they?"

"Information. If you or I hear anything—anything at all—that might be of interest to them, we're to pass it along immediately."

"Which you were doing anyway. Without my consent, I remind you. Right, okay, letting that go. So what the hell might the Silence be interested in?"

"More of a question what *aren't* they interested in. But we have discretion. Mainly gossip, I'd guess. *Cosa* gossip."

Wren sighed. She wasn't happy about that. At all. But from what Sergei had told her, it wasn't as though the Silence didn't have other Talent on the payroll...and she'd be the one to decide what got passed along. She weighed the balance, decided that she could live with it.

"In return, they will pay a small monthly stipend into your account. Don't get too excited, we're talking *small*. But it's something."

"Something's always good." He was still fiddling with the cigarette. "What?"

"And they'll protect you. If it becomes necessary."

"Pro—" Her eyes narrowed as she understood. "The Council isn't going to put a price on my head, Sergei. We talked about this." Obviously it hadn't taken in his overthick, overprotective brain.

"Maybe yes, maybe no. But if you're wrong..." She took the cigarette away from him when he started to shred it.

"If you're wrong," he said, "all you have to do is ask and they will shield you."

"And that will do what, against current?"

"If current were all-powerful, the Council would have a lot more real-world power than it already does," he said, looking her in the eye for the first time since they sat down.

Point taken. The Council's actions toward the rest of the *Cosa* might not be mirrored in the real world, but she'd bet that wasn't from a lack of inclination. The Council board was made up of people who had a taste for mundane power, too.

"What about the fatae...?"

"Don't push it, Wren. The Silence has no interest in supernaturals." He paused, shrugged. "Not right now, anyway. If we can prove they'd be useful..."

Wren snorted. "More likely they'd see them as something to be exploited. And let me tell you, past experience says *not* a good idea."

The waitress finally came back with their drinks, and she sipped her coffee, watching him doctor his tea to his liking. It was a ritual with him, the stirring and measuring, and soothing to watch. His hands were precise but not fussy, and she remembered the feel of them stroking her hair as she faded off into sleep.

It might have been that that decided her. The realization that something doesn't stop just when you're out of the picture. That Sergei would still be sitting there, stroking her hair, while she was dead to the world. That things set in motion don't always stop when, as he would say, the situation was finalized. She hated the knowledge. Resented it. Couldn't, no matter how hard she tried, stuff it back into its box.

"So."

"So," he echoed. "That's the deal. It's your choice, yes or no."

"Me, gainfully employed. Well, sort of." She grinned a little, then reached out to take one of those capable hands in her own. "You good with this?"

He shook his head. "No. Not really. But it's your decision."

"And you..."

"We're partners." There was a vow in his dark eyes. "Whither thou goest, etcetera. We're going to have to get that engraved on our foreheads or something, we seem to have trouble believing the other means it." His mouth twisted a little, and he sipped at his tea, put it down. "They wanted you most of all, but they'd prefer both of us. Saves on having to match you with a new Handler. The Silence is all for using what works."

She almost smiled at that, pulling back to her side of the table. "It's weird. I've been thinking about it a lot, the past couple of weeks. And..."

"And?"

"It's not about the money. Or the protection, although yeah I'll admit it's always nice to know that if I'm wrong, here's a place to run to. But..."

This time, she was the one fiddling with the remains of the cigarette. How to say what had been ticking in her brain since that moment she translocated?

"I've spent my entire life thinking small, Sergei. Me, the stuff around me. It's not a bad way to be, I guess...but if I walk away from this, this thing the Silence is offering, the chance to do some actual good in the world.... I get the feeling I'm going to always wonder—"

"What if?"

"What if," she agreed. "But when you go back to them, ask for more money first. You never know, right?"

He laughed, shaking his head. "That's my Wren." He finished off his tea and stood up. "Okay, let me see what I can do."

Two weeks later, Wren placed a stem of lilac on the sidewalk. Her fingers lingered on the bloom before pulling away, standing up.

"Why lilac?"

She shrugged, feeling the bandage pull as she did so. The sling was long gone, but she still didn't have a full range of movement back. "Seemed more appropriate than roses."

There had been the faintest whiff of something floral, when Jamie finally disappeared. She had spent half an hour in the florist this morning, trying to recognize it.

Sergei reached forward to place a fist-sized chunk of smoky quartz beside the flower, his fingers brushing the small brass plaque workers had affixed to the side of the building just that morning.

"James Koogler. 1927 to 1955." He shook his head, dark glasses hiding whatever expression was in his eyes. "You'd think they could have done more for the man who gave his life for this building."

"Hey, you don't want to go around telling people a man was killed in the very spot where they work. People might start talking about ghosts, or curses, or something."

Wren's attempt at humor fell flat.

"It's not enough, is it?"

"It has to be," she said. "For now."

She had told him that first night, crying in his arms, about the deal she'd struck, the oath Oliver Frants had sworn. With her as the only living witness, there wasn't any way to ensure he would honor it, despite her blood-thirsty thoughts at the time. But somehow, Sergei still thought it would all work out in the end. He believed in karma, did her partner. And justice.

She wasn't sure what she believed in. And she really wasn't sure there was any justice at all in the world. Not the kind that satisfied. But that was what she hoped to find with the Silence. Maybe.

"I'll watch him, Jamie," she promised. "And I'll never let him forget."

As though on cue, a jacketed security guard came out of the building. Not Rafe.

"Excuse me. I'm going to have to ask you two to move on."

Sergei looked at him over the tops of his sunglasses, and the smaller man blinked but didn't retreat. "Please. I really don't want to have to have you arrested for trespassing."

"It's okay," Wren told her partner. "We can go. It's no big deal."

He held the guard's gaze for a long moment, then let him go. "You want coffee?" he asked Wren, as though they had never been interrupted.

"Do I ever not? But back to my place. Jackson's had an order delivered, including this new blend he swears will put curl in my hair."

As they walked away, Sergei glanced back. The guard had already removed their offerings, tossing them into the city trash bin on the corner. He thought briefly about arranging with a florist to have more lilac delivered the next day. And the next, and the next, until they got tired of tossing them. Then he let the idea go. It wasn't needful. Jamie, if he was still there at all, knew the attempt had been made.

There were other things to worry about.

"So." She took his hand, lacing her fingers through his. "All done?"

"All but the handshake. Astonishingly, I think everyone's pretty well pleased with the result," Sergei said in wonder. "Although if I never have to go through a negotiating round like that again…"

"We did good, huh?"

"Yeah." Sergei nodded. "I think maybe we did real good."

"Excellent." She leaned a little against his shoulder. "Take me to dinner."

"Why should I do that?"

She bit the inside of her cheek and looked up at him thoughtfully.

"Because you love me, and worry that I'm not eating right."

Behind them, just far enough down the street and in the shadows to be unseen but near enough to be helpful if something happened, P.B. rolled his eyes and made a rude noise only he could hear. But his black button nose was scrunched in amusement, and his eyes rested on the two figures with affection.

They weren't bad, as humans went. He rather thought he might keep them.

* * * * *

**Hidden in the secrets of antiquity,
lies the unimagined truth...**

Introducing

ROGUE
Angel™

a brand-new line filled with mystery
and suspense, action and adventure,
and a fascinating look into history.

And it all begins with DESTINY.

In a sealed crypt in
France, where the
terrifying legend of
the beast of Gevaudan
begins to unravel,
Annja Creed discovers
a stunning artifact
that will seal her destiny.

*Available every other
month starting
July 2006, wherever
you buy books.*